# Daughter of the House

By the same author:

*Celebration*
*Follies*
*Sunrise*
*The White Dove*
*Strangers*
*Bad Girls, Good Women*
*A Woman of Our Times*
*All My Sins Remembered*
*Other People's Marriages*
*A Simple Life*
*Every Woman Knows a Secret*
*Moon Island*
*White*
*The Potter's House*
*If My Father Loved Me*
*Sun At Midnight*
*Iris and Ruby*
*Constance*
*Lovers and Newcomers*
*The Kashmir Shawl*
*The Illusionists*

# Daughter of the House

## Rosie Thomas

THE OVERLOOK PRESS
New York, NY

This edition first published in hardcover in the United States in 2015 by
The Overlook Press, Peter Mayer Publishers, Inc.
141 Wooster Street
New York, NY 10012
www.overlookpress.com

For bulk and special orders, please contact sales@overlookny.com,
or write us at the above address.

First published in Great Britain by
HarperCollins*Publishers* 2015

Library of Congress Cataloging-in-Publication Data
Thomas, Rosie.
Daughter of the house / Rosie Thomas.
pages ; cm
ISBN 978-1-4683-1174-7 (hardcover)
1. Young women--Fiction. 2. Psychic ability--Fiction. 3. London
(England)--Social life and customs--20th century--Fiction. I. Title.
PR6070.H655D38 2015
823'.914--dc23
2015023975
Manufactured in the United States of America

2 4 6 8 10 9 7 5 3 1
ISBN 978-1-4683-1174-7

For James and Flora
14 February 2015

# PART ONE

# CHAPTER ONE

*Kent, 1910*

Mr and Mrs Devil Wix and their three children made a vivid picture as they strolled towards the steamer jetty. Devil wore a loose blue flannel coat with patch pockets, and a straw hat that he tipped to the other holidaymakers. His wife Eliza's short steps were dictated by the fashionably narrow hem of her rose-pink and dove-grey hobble skirt. She had dressed her hair under a grey turban with a matching pink feather cockade.

Arthur, the youngest child, dashed ahead in his enthusiasm to get aboard the pleasure boat before doubling back to chivvy his family. Cornelius and Nancy trailed behind with Phyllis, their paid companion. Cornelius's slumped shoulders revealed how much he would have preferred to spend the morning out on the heathland with his butterfly net. He was gloomily asserting to Nancy that with the swell that was running out in the bay they would certainly all be seasick. It was very like him to adopt nautical terms without having ever ventured out to sea.

Nancy only half-listened. She was watching the little

procession of guests strolling from their hotel towards the sea, and to her dismay she saw that the Clares and Mr Feather were also planning to take the excursion. Her mother, Eliza, had chatted to Mrs Clare on the hotel terrace, and on one or two evenings Mrs Clare had invited Eliza to sit with her after dinner in the drawing room. Once the two men had enjoyed their cigars they had joined them too. Devil had not been present to keep Eliza company, of course. He was almost always in London, because of the theatre. He was only here with his family now because it was a Sunday afternoon and there would be no stage show until tomorrow evening.

Nancy and Cornelius and Arthur had been introduced to Mrs Clare and to her husband and brother, and they had endured the usual polite conversations. Arthur and Mr Clare talked about cricket while Mrs Clare's pale blue eyes assessed Nancy's clothes. Nancy knew she was dressed too brightly. Her cerise coat marked her out, instead of concealing her in mouse-grey or mole-brown folds like the daughter of a conventional family. She tried not to mind about this, noticing on her own part that Mrs Clare looked quite prim and colourless next to Eliza's abundant glamour.

Mr Feather was Mrs Clare's brother, and it was his presence more than the others' that made Nancy feel uncomfortable. Mrs Clare was always anxiously glancing at him, almost as if she suspected he might be angry and she was obliged to soothe him, but whenever Nancy looked in his direction he was staring at *her*. She couldn't help returning his look even though she tried very hard not to. His dark eyes seemed to drill into her temple or the back of her head. Whenever he spoke to her it was always in a low voice and with a sympathetic half-smile, as though she had already confided something incriminating to him. His manner seemed to suggest they held an experience in common, and Nancy particularly hated this because she did have a secret. But she held it so deep within herself that she had never told a soul, and certainly not Mr Feather. How could the man know about her Uncanny? And if he didn't know, why did he watch her with such close interest?

His presence was like one of her father's hidden stage magnets, dragging her closer and weighing her down, and now he was coming on the steamer trip with them. Was she never to take a step in any direction without the man's unwelcome concern reaching out for her, like the tentacles of an octopus? She could feel the tickle of one on the back of her neck right at this moment. She wanted to slap it away.

'Come along, dear,' Phyllis said.

The companion was clutching the frame of her bag in two hands and looking as if she was already seasick. Poor thing, Nancy thought. Why must her father always sweep them all along with his enthusiasms? The steamer trip had been his idea and Eliza had taken some persuasion before she agreed to it.

The Wixes joined the short queue to board the steamer. Arthur struck up a talk about the Eton versus Harrow cricket match with two boys of his own age. Devil had promised to take his sons to Lord's for the Schools' Day in a month's time and Arthur was already working himself into a froth of excitement.

'Half a crown's on Eton,' one boy taunted and Arthur feinted a punch at him. The three of them chased up the short gangway and sprang down into the launch.

When it was Nancy's turn a seaman with a full beard took her hand and called her 'miss' as she stepped down to the rocking deck. She hesitated. Although she couldn't see anything out of the ordinary the smells of engine oil and seawater and boat varnish were overpowering, and that was always a sign. All her instincts were to leap back to safety on dry land.

The man's grasp tightened.

'I won't let you fall, missy. Step this way.'

Salt-caked sisal matting was laid on the deck in case any of the ladies should lose her footing. Nancy felt she had no choice but to take the seat that was offered to her. Hampered by her fashionable skirt Eliza needed a helping hand on either side before she could step down. Devil escorted her to a cushioned bench under the awning and Phyllis nervously sat further along towards the rail.

Nancy watched the boatmen making their preparations for departure. Heavy ropes dragging swags of weed were hauled through the water and thick-legged boys in ragged trousers applied their backs to the capstan. The air was thick with more layers of stink, of tar and brass polish and coal smoke. Nancy had to swallow hard.

Devil chose a seat in the open nearer to the bow. He beckoned to some of the younger children and they sidled towards him. He winked at his little audience, making a show of flexing his fingers and pushing back the cuffs of his coat. One of Arthur's new friends was playing with a cricket ball and as soon as he spotted it Devil held out his hand. The boy was reluctant but at a stern nod from his father he passed it over. He watched apprehensively as Devil tossed the ball high in the air. Even though the boat was rocking he caught it without an upward glance, as Nancy knew he would. With a casual flick of the wrist he threw the ball a second time, higher still. A big wave slammed the boat against the jetty, causing a gentleman to stumble as he squeezed between the crowded benches, but again the ball was drawn back to Devil's hand as if magnetised. Three more times he threw and caught, defying the boat's pitching. The owner of the ball had relaxed enough to smile as the ball flew upwards one more time.

There was a beat, stretched by the breeze and the shriek of a gull gliding overhead. This time there was no satisfying slap from the leather dropping into Devil's cupped palm.

Devil took off his straw hat and peered inside it, scratching his head in astonishment. Several children looked down to the deck and others peered over the side, but there was no clatter or splash.

'It's gone,' the owner wailed.

Devil replaced his hat.

'Sorry about this, old chap,' he murmured to the boy. 'I'll make it up to you somehow.'

Peering around, he noticed a girl with a posy basket set on her lap.

'May I perhaps have a look in your basket, miss?'

Seated a little to one side Mrs Clare raised her eyebrows at her brother and almost imperceptibly pursed her lips. No one else was meant to see, but Nancy did. She hated it when her father chose to be conspicuous in this way – even though he had always been the same – and she turned her head in anguish. A yard away, on the jetty, the bearded captain and one of the other sailors spoke urgently together. They had been considering the wind and the sky but the bearded man indicated the full boat and the jaunty pennants snapping in the breeze. With his big sea boot he kicked the boat away from the moorings, leaping inboard over the widening gap at the very last moment. There was a roar from the engine and a churn of green water, a sailor snatched up the last end of rope and dropped it into a loop, and the steamer's bow swung out into the bay. Nancy sneaked a look towards her father and saw that – of course – he had produced the cricket ball from the little girl's basket. The boy grabbed it back and stowed it inside his coat as Devil bowed over his doffed hat.

Please, no more, Nancy prayed with a twelve-year-old's disloyal fervour.

It seemed that she was heard because Devil came back to sit beside Eliza under the awning.

Arthur and his companions were gamely ragging each other and Cornelius had never looked up from his book. The steamer ploughed the length of the pier and then drove out into the stiff wind. Spume flew and Phyllis's hands tightened on the cane handles of her bag. In trying not to look longingly at the pier amusements Nancy made the mistake of meeting Mr Feather's eye again. Beadily he held her gaze and she thought there was a glimmer of superior amusement, as if the pleasure craft and the crew and the benches lined with ladies and gentlemen in their holiday outfits had all been placed there for just the two of them to observe, and enjoy.

It was intolerable.

The prow reared upwards. The view of the houses clustered at the side of the bay vanished behind a wall of green as a huge wave lifted the steamer. Spray scattered over the laughing gentlemen and bolder boys in the forward seats, sending them scurrying for the shelter of the awning even though a crewman shouted that they were to hold tight and keep their places. A second later the boat pitched down – and down – into the wave trough. Phyllis let out a mouse's squeak of alarm. Nancy wondered if the budding apprehension she was experiencing inside her ribcage, like a dark flower beginning to unfurl, might be the beginning of seasickness. It was *not*, she told herself firmly. At least Mr Feather had transferred his attention to Mrs Clare. He was patting his sister's hand and reassuring her.

Cornelius raised his head. Another huge wave lifted and tossed the boat down again. Eliza was the only one of the ladies who did not show any sign of dismay. She sat upright, seeming quite ready to meet the salt wind and the flung diamonds of spray.

The land dropped further behind them. After a few minutes Nancy grew used to the motion. It was even quite exhilarating to watch the glassy rollers with their curling lips of white foam as they swept towards them, and to feel the sharp upwards swing and then the answering downwards plunge as the boat cleaved through the water. The beat of the engine was steady, and her bearded sailor stood squarely in the wheelhouse with his pipe between his teeth and his eyes on the horizon. He looked just like a hero in a book.

'I say!' Arthur sang out. His childish grin split his face. Arthur loved all kinds of roughhousing.

Phyllis's face had taken on a sweaty glimmer. She left her seat, treading with exaggerated care, and the gentleman next to her supported her arm and handed her closer to the rail. She sank down, her handkerchief to her mouth.

'Oh dear, poor Phyllis,' Eliza murmured.

She stood up too and took short, swaying steps to the companion's side. Phyllis fended her off, clearly indicating that she preferred to be left to suffer alone. Eliza returned to her husband. The steamer turned slightly in its circuit of the bay and immediately pitched even more threateningly as the waves caught it broadside. Mrs Clare got unsteadily to her feet and joined Phyllis. One of the gentlemen had to make the same move and Nancy became aware that the talk and laughter had faded. Most of the passengers were sitting in silence. The stink of smoke and hot oil was not helping matters. Nancy uneasily scanned the faces, and black petals further unfurled in her chest. Two sailors passed down the twin gangways, moving with easy confidence. One of them ducked into the wheelhouse and conferred with the captain.

'Pappy?' Nancy said. His nod reassured her.

Mrs Clare leaned miserably over the rail. As if she set the proper example in this and in all other social matters, some others followed suit.

The bearded captain surrendered the wheel and took a megaphone from its cabinet. Bracing himself at the wheel-house door he announced, 'Ladies and gentlemen, the sea is not going to be our friend this morning. We'll make an early turn about. We don't want any of our passengers to feel uncomfortable aboard *Queen Mab*.'

The engine laboured as they swung round in an arc, the churn of water at the stern swallowed by a wave that broke over the gunwale as it surged past them. The steamer bobbed and rolled, seeming for the first time unequal to the job of keeping afloat.

Devil said merrily, 'Will we get our shillings back, do you think?'

At least the waves now swept them towards the welcome shore. Phyllis laid her forehead against the rail. Within quite a short time they were nearing the seaward end of the pier, where the strollers and fishermen were clearly visible. Cornelius's book was closed in his lap but he held his place with his forefinger.

There came a lurch and a shriek of protesting machinery, and then a rending noise like metal plates being crunched up and pitched on a metal floor. When this din stopped the engine had stopped too, and in the strange quiet the buffet of wind and the waves churning beneath the pier sounded even louder.

From Cornelius's expression Nancy knew that something must have gone seriously wrong.

The steamer rolled heavily as its prow turned through the water, unable to make headway without engine power. Two sailors dashed to the rail, pushing aside the passengers in their hurry. One of them grabbed a fender and the other took a boathook. Turning to her hero, Nancy saw that the pipe was gone. He fought with the wheel, trying to bring his boat round, but wind and current swept it towards the pier supports.

A woman pressed her hand to her mouth, stifling a scream.

The male passengers began shouting and dashing to the seaward side, propelling their children and womenfolk away from the looming pier. The people on the walkways were now far above them and at the lower level yawned an underworld of heaving water and dripping iron stanchions.

Devil caught Eliza tightly at his side. Arthur was trapped in the press of people who had fled to the far rail.

'For God's sake hold on,' Devil bellowed to his family.

The sailor made a stab with his boathook, but the sturdy pole splintered as the *Queen Mab* smashed into the pier.

The force of the impact threw the steamer sideways. The outer rail dipped and water flowed over it before the vessel sluggishly rolled in the opposite direction, sending bodies tumbling across the decks and falling against the benches. Cornelius lunged towards his sister and caught her by the arm to stop her skidding down the crazily angled gangway. A confusion of shouts and screams tore the air. Water poured everywhere, covering the decks and the seats and flooding into the wheelhouse.

Devil supported his wife as the water rose past his knees. She was trapped by the weight of her sodden skirt. A barnacled ladder on the nearest pier support rose to an opening that was already jammed with shocked faces. An arm reached down with a dangling lifebelt and Devil somehow hoisted Eliza up the lowest metal rungs. She grasped the lifebelt and men began to haul her up from above. Only when she was safe did Devil turn to look for his children.

Nancy saw all this, as if from the depths of the Uncanny.

Cornelius shouted her name as icy water sucked round her knees. A wave slammed into her chest; she was torn away and thrown against the submerged rail. All around there were people in the water, splashing and flailing as the *Queen Mab* went down.

To her horror she saw Arthur amongst them. His blond head was darkened with the hair plastered against his skull. Nancy let the next wave lift her free of the sinking vessel. Her skirt caught between her legs as she tried to kick out. She was submerged, sinking into bubbling depths with her hair fanning out like seaweed. Somehow she freed her limbs and frantically fought her way upwards. Her face broke the surface and she gulped for air.

There were boats approaching, and at the same time men with ropes came swarming down the pier stanchions. A half-submerged dark shape was bobbing close at hand and she recognised it as one of the boat's wooden benches, the green seat cushion still attached. She launched herself at it and somehow caught hold. She took a sobbing breath, trying to remember where she had seen Arthur in the water. Clawing back the hair that clogged her eyes and mouth she yelled his name.

The waves were dotted with hats and cushions and a dark floating web that had been a woman's shawl. Rotating as far as she could without losing her hold on the seat she caught sight of him. He had torn off his coat and his shirt billowed in the swell. When she glimpsed his face it was dead white, frighteningly like a corpse.

But Arthur knew how to *swim*.

She screamed again, 'Arthur. Here, Arthur. Swim to me.'

He caught sight of her and tried to reach out, a splashy scramble that brought him no closer. He was already exhausted by his efforts to stay afloat. His head seemed to sink lower in the water.

Powered by desperation Nancy kicked towards him, towing her makeshift raft. Arthur's shirt ballooned as another wave caught and released them. They were only a yard apart now. Filling her lungs with a huge breath Nancy let go of the bench. She splashed frantically to her brother and at last caught hold of him. They clung together and there was a long, suffocating and terrible moment when it seemed certain they were going to drag each other down. But then Arthur seemed to revive a little. He struck out with his free arm and Nancy followed suit and somehow they propelled themselves through the water to reach the floating bench. They grabbed it at the same instant. The seat wallowed and sank deeper but it was just buoyant enough to support them both.

A rowing boat swayed on the crest of the next wave.

'Two children here,' a man at the prow shouted.

Nancy's layers of clothes were dragging her down. It took every ounce of her strength to keep her head above the waves, but somehow she managed also to watch Arthur and make sure his grip was secure. He shuddered and coughed as the waves tipped their raft up and down.

Water sluiced over his head and she screamed at him to hold on.

An oar thrust past Nancy's ear and then a grappling hook caught the slats of the bench. A man's hand reached for and snatched the collar of her coat. She felt herself being towed in to the side of the rowing boat where more sturdy arms supported her. The boat rocked fiercely and she howled at her rescuers, 'Save my brother.'

'Your brother'll be right enough,' someone shouted back.

A man in a jersey leaned right down into the waves and tried to lift her, but it took another fellow to help him and they hauled on her wrists and arms and then her heavy body until her hips cleared the side and she tumbled into the bottom of the boat. Her petticoats and even her drawers were all on show but she didn't give it a thought.

'Arthur!'

She fought to sit upright and her rescuers steadied her.

'We've got 'im. You'm a brave girl, ain't you?'

A sodden, inert mass was hoisted and deposited beside her.

Sobbing and spitting up water she half-crawled to him. His shirt was twisted up to his armpits and his exposed skin was mottled but his eyes opened, startlingly blue in his blanched face. Two of the boatmen bent at the oars and Nancy glimpsed the looming corner of the pier as they swung away from the wreck. The third wrapped a coat around the shuddering boy, and then did the same for Nancy.

'You'll be good as new,' their rescuer said.

The grim faces of the three men told Nancy that they were the fortunate ones.

Arthur lay half in her lap with his eyes fixed on her face. His breath came in shallow gulps but he was clearly reviving. Through chattering teeth he gasped, 'Mama? Where's Mama?'

Nancy stretched upright to look back at the pier. Eliza

had reached the ladder and the lifebelt, and must have been saved.

But where was Cornelius? Phyllis? And their father?

The water was dotted with floating debris and rescue boats that had made the short trip out from the beach. She saw some steamer passengers in the other boats, and others being helped up to the pier walkway, but she recognised none of them. The *Queen Mab* was almost submerged. The funnel and the wheelhouse tilted at a crazy angle, and the jaunty awning had been torn to tatters by the force of the waves.

The black flower grew so big that it filled her whole chest.

Their boat rode a wave close in to the beach and a man in big rubber waders strode out to them. He swept Nancy into his arms and carried her to the shingly rim, where she was passed along a chain of hands and finally set down on the sand where a blanket immediately enveloped her. Arthur was given the same treatment, and the boat pushed out again.

'My father,' Nancy screamed. 'Where is he?'

Her legs gave way beneath her. A woman in an apron knelt to take her in her arms and wrap the blanket tighter. Nancy thought she recognised her from the cockle stall on the beach corner.

'There you are, my love. You'm all right now. Don't you worry.'

'*My father.*'

She was shuddering now like Arthur, great uncontrollable waves of cold and panic sweeping over her. 'My other brother. I have to find them. Phyllis was with us too. Where are they?'

'Your daddy will be here, I'm sure. Where are you staying, my darling?'

Someone else was trying to make her drink warm milk out of a thick white cup. The smell of it was unbearable. Her teeth rattled on the rim before she managed to turn her face away. Arthur drank his although his head was hanging and he seemed too shocked to speak.

'Terrible,' a voice said nearby. 'I seen one drowned at least.'

'Not now, Mary,' another reprimanded.

The little boats straggled back to the beach with the last of the rescued passengers. Women and children were passed ashore as Nancy and Arthur had been, to be immediately swaddled in makeshift coverings. Arthur's friend with the cricket ball was amongst them. He was crying and trying to hide his tears. Nancy sat with her arms wrapped round her knees in an attempt to control her shivers. Her eyes stung from the salt and the effort of scanning the beach for her family.

A shadow fell across her. Mr Feather loomed tall and black like the gnomon of a sundial. One of the rescuers had draped a rough blanket over his wet clothes, giving him the look of an Old Testament prophet. The resemblance was strengthened when he raised one hand and brought it to rest on the top of her head. The uneasy sense of being weighted down that she felt in his presence now became real. She tried to duck away but his hand pinned her beneath it like one of Cornelius's butterflies in a case. In the shingle beside her feet she saw a pink shell, the size and shape of a child's fingernail.

In a hoarse voice he begged, 'She slipped away from me. Where is she now? Tell me what you see. Is she here or has she passed?'

'I can't see anything.' Nancy was close to sobbing. The man did know her secret, her way of seeing with her inside eyes, into places no one else saw. Ever since she was a little girl she had possessed the ability. When she was small she linked the waking dreams with her sleeping dreams, and she assumed that everyone had the two different kinds. She was almost thirteen now, and as she grew away from childhood she understood – because no else ever mentioned such a thing – that the wakeful dreams were somehow hers alone.

He crouched to bring his mouth closer to her ear. 'Yes, you can. As soon as I set eyes on you, I knew you were a seer. Where is my Helena?'

She tried to shake off his hand, but she was paralysed. It seemed that her head was no longer made of bone and skin because it was softening and lightening to the point where it threatened to float off her shoulders. The blood noisily surged in her veins.

The beach and the rescuers melted away. Instead of the sand and a slice of busy sea she saw billows of mud with the skeletons of trees poking up like crooked fingers. At the same time a foul smell wrapped round her. She coughed in disgust and tried to pull away, but Feather still restrained her.

The smell became overpowering, nauseating. She blinked and the mud churned and there were broken men lying in it. Dozens of them were strewn as far as the eye could see, dying and already dead, with smirched or shattered faces gazing up at the white sky.

She had no idea where this horrifying place could be. All she knew was that this inside vision was made somehow sharper and more real by the man's hand resting on the top of her head.

She screwed her eyes shut. Tears burned the inner lids. She whispered, 'Please. Please make it stop.'

Mercifully the scene was already fading. It had been no more than a glimpse. As swiftly as it had come the smell ebbed away, carrying the mud and the wounded and dead with it. Her head grew heavy once more and wobbled on her neck, and the man's hand lifted at last.

He murmured, 'Don't be frightened. You are a seer. You might even think of your ability as a gift. Some of us do.'

She didn't want to be any sort of *us*, not in a company with this man who excluded her father and mother and even Neelie and Arthur.

Then to her joy she saw Devil. He was searching the knots of people lined up on the beach. She scrambled to her feet and now Feather did not try to hold her back.

'Pappy! We're here.'

She ran at him and pressed her face against his soaked clothes as he hugged her. Neither of them could find words. Arthur came more slowly, white with shock, and Devil bent his head over his two children.

'Thank God,' he murmured.

'Mama?' Arthur managed to ask.

'She is safe. Cornelius is with her.'

'And Phyllis?'

Nancy's question was not answered. Devil thanked the cockle seller and her helpers and shepherded his children away from the rescue scene. At the pier entrance Eliza and Cornelius had been searching amongst the passengers who had been brought in that way. As soon as she saw them Eliza ran, tripping up in the constricting skirt. Tears were running down her face, her smart turban was gone and her hair had come down in thick hanks. Nancy had never seen her composed mother in such a way and the sight was deeply shocking.

18

Devil hustled them away from the beach. Nancy didn't look back to see if Mr Feather was still searching for his sister. Devil said they must get back to the hotel immediately, to warmth and dry clothing. Some of the townspeople had brought drays and fish wagons down to the promenade to ferry survivors, but these had now set off and it seemed that the Wixes must either walk or take the little pleasure tram that ran to their hotel from the pier. Its driver looked incongruous in his smart braided uniform as he tried to hurry their shivering group towards it.

'But where is Phyllis?' Nancy demanded. Eliza was trying to massage some warmth into Arthur's blanketed body. Cornelius took Nancy's hand and tucked it under his arm.

'We don't know,' he said.

'*Where is she?*'

'The men are looking for her,' Devil answered.

'We can't go without her,' Nancy flamed.

Her father's face darkened. 'There's nothing you can do here, Nancy. Do as you are told.'

The toy tram trundled towards the hotel, leaving behind the rescue scene and the stricken steamer. It was wrong to be perched like carefree holidaymakers under the little canopy. In Nancy's head the wind seemed to chivvy the fragments of the day, briefly pasting lurid, disjointed images of the steamer and their escape from it over the innocent seaside landscape.

Arthur had still barely spoken.

Eliza told him, 'You're safe now. You did very well, you know, to take care of your sister. Papa and I are proud of you.'

The tram rocked around the curve of track. Arthur turned his coin-bright profile towards Nancy. There was a tick of silence during which she prepared to accept whatever he would say. He was younger than her by fifteen months, but she was only a girl. Cornelius was watching her too from beneath his heavy eyelids. Cornelius often saw more than he would afterwards admit to.

'I didn't take care of her,' Arthur said.

It must have been the salt in his throat and chest that made his treble voice crack and emerge an octave lower.

'Nancy saved *me*. She was safe but she let go and came for me. The boatman told her she was a brave girl.' There was another silence before he added, 'So you see, actually I was rather useless.'

The last words came out in a boy's piping voice once more.

Nancy noticed that her skirt was beginning to dry, leaving wavy tidemarks of salt. She was thinking that from today – or from the day before yesterday, really – everything would be different. You could never un-see what you had seen; that much was clear without any intervention from the Uncanny or Mr Feather.

'No, Arthur, you weren't useless at all,' she mumbled.

Eliza cupped Nancy's chin and lifted it so their eyes met. Her fingers were icy cold and the grey in her matted hair was revealed. With the blanket over her shoulders she could have been one of the cockle women, but still she commanded attention. Nancy yearned for the warmth of her approval.

Eliza asked, 'Is that what happened?'

Arthur's honesty was brave because it had cost him something. Nancy had done what she did without thinking, and therefore she hadn't really and truly been brave at all. So she reluctantly nodded because to claim any more would have felt like an untruth.

'Good girl,' Eliza said, and Nancy stored up this praise like treasure.

'Well done, Zenobia.'

At her father's insistence Nancy had been named after the queen of the Asian desert kingdom of Palmyra, and Devil invariably used her formal name on significant occasions. But there had never been a day like this one. Nancy shifted closer to him on the narrow seat, he put his arm round her and she nestled against him.

At the hotel Eliza took charge of running a hot bath in the clanking bathroom at the end of the corridor. Usually it was Phyllis who filled baths and laid out nightclothes and brought hot-water bottles when they were needed. Her absence shouted at every turn.

When Nancy was dressed Cornelius and Arthur came to her room. Cornelius settled himself at the foot of his sister's bed and Nancy rested her feet against his solid thigh. Of all of them he seemed the best survivor – he told her that after he had lost sight of her and Arthur he had paddled to the pier ladder and clung on to the lowest rung until all the women and children had climbed to safety. Devil had swum several times between the pier and the stricken steamer, desperately searching the water for the two of them.

Arthur remained silent, standing with his back to them and apparently staring out at the heathland. Finally he spun round.

'*I* want to be a brave man,' he blurted out.

The possibility that he might not be, that bravery was not the automatic right of boys of his sort, was deeply disturbing to him.

Cornelius blinked behind his glasses. Nancy said quickly, 'Of course you will be.'

Arthur's mouth quivered. He was on the point of tears. 'And I want Phyllis to come back.'

\*     \*     \*

21

Late that afternoon Devil and Eliza broke the news to their children that the companion's body had been recovered from the sea.

Four of the forty people aboard the *Queen Mab* had lost their lives. The others were Mr and Mrs Clare and the youngest passenger, the little girl with the posy basket. Nancy couldn't put out of her mind how Devil's first thought had been for Eliza, and she imagined how Mr Clare must also have struggled to save his wife, never giving up until the waves claimed him too. That evening, the Clares' usual table in the dining room was covered with a cloth but left unlaid.

In her bed, after the strange dinner where almost no one in the room spoke or ate much and the rattle of cutlery seemed too loud to bear, Nancy was unable to sleep. For the last year Phyllis had been with her to make sure she brushed her hair and placed her shoes side by side under her chair. Now the gaunt little hotel bedroom was full of strange shadows, and although she forced herself to lie still her head seethed with unwelcome images.

She lay awake for so long that sleep seemed impossibly remote. The procession of images through her mind led her to the Palmyra, to one of the theatre's private boxes. She was watching a performance but she wasn't enjoying the stage spectacle because Devil was in danger, and she was the only one in the audience who knew it. When she tried to call a warning no sound came because her voice was stuck in her throat. Nor could she run to save him because her legs and arms were frozen. The audience was shouting, black mouths flapping open as waves of noise crashed over the stage. Nancy sweated and gasped as she struggled to break out of her paralysis.

Her father grinned straight at her and then glanced up

into the shadowed recess above the stage where scenery and mirrors were suspended out of sight. He swept off his silk hat and began to make a bow.

There came a terrible rush of air and a black pit opened at his feet. Nancy had once been shown the dark realm of machinery and pulleys and ladders that lay beneath the stage. Devil tipped forwards, slowly, like a giant puppet, and disappeared into the darkness. Too late, her voice tore out of her throat. The roaring filled her mouth with scarlet noise and she thrashed in the coils of her clothing that had now become slippery and voluminous.

Phyllis appeared in the audience, her face white and round as the full moon, and then she was gone and Nancy's face was pressed up against the cold bars of the box. To her relief she found that the metal bars belonged to the hotel bedstead, not a box at the Palmyra. She was tangled up in the bedcovers and she writhed to set herself free.

She had fallen asleep after all and it had only been a nightmare, nothing more.

She had no idea of the time, but the depth of darkness suggested that it was the lowest hour of the night. She was sweating and shivering and her mouth was parched. Her water glass was empty. Phyllis had not filled it up for her.

Phyllis was dead.

Nancy slid out of bed and haphazardly drew on some clothes. She set out for the distant bathroom but in her confused state she remembered there were windows on the half-landing just beyond it. She was taken with the idea of looking out of one of the windows at the shifting sea. It wouldn't be soothing, but it might be something like looking the enemy in the eye. Feeling her way along the wall she shuffled through the darkness. In an angle of the stairs a little triangular bay jutted out towards the sea. She sank down on a window seat and pressed her forehead to the cold glass.

There were bobbing lights out on the water but she thought at first that the beach below the terrace was deserted.

Then, looking harder, she saw that there was someone out there. A figure like a black stone pillar stood alone, staring in the direction of the pier. From the set of his shoulders, the angle of his head, Nancy knew it was Mr Feather.

She watched him for a long time but he didn't move. The black flower was withering in her chest, its petals falling into soft dust.

# CHAPTER TWO

A month later, on the Saturday of the Eton and Harrow Match, Devil left the house very early without telling anyone where he was going. Arthur boiled with fury and anguish, demanding of Eliza every five minutes when she thought he would come back.

'We'll be late, Mama. I can't bear it. He *promised*, you know. He did, didn't he?'

'Hush, Arthur. Mama doesn't know any more than you do,' Nancy said. She could see that Eliza was particularly weary this morning. Her mother suffered from back pain and other ailments that were not discussed, and the holiday in Kent had been planned so she could rest and recover some strength in the sea air. The loss of the *Queen Mab* had been the end of that, and Phyllis's death had left the Wixes' London house muddled and freighted with unacknowledged grief.

It was ten-thirty before Devil reappeared. Cornelius had been out with his butterfly net to a patch of buddleia that grew on the canal towpath near to the house, and he saw the surprise first. He hurried in to find Nancy.

'You'd better come and look,' he called. She followed him outside to see what was causing a commotion in their quiet road, and she was not amazed to discover that it was her father.

Devil beamed behind the steering wheel of a motor car. He wore gauntlets and a tweed cap and he looked delighted with the world and himself. Arthur had already vaulted into the passenger's seat. Devil leaned out to kiss his wife on the lips.

'What do you think?' Without waiting for an answer he called over her shoulder to Nancy and Cornelius, 'Quite a handsome machine, eh?'

Arthur's tow-blond head bobbed up and down. 'Pappy says it's a De Dion-Bouton landaulet,' he shouted.

Two or three of the men from the street, hands in pockets and hats on the backs of their heads, were murmuring over the long, polished bonnet. Brass fittings glittered bright in the cloudy air. Devil kept the engine running and the machine purred and shivered like a big sleek animal. Nancy jumped on to the wooden running board. There was an open seat at the back, reached by its own door. Cornelius sprang in at the other side and they jigged up and down on the leather upholstery.

'Can I drive?' Cornelius demanded.

'D'you fancy the job of chauffeur, Con?' Devil laughed. 'Let me show you how she runs first. Arthur, sit in the back, please. Make room for your mother up here.'

Eliza was all cold lines. She hesitated, but found no option other than to step up into the seat next to her husband.

'Where are we going?' she icily demanded.

Devil grinned. 'To Lord's, where else? We're all dressed up and ready for Arthur's special day, aren't we?'

He eased a lever and the car rolled forward. He swung

the wheel and they were soon bowling along the high road, overtaking a tram with a blast on the horn and a rush of speed. Cornelius sat with his palms flat on his thighs, rocking with pleasure, and Arthur chanted 'De Dion-Bouton' over and over.

'She ran smooth as silk, all the way from the chap in Sydenham who sold it to me,' Devil preened.

Eliza said, 'Please tell me you haven't paid good money for this motor car.'

'It's not new. Built in 1908, but hardly driven. Rather a bargain.'

Eliza's voice rose. 'You've bought it? A *car*, at a time like this?'

The three children glanced at each other.

'What better time? We deserve to be happy. Everyone has been so cast down since the steamer, I thought a surprise would cheer you all up.'

Eliza's gloved hand struck her husband's arm.

'Damn you,' she hissed.

He looked down at her, and the car briefly swerved and rocked before he corrected it.

'Don't be a shrew, Eliza.'

She sat in silence all the way to the cricket ground. As they drew near to it the crowds heading for the match turned to stare at them. Devil waved as if he were the King.

'Let's have a happy day, shall we?' Devil pleaded with her. 'Arthur will soon be at Harrow, Cornelius is leaving school. We should enjoy being together while we can.'

As usual, Nancy was not mentioned. She was the middle child, and a girl.

Eliza was looking forward to meeting her sister Faith, with her husband Matthew Shaw and their three children, and to sharing a picnic luncheon with them. It was her choice either to enjoy herself or to let Devil's misguided gesture mar the day. The two small vertical clefts between her eyebrows melted away.

'We'll talk about this machine later,' she said, allowing her husband to help her down. Devil winked over his shoulder at Nancy and Cornelius. Arthur had already run to the gate, unable to contemplate missing a single ball.

It was a chilly day for July, with low clouds seeming almost to touch the roof of the pavilion. Under the muted sky the grass flared with a saturated, emerald brilliance. In the luncheon interval, when the ladies left their seats in the stands to mingle in the outfield with the other family groups, they covered their shoulders with wraps and kept their parasols furled.

After their picnic the sisters strolled arm in arm, drawing plenty of interested glances from the other spectators. Faith's vast hat was festooned with flowers and veiling while Eliza had chosen a tall, narrow toque with a single extravagant plume that curled almost to her shoulder. The hat made her look like an Egyptian queen.

Nancy and her cousin Lizzie Shaw followed them, arms linked in an unconscious reflection of their mothers. Nancy had turned thirteen last week and to mark this milestone Eliza had given her a pair of glacé leather shoes with raised heels, and her first pair of silk stockings. After her usual lisle bulletproofs the whispery silk left her ankles feeling naked, and she stepped a little unsteadily on the unaccustomed heels. The day was supposed to be a celebration of Arthur's imminent entry into Harrow and the ranks of public-school men, but for Nancy it retained the queasy, brittle veneer that had become familiar since the loss of the *Queen Mab*. She did what was expected of her, at school and at home, but she couldn't shake off the sense that none of it mattered. What did it even mean to be alive, she wondered, when death always hovered so close?

Phyllis had disappeared as if she had never existed, and they hadn't even attended her funeral. Nancy had asked Eliza if she might go, but Eliza had replied that it would not be suitable. If Nancy even tried to talk about the companion, Eliza shook her head.

'My poor Nancy. It's hard to come to terms with it at your age, but people do die. The best way is to look forwards, and try not to dwell on the past.'

Nancy began to wonder about the events in her parents' history that made them so fiercely intent on the here and now, and so unwilling to acknowledge what was past.

Lizzie tugged at her wrist and flashed a grin. Miss Elizabeth Shaw was a red-lipped young woman of twenty-one, with dark eyelashes and a ripe giggle. She had trained as a shorthand typist before taking a job with the managing director of a tea-importing company. She liked to describe herself as a career woman, tilting her head on the stalk of her pretty neck as she did so and laughing in a way that was not in the least self-deprecating. Lizzie declared interests in the suffragist movement, although Nancy privately believed that this might be as much to discountenance her conventional parents as from real conviction.

'Guy Earle is a handsome boy, don't you think?'

She was referring to the Harrow captain, at the same time as observing the progress of a pair of uniformed young army officers who were strolling in the opposite direction.

'Is he?'

Lizzie let out a spurt of laughter. 'Come off it, Nancy. You're not a baby. You like boys, don't you?'

'I like my brothers and my cousins. I don't know any others.'

Lizzie's brothers Rowland and Edwin were sleek young City men in their mid-twenties, one a stockbroker and the other employed in a bank.

Her cousin laughed again. 'Oh, darling Nancy. You will, I promise.'

Their fathers leaned against the front wall of one of the stands, smoking as they watched the crowds passing in front of them. Devil had never been interested in cricket and barely understood the rules of the game, but he was quite happy to issue his thoughts on the bowling.

Nancy's uncle Matthew Shaw was hardly any better informed. He was a solid, uxorious man who had long ago – when the Shaws and Eliza first met Devil Wix – been the manager of a waxworks gallery. Since those early days he had taken over the running of his late father-in-law's wholesale greengrocery business and was building up a sideline in fruit importing. He was a capable businessman and Devil had more than once tried to recruit him to manage the theatre – in tandem with himself, naturally. Matthew always rejected these advances. He loved Eliza Wix as a sister, but he considered his in-laws to be a racy and a risky combination. Matthew was aware that the Palmyra was forever on a precarious footing, and it mystified him that year after year Devil was able to keep it afloat, constantly reinventing and rejuvenating what was (for all its proprietor's claims) a Victorian variety hall.

'Arthur's happy,' Matthew observed.

The boy could be seen at the foot of the pavilion steps as he tried to catch an off-pitch glimpse of his team heroes.

'He's got good reason. This match is in the bag.'

Matthew nodded. They all knew that Cornelius was not quite like other boys and would never tread the conventional path, so Devil had determined that his younger son should go to a great public school. Arthur was a gifted cricketer but he was only average at his lessons, unlike Cornelius who was an encyclopaedic authority on the few subjects that interested him – Lepidoptera and the classical orders of architecture amongst them. So it had been a day of rejoicing in the Wix family when after months of tutoring Arthur narrowly passed the Common Entrance exam for Harrow. For Devil and Eliza it was a measure of how far they had risen in the world.

Eliza's late father had been a wholesale greengrocer and Devil's course had been even more dramatic. He ran away from a bleak village childhood, and in his early days in London he had slept in the streets. Now that he was a theatre impresario, even though the foundations of his prosperity were not as secure as they appeared, these precarious origins were not much recalled – even with Faith and Matthew. Arthur was now only weeks away from entering Harrow School, and although he and Faith thought it both pretentious and extravagant of the Wixes to be sending their boy to one of the great public schools, Matthew had to acknowledge that Devil's partisan attitude was justified today.

The Shaw brothers reappeared from their excursion to the Lord's Hotel, carrying a beery waft with them. Rowland laced his hands behind his head and stretched his legs beneath the seat in front. He swallowed a belch.

'I'm quite ready. Play can resume.'

Arthur raced round the ellipse of grass and bounded up to his family.

'Earle and the rest of our fellows are pretty confident,'

he announced, as if he had taken his lunch in the pavilion with them.

Bats under their arms, two Eton men strode out to the wicket.

Eliza had taken a glass of hock with her picnic. She remarked, 'How lovely it is to be all together like this. We must come again next year, don't you think?'

'Please, Mama, hush,' Arthur cried in anguish.

Nancy rested her chin on doubled fists. She longed to lose herself in the game like everyone else, but the scent of mown grass rose and surged into the crannies of her head. A tilt of perspective replaced the cricket pitch with mud and shattered trees and the sad remains of men.

She resisted the swamp with all her strength, clenching her teeth until her jaw creaked. No one was looking at her. Flags in front of the pavilion stirred in the summer breeze and she heard the cheering for a boundary as if it came from a long way off.

Perhaps strength of will was what was needed. The Uncanny mustn't be allowed to claim her.

From now on, *she* must try to be the one who claimed *it*.

The white figures of the cricketers swam against the grass but they remained themselves. The smell of grass was now only a midsummer scent mingling with strawberries and her mother's perfume.

I won't think about the other place, she repeated. I shall try to be more like Arthur and Lizzie.

As if to endorse her strength of will her father nudged her and winked.

'What do you think of this, eh?'

She swallowed hard. 'So exciting.'

Bob Fowler, the Eton captain, was finally caught out.

'Now we're secure,' Arthur crowed.

But Eton's tenth-wicket partnership suddenly began to hit the Harrow bowling all over the field. Astonishingly, fifty runs were put on in only half an hour.

In the tea interval Devil and the three Shaw men walked to the boundary to watch groundsmen dragging up the heavy roller. The sky was lightening at last and a pale bar of sunlight crept between clouds to fall across the face of the Grand Stand. In a state of unbearable tension Arthur could only jiggle in his seat. The Shaw men stopped ribbing him.

A succession of wickets fell before the Harrow captain came out to bat. He staunched the flow with a score of thirteen, but then he was caught off a savage yorker.

Arthur could not help himself. He jumped up and yelled, 'No! Earle's not out. It was a bump ball, I saw it. Not out, I say.' Faces turned to him.

'Arthur,' Devil said sharply. He knew enough about cricket to recognise unsporting behaviour.

Harrow's tenth man could be seen sprinting out of one of the tea tents with a cream bun still grasped in his hand, urgently summoned to prepare for his innings. The last stand put on a desperate thirteen runs.

'Come on,' Arthur gasped.

But then, at one minute to six, the end came. The batsman played inside a ball that did not turn as expected, and was caught in the slips. The roar from the crowd was loud enough to lift the roofs. It swelled over Regent's Park and the villas of St John's Wood. Eton had won the match by nine runs.

Arthur blinked at the tumult of Eton boys and families surging on to the pitch. He pulled his straw hat down towards his ears until the crown threatened to split from the brim.

'I don't know how that happened,' he whispered. 'It's beyond comprehension.'

Cornelius placed his bookmark.

'Are we going home now?'

The pandemonium in the ground was growing and the exuberant crowds seemed denser than they had done all day.

'It will take for ever to make our way to the underground in this crush,' Matthew complained.

'And I am afraid I must leave you and take the De Dion to the theatre,' Devil apologised. He adjusted the brim of his hat with the Harrow colours to a more rakish angle and smoothed the flanks of his striped blazer. In less than an hour he would be in his white tie and tailcoat, ready to step out on the Palmyra stage as the evening's master of ceremonies.

'I'm glad you have your motor car, and the rest of us are in no hurry,' Eliza observed.

Devil kissed her on the cheek and offered Faith the same salute. To Arthur he said, 'Next year, there will be another match. And in five years' time you will be lifting your bat in the Harrow eleven.'

Arthur set his smooth jaw as he stared into this dizzy future. A second later Devil had vanished into the crowd.

The rest of the party agreed that they might as well allow the hubbub to die down. The four women took a stroll round the outfield. Lizzie was saying that her boss Mr Hastings was a tremendous oarsman and she greatly preferred rowing to cricket as a spectator sport. Perhaps next year Nancy might like to come with her and some lively girls to Henley? This year they had had so much fun – a broad wink – and she was sure Nancy would adore it.

A man was standing beside the perimeter wall, shading his eyes from the weak sun as he looked towards them.

His dark coat made him incongruous amongst the other spectators in their light summer clothes. As they drew abreast he stepped into their path.

'Mrs Wix? Nancy?'

It was Mr Feather.

He tried to lock his gaze with Nancy's but after the smallest nod in his direction she fixed her attention on the pavilion roof. Her heart banged uncomfortably against her ribs. Faith and Lizzie politely withdrew a little distance.

'How are you?' Eliza murmured to him. The man's gaunt appearance startled her. 'I am so sorry about Mrs Clare.'

'Thank you. It was a terrible . . . it is not . . . I had hoped . . .'

He struggled for the words and then bowed his head. In a man who had been so fluent the inarticulacy was even more shocking than his altered looks.

Eliza placed her hand on his sleeve.

'Perhaps Nancy might bring you a glass of lemonade?'

Nancy stared at the buttons of his coat so as not to see his face, and still his proximity made her shiver.

*I don't want to be a seer.*

Mr Feather collected himself and sadly nodded.

'Lemonade? That is kind, but no, thank you. I should offer my condolences in return, for the loss you also suffered on that day.'

'Phyllis was our children's companion. Very sad, of course, but she was not a relative.'

Eliza's tone indicated that the topic was closed. Nancy shot her a glance, wondering how her mother could some- times seem so devoid of feelings.

A young man hurried towards them. He called out, 'Lawrence? So sorry, I had to speak to a chap I was . . . ah? Hullo!'

With an effort Lawrence Feather produced a smile. 'Not at all, Lycett. I too have bumped into some friends. Mrs Wix, Miss Wix, may I introduce Mr Lycett Stone?'

He was a tall, plump and dishevelled Etonian in top hat and elaborate waistcoat. He grinned and removed the hat with a flourish, clearly elated by the match. Unconfined by the topper his curly hair gave him the look of an over-grown Cupid. Nancy didn't want to stare, but she was struck by the young man's exuberance. She thought it would have been fun to hear his account of the game. More fun than listening to Arthur, at any rate.

The young man beamed. 'Well, I have to say, it's been a great day.'

'You must be delighted,' Eliza agreed.

'Eh? Oh dear. Your boy's a Harrovian, I assume?'

'Yes, he will be.'

Lycett Stone pursed his full lips and did his best to look sympathetic, but unruly satisfaction spilled out of him.

'Next year,' he consoled. 'There's always next year.'

Lawrence Feather looked even more sombre beside this vision of merriment. He murmured, 'I shouldn't detain you any longer, Mrs Wix. But may I call on you at some conven-ient time?'

Eliza agreed, mainly out of pity for the state he was in. The strange pair said goodbye and moved off into the crowd as Faith and Lizzie rejoined them.

'Who was that?' Lizzie Shaw demanded.

Eliza explained the circumstances in which they had last seen Lawrence Feather.

'Oh, I see. Actually I meant the other one, the Eton boy.'

'I don't know, Lizzie,' Eliza said. 'His name is Lycett Stone. Why do you ask?'

'He looked rather jolly.'

It was almost seven o'clock and the crowds were thinning out at last. The two families had planned to eat supper together but Rowland and Edwin Shaw excused themselves, saying they were going on to meet some fellows for a drink. The brothers shared a set of bachelor rooms in Holloway. Only Lizzie still lived with her mother and father, and she had privately confided to Nancy that she didn't intend to remain there much longer. As they threaded their way to St John's Wood underground station Lizzie was still volubly talking.

'We are liberated women in this family. We don't need overseeing and chaperoning every time we step out of the front door, do we? Look at your mama. Even in her day she was able to live in a ladies' rooming house and work as an artists' model.'

This wasn't news to Nancy or anyone else. Eliza loved to reminisce about her artistic and theatrical days.

The Wixes lived beside the Regent's Canal at Islington. It was a pretty house, rising three storeys above a basement area enclosed by railings. There were curled wrought-iron balconies at the tall windows, and the play of light over the water was caught in the rippled old glass. Only ten years before the canal had been busy with laden barges drawn by huge slow horses, but lately the furniture-makers of the area had begun to receive their timbers by motor wagon and the channel now bloomed with carpets of green weed.

Devil had bought the house for Eliza shortly after Cornelius was born, borrowing the money at a high rate of interest from a private bank. The heavy repayments on the loan had begun the serious undermining of the Wixes' finances. The theatre business and their home lives had rocked on more or less unstable foundations ever since.

When they reached the house Eliza had to stop and lean against the railings to catch her breath. She seemed too tired even to search for her key.

'Mama?' Nancy said in concern.

Arthur ran up the steps to ring the bell and the door was grudgingly cracked open by Cook.

'Evening, mum, Mrs Shaw, Mr Shaw.'

The cook was not pleased to see visitors for supper, especially since it was Peggy's evening off.

The Wixes kept two servants in the house, Mrs Frost the cook ('An aptly named person,' Cornelius had remarked), and a housemaid. Nancy loyally insisted that she wouldn't accept any replacement for Phyllis. A daily woman came in to do the heavy cleaning and laundry, her morose little husband did odd jobs, and a smeary-faced boy appeared in the mornings to clean the shoes and run any necessary errands.

'There's only cold cuts, mum,' Cook called after Eliza as the sisters went upstairs to take off their hats. 'I reckon I could boil up a few spuds, if you really need me to.'

In her bedroom Eliza drew the hatpins from her plumed toque and set it on the dressing table. Faith steered her to the chair at the window.

'There. Sit for a moment.'

'Matthew . . .' Eliza began.

'. . . will be glad to read the newspaper in peace for half an hour,' Faith finished for her. 'Shall I ask Cook to bring us a pot of tea?'

'By all means. She will certainly give notice if you do. It will save me the trouble of dismissing her.'

Faith only laughed. She was well used to the state of semi-warfare between Eliza and the cook.

'No tea, then. Something stronger?'

38

A silver tray with a bottle and glasses stood on Devil's dressing stand. Faith placed a weak gin and water in her sister's hand and watched her take two swallows.

'I don't know where I'd be without you, Faith.'

Eliza and her sister were close, and had become even more so in recent years. As a young woman Eliza had dismissed Faith's choice of marriage and motherhood as unadventurous, but she was generous enough now to acknowledge that for all her youthful insistence on freedom they had ended up in more or less the same place. How age *enamels* us, she would say. It builds up in layers and locks us inside our own skin, stopping us from breaking out, preventing the outside from burrowing in.

Faith said, 'You'd do perfectly well, but you don't have to because I am here. Is it bad today?'

Eliza closed her eyes. Her fingers splayed over her lower belly as if to support the failures and collapses within.

'My back aches, a little.'

'What else, then? Is it Devil?'

There was a long pause.

'No more than usual.'

Faith didn't ask, 'Who is it this time?' but she might well have done.

There was always someone: an actress or a dancer from the theatre, a waitress from one of the supper clubs, or a young girl met across a shop counter when he was choosing a pair of gloves or a bottle of scent for Eliza.

That was the strange thing.

Apart from the few years at the beginning of their married life, before Cornelius was born, Devil had been incapable of fidelity. Yet even when his pursuit of women was at its most fervent, Devil had always been – so it seemed to Faith and Matthew – utterly obsessed with his wife.

Faith said, 'He adores you.'

Eliza gave a thin sigh. It was not the first time the two of them had discussed the matter.

'That's partly the trouble. I can't satisfy his craving, and the more I fail in that the more he longs for what he imagines I am withholding.'

It wasn't just sex, although sex lay at the root of it. Once they had been well suited. But then Cornelius had come, or rather a brutal doctor with a pair of forceps had dragged him into the world, and after that there had been a change. Pain and distress made Eliza hesitant, even though she had tried to pretend otherwise, and although Devil had done his best he had in the end read her hesitancy as reluctance. He was cast as the importuner and Eliza as the withholder, and although the front line of their battle constantly shifted, sometimes dressed up as comedy and at others bitterly rancorous, there was always a battle.

Almost five years after Cornelius Nancy had arrived easily, but Arthur's birth hardly more than a year after that had been almost as difficult as his brother's.

Nowadays Devil propitiated his wife with expensive comforts and sea air. Accepting her reliance on new doctors and patent cures, he squandered too much time and energy on the Palmyra, arguing that otherwise the theatre could not generate the money he needed to care for his family. Devil regarded the diversions of motor cars and women as just that, and would have claimed – in the circumstances – they were nothing less than he deserved. Eliza didn't see it the same way, and she was angry with him. All the images of herself that she had created as a young woman had been to do with strength and freedom, and now she possessed neither. She was little better than an invalid, and she had become dependent on her unreliable husband for everything.

Eliza sat upright. She squeezed her glass so tightly that it might have shattered.

'How has this happened to me? Here I sit like a wilting girl. I'm ashamed of myself, Faith.'

'There is no shame in what you have suffered.'

'I am weak.'

Faith shot back at her, 'We're women. We're all weak. You don't have a monopoly on the condition.'

Faith was not usually so blunt. Eliza stuck out her glass, still miraculously intact. They were both smiling, almost girls again.

'We'll have to endure it, I suppose. Give me some more gin before we go down and feast on the boiled spuds.'

On the floor above Lizzie stuck her head out of Nancy's bedroom window and – to Nancy's astonished awe – smoked a cigarette.

'Do you want one?'

'*No*. I mean . . . I don't mind, but I don't smoke.'

'Terrible, isn't it? I caught the habit from some of the girls at work and now I'm completely hooked.'

Cornelius rapped on the door and Lizzie quickly ground out the cigarette on the windowsill before tossing the end into the grey air.

Cornelius called, 'Cook says to come now if you don't want it cold.'

'It was cold to start with, wasn't it?' Lizzie laughed.

The stage door was in a narrow alley that ran from the Strand towards the Embankment. Devil stepped inside. The doorman in his wooden cubicle passed over a sheaf of post and wished him a good evening.

'Who won the match, sir?'

'Eton, I'm sorry to say.'

'Mr Arthur'll be disappointed.'

'That's hardly the word.'

Devil made his way down a dark passageway lit by a single overhead bulb and up a short flight of bare wooden stairs. There was a strong smell of worn clothing, congealed grease, and mice.

The theatre owner and manager's office had brown-painted walls and was hardly wide enough for a cluttered desk. The lighting was no better or brighter than in the corridor outside. He propped himself on a corner of the desk and quickly shuffled through the mail. It was all bills, mostly final demands, and at the bottom of the heap he found a flyer for the new show at a rival theatre. The type was blocky, modern and rather eye-catching. Devil screwed the sheet up and threw it at the wastebasket.

The backstage manager Anthony Ellis stuck his head round the door.

'All right, Mr Wix?'

'Hullo, Anthony. What was the house like this afternoon?'

'Eighty-three.'

'Christ. Tonight?'

'Better. Might be two hundred.'

Devil nodded. The capacity of the Palmyra was two hundred and fifty. Its intimate scale made it perfect for performances of magic, although even when it was full it was an exacting task to make it pay well. There was no profit to be taken out of a thin house.

'Thirty until the up,' Anthony reminded him.

The stage manager withdrew. Devil heard him tread along the corridor to the door of the main dressing area. He knew every creak of the old floorboards, every scrape of a hinge and click of a switch. The other performers all made ready in one chaotic room, ducking behind screens and crowding at a single mirror. The Palmyra was not noted for its back-stage luxury. All resources were lavished on the front of house.

Devil whistled as he stripped off his blazer and soft-collared shirt. He stood in his vest at a broken piece of mirror and rapidly applied a layer of make-up, then worked over the arches of his eyebrows with a dark pencil before finally reddening his lips with a crimson crayon. When he was finished he removed his starched shirt from the hanger and slipped it on, careful to keep the folds away from his painted face. He fixed his collar with an old stud and deftly tied his white butterfly.

Once he was fully costumed he stood in front of the glass again. He rubbed brilliantine through his greying hair, the gloss turning it darker. Then he briskly applied a pair of old wooden-backed hairbrushes to the sides and top.

Devil was fifty-four years old and still a notably hand-some man.

By this time Anthony Ellis was coming back to call the ten. Devil walked through the skein of cramped passageways to the wings. Stagehands in shirtsleeves greeted him as he passed. From the pit he could hear the small orchestra tuning up. As he took his place behind the house curtain a stooping elderly woman hurried from a niche to brush the shoulders of his coat. Sylvia Aynscoe was the wardrobe mistress and dresser, and she had been employed at the Palmyra almost since the beginning.

'Evening, Sylvia.'

She gave him a compressed smile before twitching the points of his collar into place. Sylvia was an old ally of Eliza's. It was through the unobtrusive conduit of the dresser that news of everything that happened at the Palmyra found its way back to Islington.

At two minutes to the up Devil was poised on the balls of his feet like an athlete ready to sprint. He flexed his white-gloved fingers and patted the props in the concealed pockets in his coat. The rustle and chatter of the audience through the heavy green velvet drapes sounded like the sea.

The first act of the current show was a dance illusion routine. Four girls in laced satin pumps and scanty dresses of sequinned tulle softly padded to their positions behind him. The best-looking of the four, an elfin girl with a dancer's taut body, knew better than to try to attract his attention at this tense moment. She turned her head instead to catch her reflection in one of the mirrors. A tall plume of white feathers nodded from a tiny tiara, darts of radiance flashing from the paste gems.

The orchestra struck up the national anthem and the audience rose to its feet. As soon as they had resumed their seats Devil stepped out between the tabs. The bright circle of the following spot tightened on him as he smiled into the heart of the expectant house. He was glad to see that it was better than two hundred. All the stalls were occupied and only a score of seats in the gallery were empty. Pale faces gazed down at him from two tiers of gilt-fronted boxes at the sides of the stage. He let his eyes sweep over the rows of seats.

'Good evening, ladies and gentlemen. Welcome to the home of magic and illusion. We have a magnificent and intriguing show for you tonight.'

Devil pivoted. When he turned again a ringmaster's whip had appeared in his hand. He cracked the whip and a mirrored ball spun on the boards at his feet; he cracked it a second time and the ball rose like a giant soap bubble and floated away.

Laughter and applause spread through his veins, lovely as warmth in winter. Even though he was pinioned in the lights he could see out to the slender pillars that were carved to resemble palm stems, and the fronds of painted plaster leaves. Gilt-framed lozenges of bright paint glimmered at him. His voice rose into the graceful cupola surmounting the auditorium. Devil thought of his theatre as a jewel box that his audience could open, only a few feet removed from the din of the Strand. He offered them opulence in exchange for the mundane world.

He loved every brick and plank of the place.

The giant bubble sank again. Another flick of the whip broke it into real soap bubbles that drifted out over the double *fauteuils* at the front of the stalls and gently vanished.

Devil swept his bow and backed into the wings.

The curtain rose at once on the dancers. Four girls arched their taut bodies against four triangular columns. Two faces of the columns were mirrored and the third was black.

The orchestra began to play 'Let Me Call You Sweetheart'.

The columns were mounted on spindles, and in the recess beneath their feet a stagehand turned a drum and the columns silently revolved. The girls moved into their dance. Four were multiplied to eight, and the mirrors reflected their reflections until sixty-four splintered images danced into the light, were swallowed up by the turning darkness, and then pirouetted into view again. Dozens of white plumes swayed and the jewels shot points of fire.

The audience drew a collective breath and the applause for this vision almost drowned out the music.

Devil watched from the wings. The elfin dancer spun *en pointe* and her blank gaze passed over his face. But on the next turn their eyes locked for a fraction of a second. No one else saw it, but the ghost of her smile for him was multiplied into infinity.

Devil lifted his gloved hand in a small salute. He turned away through the wings, and returned to his office where the bills were still piled on his desk.

# CHAPTER THREE

The housemaid brought in the tray and placed it on the table.

'Anything else, Mrs Wix?'

Eliza ran her eye over the tea service with the pattern of forget-me-nots, the silver pot and sugar tongs, and the two varieties of cake on a tiered plate.

'Thank you, Peggy, that will be all.' When the girl had left the room Eliza said to her guest, 'Now, Mr Feather, how do you take your tea?'

The man had called on her twice before. On the first occasion she had been out at Faith's and on the second she had told Peggy to say she was not at home. When he turned up for the third time she realised that he would go on knocking at her front door day after day until she did agree to see him, so she had let him in. Lawrence Feather was not a welcome guest, but now he was here she would at least show him that she ran a proper household.

Feather was not the man to be deflected from his purpose by tea or sponge cake. As soon as he could he put his cup aside and leaned forward.

'I need your help,' he said.

She inclined her head. 'Really? In what way?'

'I think you don't believe in psychism, Mrs Wix?'

She frowned. 'I have seen plenty of stage cheats and music-hall fakery. Clutching icy hands, floating mists, bells clanging when there is no one to ring them, that sort of thing. There is no real harm in it, as entertainment for those who are so inclined. But there has never been a so-called manifestation that couldn't be explained away by hidden wires, a yard or two of fine muslin, a human arm in a black sleeve. All in a darkened room, naturally. Possibly I am too coarse to be susceptible to the real thing, Mr Feather.'

He did not flinch. He just looked at her, his eyes glowing like coals in their hollow sockets.

'I don't believe you are in the least coarse, Mrs Wix. Let me put it to you in a different way. Are you quite certain that there are no senses on the fringe of human consciousness, nothing whatsoever beyond the range of what is accepted as normal or physical?'

Eliza hesitated.

'I think none of us can be quite certain of that. I was talking about those cheap stage performances I have seen with my own eyes and know to be fraudulent. You are speaking of different matters, perhaps.'

'I am.'

The man probably conveyed all sorts of damaging nonsense to the lost and bereaved who made up his audiences. She was suspicious of him and his motives.

He lifted his hand. 'You know, of course, that I lost my sister Helena, and my dear brother-in-law, when the steamer sank. We spoke of it when we met at Lord's.'

'Yes. You have my sympathy.'

'Thank you. You and your family suffered your own loss.

48

However, Mrs Wix, I am not married. Helena was all I had. I loved her dearly. Perhaps even too dearly.'

There was a shiver of a pause. Feather's tongue moistened his lips before he smoothly continued, 'Our parents passed years ago and we have no other siblings. She was my lieutenant in my work, and she knew everything about my efforts to open a conduit from this world to the regions beyond.'

He anticipated the obvious question.

'You are wondering, since this is my claimed expertise, if I am able to speak to her now, or if she has in any way reached out to me?'

'Yes.'

His voice sank to a whisper. He seemed on the brink of tears.

'I have tried. I have tried with all my heart, and every fibre of my capacity. There is a tumult of voices out there, crying and calling, clamouring for me to open their channels, but there is no Helena.'

Eliza could not help feeling sympathy, even for a charlatan.

'Only once, on the night she passed, did I hear anything. I stood on the beach in front of the hotel and I wanted to die from grief. I hoped I would die, God forgive me. Then Helena spoke suddenly to me out of the silence. She said, "I am here."'

'Was that a comfort to you?'

He nodded. 'Yes. Oh yes, it was the greatest comfort. But that was all she said, even though I stood for hours in the same place, waiting and hoping. Since that night there has been nothing. No word and no sign – except for one significant thing.'

The calculating glance he gave her was at odds with his grieving demeanour and her sympathy faded.

'What is that?'

'I was invited at the last moment to attend the Schools

Match by my godson, the child of an old friend, a young man thoughtful in his efforts to lift me out of my sorrow. I almost didn't go, but I didn't want to reject a kindness.'

'You introduced us.' Eliza recalled the plump boy's merriment.

'I did. And there at Lord's I saw your daughter again. Mrs Wix, I could only interpret such a coincidence as no coincidence at all, but a sign from Helena.'

'My *daughter*?'

'Yes. You know that Nancy has unusual psychic powers?'

This must stop immediately, Eliza thought. She stood up, stretching to her full height.

'To encounter people by chance at a public-school cricket match is not a sign of any kind. My daughter is thirteen years old. She has no powers. I don't want you to speak of her in relation to your beliefs. I would like you to leave my house now, and never to come here again.'

A spasm of pain darted from the small of her back and travelled down her thighs and into her calves, making her gasp. She held on to the back of her chair for support. Lawrence Feather gazed into her face as if he knew and understood what she felt.

He murmured, 'Thirteen is a crucial age for a young girl. The senses are newly awakened, and the powers are as sharp and subtle as they ever will be. Nancy is a clairvoyant and precognisant, I knew it the instant I saw her in the saloon of the hotel.'

Eliza straightened as the pain released her.

'What *tripe*.'

'No, Mrs Wix. Truth. I am certain that Helena intends Nancy to be our channel. I have come here to ask you – to beg you – to let me be your daughter's control. She could be a great medium some day.'

'This is impertinent nonsense. Please go now or I shall have to call for help.'

'You won't allow me to consult Nancy herself?'

'Most definitely I will not.'

Downstairs the front door slammed.

Cornelius was at his new place of work, Devil was at the theatre and Arthur was spending the day with a friend. The arrival could only be Nancy herself. Eliza had sent her to the draper's shop at the far end of the Essex Road to buy a length of tweed for a new winter coat. Eliza had given her some other commissions to attend to on the way back, and she had only let Lawrence Feather into the house in the expectation that he would be long gone by the time Nancy returned.

'Stay here,' she ordered, hoping to intercept her daughter and send her straight to her room. But she was too late. Pink-cheeked from the brisk walk, Nancy appeared in the doorway carrying a brown paper parcel tied with string.

'I have the tweed but Ransom's is closed today for family reasons, the notice in the window says. *Oh.*'

'Good afternoon, Nancy,' Lawrence Feather said.

Nancy's stricken expression convinced Eliza that something significant had already taken place between her daughter and the medium. Unwelcome speculations raced through her mind. Nancy's childhood had been sheltered and – by her parents' standards – privileged, and she was as innocent as a much younger girl. That was what Eliza and Devil had intended for her, and they had schemed and struggled to make it happen.

Eliza thought quickly. If she dismissed the man now, he would not give up. She imagined him lying in wait for Nancy, watching her movements from a niche across the canal and springing out to seize her by the arm in some deserted street. In her own youth she had suffered a similar attack and the memory of it would never leave her.

It would be better to confront this business. She wished Devil were here, but then Devil's response would certainly be aggressive and Lawrence Feather might be better handled with greater cunning. Eliza took her seat again. She seemed to consider and then reach a decision.

'Please join us, Nancy. Mr Feather and I were talking about his sad loss and then a little about his psychic theories.'

She spoke neutrally, as if the theories related to nothing more controversial than gardening or dog breeding.

Nancy obediently sat behind the shelter of the tea table. She glanced from her mother to the visitor.

Feather didn't hesitate.

'You will recall what happened on that terrible morning, Nancy, when I found you on the beach?'

Nancy pressed her lips between her teeth. 'Yes.'

'I was explaining to your mother that I had already recognised you as one of our number. It is one of my best-developed skills, and a source of particular satisfaction to me, to adopt and encourage new practitioners in the psychic arts.'

Eliza almost smiled. The man was preeningly vain, and his absurdity immediately made him seem less alarming. Nancy was young, but she would surely see that he was ridiculous.

'That morning we shared a psychic experience, did we not? I told you that you are a seer, and you should not be afraid of your gift.'

'Is this what happened, Nancy?'

Nancy gave the smallest possible nod. She felt as if she were being goaded into an awkward place between the rock of her mother's hostility and the chasm of Mr Feather's horrible powers. Then it came to her, with a surge of rebellion, that neither of them could really know about the Uncanny. Mr Feather might have tipped her deeper into it, with his heavy hand on her head, but he didn't see inside her. He hadn't glimpsed the mud and the trees and the shattered men, nor had her mother.

The Uncanny was hers alone. The privacy of it seemed suddenly to be her strength as much as a weakness. At the Lord's match, she had even established some control over it. She didn't know what the gift really was or why it had been granted to her, but maybe the man was right. There would be a use for it.

'What else?' Eliza asked.

Nancy slowly shook her head.

'Nothing.'

'I know you will tell me the truth, Nancy.'

Eliza expected nothing less than absolute candour.

'There is nothing, Mama.'

Feather put in, 'Mrs Wix, this is not the place to discuss such matters but I assure you . . .'

Eliza held up her hand.

'The psychic arts.' Her tone was wintry, with mockery in it keen as a blade. 'Mr Feather has a theory, Nancy. He believes that there are voices from beyond the grave, and it is his work, or profession – he tells me that he is a professional medium – to channel them, as he calls it. It's in relation to this work that Mr Feather has called today to ask a favour of you.'

'Of *me*?'

Eliza was confident now. She had all the ammunition she needed.

'He believes that you can help him to speak to Mrs Clare.'

Nancy's dry lips cracked and made her wince. 'But

Mrs Clare is dead. And Phyllis and Mr Clare and the little girl.'

'Yes, very sadly that is true. Unfortunately, Mr Feather can't reach his late sister on the other side or hear her messages himself, despite his skills. He believes that you will be able to do this for him. Under his control, that is.'

There was a silence. Lawrence Feather's eyes implored Nancy. She sank lower in her chair.

Eliza asked, 'Do you think you can do this, Nancy?'

'No.'

The monosyllable dropped into stillness. With a stage artist's timing Eliza let the silence gather and deepen. At last she said, 'There you are. You asked to be allowed to consult my daughter, and against my preference you have been able to do so. You have your answer, Mr Feather.'

He started forwards in his chair. 'Nancy, please listen to me. You and I both know . . .'

Eliza cut him short. She stood again, ignoring the pains in her back. Her demeanour was so forbidding that the medium fell silent.

'There's nothing more to be discussed.'

She crossed to the door and held it open.

Only when she had seen him out of the house and watched him walking to the tram stop did she return to Nancy. The girl was hunched in her chair, her arms wrapped around herself. Eliza believed the child was telling the truth – she was too obedient to do otherwise – but the afternoon's events were still troubling.

'What nonsense. The poor man must be unbalanced by grief.'

Nancy raised her head. 'Perhaps,' she said.

Her gaze seemed clouded, no longer quite that of an innocent child.

'I ask you one more time, Nancy. Are you quite sure that nothing untoward happened with that man? Did he touch or even speak to you in any way that was improper?'

Nancy's face flooded with colour.

'No, not at all.'

'Then why does his presence trouble you? It's obvious that it does.'

'I'm not denying it, Mama. He is strange, and to see him makes me think of the steamer and Phyllis.'

It was an oblique version of the truth and Nancy reddened at even slightly misrepresenting herself to her mother.

Eliza considered. Nancy wasn't an actress, she couldn't feign distress so convincingly. The *Queen Mab* had been a shocking experience for all three children, and it was natural for Nancy to be upset by the reminder. She put her arm around her daughter's shoulders.

'I understand.'

Eliza and Devil had decided that they should not dwell on the circumstances of the tragedy. In their own experience the best way to deal with shocking events was to leave them in the past. She hugged Nancy briefly and then released her.

'You will not have to meet that man again.'

'Mama?'

'What is it?'

'*Is* there such a thing as psychism? *Can* the dead speak to us?'

Eliza hesitated. It was a long time since she had been able to command the reverie. Long ago, by emptying her mind on an exhaled breath, she had been able to slip into a peaceful dimension of intense colours. She had been a rebellious child, and she had used the ability as a shield against adult wrath and a refuge from tedium. Later when she had taken employment as an artists' model, she had made professional use of the reverie to hold her pose in the life-drawing class.

The power had gradually deserted her at about the time she fell in love with Devil, and she supposed now that the condition had been connected with the physical and emotional changes of young womanhood. She had never heard voices from the other side, and she was sure that her innocent reverie was no channel to the supernatural.

Devil had been the one who claimed that he saw ghosts. But then Devil had suffered such hardships and horrors during his childhood it was hardly surprising his imagination had turned macabre. Yet he too had grown out of his susceptibility. He had not spoken of his ghosts for many years now.

Eliza considered herself to be a rational woman with modern ideas. Her scepticism was founded in years of exposure to the tricks and devices of stage illusionists.

'No, the dead do not speak to us,' she answered at length. 'But as you already know there are some people who claim they do.'

'Why do they do that?'

She patted Nancy's hand. The naivety of the question reassured her. It was time to finish this conversation and move on to healthier topics.

'For money, or perhaps for public attention,' she smiled. 'Now, look at the time. You should go and dress, or we will be late at Aunt Faith's.'

Nancy went upstairs. Across the landing, in the larger front bedroom shared by Cornelius and Arthur, Arthur's school trunk and boxes were packed and corded ready for the carrier. Tomorrow, Devil and Eliza would drive their son to Harrow School in the De Dion-Bouton. The motor car had been polished to a state of glittering perfection by old Gibb, the chauffeur-mechanic Devil had employed to look after it.

In contrast to his brother's success, Cornelius had recently become a clerk in a shipping office. Every day he carried sandwiches packed in a tin box to his place of work and he had described to Nancy how he sat on a bench in a nearby graveyard to eat them.

'I like it. It's peaceful.'

He dismissed all questions about his colleagues or the actual work he performed, but this surprised no one. Cornelius was never communicative.

Nancy leaned on the windowsill, as Lizzie had done when she smoked the startling cigarette. From here she could look straight down into the basement area where the mangle stood under its tin roof. A little iron bridge led from the dining room across to the garden where Eliza liked to grow flowers for their fragrance. The strong perfume of night-scented jasmine was already drifting upwards.

She hadn't confided in her mother. She had the not altogether unpleasant sense of having cut her moorings.

She had said *No* to Mr Feather because it was true in the broad sense. She didn't think she could speak to Mrs Clare.

Yet she did know that there had been an unnatural relationship between Mr Feather and his sister. Helena Clare had been afraid of him; Nancy had clearly seen it in her face. Instead of the garden lying below her she saw a boathouse and a moored boat with cushioned seats. Outside, shafts of greenish light struck across lake water and in the shadowy interior two bodies grappled and then locked together. The rowing boat violently rocked. She was witnessing something horrible and wrong, and she was disgusted as well as afraid.

It was a mild evening, still early, but the hairs on Nancy's forearms rose.

She drew her head inside and slammed the window on the Uncanny. An unexpected glint of light on metal caught her eye and she crossed to her dressing table to see what it was. Lying next to her hairbrush was a silver locket she had never seen before. The chain was neatly folded but it was tarnished, as was the locket itself. She picked it up and cupped it in the hollow of her hand. There was a faint design of engraved leaves on the front and traces of dirt caught in the filigree. Unwillingly, she turned the piece over.

The initials engraved on the reverse were *HMF*.

Her hand shook but she slipped her thumbnail into the crease between the halves of the locket and prised it open. Within lay two locks of hair, twisted to form a ring and bound with scarlet thread. The tiny circlet was damp and earth was matted in it.

She closed the locket and dropped it on the dressing table. She knew whose initials these must be, and whose heads the two locks of hair had come from.

Arthur raced up the stairs, his boots skidding on the linoleum. He drummed on Nancy's door.

'Wait,' she told him.

When she glanced down again the dressing table was bare except for her hairbrush and comb.

The Shaws lived in a suburban enclave of substantial new red-brick villas to the north of Maida Vale. It was a highly respectable area marked out by pleached limes and encaustic tiles, leafy in summer and scented in winter with coal smoke and damp earth. The Shaws' house had a projecting double-height bay topped off with a conical turret roofed in slate, for which Devil had mockingly nicknamed it Bavaria after one of Ludwig's fantasy castles. Their own smaller, more gracefully proportioned house was a hundred years older but the stink of the tanneries to the east often crept around it, and decaying hovels and factories crowded at the margins of the canal basin only yards from their door. Yet Devil would not hear of a move to anywhere more rural. He loathed suburbia and claimed to have a physical aversion to open countryside.

Matthew came to the door dressed in shirtsleeves and a woollen waistcoat. He loved his home and presiding over his table, and was always a happier man on his own territory. Devil was formal in a starched collar and a fitted coat. He raised an eyebrow as the men shook hands.

'On your way up to bed, Matty?'

Laughing, Matthew ruffled Arthur's hair. Arthur bore this with good humour, even though in a year or so he would easily top his uncle in height.

'Here he is, the scholar. You'll be talking to us in Latin or Greek by Christmas, Arthur, eh?'

'I already know Latin and Greek, Uncle Matthew.'

Faith came forward, rosy-cheeked and handsome in a new blue dress.

'So we are all together again. Rowland and Edwin have come from Town specially to give you a send-off, Arthur.'

Rowland stuck out a hand. 'Arthur, my boy. We've been waiting for you. Come out for a smoke with us?'

'Rowland, please,' Faith remonstrated.

Arthur glowed. He admired his adult cousins and he liked nothing better than listening to their knowing talk about girls and business. The three of them went outside to a little stone-paved terrace bordered with azalea bushes and Japanese maples. Lizzie made a point of taking Nancy by the arm and leading her to the window seat at the other end of the room for a cosy talk. Cornelius sat calmly. As always he gave the impression of being busy with his own thoughts.

The first breath of autumn in the air gave Matthew the excuse to light a fire, and as the day faded Faith turned on the lamps under their painted-glass shades. Pools of brightness lay on the rugs and fringed cushions and upholstered stools. The crowded, homely room was stuffed with mementoes. Faith loved to arrange framed photographs on the lid of the piano, showing her children at every stage from dimpled babyhood to the latest one of Edwin on a bicycling holiday with his friends from the bank.

Later Matthew led the way into the dining room. Arthur was given the place of honour at the head of the table. Candles burned in a branched pewter candlestick and there were new napkins and a matching table runner.

Faith had only one little housemaid and a daily char and she did most of the lighter domestic work and all the cooking herself. She was an excellent plain cook and her dishes always arrived hot at the table and in the proper sequence. This made a contrast with Islington, where matters were not always so smoothly arranged even though there were more hands to do the work. Domestic comforts always put Devil in a good humour. He tilted back in his chair and grinned across the table at his wife.

Lizzie and Nancy carried plates up from the kitchen. Lizzie took the opportunity to continue the talk they had begun on the window seat, saying, 'You do look a bit cheesed off, my girl. What's up?'

*Cheesed off* wasn't exactly it, but Nancy was touched that her cousin had noticed.

'I am a little, I suppose.'

Lizzie's dark eyebrows rose.

'Battles at home, eh? Don't tell me you are getting to be

60

a rebellious creature, Nancy?' She rolled her eyes. 'If so let me tell you, life will not get any easier from now on.'

Nancy glanced over her shoulder and said hastily, 'Oh no, nothing like that. But can I ask you something?'

'Go ahead.'

She blurted out, 'Do you ever feel solitary? As if there are millions of people swarming around you, and yet no one knows who you are?'

Her cousin shrewdly eyed her.

'I used to, all the time. My dear brothers, you know, deaf and blind to half the world. My father is a Victorian figure and my mother is equally historic. Of course she is, and Aunt Eliza too. They don't understand modern life. *We* have to make our own way, and we won't allow the men to dictate to us. Gaining the vote is only the beginning of it. You'll find out you're not alone, just as soon as you start making your own women friends.'

'I won't always feel like an outsider?'

Lizzie nudged her ribs. 'You're not an outsider. You've got me, for a start. You'll grow into yourself. That's what happens.'

She enjoyed offering advice as a woman of the world.

'Tell you what, Nance. Why don't you come with me to one of my suffragist meetings? There are all sorts of jolly interesting women for you to meet, and there's no boring formality to it.'

'Aren't they evening meetings? I shouldn't think I'd be allowed to come.'

In the dining room doorway Lizzie paused and winked.

'*Shhhh*. We'll say I am escorting you to . . . I know, to an orchestral concert.'

Nancy had to laugh.

Matthew brandished the carving knife. 'Splendid.'

Nancy slid into her chair, consoled by Lizzie's brisk affection. She glanced round the circle of faces and told herself that here was a loving and happy family. The locket belonged to the Uncanny. And so did Helena Clare, née Feather.

After dinner they enjoyed some music. Matthew had a strong tenor voice and Faith accompanied him for two or three songs, and then the sisters played a piano duet. Under protest, with his voice sliding and cracking, Arthur performed 'In the Lion's Cage', a comic ditty that had been his party piece since he was six years old. Edwin joined in the choruses, miming the lion's antics until they all shook with laughter.

Finally Rowland rolled up his shirtsleeves, bit a cigarette between his teeth and crashed into a ragtime tune. He played with such wild energy that no one minded the wrong notes. The rugs had been pushed back and they were all laughing and dancing, even Cornelius. The two-step was beyond him but he hopped from foot to foot, managing not to trample on his sister's feet.

There had been a glass of wine for everyone at dinner, to drink a toast to Arthur and wish him luck, and Nancy felt the heat of alcohol flushing through her veins. She flung her arms around Cornelius's jigging bulk.

'I love you, Neelie,' she smiled.

He answered solemnly, 'And I you.'

Devil seized Faith's modern glass fire screen. He tipped it on one side and balanced it on two stools. He stroked his wrists and flexed his hands, the signal for magic.

A bright penny lay in the palm of his left hand. He threw it in the air, caught it and pressed it down to the glass. They all heard the clink.

Devil made a show of crouching close to the screen.

He slid his right palm underneath the glass so it matched the left and pressed downwards with great force. Then with a great sweep he lifted the upper hand and revealed the penny shining in the lower palm. It seemed that he had forced it through an unbroken sheet of glass.

Everyone laughed and clapped. Arthur ran to his father.

'Disguise, distraction, deception, misdirection,' he chanted.

'Very good, my boy. You are one-tenth of the way to becoming a magician.'

'And I know the other nine-tenths, Pappy, don't I?'

'*Practice*,' they all chorused.

At the door as they were leaving Eliza kissed her sister.

'That was a golden evening,' she said.

'It was, wasn't it?' Faith smiled.

In the jolting murk of the train Arthur sighed.

'I'm jolly well going to miss you all, you know.'

Cornelius frowned. 'I would say the same, Arthur, but no one would believe me.'

'Idiot,' Arthur mumbled. He was almost asleep.

Eliza's head rested against Devil's shoulder and her gloved hand lay in his.

# PART TWO

# CHAPTER FOUR

*London, 1919*

The fire in the outer office had sunk to an ashy heap with no more than a red glimmer at its heart. Glancing at the clock on the wall, Nancy set aside the sheaf of invoices she was filing. Only just four o'clock on a bitter January afternoon. The managing director's secretary was in the inner office with the door closed. Nancy stooped over the hearth to stir the embers with the poker, then tipped a scoop of coke. A rising puff of dust filled her throat and made her eyes water. She rubbed her nose with the back of her hand, but that only reminded her that she had chilblains on her knuckles and the stubborn remains of a head cold.

On the way back to her desk she stuck her head out of the door. She heard the rat-a-tat clatter of the small press running in the print room downstairs and a snatch of someone whistling before Jinny Main's hooting laughter rose up the stairwell. Nancy sighed. Up here she had only the ticking clock and Miss Dent for company. She was hardly back in her seat before Jinny herself looked in.

'Got a minute, Nance? I could do with a hand down there.'

Nancy followed Jinny down the stone stairs. Her friend's brown overall was ink-stained, pulled in at the waist with a thick leather belt. Her hair was tied up in a scarf to keep it clear of the machinery. During the war when she worked on the print floor Nancy had dressed the same, and she kept her own work coat hanging on a peg in the women's lavatory at the back of the building. But in her new position as office assistant she must wear more suitable clothing, or so Miss Dent had advised her. Uncertain of herself and hoping for the best, Nancy now dressed in a jersey with a plain flannel skirt, fixing her hair with a pair of *cloisonné* combs Arthur had brought back from Antwerp.

'Take the other end of this blasted trolley,' Jinny ordered.

Old Desmond the machine minder was shifting flat sheets ready for the collating machine and there was no one else free to help. Using the trolley they manoeuvred the finished copies of the left-wing magazine *New Measure* through two sets of doors to the dispatch room.

'That's my girls,' the dispatch manager greeted them approvingly. Frank was another old man who had worked through the war at Lennox & Ringland. 'Let's pack 'em before that van driver sticks his ugly mug in here.'

Jinny counted out the magazines in batches of two dozen, Frank wrapped them in brown paper and Nancy finished the packages with string. The job was soon done. It was only a short print run, a typical job for L & R. Frank stood upright, wincing.

'The knee still hurts, does it?' Jinny asked. She had sympathy for everyone.

'I'll live, darling. Look at you, Nancy Wix. Black smuts all over your pretty face.'

Frank pulled a handkerchief out of his trouser pocket and dabbed at her cheek. The hanky smelt bad and she craned her neck away. At least he hadn't spat on it first.

'So long, Frankie,' Jinny called, taking her arm. 'See you in the morning, eh?'

The two girls escaped the pipe-smoke fug of the dispatch room just as the van driver arrived for the magazines.

'C'mon. Let's have a quick cuppa,' Jinny muttered.

'Ma Dent . . .'

'You can tell Ma Dent we shifted and packed the whole run of *New Measure* for Frankie Fingers, can't you?'

There was a tiny kitchen beyond the typesetting benches. The girls passed behind two printers perched at the keyboards of the rattling Linotype machines, their copy pegged beside them and their hands flying over the keys. On occasions even Nancy had been called upon to work a machine shift, but since the armistice the men had come back to take up their old jobs. Jinny was relegated to the handsetting benches and Nancy made the best of the uncongenial work upstairs in the office.

Nancy filled the kettle at the single cold tap and lit the gas ring. She rinsed a pair of cups and swiped them with a drying-up cloth. The printworks floor was noisy and dirty, thick with oil and acrid fumes from the machinery, but she loved it.

There was nowhere to sit down so when the brew was ready they leaned against the sink.

Jinny smacked her lips. 'That's better. Here, Nance. Have one of these. The jam ones are good.'

She took the biscuit and ate it while her friend rolled and smoked a cigarette. Even now, this made Nancy think of her cousin Lizzie.

Poor Lizzie. Or not so poor nowadays, Nancy reminded

herself. Lizzie had been unlucky, but she had refused to let circumstances get the better of her.

Jinny's cigarette tilted in the corner of her mouth. She was squinting at her friend through a haze of smoke.

'All right?'

'Yes'.

'Nothing there?'

They rarely spoke about Nancy's Uncanny but Jinny did not dismiss it, or even seem to regard it as particularly strange.

'There are more things than we understand, I know that much,' she shrugged. 'I don't need an old freak like Mrs Bullock Dodd to make me believe or not believe. Remember?'

It was Lizzie Shaw who took Nancy to her first suffragist meeting in 1911, but by the time she was fifteen Nancy had been drawn into the Women's Social and Political Union on her own account.

Nancy knew how her mother's independent spirit had been worn down by her circumstances, and she thought that her own future was unlikely to be any different unless women came together with a shared intent.

Why should men own almost all the property and retain all the power?

The answer came to her in the clear voice of the WSPU.

Because the men gave themselves permission to do so.

Nancy and her fellow campaigners believed that change could only come if women won the right to vote. Why should there not be women Members of Parliament, even, to speak up for other women?

Her family were sceptical about her gradual political awakening. Eliza advised her that she would do better to find a steady, well-paid job and ideally a rich husband, but she made no particular objection to Nancy attending meetings in the meantime. Devil laughed and referred to 'my daughter, the radical', which was one way of not taking her seriously because she was only a girl. Cornelius was indifferent to politics and organised protest of any kind, but Arthur was opposed to all her ideas.

'Why do you want to boss men around? Men look after girls, always have done, and you should be glad of that.'

'I don't want to boss anyone. I want my voice to be heard, the same as yours.'

'What *for*?'

Her little brother was now a head taller than her. He looked down at her in bafflement.

As the years passed, at meetings and on marches Nancy made new friends. These women were different from the girls in her class at school, and even from the far less conventional company backstage at the Palmyra. They weren't like Lizzie Shaw either. As Nancy had suspected she might, Lizzie turned out to be only a part-time suffragist. She loved the rhetoric, and the mischief of behaving badly, but she was too interested in having fun to spend her free time handing out leaflets in the rain or splashing paint on banners.

Although they did not meet on that night, Jinny had been present at the first WSPU meeting Nancy ever attended. When she shyly followed Lizzie into a drab hall behind a Methodist chapel, the space was swelling with a sound that Nancy had never heard before. It was a loud chorus of women's voices, rising unconfined, uncut by rumbling male noise. Their talk sounded as exuberant as birdsong.

A woman had mounted the platform, dressed with refined elegance, a cameo brooch at her throat. Her grey hair was arranged under a felt hat with a purple, white and green badge pinned to it.

'Good evening, friends,' she said, and silence fell at once.

Nancy learned that the Honourable Mrs Frances Templeton was the chairman of this section of the WSPU. She opened the meeting with a series of reports, from news of leafleting initiatives to the present condition of hunger strikers in Holloway Prison, and Nancy had been astonished and enthralled to find herself apparently at the hub of these important protests.

After the business of the evening was concluded, Mrs Templeton had introduced a speaker. Mamie Bullock Dodd was an American Spiritualist who had lectured them on the links between their organisations.

She boomed in a rich tenor voice, 'Many Spiritualists are suffragists, and socialists too. "Those terrible triplets, connected by the same umbilical cord and nursed from the same bottle." That is a quote, but I will not dignify the gentleman by speaking his name.'

Mrs Bullock Dodd had attempted to conduct a seance but it had not been a success. The packed benches of militant suffragists did not give off the faintest whiff of psychism, and Nancy and Lizzie had got the giggles so badly that Mrs Templeton had frowned at them from the platform. Mrs Dodd struggled gamely on. Were they aware that Spiritualism was the only religious movement in the world that acknowledged the equality of women and men? They were all women of the twin spheres. A woman was a communication from heaven to earth and the spirits of the universe breathed through her lips.

A bareheaded girl had jumped up.

'Will the spirits breathe us rights at the ballot box, then? A vote's what I'm after. I'll 'andle my menfolk in my own way, thanks very much, wi'out the spirits' 'elp. 'Cept those my 'usband drinks when 'e can afford 'em. I'll worry about the hereafter when I gets there.'

Lizzie had to cram her handkerchief between her teeth to stifle her gasps. But oddly enough Mrs Dodd's vaporous claims had made Nancy feel better. As she represented them the Spiritualists didn't sound threatening or even eerie and if this was Lawrence Feather's domain, there was nothing to fear. The Uncanny still lay within her, and it was hers alone.

Once they discovered that they had both been present, Jinny and Nancy sometimes laughed about the evening. Nowadays Nancy considered Spiritualism to be an eccentric but benign cul-de-sac, although the spirits themselves were a different matter.

Nancy met Jinny Main in a café after a rally in Parliament Square. She was fifteen, and Jinny was two years older. She was struck at once by her grace. Jinny listened to what other people had to say even when it was nonsense, and she never said a bad word about anyone. She was motherless and her father was a drinker, but she never complained about her difficult life.

'I'm lucky compared with some,' she said, with her enclosed smile. She wasn't otherwise vain about her appearance but she did mind about the protruding teeth that overcrowded her square jaw.

Jinny was employed as a printer's devil. She was boyish enough to be inconspicuous in a male environment, and she worked as hard as any of the men. One evening before the next meeting her new friend took Nancy to Lennox & Ringland to show her round the printworks floor. Jinny was setting up the type for a new WSPU leaflet and Nancy watched in fascination as she demonstrated how to hand set.

'You need good eyesight and quick fingers. This is eight-point type,' she said.

Each tiny letter had to be read backwards, picked and dropped into a metal slug, spaced to form complete lines that also had to be read backwards.

'Have a go,' she invited.

Nancy fumbled her way through five words. Jinny grinned and took a pull of her efforts, then held up the result.

'*Omadood barm besarves amather*. Really?'

They laughed until they had to prop themselves up against the bench.

Nancy's version of 'one good turn deserves another' became their comfort phrase.

'Omadood barm,' Jinny would call to her as the insults and catcalls flew over their heads from the anti-suffragist masses.

Nancy left school in 1913, just before her sixteenth birthday. A dismal interval followed in which she was supposed to be learning French and, if she was to be anything like the girls she had been at school with, beginning to cast around for a husband. Neither of these activities appealed to her and she begged her father to let her do something useful at the Palmyra instead. Devil insisted there was nothing suitable. Nancy understood that his expectations were different when it came to Cornelius and Arthur. When they were much younger Devil had always been murmuring about 'Wix and Sons', and as the daughter she was being advised to train as a bilingual secretary to some businessman.

'Commerce is where the future lies. It is a much better world for you than the theatre. You will have the security of a career,' Eliza said. Infuriatingly, since Nancy knew that her mother had not placed great emphasis on suitability or security in her own younger days.

'I am never going to *be* bilingual'.

'Apply yourself, Nancy. Mamselle Schenck says that you have a good brain.'

Lucie Schenck was a middle-aged French lady who was supposed to be teaching her the language.

Then seemingly without warning, like a thunderclap out of a summer sky, the war came.

It did not end before Christmas, even though most people had been certain that it would, and Mlle Schenck hurried back to her family in a village only ten miles from Neuve Chapelle. At the same time Jinny Main told Nancy that so many of the skilled men were leaving their benches at Lennox & Ringland to join up that no one remained to print the pamphlets and journals. Dust was gathering on the typesetting machines. Within a week she had applied for a job alongside Jinny, and was employed at once as the print floor dogsbody. Jinny herself had been promoted to Linotype operator.

At the end of 1914 Jinny volunteered to be a nurse with the London Ambulance Column. From the front, the wounded men were evacuated by train to the French coast and from there brought across the Channel to be loaded on to another train. Finally the LAC met them in London and drove them onwards to their final hospital destination. At the railway stations the ambulances were sometimes overwhelmed by crowds of well-wishers who had come to cheer the men home.

The LAC organisers were used to dealing with a different class of girl, and they advised Jinny that she did not have the required nursing qualifications. But she stood her ground in the matron's office and insisted they at least recruit her as a driver. She was a country girl who knew how to operate farm machinery so they agreed in the end to let her try the work. Her supervisor later told her she hadn't been expected to last a week, but Jinny settled into it and spent many of her nights threading her stretcher cases through the dark streets. Nancy would cover for her on the days when she crawled away to sleep in a cupboard, unable to stay awake any longer.

On the busiest 'push' nights when the trains pulled in with a seemingly unending stream of smashed bones and bloodied dressings, Nancy helped out at the Column HQ in Regent's Park. She begged but Eliza had refused to let her train for proper nursing, so her work was little more than folding blankets and smoothing laundered slips on to stretcher pillows, or even making cocoa for the dispatch riders. But it was something.

Those nights deepened her friendship with Jinny. Day after day, in an attempt to bridge the chasm between the demands of the night and the ordinary working world, the two girls talked and shared their secrets.

Early one morning, as they sat in the fresh air under an unfurling chestnut tree in Regent's Park to recover from an unusually bad night, Jinny told Nancy about the grey coaches.

Tacked on to the end of some of the hospital trains from France were locked carriages with blanked-out windows. The doors were never unlocked while the regular wounded were being unloaded, but plain grey vans discreetly waited until the rest of the train was empty. The ordinary ambulance drivers did not ask questions and no one speculated about the men who must be inside the coaches. There was no cheering for them.

Nancy listened to this account in silence.

This time in the Uncanny she did not see anything clearly

and that was a mercy, but she could hear all too well. There was darkness barred with slats of light, a terrible weeping, and a husky voice that tonelessly whispered, 'All gone,' over and over. And there was a low growling, sounding less like a man than an animal, a wounded bear or some other creature she did not even know.

Jinny saw her face. 'I'm sorry,' she cried. 'It's your other sight, isn't it? I didn't mean to wake it up, Nance.'

Nancy had never told another soul, but she had described to Jinny how as a girl she had glimpsed the war long before it had begun.

She breathed deeply. 'It's all right. We're both all right, aren't we? It's the soldiers. They're dying, not us.'

Worse than dying, some of them, she now understood.

Cornelius was out there, and her cousins Rowland and Edwin. Arthur was still too young to enlist but he was already at Sandhurst on an accelerated officer-training programme. Even Arthur would soon be going to France.

Jinny clasped her hand until the voices faded. Sunshine sparkled on the grass as they walked to a café to buy a bun for breakfast before catching the bus to Lennox & Ringland.

It was at the beginning of 1915 that Cornelius had suddenly decided he must join up in the ranks.

Devil was too old to fight in France, but he believed in doing his duty. He devised a series of shows for the Palmyra that featured comedy routines, patriotic songs and choruses, and uplifting speeches from popular public figures. They were called 'Union Jack Nights', and seats were given away to men in uniform. On one of these nights, Cornelius was sitting in a front *fauteuil*. Devil had asked him to watch the performance and give him some ideas for improving the static sets. A soloist came out to the apron to perform a song about joining up. The chorus went, '*I do like you, cockie, now you've got yer khaki on.'* The women sitting in the seats near Cornelius sang and clapped and the singer marched down from the stage. Passing through the audience she stopped in front of Cornelius and handed him a white feather.

The next morning he went out to the recruitment office. He didn't tell Devil and Eliza about his intentions, and even Nancy only heard about it afterwards. He was examined by a medical officer and – to his intense humiliation – immediately classified as medically unfit.

A different man might have accepted this judgement and looked for useful war work at home, but the normal rules could not be made to fit Cornelius. As always, only his personal logic applied. Once he had decided it was what he must do, he could not contemplate not going to France. He loved motor vehicles and driving with a passion that had begun with Devil's De Dion-Bouton, and he concluded that if he was not to be a soldier he must be an ambulance driver.

He volunteered, and within days he was on the Western Front.

The field dressing stations were canvas shelters crammed with wounded and dying men. Cornelius and the other drivers collected the injured from the dressing stations and ferried them behind the lines, through the mud and chaos of the nearby battle, to the clearing hospital. The hopeless cases were set aside, and there were more than enough of those, but men with even the smallest chance of survival were roughly patched up and transferred to slow, crowded casualty trains.

Thus two people who Nancy dearly loved had formed the first and final links in this long rescue chain, and she was proud of them both.

At last the war to end all wars came to an end.

After the armistice Cornelius finally came home. Arthur also survived, although he remained in France with his regiment. Edwin and Rowland Shaw were among the many thousands of men who did not come back. The landscape of the Uncanny was thronged with lost and dead men, but if her cousins and others she had known were amongst them Nancy did not distinguish them. It was like being a mechanical conduit for images that were distressing but not connected to her, and for this she was deeply grateful.

Recalled to the present by a nudge from Jinny, Nancy collected herself. 'What were we saying?'

Jinny said gently, 'How's your brother?'

'Not bad, thank you. Some days better than others.'

Some days for Cornelius were very bad.

'Is there any more tea in that pot?'

Nancy sloshed thick brown brew into their cups.

'Why don't you come out with us tonight, Nance? Me and Joycey and some of the others are going to have our tea at Willby's and then quite likely a half-pint at the Eagle.'

Nancy liked poached eggs on thick slices of buttered toast, and the pleasant heat in the neighbouring saloon bar afterwards when Jinny's friends crowded round a beer-ringed table to argue about communism or rights for women. The war had changed the group's political objectives, as it had changed everything else, because women had the vote now – or some of them did.

'There's still a lot of work to be done,' they agreed.

For the last two years the group had been all female, but just recently one or two soldier boyfriends had reappeared. The men perched suspiciously on the edge of the circle and their presence changed the whole atmosphere.

She shook her head. 'I can't tonight. Ma's expecting me home.'

'Fair enough. Better get back to it, I suppose.'

'See you tomorrow.'

Miss Dent was at her typewriter. The keys clacked like hailstones on cobbles and the carriage return pinged every few seconds.

Mr Lennox strolled out of his office.

'Find me the Platt correspondence file, Miss Wix, please.'

She knelt at the lowest drawer of a tin filing cabinet and extracted the folder. His shoes looked as though someone polished them every morning and she wondered whose job this might be. Most certainly Mr Lennox did not shine his own shoes. There weren't many domestic servants these days, but perhaps his wife did it for him.

It was twenty to six. Miss Dent collected Mr Lennox's signature on a handful of urgent letters. 'Shall I take those down to the post?' Nancy asked.

Five minutes later she had completed her errand and was free to make her way home. Although it was an easy bus journey to Islington from the printworks in an alley behind Fleet Street, Nancy usually preferred to walk. She told herself she was saving the fare and she needed the exercise, but the truth was that she was in no hurry to get back home.

Pulling up her coat collar against the rain she headed towards St Paul's. The pavements were crowded with home-going workers, the street lamps down Ludgate Hill burnishing their wet umbrellas so that they resembled insects' wings. Nancy had no umbrella. She lifted her face and let the thin, cold drizzle wash away the grime of the day.

Fleet Street was always busy but tonight the road was at a standstill, choked with idling buses and wagons bearing great webs of paper to the newspaper printworks. She stopped for a moment at the kerb, intending to cross over to buy Cornelius an evening paper from an old news vendor who always gave her a cheerful good evening. But the stationary vehicles offered no room to pass. In the distance she could hear shouting followed by a ragged burst of cheering.

She became aware of a big cream-coloured car standing motionless just three feet away. A man was leaning forward in the rear seat, and she noticed the chauffeur's peaked cap as he tilted his head to listen to what his passenger was saying. A deep blast on the car's horn followed. Hooting was perfectly pointless, she thought impatiently, because anyone could see that the road was blocked all the way to Ludgate Circus. She was about to step off the pavement and somehow worm her way between the vehicles and through the clouds of exhaust fumes, but she hesitated for two seconds for a last look at the elongated curves of the cream bonnet. The raised black eyebrow of the wheel arch was close enough for her to have stroked it with her fingertips. As she hung there, the car door was thrown open and the passenger stepped out. The polished handle just grazed her elbow.

'I am so sorry. I almost knocked you over.'

The man was tall, wearing a soft hat. He lifted it politely and she saw smooth fair hair and a narrow, chiselled face.

'It's all right. I was staring at your car instead of crossing the road.'

'Were you? Do you like it?'

'My father would. He loves cars. He used to have a De Dion-Bouton before the war but he had to sell it.'

'Poor chap, that must have been hard for him. They are beautiful machines.'

81

'He has a Ford now.'

The man raised a sympathetic eyebrow. 'Quite serviceable, I should think. This one is a Daimler, the new model.'

As he spoke, the car gave a shudder and the engine stalled. The man gently shoved the running board with the shiny toe of his shoe. 'Not as reliable as a De Dion, as you can see. What's the trouble this time, Higgs?'

The chauffeur hurried to unclip and fold back the bonnet.

'Spark-ignition again, Mr Maitland, I'd say. Don't like the rain, it seems.'

Mr Maitland stared down the street.

He asked Nancy, 'Do you know what's causing the delay?'

The chanting and cheering was louder and she could hear the shrill, familiar blasts of police whistles.

'A march or protest of some sort. Heading for the Embankment, probably. Is there a vote in Parliament tonight?'

He frowned. 'Yes. I wonder who it is this time? Jobless ex-servicemen, coal miners? Suffragettes?'

She disliked this form of the word. 'I would know if it was suffrag*ists* because I would be with them. But women do have the vote now, you know. Some of us do, at any rate.'

'Not you, you are too young.'

'I am twenty-one.'

He looked at her, and she found herself staring straight back. She had to tilt her head to meet his eyes.

He added, 'I'm not unsympathetic to unemployed men, by the way, or to the miners. I shouldn't have let impatience with the car and the hold-up get the better of me. I apologise again.'

Nancy marched a few steps on the spot to indicate how free she was, not encumbered even by an umbrella. The felt brim of her hat was beginning to droop with the weight of damp.

'I usually find walking is the best way. It's fast, free and good for you.'

'Yes, on this occasion you'll certainly get wherever you are going before me. Are you in a hurry?'

She hesitated. 'Not really. I'm on my way home.'

'I *was* in a hurry. But I'm already late, and I expect I'll be invited to plenty more dull City dinners.'

Poor Higgs folded a piece of sacking to protect his trousers and knelt to peer underneath the Daimler. The buses and lorries had not moved which meant the police must have closed the road.

'Would you like to come and have a drink?'

*No*, Nancy prepared to say, but another unexpected instinct shouted *Yes, oh yes*.

'There's a place just down that alley,' she pointed.

'Very good.' Mr Maitland cheerfully told Higgs that they would be waiting inside, out of the rain, and swept Nancy towards an inviting doorway.

The pub was well known to Nancy and she didn't think about the row of workmen at the bar, or the cindery fire, or the reek of spilled beer rising from the bare floorboards. But the man took all this in before pulling out a chair for her at the table closest to the hearth. Only when he had made her comfortable did he remove his own coat and white silk scarf. He was wearing immaculate evening dress, quite different from the kind Devil wore on stage. He spoke two words to the usually surly publican who came running with kindling to restore the fire. He called Mr Maitland 'sir' without a flicker of insolence.

Nancy asked for a half of bitter, and two polished glasses were set in front of them without any spillage on the table. This man was used to being served.

'Do you usually drink beer?' he asked her.

'Yes.' It was hardly worth pointing out that she liked whisky but couldn't afford it, or gin, or even sherry.

Although he didn't smile readily, he had an unusual dimple high on his left cheek that seemed to deepen when he was amused. Nancy took off her sorry hat and her hair came down with it. He looked more closely at her.

'My name is Gil Maitland.'

'How do you do? I am Nancy Wix.'

'I am pleased to meet you, Miss Wix.'

She could almost believe this, because he seemed suddenly to be in a much better humour. A slow tide of blood rose from her throat to her cheeks. The warmth of the bar made her nose run and her chilblains itched almost unbearably. She had to sniff, and clench her fists to stop herself clawing at her knuckles. Gil Maitland took out a folded handkerchief and handed it over. It was thick and starched and almost certainly monogrammed.

When she tried to hand it back he said, 'Please, keep it.'

There would be plenty more handkerchiefs where this one had come from, she thought, laid in a tallboy by a laundry maid overseen by the valet. From this single detail she found she could imagine all the ease of Gil Maitland's life. With Jinny Main and their other friends she would have dismissed him as the enemy, but now she felt oddly benign towards him. He was only a man, another human being, and his high assurance didn't repel her in the least.

The exact opposite, in fact.

She wanted to laugh, from amusement and happiness,

and he saw it and now he did smile. Gil Maitland would not miss much, she realised.

'Well, Miss Wix. Who are you and what do you do?'

Because he asked questions that were sufficiently interested without being over-inquisitive, and because he listened to her answers, she confided far more about Lennox & Ringland and her family and the Palmyra than she would ordinarily have done. Mr Maitland smoked two cigarettes, gold-tipped with black papers, and drank his beer.

'Now it's your turn. Who are *you*?' she asked at the end.

'I'm afraid I have nothing so exotic to tell.'

Nancy had never thought of her background as anything of the kind, and the notion was surprising.

All in all Gil Maitland was a surprising person.

'I am just a businessman,' he added.

'No, that's not fair. You let me babble on for ages so you should tell me your story in return.'

Was she being rude? Nancy wasn't sure. She just wanted to go on sitting here, looking at him and talking.

There was the cleft in the cheek again. 'I am afraid of boring you. What would you like to know? My grandfather made his fortune importing Indian cotton and setting up Manchester factories. My father was a chemical engineer, and he developed and patented the Maitland Process.' He cocked an eyebrow at her. 'Can you really be interested in all this? The Maitland Process is a method by which large quantities of fabric can be cheaply and permanently dyed and printed.'

'I see.' She could imagine, at any rate.

'I am an economist. I have broadened the scope of our businesses and I am investing in new methods of manufacture. Maitland's creates employment and generates wealth, you know. Perhaps you disapprove of capitalism?'

'Of course I do.'

After a moment Gil Maitland laughed, and so did she.

'I'd have been disappointed to hear otherwise,' he said.

She would have liked to begin a debate, as she had done several times in this very pub, with such a plum representative of the other faction. She was disappointed when she saw the chauffeur discreetly approaching.

'Excuse me, Mr Maitland. Just to let you know the car's running again, and the road is open.'

Did she imagine it, or was Gil Maitland also disappointed?

'Thank you, Higgs.'

Mr Maitland helped her into her coat and she did her best to fix her hat. His eyes were steady as she twitched the hopeless brim.

'I hope you will let me give you a lift?'

Nancy buttoned her gloves. She was trying to work out how old he was. Perhaps in his mid- to late-thirties, she decided.

'Well . . . thank you. I'd rather like a ride home in a Daimler. I'll be able to tell my father all about it.'

The big car glided up Faringdon Road. Perched in the leather interior Nancy wondered what it would be like to be married to a man like Gil Maitland. He hadn't mentioned a wife, and she had deliberately not asked him.

It would be rather wonderful, she thought.

For the first time, Eliza's perennial advice to look for a rich husband made sense. Fortunately the darkness hid her blazing cheeks.

*Don't be so bloody ridiculous*, she told herself. *That's not what you want at all.*

The car drew up much too soon beside the canal and Higgs opened the passenger door for her.

'Thank you. That was very interesting,' she told Mr Maitland as she stepped out.

'It was interesting for me too. Goodnight, Nancy.'

The car slid away. It was still raining.

*Goodnight, Gil,* she whispered to herself.

# CHAPTER FIVE

Puddles of molten metal lay on the steps of the house. It was only rainwater caught in the worn hollows of the stone, but ever since she could remember she had thought it looked like mercury in the lamplight. Devil used a phial of mercury in one of his illusions, and when they were small she and Cornelius had loved the way the metal broke up into tiny globules before a twitch of the glass saucer collected it into a seamless pool again.

Smiling at this memory as well as with the residual pleasure of her encounter with Mr Maitland, Nancy put her key in the lock. The door swung open into the quiet house.

She took off her coat and shook it out before draping it on the hall stand. Droplets darkened the dusty runner. Rubbing her inflamed knuckles, she made her way down a flight of stairs to the kitchen. It was empty but the room was warm at least. This was no longer the steamy domain of the cook and housemaid. Peggy was at home in Kent with her widowed mother and almost as soon as the war started Mrs Frost had left to work in the munitions.

Nowadays Eliza and Nancy ran the household between

them. Devil spent long hours at the Palmyra, Arthur was still abroad and Cornelius – Nancy's lips tightened – Cornelius was not likely to care whether or not the steps had been swept or if the butcher's boy had brought the wrong order yet again.

She flung open the door of the iron range and stoked the fire. She thought what a great deal of making and tending fires must have gone on all through her childhood, yet she had never paid any attention to the work.

There was a saucepan pushed to one side of the hob and she peered at the contents. Enough of an Irish stew remained to make a meal for the three of them if she added some more spuds and a few carrots. The situation was really quite promising.

Nancy went up two flights of stairs and knocked at her mother's door.

Eliza had been reading. She took off her spectacles and laid them on the table, pinching the bridge of her nose and blinking. Her dark hair had turned grey and the hollows in her cheeks had deepened. Eliza still drew glances in the street, although she claimed not to care in the least about her appearance. Whether she did or not she had retained her theatrical way of piling on colour on colour, twisting a pair of necklaces together and sticking a discarded bird's feather in a hatband. These days she looked rare, and not a little forbidding.

'I thought you might have gone out with your friend Jinny.'

When Cornelius first came home, Jinny had called several times to sit with him. She understood something of what he must have experienced, and Cornelius would sometimes talk to her when he could speak to no one else. Eliza had been grateful for this intervention – grateful for anything at all that seemed to help her son – but she still didn't quite approve of Jinny. The girl was a suffragette, a radical, a print shop assistant, and she was not likely to help Nancy up in the world. Rather the opposite. Now the war was over Eliza thought Nancy should be putting her expensive education and refined upbringing to better use.

Nancy said, 'No, not today. How has he been?'

'Quiet.'

Eliza shuffled to her feet and Nancy immediately went to her. Under her hands her mother's arms felt thin enough to snap. For a brief second they embraced, wordlessly holding each other close. Nancy thought, *let me hold you*, but Eliza moved to the door in order to listen to the silence of the house.

'He must be asleep,' she said. 'There's a letter from Arthur, by the way.'

Nancy took it and eagerly skimmed the flimsy blue pages.

Arthur was at the Brigade HQ in Belgium, to which his regiment was attached as part of the mopping-up operations that must continue for months to come. As always he wrote cheerfully about his superiors and their eccentricities, about excursions into the nearby town with his brother officers, and the football matches and other entertainments laid on for the men.

*Pa, there is an officer here called Bolton who is quite a decent conjuror. Have I told you about him? He's not in your class of course, but he can do some party tricks with a pack of cards and a trio of handkerchiefs. On Saturday I helped him out with a show (in truth I dressed up as his female assistant in skirts and a fetching wig) and the men all howled with laughter. I advise you to book us for the old Palmyra while you still have the chance.*

Nancy slipped the letter back into its envelope. Arthur never spoke about the real work he had to do. For the soldiers still in France there were so many bodies to be collected, identities to be established, graves to be dug and information to be filed. But at least Arthur was alive and safe. It was hard that Aunt Faith had to grieve for both her boys.

Nancy smiled at Eliza with all the brightness she could muster. 'We can have dinner, Ma, as soon as the vegetables are done.'

'Leave that to me. You go up and see him.'

Cornelius still occupied his boyhood room. She put her mouth close to the door and spoke in a low voice. He could not bear loud noises.

'Neelie? Are you awake?'

He was sitting in his usual place in the chair beside the bed. His shoulders slumped and his big red hands hung between his knees.

'How are you tonight?' she asked gently. He blinked at her. Behind his spectacles his eyes were swollen.

'Is it time? Do they need us? Wait, I'll fill my water bottle. Some poor fellow will need a drink.' He looked at the walls, his face quivering with confusion, before seizing her hand. He was in anguish.

'What are you doing here, Nancy? It's not safe. So close to the guns. Can't you hear them?'

Fresh tears ran down his face.

'It's all right, Neelie. You're at home with us now, remember?' She drew his head against her heart and stroked his hair. The rhythm of her heartbeat seemed to comfort him.

Uncertainly he whispered, 'What's that?' And then, 'I must have been dreaming.'

Cornelius's waking dreams were so intense that he lived in them more than in the present world. She understood that, of course.

Cornelius drove his motor ambulance for three years, with only short breaks for recuperative leave. When the end of the fighting came he was the longest-serving driver in his detachment. Only when he was no longer needed, when there were no more stretchers to load under the canvas roof of his ambulance and when he did not have to sluice any more blood and human debris from its metal floor before setting off on the next outward journey, only then did he crumble from within.

Cornelius had not come home in one of the grey coaches. He had travelled alone by passenger ferry, telling no one that he was on his way. One evening in Islington Nancy had opened the front door to find him standing there, his pack at his feet as if he couldn't carry the burden another step.

It seemed at first that he was nearly himself. A little subdued, but that was not a surprise. He had never had much to say during his short home leaves. Then day by day he seemed to be losing an invisible battle of his own. He retreated to his bedroom and began to weep.

'Yes, Neelie, you were dreaming.'

She didn't know whether to wish him consciousness or oblivion.

The Wixes' doctor prescribed rest and sedatives, but the medicine only sent Cornelius into a heavy sleep from which he woke up dulled and tearful. The only times he seemed a little better were after Jinny's visits, when the two of them sat and talked behind a closed door.

Nancy would try to help him to talk by asking, 'Neelie? What were the other ambulance drivers like?' or 'Tell me about that little town, remember, the one you wrote to me about? With the lace half-curtains at all the windows and the one bell ringing for Mass?'

He would only shake his head and she understood that she was clumsy, although she did not know what she could say that would be any different.

There were a few hopeful signs. He seemed to enjoy Devil's reminiscences about drives in the old car, or his eyes would settle on his mother's gaudy scarves and glint with sudden wild amusement. He had a shelf of his old books and sometimes he would take one down and stare at the pictures of butterflies. He no longer drew architectural details, even recoiling from the sketch tablet and pencils when Nancy found them for him.

His family could only offer the security of home, and pray that the tears would stop in time.

'Would you like some dinner?' she asked.

Cornelius's head jerked as if he was surprised to notice the green velvet curtains and the jug of water placed on his night table. He stared at the empty bed on the opposite side of the room.

She told him, 'There's a letter from Arthur. He's been doing magic shows for the men.'

'Magic? Is that so?'

Arm in arm they slowly descended. In his carpet slippers Cornelius shambled like an old man.

Eliza had set knives and forks on the little gate-legged table in the kitchen corner where Cook and Peggy used to sit in the afternoons to look at the penny papers. The family rarely used the dining room these days except when Devil glared and complained that it was not much different from living in Maria Hayes's place, back in the old rookery of St Giles. When Devil next ate dinner at home Eliza laid the table upstairs with the best plates and lit two candles in the silver candlesticks. He smiled a little sadly at the sight and kissed the back of her neck.

Nancy guided Cornelius to his chair as Eliza ladled stew. He dipped his head and ate quickly, anxiously glancing at the clock between mouthfuls.

'Can't sit here all night. They'll be lined up, you know. Rows of them.'

Eliza ate hardly a mouthful. She didn't watch her son but it was clear that every bone in her body shivered for him.

'Did you go out today?' Nancy asked her. Cornelius didn't need someone to be with him all the time. He seemed less distressed if he was left in peace.

'I walked up as far as the market. I had to get soap and matches and lard and about a dozen other things.'

'You didn't carry all that shopping home, Ma, did you?'

Nancy didn't know much more about Eliza's afflictions than she had done as a girl, but she was certain that she was not allowed to lift anything heavy. Eliza waved a dismissive hand.

'It was very busy. Crowds of miserable people, looking sick and exhausted. A woman right in front of me was coughing like a walrus.'

Nancy laughed. 'Do walruses cough?'

Cornelius suddenly lifted his head. 'They do. Although perhaps it's more of a *bark*.'

The women smiled in astonishment. It was an unexpected glimpse of the boy he had once been, to be authoritative about walruses. Eliza covered his hand with hers.

'My dear son,' she murmured.

Very quietly Nancy pushed back her chair and slipped out of the kitchen.

Up in the drawing room she idly parted the curtains so she could look down into the pitch-black garden. She could see no further than the twigs poking up from the iron balustrade and these were overlaid by reflections of the room behind her. She caught an overpowering scent of summer roses and damp earth as one of the tall doors suddenly swung open and a child came in from the darkness.

It was a little girl. Water streamed from her hair.

Nancy stood transfixed. The apparition was so lonely and small. A long time seemed to pass.

'What do you want?' she asked at last.

The child didn't speak. Instead she reached out her small hand. It seemed she was trying to lead Nancy outside. Although she was not afraid of her, Nancy could not help but recoil.

'I can't come with you.'

Nancy could see the pallor of the child's scalp where the locks of wet hair parted. She shivered. The desolation emanating from the little thing chilled the room.

'Tell me what you want,' Nancy begged.

She shook her head and her small hand drew back. A sharp gust of wind stirred the heavy curtains as the girl stepped out into the night.

As soon as she was gone frustration swept over Nancy. It was deeply distressing to have seen the apparition and yet been unable to help her.

She sat down in her father's armchair, closing her eyes to allow herself to recover. The scent of flowers faded.

Nancy feared the Uncanny much less than she had done when Mr Feather placed his hand on her head. She had borrowed Cornelius's big dictionary to look up the terms associated with psychism, '*clairvoyant*' and '*telepathy*' and '*precognition*', puzzling over the definitions set out in what she had later learned to recognise as tiny six-point type. Clairvoyant took her to *'mentally perceiving objects or events at a distance, or concealed from sight, or in the future, attributed to certain persons'*, which might account for her glimpse of the trenches long before they had been dug but still fell quite a long way short of explaining the Uncanny. *'Communications from one mind to another'* and *'foreknowledge'* did not illuminate much either.

There was no defining the state, she concluded, any more than there was any way of properly controlling it. It was something that happened to her, like the fits Cornelius had occasionally suffered when he was much younger. The difference was that her fits were invisible to everyone else.

Her private theory was that perhaps past and present and future time did not run in a straight line. She imagined that they streamed in curls and loops, doubling back and crossing over each other, and that there were tiny flaws in the gossamer membrane that held them apart. Through these cracks, was it not possible that glimpses of different times, shadows of people who were gone or had not yet arrived, might seep into the here and now? And equally, might not the curls and loops shift as time spooled by, causing the cracks to close again?

Some people might be more than usually sensitive to such leakages, she reasoned. It was not a lucky gift, at least not as Mr Feather had suggested. She remembered a girl at her school admired by everyone for having perfect musical pitch, but the same girl found it almost physically painful to listen to off-key playing. She would shudder and put her hands over her ears.

Such gifts were not always welcome, or comfortable to possess.

'Nancy?'

Eliza was shaking her.

'He's gone upstairs to bed.' Eliza was rubbing her hands together, her shoulders drawn close to her ears. 'Why is it so cold in here?'

Nancy struggled to collect herself. 'Has he? Is it?'

The corners of Eliza's mouth turned down. Nancy knew how capable she was of kindling her mother's irritation, but it saddened her to be made aware of it over and over again. Eliza unconditionally adored her sons but she measured her daughter against her own yardstick. Nancy must fulfil her mother's ambitions for her, which had once been Eliza's for herself. Eliza particularly disliked the notion that her child might be keeping something from her.

'What are you hiding?' she had once snapped when Nancy was much younger.

Flippantly Nancy had held out her upturned palms to show that there was nothing concealed there.

Eliza slapped them.

'That's enough. You are not a *conjuror*.'

Nancy wished she could be more the daughter Eliza wanted. She regretted the distance between them because it seemed so small, and yet was so impossible to bridge.

She took her mother's hands now. 'Ma?'

Eliza's fingers were dry and hot. Nancy touched her forehead and found that it was burning too.

'You're not well.'

Eliza's head drooped in defeat. She sighed, 'Nancy, I am so tired of illness.'

Eliza let herself be led upstairs to bed. Their roles could suddenly reverse and in one second switch back again.

Once she had settled her mother under the eiderdown and listened at Cornelius's door, Nancy wandered back through the darkened house. She was too concerned about

Eliza to spare much thought for the little apparition, but she went into the drawing room and stood on the same spot. There was nothing there now and when she opened the doors overlooking the garden only cold, damp air swept in. But there was something at the back of her, like the palm of a hand moving just a hair's breadth away from her head. She spun round, almost crying out, and searched the empty room. She walked the length of it and opened the front curtains.

A man in a long overcoat stood next to the railing topping the canal embankment. At first his face was hidden under the brim of his hat, but then he seemed to sense her watching him and looked up.

It was Lawrence Feather. She knew him at once, even though she had not set eyes on him since the day Eliza dispatched him from this room, more than eight years ago. He had stood in just the same way, motionless and intent, on the beach outside the hotel and she had looked down on him from a bay window.

A cold current crept through her, raising the hairs at the nape of her neck. The Uncanny was powerful, closer than it had been since the day of the *Queen Mab*. She had thought for a long time that she controlled it but now it spilled through the air and possessed her.

Feather stood for another moment, locking her eyes with his. Then with an exaggerated gesture he raised his hat to her, and walked slowly away.

Inside her head Nancy tried to defy him. She watched him turn the corner where the canal entered the tunnel and she thought – or perhaps she spoke the words aloud – *if you are dead you can't affect us. If you are not, there is nothing here that concerns you.*

She closed the curtains tight, leaving not a chink between them, and continued her way downstairs. In the kitchen she made herself comfortable in a chair close to the range where she could hear the soft hissing of coals.

She had been sitting deep in thought for perhaps half an hour when her father came in. Devil was in his old tweed overcoat, his face not quite scrubbed bare of stage make-up and his regular smell of bay rum and cigar smoke spiked with fumes of brandy.

'You're up late, Nancy.'

She found a smile.

'I was about to make a cup of cocoa. Would you like one?'

'Keeping up your wartime skills, eh?'

He teased her, but he was proud of her work for Jinny's column. Unlike Eliza, Devil was fond of Jinny. He asked about her while Nancy warmed and whisked the milk.

'Got a young man yet, has she? A nice warm armful like that, she must have someone.'

'Pa.'

Devil chuckled. 'A young girl then?'

'I don't know. Don't be nosy.'

They both laughed and Nancy forgot her anxieties. She loved the rare occasions when she had her father to herself. She handed him his cocoa mug and he thoughtfully sipped.

'It would taste much better with a splash of brandy.'

She ignored him.

'And you?' he asked.

'Do I have a nice young girl?'

Devil had the grace to look slightly abashed.

'I'd like to see you with a couple of admirers. You're young and pretty. You should be having some fun and misbehaving, kissing someone under a full moon, instead of going off to work every day at your printers and coming home to your mother and me and Neelie. Eh?'

He sandwiched her feet between his on the rag rug.

She smiled. 'Misbehaving? Is that what fun is?'

Until tonight the only men Nancy had known were just back from the war, no longer eager to snatch every opportunity for a kiss and a joke. Now they were home for good they seemed aware of an uncertain future.

Gil Maitland was different, and she thought he was thrillingly unlike any male she had ever encountered. Unfortunately there had been no glimpse of any moon, and he had not been remotely eager for a kiss.

Devil raised an eyebrow. 'Of course. What's wrong with dancing to jazz bands, may I ask? Dressing up and drinking cocktails?'

'Nothing at all.'

She told him about having tea and a jam biscuit with Jinny, and the puddle of rain on the steps that looked like mercury. She wanted to keep the Daimler and its owner to herself. Nor did she say *I saw a ghost. Maybe two.*

Devil didn't notice any reticence. He loved to reminisce about his old tricks.

'Mercury, eh? Ah, that was a good illusion, the Melting Wand. Maybe I should bring back some of the old favourites. Nostalgia plays well, or it used to. Listen to me, I'm getting old. Modern is what counts nowadays, isn't it?'

'Was it a decent house tonight?'

Like Eliza, Devil had gone grey. It was only when he smiled that he looked as rakishly handsome as ever. He didn't smile now.

'No,' he admitted.

The Palmyra was going through a particularly thin time. Public tastes had changed, and it seemed that spectacular magic shows belonged to a happier and less cynical age.

'Are you worried, Pa?'

He tried to shrug off the question. 'Luckily I am not the worrying kind. Otherwise I'd have worn myself into the grave long ago.'

Nancy couldn't remember a time when even the air they breathed had not been clouded with uncertainty about the theatre. But their impending poverty was usually Eliza's refrain, and Devil's chorus had always been that they should spend money and leave the making of it to him.

Tonight was different, though, in so many respects.

'What can we do?'

'My lovely girl. Thank you for that "we", but the Palmyra is your old dad's concern. Always has been.'

Once it had been his and Eliza's together. Nowadays his wife was too infirm. Cornelius couldn't help, and Arthur was doubly absent because they had chosen to make him inviolate. Arthur was now an army officer, with a classical education. He would never be allowed to step back across the divide into a disreputable and precarious life in the theatre.

A quick rush of love for her father caught in Nancy's throat. To hide her emotion she gathered up the empty cups and took them to the sink.

'How was your mama this evening?'

'She wasn't very well. I saw her into bed.'

Devil leapt to his feet.

'What? Why didn't you tell me?'

His wife, and the theatre. Always Devil's true, twin poles.

'She's asleep now.'

'I'll go up to her. Goodnight, my girl.'

His lips brushed her forehead and he hurried away.

Nancy washed up the saucepan and crockery and left them on the scrubbed draining board. She damped the fire, and looked around the room for what needed to be done in the morning before she quietly made her own way to bed.

# CHAPTER SIX

Devil came to Nancy's room long before daylight.

He said hoarsely, 'Your mother is ill.'

Nancy pushed back the bedcovers and ran. She found Eliza sweating and semi-delirious. When she put her hand to her forehead she moaned and twisted in the soaking sheets.

Devil asked, 'Where has she been? What did she do yesterday?'

Nancy's mouth went dry with fear. There had been a woman who coughed like a walrus. Cornelius had raised his head at the word.

'She went to Chapel Market.'

A crowded place, ripe for the spreading of infection.

Eliza's skin had taken on a strange blue tinge and she fought to draw in air through lungs that audibly bubbled with mucus. The intervals between each breath and the next seemed endless.

Father and daughter stared at each other across the tumbled bed. Neither of them uttered the word, but they didn't need to. Devil's face turned the colour of clay.

Through her rising terror Nancy tried to speak calmly. She would have to take charge of the situation; instinctively she knew that her father could not. 'We must cool her down and help her to breathe. Bring me some water, washing cloths, towels.'

He hurried away, his slippers flapping on the linoleum of the landing.

Nancy slipped her arm beneath Eliza's shoulders, and her heart twisted with love as well as fear as she supported their negligible weight. Eliza clutched at her wrist. Her eyes were wide and wild with fever.

'Carlo?' she gasped. And then another word that might have been *Christmas*.

'Hush, Ma. Just try to lie still and breathe. We're taking care of you.'

Devil returned as Nancy peeled away the sodden bed-clothes.

'Now bring some dry sheets and a clean nightdress.'

He seemed relieved to do whatever he was told. She heard him fling open the doors of the big linen press on the landing.

Nancy wrung out a washcloth in an enamel bowl. She sponged her mother's forehead and chest and then drew the sheet from beneath her before wrapping her in the towels. All the time she murmured as if to a distressed child, *there, let's get you dry, we'll take care of you, I know it hurts.*

She held her close, her lips against her burning forehead. Already the skin was pearled with fresh sweat. Nancy's eyes met Devil's.

'You must go for the doctor.'

His nod held all their misgivings. Medical attention was not easy to find. Many doctors were still in France, attending to soldiers who couldn't yet be brought back home. Others had dispersed to the overflowing military hospitals, and the voluntary nurses as well as the paid ones had mostly followed them.

Devil pulled on trousers over his pyjamas. 'I'll ask Cornelius's man to come, shall I?'

'Be quick.'

'Carlo,' Eliza muttered again, and then 'Jakey? Jake, speak up. They can't hear you in the gallery.'

She gave a sudden wild laugh and just as abruptly a spray of reddish foam came out of her mouth. Nancy wiped her lips and chin.

You are not going to die, she silently insisted. Don't even consider it, because I won't let you. I need you too much.

She held her until she seemed calmer. Racking shivers followed on from the sweating. Gently she laid her back against the pillows and pulled the hem of the soaked night-dress up to her mother's thighs. Eliza's hand descended like a claw and tried to prevent her from lifting it further.

'It's not Carlo, Mama, it's me,' Nancy whispered. 'No one else is here to see anything.'

Tears rolled from the corners of Eliza's eyes but she was too sick to protest further. Nancy lifted her mother's hips and pulled up the nightdress. What she saw made her catch her breath in shock. Eliza's belly was a pillow of white flesh scored with deep creases. Nancy knew only her own neat anatomy, and the glimpse of her mother's damaged body made her gasp with shock.

Even in the grip of the fever Eliza knew what was to be seen. Her lips stretched in a rictus of distress.

'I'm sorry.' Nancy removed the garment and threw it aside, then as gently as she could she towelled her mother's body and dressed her again. She spread a clean sheet on

Devil's side of the bed and hoisted her on to the fresh bedclothes. She covered her with the blankets, smoothed her hair off her face and held her in her arms, wordlessly praying. Eliza's eyes were half-closed. Each successive breath seemed to be dragged out of her body.

Nancy listened to the steady ticking of the bedroom clock, counting the seconds as they built into slow minutes.

At last she heard the front door rattle and two pairs of boots treading up the stairs.

Dr Vassilis was a very old man with straggling whiskers and a bald domed head. He had clearly dressed in haste. His metal-framed spectacles chafed flaky patches at the bridge of his nose. The Wixes knew that he was kind, because Cornelius was not afraid of him, but he was not the best doctor in London.

He put his bag down on the end of the bed and took out a muslin mask that he hooked over his ears. Eliza saw his half-blanked face and writhed away in terror. Devil and Nancy had to hold her down so the old man could lower his stethoscope to her fluttering chest.

The doctor stepped back after making his quick examination.

'Spanish influenza is highly contagious,' he muttered in his Greek-accented English. 'To nurse her I advise you both, three layers of muslin, so, over the nose and mouth.'

'To hell with the muslin, tell me about my wife.'

Vassilis shook his head at Devil. He looked like an old sheep.

'You will do no good to be sick like she is.'

'What can we do?' Nancy begged.

'Aspirins is the best medicine. Keep her warm, if she will drink let her have it, watch her carefully.'

'Is that all?'

Vassilis nodded sadly. 'I can tell you, it is in a way hopeful that your mother is older and not so strong. This flu, I don't know why – and I am only a doctor, perhaps it is God himself who understands these things – it seems to like the young and the strong best of all. They die like this,' he clicked his bony fingers, 'and the weaker ones, babies and old people, they stay alive.' He shrugged.

Devil gripped one of the brass bed knobs so tightly that his knuckles whitened. For once he was completely in the room, no other concern colouring his expression, his face stripped naked by anxiety. Nancy's thoughts flicked to her mother's ruined body and just as quickly she steered them away again. She could read love for his wife plainly written in Devil's face. He would be a smaller man without her. Nancy had always assumed that it was Devil who led the way, charming other people and pleasing himself, while Eliza resented his glamour. Now it occurred to her that he was only trying to deflect some of the power she held over him.

What a complicated measure men and women were obliged to dance, she thought. She didn't include herself in this company, or even wonder when her own dance might begin.

The doctor took a brown vial from his bag. 'Two of these for her, every four hours. A high dose but it is best in such a case.'

At the door, as Devil was showing him out, he asked, 'How is Cornelius?'

'The same,' Devil told him.

But that was not quite true. When daylight came and it seemed that Eliza was poised on the very margin between life and death, Cornelius slipped into the room.

Nancy got up from the bedside to try to warn him or

107

perhaps to shield him but he gently put her aside. He studied his mother's congested face and listened to her breathing, then lifted her wrist to count her pulse. He was composed, although he understood how ill she was. Eliza opened her eyes and saw him.

'There, Ma,' Cornelius soothed. 'I'm here.'

The winter light crept across the floor. The three watchers sat in silence until Devil's chin drooped on to his chest and he fell into an exhausted doze. Nancy tensed with Eliza's every breath but Cornelius remained impassive. When Eliza coughed so hard that she retched up mouthfuls of pink mucus he wiped it away and afterwards moistened her lips with a few drops of water.

An hour passed and then another. There was no change, but Eliza still breathed.

'We should send for Aunt Faith,' Nancy said at last.

Devil lifted his head. 'I will do it.' He was glad of anything that was not just waiting.

It was time for another dose. Cornelius took the bottle from Nancy and administered the pills, doing it more deftly than she could have done. She saw that he had somehow been hooked from his despair into the detached state that must have allowed him to do his work in France. It was odd to feel any satisfaction on this terrible morning but she did feel it, and it grew stronger when her brother touched her arm and said in a voice that was almost his own, 'She is holding on, you know.'

When Faith arrived two hours later in response to Devil's telegram, Eliza had fallen uneasily asleep. Her features were sharp and her eyes had sunk deep into their sockets.

Nancy and Faith wordlessly hugged each other.

Faith was wearing the dark clothes she had put on after Rowland was killed on the Somme. His death had come only a little more than a year after Edwin succumbed to his wounds at Ypres. Faith's happiness now was all in her grandson, Lizzie's child, although there had not been so much satisfaction when the baby came far too soon after Lizzie's hasty wedding. The marriage had not lasted many months into the war and the whereabouts of little Thomas Shaw Hooper's father were not now known.

Matthew Shaw said, 'You couldn't trust that man as far as you could throw him. I knew it the minute he walked through my front door.'

Nowadays Lizzie never spoke of Jack Hooper, although when she first met him she had talked of nothing else. She had breathed in Nancy's ear, 'God, he's so handsome. He makes me feel like a queen and a she-devil, both at the same time.'

And then she had laughed, a strange glittering laughter that made Nancy jealous. Nancy had not then been able to imagine what passion must feel like, but now it occurred to her that she had experienced the softest premonitory whisper of it. Was it only a matter of hours ago that she had sat talking to Gil Maitland? Yesterday evening seemed to belong in another life.

Devil made room for Faith at one side of the bed and Cornelius sat opposite them. There was no space for Nancy, so at Faith's suggestion she slipped away to make tea. The fire had gone out and the kitchen was chilly. She brought in a basket of kindling from the lean-to in the back area, lit a twisted horseshoe of newspaper and set the kettle on the hob. Her chilblains flared and she clawed absently at them. While she was waiting for the water to boil she rummaged in the drawers of the old dresser and after quite a long search found what she was looking for, a small roll of butter muslin that Mrs Frost must have used for making raspberry jelly. Devil liked jelly, although none had been made in this kitchen for several years. She laid the muslin to one side, acknowledging that it was too late now to try to protect anyone from infection. But it was the memory of sweet red jelly that prompted her to carve slices off yesterday's loaf and toast them in front of the yellow fire. She laid a tray with butter and shop jam and carried it up to the drawing room, not even glancing out of the window at the spot where Lawrence Feather had appeared last night.

Eliza was still fitfully sleeping. Her mouth hung open and her jaw sagged. Nancy gave a cup of tea to Faith and sent Devil and Cornelius downstairs for theirs.

Nancy murmured, 'I've heard that the first twenty-four hours are the worst. If she can survive the night, you know . . .'

Faith answered, 'Your mother will, if anyone can. I have seen her do it before. After Cornelius was born she was more dead than alive, then a few hours later she was sitting up and trying to nurse him and insisting that he was going to live too. Matthew and I sent for the priest to baptise him, we were so certain that he wouldn't last the day.'

'Was she always the same?'

Faith said, 'Yes. Always.'

Nancy almost smiled. There were no compromises in Eliza except for those forced on her by life's reverses, and she bowed under those with little grace.

Eliza's fits of coughing shook the house. They could only hold her arms and hope that the spasms would not crack her ribs. When the latest one subsided Faith folded a damp cloth with some drops of eau de cologne and placed it on her forehead while Nancy sponged her wrists with cold water. The pillow was sweat-soaked so they placed a fresh towel under her head.

The two women talked in low voices.

Nancy asked, 'Carlo was the dwarf, wasn't he? She keeps saying his name.'

'Carlo was your father's stage partner in the very first days of the Palmyra. Eliza and I went to see them perform an act called *The Philosopher's Illusion.*'

Nancy had often heard it described. The trick turned on the dwarf's miniature stature, which he concealed from the audience throughout by walking on stilts.

'Carlo was in love with her, poor fellow. They all were,' Faith added.

'Who was Jakey? Ma talked about him too.'

Faith was distracted. 'The boy? He was in the company back then. He could act rather well. I think he went on to another theatre and much bigger things.'

Nancy bent her head and laced her fingers with her mother's. Eliza's wedding ring was loose on the bone.

Devil and Cornelius came back, somewhat restored by toast and tea.

The day wore on. At the end of the afternoon Nancy walked up the road to the post office. The cold air was like a slap after the close fug of the sickroom. She telephoned Miss Dent, to let her know that she would have to be away from work for as long as her mother needed to be nursed. Miss Dent accepted her apologies with a brief word of sympathy and didn't ask her when she expected to return to work.

At home again Nancy found Faith busy in the kitchen and hearty smells of cooking drifting up through the house. She tried to thank her, but Faith would hear none of it.

'Who else needs me? Not Lizzie. And Matthew can look out for Tommy just as well as I can.'

Nancy put her arms around her aunt's plump shoulders.

'All the same, thank you,' she said.

Soon there was a hot meal ready for Devil and Cornelius. The men ate quickly and gratefully. Cornelius brooded in silence but at least he didn't mutter about the wounded waiting for his help, or watch the clock as if every spoonful might cost a man's life.

Devil didn't even contemplate going to the Palmyra for the evening performance.

'Anthony will have to manage,' he shrugged.

The evening slid into night. Devil dozed at the bedside with his head on his folded arms and Nancy and Faith took it in turns to lie down in Nancy's bedroom. Cornelius padded between his own room and Eliza's, and Nancy found his withdrawn vigilance oddly reassuring. He picked up the latest letter from Arthur and scanned it.

'Have you sent for him? He would get compassionate leave, I think.'

Devil briefly shook his head. They all understood that he delayed because Arthur was to be shielded as far as possible.

'Ah. Well, maybe it's for the best. I think the crisis may be almost over.'

It seemed that Cornelius was right. The next time Eliza woke she was too weak to lift her head but she knew them all. Her eyes always came back to Devil.

Dr Vassilis was visibly surprised when he called the next day, but he pretended to have foreseen the improvement. He examined her before stepping well back to remove his muslin mask.

'Yes, you see, it is just like I told you. It is not the strongest ones who survive. Last night I have a young man die, sick for one day and *pfffff*, he goes like blowing out this.' He pointed to the candle in its holder on the night table. The family stared at him, not at all comforted, and the doctor snapped his bag shut. To Cornelius he said in a more cheerful voice, 'How are you, my friend?'

Cornelius considered the question.

'There has been more than enough dying, doctor. To sit and brood on it as I have been doing is not helpful. I find nursing my mother a more useful occupation.'

Vassilis looked shrewdly at him.

'That is a fine discovery, Mr Wix.'

The doctor bowed and wished them good day. After she had seen him out Nancy gave way in private to tears of relief. To manage her feelings for Devil and Cornelius's sake she set herself the job of laundering all the soiled bed linen and towels. In the scullery she put water on to boil and found a kind of painful oblivion in plunging her arms deep in the enamel wash tub and scrubbing with the laundry soap until her muscles ached. She tipped the scummy water down the stone sink and ran a fresh tub. She rinsed everything twice and fed the clean items through the mangle, leaning down on the heavy handle with all the weight of her body. She pegged out sheets under the tin roof that partly covered the back area and draped the towels on the wooden maiden suspended from the kitchen ceiling. Her arms were scalded crimson to the elbows.

Faith found her as she was finishing the work.

'Nancy? Look at you. Doesn't Eliza send out to a laundry?'

'The boy came for it yesterday when we were all too busy. Anyway I needed to do it myself, and it's made me feel much better. Is Ma sleeping?'

'She is. Cornelius is with her. Your father's exhausted so I told him to lie down in your room.'

'That's good.'

Faith regarded her with an odd expression.

'Aunt Faith? Is something wrong?'

'You are so like her, you know.'

Nancy was taken aback.

Her whole life was coloured by being unlike her mother and by wishing to resemble her more closely.

'Not in your looks, although since you have grown up I see more of her in you every day. In your stubbornness, I mean. You won't ever give up once you have fixed on an idea. Even when you were tiny, if you wanted to play with a toy you would have it, however hard the boys tried to take it off you. You wouldn't yell, but you kept your eyes and your little hands fastened tight on it. Lizzie always understood the power of a bargain. She'd hand over the ball so as to get herself something better. You have your mother's energy too.' Faith pointed at the white ramparts of sheets, stirring in the wind. 'She would have done that, before her strength went.'

'Poor Ma,' Nancy sighed.

She hadn't been aware that she possessed Eliza's iron will. Nancy's own impression was of inhabiting the margins of her family. She stayed on the outskirts and kept quiet, mostly because of the Uncanny and her conviction that she had to protect it and keep it secret. Her way of camouflaging her difference was to be unobtrusive in plain sight.

She took it for granted that her father loved her, in the way that fathers always loved their only daughters, but she didn't think he knew or understood her particularly well, any more than Eliza did. Most of her parents' energies, after all, were applied to each other. The memory of the *Queen Mab* returned, and how her father's first and strongest instinct had been to save his wife.

Nancy wiped her damp forehead with the back of her

hand. Her shoulders ached from lifting and mangling wet towels, and there was a new and less manageable ache in her that she did not yet recognise. She wondered how it ever came about that you loved someone like a husband or wife, and were loved back. It seemed too complicated to happen very often and yet the suggestion of it was everywhere, except in her own life.

Faith saw her expression.

'Nancy, dear. You're very tired. You'll be ill yourself if you don't take care.'

'It's not that, Aunt Faith.'

'What is it, then?'

Faith's motherly concern touched her, and the ache faded a little. But Nancy's instinct was always to parry a direct question so she turned aside and asked, 'Will Ma get well?'

Faith used a folded cloth to lift a pan of scalding water. Clouds of steam billowed between them.

'I believe she will recover from this bout, yes.'

Nancy could see that her aunt was disappointed by her reticence.

The next day Eliza was a little better. The sweating and shivering stopped, although the terrible cough persisted. The day after that Faith held her while Nancy fed her two or three spoonfuls of soup.

The household adjusted to the rhythms of nursing Eliza. Faith spent the days helping Nancy and Cornelius in Islington, but she returned to Matthew every evening because he complained so much about Lizzie's cooking and standards of housekeeping.

After the end of her marriage Lizzie went back to her parents, although she confided to Nancy that it was difficult to live in a house that had become a shrine to Edwin and

Rowland. Their boyhood possessions were preserved like relics and there were photographs of the dead sons everywhere. Nancy couldn't say much in response to this, because Lizzie must think it unfair that Cornelius and Arthur were both still alive.

Lizzie had adopted a brisk manner that could make her seem a little hard. She had to give up her beloved job with the tea importer once she became a mother, but afterwards she had quickly yielded the daily care of Tommy to Faith, in favour of helping her father with the family greengrocery. The loss of his sons had aged Matthew Shaw, and Lizzie had energy and an undeniable talent for business. She made herself useful and then indispensable and she claimed a healthy wage for her efforts. Her short tenure as Jack Hooper's wife had left her with a fierce desire for independence.

'Mama shouldn't have to run back and forth every day like this. My father could quite easily fry himself an egg,' Lizzie said when she called one evening to see Eliza. 'Although he doesn't believe eggs and frying pans should be a man's work.'

Nancy had sewn a set of muslin masks and her cousin wore one as she hovered uncertainly at the bedside. The women all agreed that little Tommy must be protected from infection, but there was also an understanding that Lizzie couldn't be involved in caring for anyone who was ill. She was not a nurse, she would have insisted, and she had no talent for such things.

Lizzie had been unable to hide her shock at Eliza's changed appearance. She chatted to her a little too brightly and disconnectedly through the layers of her mask, and was relieved when Nancy led her away before Eliza got overtired.

The cousins retreated downstairs. Lizzie stood by the kitchen range, tapped a cigarette on her thumbnail and expertly clicked a lighter. She had shortened her skirts and her hair and had recently started painting her lips. The dark lipstick stained the butt of the cigarette.

Exhaling sharply she exclaimed, 'Poor Nancy. What a ghastly time you have all been through.'

Nancy accepted a cigarette and puffed inexpertly.

'She's getting better, that's all that matters.'

'She looks terrible.'

Lizzie was always blunt. To change the subject Nancy said, 'What about you?'

Lizzie shrugged. 'Tommy's happy. He'll start school in the autumn. *My* life's all work, more's the pity. I'd like a nice new boyfriend. I expect you would too, eh? You and I are both going to deserve some proper fun quite soon, darling.'

Devil had said the same thing.

'Soon,' Nancy said. She would have liked to believe it, and sometimes as she did the endless household chores she allowed herself a fantasy in which Gil Maitland's cream Daimler drew up outside the house or in front of Lennox & Ringland. He knew where she lived and her place of work, but as the days passed and there was no evidence of him she told herself that of course a man like Gil was not going to materialise and sweep her off her feet. He had whiled away an hour in her company and given her a lift home because it was raining. Nothing more.

*You are not Cinderella or a princess in a fairy tale. You are Nancy Wix. You can dream, but a dream is all it is.*

Lizzie winked at her and began to talk about business. She quickly became animated. People needed novelty and some little luxuries, she declared. With the shipping routes open again and overseas trade growing, she was establishing a network of relationships with importers of exotic fruits. Pineapples from South America, mangoes from India, figs from the Mediterranean shores, all these could be brought in the holds of cargo ships and unloaded at the London or Liverpool docks. The dewy fruits would make their way, via the modern wholesale warehouse Lizzie had encouraged her father to acquire, to every quality greengrocer in the country. The miracle of refrigeration made all this easy, Lizzie explained, waving her hands. She still wore her wedding ring, Nancy noted.

'Just wait and see. There will be a fresh pineapple or a peach on every table, I promise you. Not only in the great houses where the dukes and lords have their own hothouses.'

Nancy wondered if the war had been fought even partly to make a pineapple available to everyone who might desire one, but she said nothing. There had been so many unexpected outcomes of the conflict that the real impact seemed impossible to discern. Married women and those over thirty could vote and one of them had even been elected to Parliament. After all the suffragists' meetings, and the broken windows and arson and arrests and prison sentences, it had taken the greater war to win the battle for them.

'The how doesn't matter,' Jinny insisted. 'It's the what that counts.'

After a week at home, during which his growing distraction and restlessness reflected Eliza's steady recovery, Devil announced that he must get back to the Palmyra.

'Anthony Ellis does his best,' he said, which meant that the manager's best wasn't good enough.

He confessed to Nancy that there was a crisis of loyalty to deal with because some of the artistes had not been paid for their most recent performances. They had refused to go onstage and he had been forced to cancel shows. There was an embarrassment concerning available funds, he said. Audiences had been sparse for weeks because people feared the influenza, but an almost empty theatre still cost the same to run as it did when full.

It was nothing really, he insisted, only a short-term problem. Once the bitter weather and the threat of infection receded, the seats would fill up again. He was sure he could persuade his players and creditors to be patient.

'No need to mention this to your mother. She'll only worry.'

'I know, Pa. In the fever she thought she was at the theatre, but back in the old days. She often mentioned Carlo, and someone called Jakey. Who was he?'

Devil gave her a glance. 'Jake Jones? He was a street boy. Out of the kindness of our young hearts your mother and I took him in. Sylvia Aynscoe even taught him to read. He worked his way on to the stage and before Eliza and I knew it he was off to join Beerbohm Tree at the Haymarket company, if you please. He's done well for himself, has Jakey Jones. Haven't you heard of him?'

Nancy shook her head.

'Dear me. I should take you out and about more. He's in the films now, I believe. Mr Jones's Hamlet is celebrated, and he was a very good performer in Mr Wilde's plays if that sort of thing happens to be to your taste. I really should look him up,' Devil added thoughtfully.

Eliza's strength slowly returned but she was not an easy or accommodating patient. She was always asking what time Devil was expected home, even in the quiet hours when Cornelius read to her or simply held her hand as she drifted in and out of sleep. Nancy became the focus for her complaints. Her bones ached so horribly, why couldn't Vassilis give her something stronger to stop the pain? Her food was cold, the bed was crumpled and her pillows were always flat. Why was the sunlight so bright in her eyes, or why was the room so dim that she couldn't see a thing?

Nancy did her best, but her temper sometimes flared. If she did forget herself enough to snap at Eliza her mother sank back with an expression of shock and pain that made Nancy want to chop out her own tongue.

'I'm sorry, so sorry,' she would murmur, trying to gather her up and hold her close, but Eliza's fragile body could no longer bear the pressure of even the lightest embrace.

Cornelius tried to tell his sister that she shouldn't mind. Eliza needed all her attention and sympathy for herself, he said, to help her to recover. She wasn't trying to imagine herself in Nancy's shoes or she wouldn't be so harsh.

Nancy said sadly, 'It's my fault. After what she has been through I ought to be more patient with her.'

He patted her shoulder and told her that she had been cooped up indoors for too long. She should go out for a walk by the canal, or to meet Jinny Main and her friends. Nancy thought it was Cornelius who should go out more – in the months since he had come home he had hardly left the house. But when she casually suggested it he refused at once, unable to conceal a flash of panic.

He preferred to stay with Eliza, he insisted. When he was not at her bedside he was teaching himself to cook. He made himself at home in the kitchen, creating a great deal of mess by preparing toast and porridge and stirring experimental concoctions that Nancy and Devil gamely consumed each night.

One evening Nancy had to ask her father for some money to pay the butcher and the coal merchant, and he conjured ten shillings from his waistcoat pocket.

'I must be out of practice,' he said without smiling. 'It used to be five pounds, didn't it?'

The time came when nursing Eliza and keeping house no longer called for two people, and Nancy decided she should go back to work to bring in some money. That same day she rang up Miss Dent. The secretary was non-committal on the telephone. Nancy put on her flannel skirt, pinned up her hair with the *cloisonné* combs and returned to Lennox & Ringland. The welcome clatter of the Linotype machines sounded as lovely as a symphony and she was humming as she ran up the stairs.

As soon as she entered the outer office she saw that a change had taken place in her absence.

Miss Dent had moved to Nancy's old corner away from the fire, and in the secretary's place stood a handsome mahogany desk with a leather top. There was no one seated at it, but it was clearly intended for someone important.

'Would you go straight through to see Mr Lennox?' the secretary said. She didn't meet Nancy's eye.

Mr Lennox closed a folder and leaned back. His chair creaked on its claw feet.

'Ah, Miss Wix. Won't you sit down?'

He had never asked her to sit before. She couldn't remember that he had ever given her more than a casual glance. She took the chair opposite his desk.

'I can't keep your job for you.'

He had more to say, but she didn't really listen. The man's son had been discharged from the Royal Navy and was returning to work in the family printing business. The desk in the corner was intended for him, and Nancy was no longer required in the office. In any case she had responsibilities at home, to her mother, didn't she?

'I'm so sorry I was absent. She is almost recovered now. Can't I work down on the print floor with Jinny?'

Mr Lennox shook his head. 'The men are coming back. You young ladies have done well, but it's men's work.'

Nancy might have retorted that it had been women's work for as long as they were needed to do it, but she knew there was no point. Perhaps even Jinny's job wouldn't last much longer. She got to her feet as Mr Lennox stood up and came round the desk to her. Placing his hands on her shoulders he turned her towards him and his forearm brushed her breast.

'It's a shame, my dear, but a girl like you will want to find a husband and have a family.' His breath was meaty on her face. She shook him off and stepped out of reach.

'I see. You'll want me to work my notice, I suppose?'

No, she would receive a week's pay instead of notice. Trembling, Nancy found herself back in the outer office. Poor Miss Dent looked wretched. Nancy went back down the stone stairs and found Jinny in her brown overall, performing the menial task of hand setting type for a theatre playbill. Nancy was reminded of the posters Devil liked to design for the Palmyra before the war.

'I've been sacked.'

Jinny slammed the form against the bench with a crash that shook the type out of line.

'That bloody old bastard.'

Nancy hushed her. It wouldn't help Jinny to be overheard cursing the managing director. Jinny left her bench and steered Nancy towards the kitchen.

'I need a minute,' she said to the frowning foreman as they passed him. 'Women's reasons, all right?'

The man turned red in the face.

The two girls leaned against the old sink as they had so often done before. There would be no cup of tea today.

'What will you do?'

Nancy did her best to be optimistic although she was close to tears. Given the situation at home she badly needed to work. 'I'll find another job. Can't be a lady of leisure, can I?'

'This place isn't what it was anyway. You'll get something better, easy. You can speak French, for God's sake.'

'No, I can't.'

Jinny huffed with frustration. 'Come here.' She held out her arms and gave Nancy a rough hug.

'Thanks, Jinny. You should get back to work.'

'Yeah. Look. Now that your ma's so much better, and Cornelius as well, you can come out with us, can't you? There's an equal franchise meeting on Thursday night . . .'

Nancy didn't have much appetite for one of Jinny's political gatherings. She nodded in a non-committal way.

'I'll see.'

'That's good. We need you. Omadood barm, eh?'

'Omadood barm,' Nancy reluctantly smiled.

'Oh, by the way. I forgot to say. A man called here, wanting to see you. He looked in at the dispatch office and Frank sent him through to me.'

Nancy gaped. Her heart was skipping against her ribs.

Gil Maitland had come at last. She kept his laundered handkerchief in her pocket and her fingers closed on the folds of it. Her mind was racing ahead, to how she would tell him about Eliza's illness and losing her job, and the luxury of his listening to her.

'Nance? He was quite an odd-looking fellow, in a long

overcoat and one of those big old hats. He said he knew you very well, so I asked him why didn't he go to your house?'

Her heart slowed until it was heavy as a stone. The caller wasn't Gil at all.

'He left his card for you. Hang on a sec. What have I done with it?'

Jinny rummaged through the pockets of her ink-stained overall and at last found the creased card.

'Thanks.' Without glancing at it Nancy knew that it read *Lawrence Feather, Medium*. So it had been him in the flesh on the night Eliza fell ill, looking up at the window until he was sure she had seen him. The intensifying of the Uncanny, the way it swirled around her after having seemed almost dormant, must be to do with him.

'Who is he?'

'No one,' Nancy said sadly.

Before she left Lennox & Ringland for the last time she made a quick tour to say goodbye to her friends. The older men were sorry to see her go and they all demanded a kiss, but even in the three and a half weeks of her absence the workforce had changed. There were two unfriendly new type-setters, and an odd-job man with a big broom who didn't even glance up from his sweeping as she passed. Fifteen minutes later she was making her way back down the alley to Fleet Street.

She hesitated in the roar of traffic. Grimy-faced print workers from the early morning shift were elbowing their way out of the newspaper buildings and heading towards the pubs for a liquid breakfast. Following the bitterness of her disappointment about Gil Nancy wanted to find her father and at least confide in him about her lost job. She turned west and began to trudge through the scurrying crowds towards the Strand. Devil would commiserate with her, and then make her laugh so she would briefly forget getting the sack from a menial position that she had liked. He would steer her across the street to the Lyons' Corner House and they would take a table by the window. She could already taste the sweet white icing on the finger bun she planned to order with her coffee.

Preoccupied with her thoughts and with threading her way through the throng, she didn't look up at the theatre until she was almost at the steps. It was the foyer attendant's job to keep them swept, but today they were gritty and littered with cigarette ends. The wind had pasted a crumpled sheet of newspaper and a greasy bag that had once held chips against the big doors that opened into the green-and-gold foyer.

Nancy lifted her head. The brass door handles were chained and padlocked. A notice had been stuck behind the glass. It read simply '*CLOSED*'. One corner of the notice hung down like a dejected ear.

The Palmyra was not only closed and deserted, it already had an air of dereliction.

Shocked by the sight, Nancy hurried to the stage door in the side alley that sloped steeply down to the river. This door was also closed and padlocked. By this time of the morning, even if the theatre front was still shut the stage door would normally be open and the doorman ensconced in his cubicle with his pungent paraffin stove warming his feet. She could almost hear him calling out, 'Mornin', Miss Nancy. Ow've yer bin? Yer dad's in 'is hoffice.'

But there was no one there and the theatre was *closed*.

It was as if she had come down the Strand and found that her father's heart had stopped beating.

A tug towing a barge loaded with timber was making

its way upriver. Nancy watched it, trying to work out what must have happened and why Devil hadn't told anyone. She had been preoccupied – perhaps he *had* tried to tell her, and had given up because he didn't have her attention.

She walked home through the insistent drizzle. For all the glitter of the shop windows and the shimmering reflections in the puddles she did not think London had ever looked so dismal.

In Islington a surprise was waiting for her. An officer's cap with a highly polished badge lay on the hall stand with a pair of soft leather gloves beside it. A khaki greatcoat hung on one of the pegs.

She shouted, 'Arthur, is it you? *Arthur?*'

# CHAPTER SEVEN

The three of them were in the drawing room, seated in the window overlooking the water. Eliza was out of bed, dressed up like a Gipsy dancer in a full-skirted coat and multicoloured layers of scarves. There was a languid gaiety about her that Nancy put down to delight at seeing her second son.

'Look who's here,' she called.

'Arthur, it *is* you. How wonderful. Welcome home.'

Her brother came to her with his arms outstretched and his tunic buttons glittering, bright as a ray of sunlight in a mineshaft. His fair hair was combed to a sharp parting, his moustache was trimmed with geometric precision and she could only marvel at how handsome he was. Cornelius looked on, his face slack with happy relief. His brother was here, straight-backed and able-bodied, direct from France and bringing with him nothing worse than the scent of soap and military laundry.

'I say, Nancy. Darling Nancy,' Arthur murmured. He folded her against him and she laid her cheek against khaki and creaking leather.

'I'm so glad you've come. How long can you stay?'

'Four days' leave. I put in as soon as I got your letter, and the old man was really very obliging.'

Without consulting anyone Nancy had written a few careful details about how ill Eliza really had been. It had seemed all right do so once their mother was positively out of danger.

As Arthur squeezed her arm he murmured in her ear, 'I think you didn't tell me the whole truth when you wrote before.'

No one in this family tells the truth, Nancy thought. Not one of us.

'Pa and I were here. Neelie did an awful lot. There was no reason to worry you.'

'Don't whisper, you two,' Eliza rebuked. 'Nancy, why have you come home at this time of day? Now you are here, don't you think we should celebrate your brother's visit with a glass of something special? I'm expecting your father to look in before this evening's show – we must drink a toast to all being together again.'

'I'll fetch a bottle in a minute, Ma,' Cornelius replied. He needed plenty of time to shift from the expected route to a different track.

Nancy said, 'I'm back early to see you up and dressed, Ma. Did you feel well enough?'

In reality Eliza was so gaunt that her skin puckered over her sharp bones. She had twisted her hair in a bun and skewered it with what appeared to be a red lacquer chopstick. The ensemble was completed with one necklace of amber beads and another of coral, and a set of carved bangles that rattled when she flicked her scarves. It was the first time since the influenza that she had assembled a complete outfit, and she was making up for missed opportunities.

She waved her hand. 'Vassilis came this morning and

gave me something. I'm feeling not far from on top of the world.'

'Svalbard?' Cornelius murmured to no one in particular.

Nancy parcelled up her concerns and placed them to one side for the time being.

'Of course we must have a drink to welcome Arthur home.'

Cornelius finally lumbered to his feet. 'I am on my way.'

He took responsibility for more and more of the household duties and he didn't like to be interrupted or deflected from performing them.

While he was gone Arthur laughed about the intransigence of French railway officials and the horrors of the Channel crossing.

'Rather than enduring the saloon I set up a camp in one of the lifeboats. It was cold but there was no frightful music and almost no one was being sick. As soon as they tied up at Dover I dashed down the gangplank and into a hotel. I had a wash and shave and a plate of sausages and bacon.'

Eliza giggled like a schoolgirl at these mild anecdotes.

Nancy asked, 'So that's how you look so immaculately scrubbed?'

He smiled. 'Ah, to be clean and shaved is the greatest luxury in the world. I didn't understand that until I was regularly filthy. Now I'd choose a bowl of hot water and a sharp razor over the finest Cuban cigar any day.'

She had heard from Jinny about the wounded men's rags of battledress, often crawling with lice. She understood why Arthur's hair was barbered so close to the nape of his neck and why his fingernails were scraped almost painfully clean. Involuntarily she sat on her own hands, fearing they might be blotted with printer's ink, and then recalled that that wouldn't be happening any longer. Cornelius puffed back into the room. He had assembled a butler's tray with several mismatched glasses, a stone bottle of lemonade, a jug containing some tufted celery stalks and the prize of a dusty bottle of port. He frowned in concentration as he drew the cork and sniffed it.

'Port and lemonade.' He smacked his lips. 'It tastes of Christmas. Christmas like it was a long time ago, I mean.'

'You're right,' Eliza beamed. She put out her hand for the drink. 'I am so happy,' she added.

They held up their glasses, leaning into the circle until the rims clinked.

When she laughed Eliza seemed her old self again. Looking at her family Nancy knew how much she loved them. The war was receding and the dark ripples from it they would somehow find a way to deal with – there wasn't a family in the country that was not doing the same thing. They were here and together, that was the only thing that mattered.

Cornelius whipped a celery stalk from the jug, spraying droplets of water all over the tray and nearby cushions. There was plenty of grit clinging in the furrows but he bit into it anyway.

'I do like something to chew on, with a drink,' he explained.

Into this celebration Devil suddenly arrived. He tossed his hat and coat on the nearest chair and bear-hugged his son, then kissed his wife and told her that she looked ravishing.

'Nancy? I thought you'd be at work.'

She avoided her father's eye.

'Well, Arthur's home.'

Stating the obvious was enough to deflect him. Devil did a stagy double take when he saw what they were drinking.

'What's this? Don't we have champagne?'

'No, we don't,' Nancy said.

'That's a pity. Never mind. Welcome home, my boy. It does my old heart good to see you.'

It clearly did. Devil and Eliza drank and bravely nibbled the celery stalks. Arthur talked about his friend Captain Bolton and their performance of magic tricks in an out-building of the farm that was their present divisional HQ. His men liked the cards and silks pretty well, Arthur said, but what they loved above all was seeing their officer done up in short skirts and a blonde wig. He leapt up to demonstrate a dip and swing of the hip.

'I'm received with total rapture, let me tell you,' he grinned. 'I think I may have a brilliant performing career ahead of me. What do you think, Pa? A stage burlesque for the old Palmyra?'

Devil didn't falter. 'Quality acts like that are very costly to book. What would Captains Bolton and Wix charge by the week, do you think?'

It was almost two hours before Devil slipped his watch out of his waistcoat pocket. He made the familiar announcement that he was expected at the theatre before curtain up. Nancy thought of the littered steps and padlocked doors down in the Strand and she stiffened when her father stooped to say goodnight. He didn't notice that she kept her face turned aside.

After Devil had gone, whistling on his way down the steps as if there were nothing unusual about the day, Cornelius cooked a dinner of fried liver and mashed potato. Eliza only played with her food but she chatted brightly. Arthur ate everything on his plate with apparent relish, although Nancy guessed he would be used to better fare in the officers' mess. He would be used to being waited on, too. Later she was touched when he removed his belt and tunic and rolled up his shirtsleeves to help her with the washing-up. Seeing the old kitchen through her brother's less accustomed eyes made her realise how dingy it had become. The sink was greasy and the distemper was flaking off the ceiling in leprous patches. She must do something, she told herself. It wouldn't cost too much to have a man come in to paint the walls, and the difference would lift their spirits. Perhaps old Gibb would know someone she could ask.

Arthur threw aside the dishcloth. 'Come on. Let's all go out for a drink. Neelie, what do you say?'

Cornelius was sitting with a book. His feet were planted flat on the floor, his elbows glued to the arms of the chair.

'No. You two go.'

He spoke evenly, but Nancy saw his fear.

The crisis of Eliza's illness had brought him out of his room and given his days a point. It was weeks now since he had suffered a proper bout of weeping, and he seemed able to distinguish the present from the past so long as he kept a close focus on the daily work of the house. He didn't do the work particularly well, and that didn't matter in the least. But he never went out, and she knew that it was because he was afraid to. He didn't like loud noises or strangers, or any sequence of events that threatened to develop beyond his control.

Arthur said, 'Shall we, Nancy?'

She was relieved that he didn't try to force Cornelius to come with them. They went upstairs to say goodnight to Eliza. Her earlier animation had drained away and she was in bed, wrapped up her shabby old red robe. When she was a little girl Nancy used to think the robe was the finest garment in the world because it had a fire-breathing fanged Chinese dragon embroidered on the back.

132

'We're going to the pub, Ma. Neelie's downstairs. Will you be all right for an hour?'

'Of course I will.' She lay back and closed her eyes. Her eyelids seemed almost translucent.

Without conferring, Nancy and Arthur turned away from the local places where they might be known and walked south towards the city. The picked a large establishment on the corner of a busy street and pushed past etched-glass panels into the saloon bar. There was ornamental plaster-work with mahogany fittings, a billow of companionable smoke and a hum of talk. Out of sight in the public bar someone was thumping on a piano. Nancy's spirits rose.

'What'll it be?' he asked.

'Scotch. A large one, if you can afford it.'

'Good girl.'

She found a table while Arthur went to the bar. An enormous woman winked at her.

'Got your sweetheart home, darling? You're the lucky one.'

'He's my brother.'

The woman's gaze followed him, her cushiony red lips pursed. 'I see. Has he got a girl?'

'I'm not sure. I should ask him, shouldn't I?'

Another wink and a broad smile. 'If you don't, I will.'

Arthur put down their drinks and settled himself so his khaki shoulders blocked the woman's view. After a long draught from his pint he took out his case and lit two cigarettes. Brother and sister studied each other through the smoke.

'Now then. Why don't you start with Neelie?' Arthur said.

It was such a relief to talk. She didn't try to censor her words, for once. He listened and nodded and at the end he said, 'What he has been through is almost beyond imagining. It would unbalance any man.'

The pub's smell of stale beer and smoke and old clothes swirled powerfully around them. Through the brown linoleum floor Nancy glimpsed a flash of white sky and shattered trees.

'Nancy? Are you all right?'

She took a slug of whisky. 'Yes. Isn't it the same for you?'

Arthur knuckled beer froth from his moustache. His neatness, his air of cheerful authority, even his physical mannerisms, seemed too mature for a man of only twenty. Although he said almost nothing about it she knew what his daily work entailed. Slain men lifted from amongst the debris and live shells, and the final consignment of their bodies to graves in the French fields.

'Those poor soldiers are all dead. There's no suffering any more, not like in the dugouts and field hospitals Neelie was seeing. Anyway I'm not a complicated sort of person, am I? I'm a decent soldier and a solid batsman, and that's about it. I don't have nightmares. Not too many, at any rate. I'd be a block of wood if some things didn't get to me, but Neelie's a different person. There are specialist doctors who are helping some of our chaps through the worst. I suppose we could try to get him to one of those, if you and Ma and Pa agree? My own hope after seeing him today is that he'll recover, given time, in his own way.'

They both understood that Cornelius's way was not the same as theirs, and was never likely to be.

'I hope so too,' Nancy said. There was no money for specialist doctors, she knew that much.

'Another one?' The piano was louder and someone was singing. She drained her glass and handed it over.

'Next one'll be on me,' she promised.

'Nancy Wix. What did you learn at those suffragette meetings?'

'Cheek. I'm much older than you.'

'A whole year and three months.'

His next question was, 'What about Ma?'

'She was better today. Almost as if someone had waved a healing wand. That would be you, of course.'

'I really wish you had told me earlier about the flu. I should have been here. You can't manage everything yourself, Nance.'

Whisky disarmed her. She said humbly, 'I know. I'm sorry. I'll try not to try to in future.'

She might have said that the tradition of sheltering Arthur was their parents' legacy and she and Cornelius carried it on, but that would only be pointing out what must be obvious to him too. Arthur was older than his years, and perceptive in ways she hadn't given him credit for.

After a small silence he said in a low voice, 'If it's not Neelie or Ma, what else is up?'

'I lost my job today.'

Arthur's face clouded. 'Bugger. What happened?'

'The big boss's son came back. Everyone else moved down one rung on the ladder and I fell off the bottom.'

There was no need to say more; the same was happening everywhere.

He covered her hand with his. 'Bad luck. I know you liked the print. Don't worry, you'll find another job in no time.'

'Of course I will.' She took a deep breath. In the public bar they were bawling a chorus. 'It had better be soon. The Palmyra's closed down.'

He stared. 'Closed?'

'I was there this morning. I wanted to see Pa, you know, after I was sacked.'

She described the scene.

As they talked they acknowledged that the theatre and its fluctuating fortunes, with its equally mercurial cast of magicians and tenors and sylph-like dancers, had been the shimmering backdrop to their entire lives. Neither of them could properly comprehend that it now lay dark and silent.

'He sat at home with us all afternoon and never gave the tiniest hint,' Arthur marvelled. 'The old chap's a better actor than I realised.'

This struck them as funny. Nancy coughed into her whisky and with the release of tension they began laughing so hard that the fat woman leaned over to see if she could join in the joke. Nancy went to the bar to buy the next round and while she waited she peered past the glass screens to catch sight of the revelry in the adjoining room. The bar was a sea of red faces and swaying bodies and she envied so many people who were clearly having a good time. She leaned over her brother's shoulder.

'C'mon. Let's forget our troubles and go next door for a bit.'

He seized their drinks and led the way. The heat and noise rolled over them as they edged into the room. The singing was too loud for talk so they joined in the next chorus instead.

'If he's not asking you'd better dance with me,' a man roared at her. Nancy let herself be drawn into the jigging crowd just as a girl grabbed Arthur and hung off his arm. Over her head Arthur winked.

'That's it darling,' Nancy's partner shouted in her ear. 'Why worry, eh?'

A second pair of hands seized hers. These belonged to a boy who knew how to steer and she let herself go with him and the music until the room whirled. It was a relief not to think. Finally Arthur came to reclaim her and as they linked arms she remembered that the last time they danced together had been at Bavaria, as Devil always called the Shaws' house, on the night before Arthur went away to Harrow. Now her little brother was a handsome officer who was being given the eye by every girl in the pub. She smiled, and her previous partner saw it and blew her an imploring kiss.

'Last orders, ladies and gents, please.'

'One more?' Arthur mouthed.

Amidst protests from their new friends they retreated to the quieter bar.

'You were appreciated, Nancy.'

'Me? What about *you*?'

'They only see the uniform.'

That wasn't the case, but it was true that although the war itself was becoming an unpopular memory the men who had fought it were admired everywhere. She felt a tick of fear for Arthur.

'Don't get hurt, will you?' she begged, made vocal by the whisky. Arthur didn't respond directly.

'Do you remember that night at Aunt Faith's, before I went to school?'

'I was just thinking about it.'

'Were you really? Rowland and Edwin are so often in my mind.' Abbreviated young lives were familiar to Arthur and he moved smoothly on. 'And the Schools Match, too.'

His dream of playing at Lord's had never been realised. There had been no Eton and Harrow match for the duration of the war, and half the schoolboys who had played in Fowler's great game were now dead. Instead of reassuring her that of course he would be safe, he remarked, 'You saved me from drowning.'

Nancy flushed. 'I did nothing of the kind. The fishermen in the rowing boat were right beside us.'

'Yes, you did. The *Queen Mab* was our brush with it, you know. We didn't survive that, all of us, only for me to step on a shell, or for Cornelius to be blown up in his ambulance, or Ma or you or Devil to fall victim to Spanish flu. Here we are, and here we'll stay. That's what *I* believe.'

Simple, she thought. And as reasonable a belief to adhere to as any other.

'Arthur, I'm so glad you are home.'

He touched her hand. 'I'm happy to be. Tomorrow we'll have a quiet word with Pa, but I think we should perhaps not say anything yet to Eliza and Neelie. Are you ready to go?'

She laughed. 'If I can walk.'

He took her by the arm and they made their unsteady way into the sooty night.

The next morning Devil left home very early and Nancy and Arthur went down to the Palmyra in the certainty that they would find him there. It would be better in any case, they agreed, to talk about the business away from Islington and Eliza.

Arthur put his shoulder to the stage door but it yielded easily and he almost fell inside. They stepped in from the alley and secured the door behind them. They groped their way in semi-darkness through the labyrinth of passages to the door of Devil's office. It stood open and the light was on, revealing his old desk mounded with papers and folders. Nancy listened to the silence, feeling its physical pressure on her eardrums.

'Where is he?'

Arthur coolly glanced through some of his father's papers and clicked his tongue at what he saw.

They made their way on towards the stage. Through the slips they saw that a single bulb burned overhead, throwing a dingy wash of light over the boards.

Nancy looked out into the auditorium over the empty rows of seats. The gilded fronts of the double tier of boxes faintly glowed. Slowly she tilted her head to gaze into the little cupola. At the back of the gallery a creaking seat made her jump.

'Centre stage suits you,' her father's voice remarked.

She squinted upwards. Arthur came out on to the stage to join her.

'Pa?'

'You too, Arthur. You ought to be in the films.'

'Come down, Pa. Come and tell us what has happened.'

When he appeared he was dishevelled and his eyes were bloodshot. Nancy tried to embrace him but he held her at a little distance and she knew at once that he had been drinking.

'Why are you here?' he asked.

She told him, 'I came down yesterday because I got the sack and I wanted to see you. I found everywhere locked up. Arthur came with me this morning.'

'I see. I'm sorry.'

He turned aside and waved at the green-and-gilt interior. 'It's only temporary. Flow of cash, you know, artists being intransigent and refusing to go on without pay. A small crisis, but we've weathered plenty of those, eh? I intend to sort out some temporary funding and we'll soon be on our way again.'

Arthur considered this but Nancy burst out, 'What about the rest of the company? Anthony Ellis? Miss Aynscoe?'

These were the people who had worked for her father for many years.

'Anthony found a job at the Duke of York's and I advised him to take it. It's not well paid, but better than the princely sum of nothing, which is all he's been getting here lately. And as for Miss Aynscoe –' Devil turned aside, patting his coat pocket where the bottle lay concealed. In a lower voice he said, 'Sylvia offered me her savings. That was what convinced me to close up. Just temporarily, you know. I'll borrow from someone who can afford to lend.'

Arthur spoke for the first time.

'Shall we not stand here amongst all the ghosts? Let's go somewhere else where we can talk.'

He put his hand to his father's sleeve.

Ghosts. Nancy thought it was a surprising word for her brother to choose. It was on this stage that their father's old partner Carlo had bled to death after the Bullet trick. Devil was staring out into the wings as if he too saw troubling sights.

'Come on, Pa,' she repeated, and between them they steered him off the stage.

The Corner House across the Strand wasn't crowded. Devil was able to flirt with the nippy as they took a table next to the window and by the time the girl returned with her tray he was apparently recovering himself. He smoothed back his hair and settled the knot of his tie so that he looked spruce and almost sober again.

'It has been a setback, I won't pretend otherwise. To have my performers turn against me and to have to let my trusted employees go to work elsewhere.'

He had to assume a stage persona, Nancy thought, even to sit down in a teahouse. He was rouged and pomaded under the lights, reprising his famous role of rakish theatre manager and magician for an audience of two people. She wanted to shake him and say *Stop it. Be natural. It's us, your children.* Too often these days she felt that she was the parent and Devil the contrary child.

He grinned at them. 'Of course I should have said something, and I would have done when the moment was right. I'm an old hand, you know. I have successfully managed quite a few of these – ah – episodes before.'

'Have there been other episodes in which your acts walked out because they haven't been paid and your wardrobe manageress felt she had to offer you her savings to keep the theatre open?'

'Zenobia? You attack your father when he's down?' Devil started back in exaggerated dismay. Arthur minutely shook his head, but Nancy's irritation got the better of her. Even in his protests Devil was still acting. He had been playing his rogue's role for so long that he was unable to separate himself from it.

'Rather than borrowing even more money, why don't you just sell the Palmyra?'

This time Devil's smile bared his teeth.

'I'd sell our house first.'

He looks like a wolf, Nancy thought. The absolute devotion she had felt for him in her childhood had shifted into a more critical adult knowledge, but her father was still close to the centre of her existence and it was painful to glimpse how his vulnerability was coupled with guile. She remembered the bank manager or shopkeeper fathers of her envied school friends, and wasn't sure even now that to have such a figure wouldn't have been preferable.

'What will happen to Ma and Cornelius if you do that?'

Devil pounced. 'Exactly. Your mother has been too ill for me to consult her and my first concern is to care for her. Cornelius needs a safe home and I will do anything to preserve it for him. To shield them both from anxiety, I battle on against the financial tide. You two are different, and if you are genuinely concerned I can tell you that I am about to talk to an influential person. I think this person will be eager to help me through a temporary crisis. We'll be Wix and Sons after all. The Wix *family*,' he amended, with a glance at his daughter.

Devil made a pass with his hands as if he was about to conjure a bouquet of hothouse flowers from the coffee pot. He checked the room as he did so, seeming to invite applause from a wider audience. It was the manner of a man who was used to being watched and admired, mostly by women. He didn't see that those few who did turn in their direction were interested not in the grey-haired father but in his son – even though Arthur was a civilian today, in a soft-collared shirt and his old tweed coat from before the war.

Nancy's heart turned over with sadness, for themselves and what seemed to be the wider pain of life.

'Who is this person?' Arthur wanted to know.

Devil was pleased to tell him. 'He is an actor in the moving pictures.'

Even before Arthur asked him to elaborate, Nancy was able to work out what must have happened. In her fever Eliza had remembered Mr Jake Jones, and she herself had innocently reminded Devil of his one-time protégé. Assuming that success was lucrative, Devil must have seized on the idea of touching Mr Jones for a loan. Or quite possibly had already done so. Nancy felt the familiar pang of embarrassment. She listened miserably to Devil explaining to Arthur how he had given the actor a wonderful start and thereafter taught him everything he knew.

At the end she asked, 'So, did you just call on him out of the blue? Backstage, or at his home? And did he remember you?'

Her father looked hurt. 'We're theatre people, Nancy, moving in the same world. Jake and I never lost touch, not really, except when he went to America during the war. He's appearing now in some little modern play at the Duchess, likely to be a *very* short run, I'd say. I wrote a note and left it for him at the theatre and he responded warmly with an invitation for Eliza and me to weekend at his house in the country. It is a few years since we last met, but Jake Jones has always had a particular fondness for me, you know.'

Devil sat back to survey the room again.

'When is the visit to take place?' Arthur asked. Nancy and he did not look at each other.

'The weekend after next. Of course Eliza is not well enough to accompany me and I would have asked you to take her place, Arthur, if you were not going back to France.'

Arthur apologised and Devil continued, 'Perhaps you would like to come as my companion, Nancy? We have been asked for dinner and dancing and we'll stay overnight because Jake's house is outside London. I'm sure there will be some interesting people for you to meet.'

This was a prospect so beyond Nancy's normal routine that she knew she couldn't refuse.

'Of course, Pa. I'd love to come with you to meet a famous actor.'

Devil glanced at her skirt and jumper.

'Your mama can fix you up with a frock, I dare say?'

Arthur's mouth twitched and Nancy kept a straight face by not thinking of scarves.

'Yes, I expect so.'

'Then that's settled.' Devil summoned their waitress and told her that she had magnificent eyes as he counted out shillings for the bill.

Nancy looked through the big plate-glass window, past

143

display pyramids of tins of tea. Propped against a pillar in the rain a man with a wooden crutch was playing a mouth organ. He looked quite young. The lower half of his empty trouser leg was neatly pinned up and he wore a cardboard sign round his neck that read '*JOBLESS*'.

Arthur followed her gaze.

He murmured, 'I wonder which show he was in? Poor fellow. What is he supposed to do? There's nothing in England for any of them.'

# CHAPTER EIGHT

Devil and Nancy drove along the Great West Road before turning north into a series of smaller roads. The Ford which had replaced the De Dion-Bouton was a small black tourer with a varied history that included having been used as a courier vehicle in France. The car's little frame shuddered and bucked until Nancy thought her teeth would be shaken out, but she was still enjoying the drive. She didn't often get out of London and there was a pioneering edge to this excursion; her face was swathed in scarves and Devil had pulled his motoring cap down over his ears. He whistled as he steered and waved to the few oncoming vehicles.

Once they left the smoke of London behind the country-side began to shimmer with the first hesitant suggestions of green. The sap-thickened branches of trees stood out with extra clarity against pale skies, and wan clumps of primroses lay beneath the hedges. Nancy sniffed the keen air and the windborne gusts of ploughed earth and manure. Men were working in the fields and in the scattered villages children played outside whitewashed cottages. After London's dirt and clatter the placid emptiness was appealing.

The road wound uphill and looped back for several turns. Beech trees interlaced their branches overhead. Devil stopped in the furthest village and asked directions from an old man leaning on his stick beside a gate. He pointed down a narrow lane and Devil thanked him before the Ford nosed between tall hedges. At last they reached a pair of red-brick gateposts. A trim sign fixed to the left-hand pillar read *Whistlehalt*.

'This is the place,' Devil announced.

They rattled up a short curve of driveway, passing a gardener with a wheelbarrow. The house stood in a knot of trees, their topmost branches clumped with rooks' nests. It was built of red brick with thick vertical beams of exposed wood, a steep pitched roof and towering brick chimneys.

'Well, just look at this,' he murmured.

The front door had a small porthole let into it. A face swam briefly behind the glass before the door swung wide open.

'Hullo there!' a man called.

He had a thick mop of curly hair and a smile that seemed also in some way curly. Nancy knew she had seen this face before, but she couldn't recall where.

The man strode out to meet them and patted the bonnet of the Ford as if it were an amusing pet.

'Jake told me you'd be here. He's gone for a tramp in the woods, ha ha. Shouldn't be too long.'

Devil stepped down and the two men shook hands.

'I'm Devil Wix, and this is my daughter Zenobia.'

'Really?'

Quickly she said, 'People just call me Nancy.'

'I like that better, I must say. How do you do, Nancy?'

His eyes met hers and held them. 'I'm Lycett Stone, and people mostly call me Lion. By name not nature that is, although I'll have to leave you to judge, ha ha.' He laughed uproariously and Nancy struggled to recall where their previous encounter could have been. 'Come on inside, won't you?'

By the time they stood in a broad hallway hung with modern pictures that were incongruous between the oak beams and small-paned windows, she had it.

The Schools Match, almost nine years ago. This man was Lawrence Feather's godson. What did it mean that Feather insinuated himself into her life seemingly at every turn, even here where she had never been before?

Angrily, she wondered if she would ever be free of him.

Lycett Stone showed them upstairs to a pair of bedrooms and invited them to come down whenever they were ready and have some tea. He seemed very much at home at Whistlehalt. Nancy's room looked out over a hard tennis court and flower beds to a point where the ground dropped steeply away. Far below, over the broad tops of more trees, she could see the silvery curve of a river. She could hear the crunching of gravel as a procession of cars arrived.

'What's that river?' she asked Devil when he came to find her. She had tidied her hair and put on her best dress.

'It's the Thames, darling. The very same one as ours. Mr Jake Jones is doing well for himself, I must say.' Devil rubbed his hands together. She guessed he would be increasing the size of the loan he planned to ask for.

'May I?' Her father offered her his arm, and they descended the wide stairs together.

There was a hum of talk and loud bursts of laughter from the opposite end of the house. A pair of doors opened on to a large, low-ceilinged drawing room. Nancy had a confused impression of numbers of elegantly dressed young people draped over sofas or propped against a carved

147

mantel. They were drinking cocktails, ignoring a tray with cups and a silver pot placed on a low table. Jazz was loudly playing on a gramophone.

She hesitated on the threshold, suddenly shy.

To her relief Lion sailed forward and seized her by the hand.

'Here you are at last. You look nice in that frock. Now then, let me introduce you to some of these dreadful people.'

Her father appeared already to know several of the guests. He kissed the hand of a woman with bobbed hair, making her hoot with laughter. Lion shepherded Nancy to a sofa where several people were perched. Ice rattled as one of them agitated a silver shaker. She saw silk stockings and tennis shoes and one pair of pretty bare feet with gold-painted toenails.

'This is Dorothy, and Freddie. Take no notice of him, by the way. And Suzette, and Caspar with the execrable beard.'

Well-disposed but incurious faces nodded and smiled in her direction. With twin circles of rouge and a plait of black hair Suzette looked like a doll that had once been Nancy's favourite.

'This is Nancy Wix,' Lion explained.

The man called Freddie drawled, 'Are you Devil's daughter?'

'Do you know my father?'

They laughed. 'In the theatre we all know each other, darling, whether we have been introduced or not.'

'I am not a theatre person,' Dorothy pouted. She wiggled her gold-tipped toes in emphasis.

'What are you, dear?'

'Fred, you know perfectly well that I am now the house model at Vionnet.'

'A thousand apologies. I had entirely forgotten. Now, what will new Nancy have to drink?'

Nancy looked quickly, and pointed at Suzette's glass.

'The same, please.'

A space was made for her amongst velvet cushions and sprawled limbs on the sofa, and she accepted a cocktail with a green olive suspended in it. The glass was chill and silvery with condensation. She took a sip.

'Gin martini. You like?' Freddie raised a plucked eyebrow. 'I do.'

'Oh, good. You are one of us. What a *very* lovely mouth you have, by the way.'

The directness of this compliment might have disconcerted her had the man not been so obviously what her father called a bertie.

'Devil would tell you it's my mother's.'

'I think I saw her once. *Quite* a vision.'

Nancy slowly relaxed as warm wires of alcohol threaded through her veins. There was a lot of chatter about people she didn't know, but the witticisms basting the talk did make her laugh. Lion sat on the floor with his back resting against her shins, and when he spoke to her he hitched his elbow on her knee as if they had known each other for ever. It was the first time she had been so openly singled out by a young man, and she was flattered. The music was turned up when two people pushed back a rug to dance on the parquet, but after one song they drifted away. Evening light briefly slanted into the room before the lamps were switched on.

Someone was saying that they should play a game when a man slid into the room.

He was middle-aged, of medium height with colourless hair combed almost as precisely as Arthur's. He was dressed in an open-collared grey shirt, flannels and tennis shoes, like an unassuming undergraduate. His face was pleasant, with slightly hooded eyes and a full lower lip, but there was nothing remarkable in his appearance.

Even so, Nancy knew that someone important had just entered.

'Here he is,' Freddie murmured, as if to confirm it.

'Sorry. I've been neglecting you all,' the new arrival apologised. His voice was clear, resonant, and neutral. He didn't speak like a working man or a member of the upper classes and no external colour attached to him.

He said to Freddie, 'Has everyone got a drink? What about you, Caspar? That's good. Now, is it really you, Devil?'

Nancy noticed that her father leaned forwards, tipping his head to one side like a dog eager to be patted. He was anxious for the younger man's approval in a way she had never seen before.

So this was the actor, Jake Jones.

When Devil introduced her Jake took her hand between both of his. His gaze was direct.

'Welcome to Whistlehalt. I haven't seen your mother for many years, Nancy, but you look remarkably like her. Have they been looking after you?'

Freddie had only a moment ago handed her a second martini.

'Yes, thank you. It's a beautiful old house, Mr Jones.'

He flicked her a smile, and suddenly he was animated. There was a ripple under his skin that put her in mind of a stag or a greyhound.

'It pretends to be. In fact it was built ten years ago and the appearance is an illusion. It matches its owner in that. You should call me Jake, by the way, we're all friends here.'

150

Suzette claimed their host's attention, and the guests moved on and melded into new groups. Nancy tried to remember the names of all the people she met.

'Would you like to dance?' Lion asked her later, nodding at the square of parquet. They moved on to the improvised floor together. Suzette and Dorothy were there, giggling and holding their half-finished drinks aloft until Freddie slid between them. He didn't so much dance as undulate, Nancy thought.

Instead of being formally served dinner at Whistlehalt was laid out by discreet staff in the adjoining dining room. People drifted by in twos and threes and helped themselves from silver dishes on a sideboard. Fire dogs stood in a wide hearth and French doors overlooked darkness. Nancy put her face to the glass and peered out. She glimpsed a stone terrace and steps leading down to a lawn but mostly she could only see reflections of the throng behind her. The party was growing lively. She had never been to a gathering remotely like this, and she was enjoying herself – it didn't matter what you actually said or did, she realised. The important thing was to do it amusingly or provocatively. Preferably both.

'I'll show you around the gardens tomorrow,' Lion promised.

'I think we have to go back to town early in the morning, unfortunately.'

He ran his fingers through his thick curls and turned down the corners of his expressive mouth.

'That's a blow.'

She liked his attention, even wishing she could feel more drawn to him than she actually did.

'I know,' she smiled.

He helped her to a generous plateful of cold beef and

some sliced potatoes baked in cream and gilded with a crust of cheese and herbs. The food was negligently rich and delicious and she ate greedily, letting the weight of it subdue the gin in her stomach.

'Are you an old friend of Jake's?' she asked.

Lion waved a fork. 'Not at all. My aunt Frances, my mother's sister that is, is married to the chap who owns all the land hereabouts. Their place is about half a mile up the river. Jake is their tenant.'

Of course, Nancy thought, there would be a grand house hereabouts.

'My uncle, Frances's husband, is Everard Templeton. He's a barrister but his people have been here since Edward the Confessor or some such. Absurd, isn't it? I mean, I'm not surprised people go on strike and so forth. It seems quite unfair even to me, and I stand to inherit a couple of acres when the old man dies. Not that I've got a bean to keep the estate running. None of us does. It's only people like Jakey who have any proper loot nowadays.'

Nancy *did* like him, even if not in that way. As well as being nice to look at he was good-humoured, and not too pleased with himself.

'Is that the Honourable Frances Templeton?' she asked.

'That's the bird. Do you know her?'

'I used to go to her suffragist meetings with my cousin and some other girls.'

What would Jinny Main think of this gathering? Nancy imagined that she would – reluctantly – rather enjoy it.

'Lord, yes. Auntie Fra is no end of a politico. The latest is that she is planning to stand for Parliament. So you are one of these votes-for-women women, are you?'

This time she met Lion's bright eyes. Even as they laughed together she thought of Gil Maitland, and how different he was from this hearty boy. It occurred to her that no one she met ever had – or ever would – measure up to a man with whom she had spent a single hour of her life. And she would probably never see him again.

'Some women have the vote now, you know.'

'So they should,' he said equably. 'So *you* should, darling.'

They went back to the drawing room where the dancing was hotting up. Jake and Freddie stomped and shimmied together and Devil was in the thick of it too, shirtsleeved and partnering a buxom young woman in a skirt that exposed her legs far above the knee. He winked over her shoulder as he caught sight of Nancy. He was tight, but in control of himself and the tick of anxiety that had started up in her at the sight of him died down again. She noticed that his pockets were turned inside out, coat and trousers, and the empty flaps bounced as he moved.

Dorothy and Suzette caught Nancy's arms. 'C'mon. Planchette.'

'No,' Lion protested. 'We have to go out to look at the moon, Nancy, don't we?'

'Planchette first, Li, don't be such a damp squib. It'll be fun.'

Nancy knew a little about the craze and she didn't in the least want to play, but Lion let himself be drawn in without further protest and she couldn't think quickly enough to extricate herself. Seconds later, it seemed, she was in a room like a library, except that the books lining the shelves were nearly all replicas with painted spines. Looking more closely at the ones close to her shoulder she noticed the titles were rude puns.

A board painted with strange symbols and the letters of the alphabet lay on a circular table, and eight of them gathered round it.

Dorothy put on a solemn face.

'Place one finger here, everyone.'

*Here* was a wooden plate in the shape of a teardrop. A pencil was slotted through the centre and the whole moved freely on small castors.

Each of them rested a fingertip on the wooden teardrop. There was a long second of stillness before the contraption violently juddered and shot across the board. Nancy wanted to pull back, but she told herself it was only a game. She kept her finger lightly resting in its place.

Dorothy closed her eyes.

'Is there any spirit present who would like to come to the board?'

The planchette careered wildly and Caspar tutted.

'Do behave, whoever it is doing that. I suppose it's you, Lion?'

Another swerve.

'*Lion.*'

'I'm not bloody well doing anything.'

'Hush. You have to concentrate. Who do you want to speak to? What is your name?'

Again the planchette swerved. It came to an abrupt stop at the edge of the board with the tip of the teardrop over the letter H.

'A spirit,' Dorothy murmured.

Another swoop indicated E and then L. A cold finger caressed the back of Nancy's neck and then danced its way down her spine. E, N and A followed.

She snatched her hand away and scrambled to her feet.

'Sorry. I need some fresh air.'

She fought her way through the revelry in the drawing room and escaped out on to the terrace. There was no moon to look at, and the darkness was heavy with the unfamiliar scents of open countryside. A footstep sounded behind her and she whirled round, fearful of who or what she might see.

'Forgive me?' Lion begged. 'I am an oaf not to have realised you might be scared by that. It's only Dorothy's nonsense, you know. There's no real harm in it.'

'Of course,' she managed to say.

He came closer, solid against the dark foliage, and drew her into his arms. His mouth met hers and they experimentally kissed.

Nancy hadn't been kissed often enough, and then only by soldiers on leave. She leaned closer, a little giddy from drink, and felt a lazy flick of physical arousal that didn't reach her head or heart. But she still remembered the planchette's quick, decisive swerves across the board. She hesitated before turning her head aside to glimpse a black shape swooping low over the shrubs beyond the terrace. She had never seen one before but she guessed it must be a bat. Caught off balance she took an uncertain step backwards.

'How is your godfather?' she blurted out. 'Mr Feather?'

It was an absurd question although Lion fielded it.

'He's pretty well, thanks. How do you know Lawrence?'

'I met him before the war. You too, actually.'

'Oh Lord, I don't remember. I'm so sorry. When? Was I very badly behaved?'

She reminded him about the day at Lord's.

'Fowler's match, of course. 1910. Darling Nancy, you must hardly have been out of the nursery.'

'I had just turned thirteen.'

'All right. Not exactly a baby, but still – you know – not of an age to attract my attention in those days. I was more interested in hanging around stage doors on the hunt for actresses. Optimistic, innocent ninny that I was.'

'You must have known Mr Feather's sister, of course.'

'Aunt Helena? My father is a lot older than Lawrence, but many years ago he was interested in theosophy, Spiritualism, all that sort of thing. He was very impressed by Lawrence and they became friends. He went so far as to make him my godfather. Perhaps to ease my future transition to a better place, or some such. I've never been very interested in any of his theories, but I have to say that Lawrence stuck by me when I was a boy and out of favour with the family because of my bad behaviour. I was sorry for him when he lost his sister, although I barely knew Mrs Clare herself.'

In the thick silence that followed, the music drifting out through the drawing-room doors was damped by the night air. Somewhere near the terrace's brick balustrade a tiny rustle might have been a shrew or a field mouse creeping in the flower bed.

A thought dawned on him. 'Oh, *Helena*. I see. Well, you know, there are all sorts of explanations for *that*. It's not an uncommon name. Or it might have been my unconscious at work, or yours, even poor old Dorothy's, influencing the planch-whatsit. Jake and Freddie and this set all know Lawrence because he's an old theatrical rogue, even though he dresses the business up as spiritualism. He's rather in demand these days, as you can imagine, although I believe he also has a few rather vociferous detractors. You probably know Aunt Helena is on the other side, as Lawrence would put it? She drowned, sadly.'

'I know. My family and I were aboard the pleasure steamer that day.'

That was enough to startle even Lion Stone.

'Good God. I mean, how terrible for you all. But that does rather support my argument, wouldn't you say? Unconscious, and all that?'

'Perhaps,' Nancy said. Her best dress was flimsy and she was cold. She pressed closer into Lion's warmth and he eagerly held her.

'I say, you don't believe in the spirit realm and survival and all that, do you? You seem far too sensible to me.'

'No, I don't.'

'Of course not. Look, you're shivering. That won't do.' He kissed her, thoroughly and quite enjoyably, before taking her hand. 'Come on inside.'

The party was reaching its peak. Through the throng Nancy saw her father propped against the mantel. He had passed from being merely tight into drunkenness, and his face drooped with terrible melancholy as he surveyed the room.

'Excuse me,' Nancy said to Lion as she broke away from him. He was tactful enough to let her go.

'Pa?'

Devil closed one eye, then the other. He swayed precariously and she steadied him.

'Damn it all,' he muttered. His handsome face was ravaged.

'What has happened? Hold on to me. Let's sit down here.' As she guided him to a padded seat in the chimney alcove she saw that his pockets were still turned inside out. She tried unsuccessfully to tuck one of them away as Devil sagged against the cushions.

'Nothing there. Empty. Thin air. I'm sorry, old girl. Life's no more than a game of cards, you know. Somehow forgot to prime the deck after all these years. How did that happen? Foolish. No fool like an old one, eh?'

'Pa, it's all right. You need to get to bed. Everything will seem better tomorrow.'

'My Zenobia, queen of the Palmyra. Your poor, deserted

157

realm. But I will win it back for you.' He wagged his finger. 'There is a trick or two still to play, trust me.'

'Of course there is. I know that.'

'I asked our friend Jakey Jones for a loan.'

Devil tugged at the limp ears of his empty pockets.

'I showed him how it is. Jake and I have history, you know. He used to sleep under a market cart or curl up at the back of the Palmyra stage. Now here he is.' One flick of a finger took in the vases of hothouse flowers, the bucket of ice replenished by a quiet servant, the jigging or sprawling guests and the essential gramophone. 'You know what he said? He said that he would if he could, but he can't. It's all borrowed. No real cash. You have a name, a label, a role in the world and the money falls over itself in its rush into your pockets. All you need is a bright and shiny name. Jake claims to have no more real money than Devil Wix, but he's on the stage and in a moving picture or two and his credit is good. And you know what?'

Devil sucked in a deep breath and then exhaled a bitter gust of laughter.

'I believe him.'

Nancy believed it too. There was an unsettling fragility about the solid brick and oak house and a brittle quality to the evening. All these revellers might vanish, like Cinderella's trappings on the stroke of midnight.

She hoisted her father to his feet.

'Time for bed,' she insisted, as if speaking to a child. Without demur, stumbling only a little, he allowed her to lead him upstairs. They found his bedroom at the second attempt and she removed his coat and undid his white tie for him. He lay down with a sigh on top of the satin eider-down and flung his arms wide as she eased off his tight shoes.

'I wish your mother was here.'

He was always sentimental about Eliza when he was drunk. Nancy had seen him earlier with the girl in the short skirt, and others.

'Tomorrow,' she repeated and left him to sleep it off.

Nancy hesitated on the landing. A bronze nymph holding a torch bulb aloft provided the only illumination. She jumped when she saw a man in the shadows at the head of the stairs.

'It shouldn't be a daughter's job to put her father to bed,' Jake said. 'Freddie came to tell me you might need some help.'

'Thank you. It's all right, though. He'll already be asleep.'

The animal quiver had faded and the actor seemed entirely unmemorable. Nancy thought that if she closed her eyes she would be unable to recall his features. Jake's utter ordinariness was reassuring and she stood quietly beside him, resting her forearms next to his on the banister rail as they gazed down into the hallway.

A sobbing girl dashed beneath them, pursued by her friend who wore a man's tailcoat with a monocle swinging on a satin ribbon. Freddie strolled in the opposite direction, a cigarette in the corner of his mouth, and then Caspar emerged with a poodle on a jewelled lead and let himself out of the front door. A great billow of sound set the oak boards shivering as someone turned up the gramophone to full volume.

Jake remarked, 'A party is rather like a brief, jazzed-up version of life, don't you think? Predictability interspersed with moments of high drama.'

She noticed that he had green eyes with hazel flecks in the irises.

'I haven't been to many parties.'

He laughed. 'That will change, I'm sure. There will be plenty of parties. People want to enjoy themselves now. They might as well, while they can.'

'You don't sound very optimistic.'

'About the future? No, I'm not.'

The music was silenced and raised voices followed. The party was clearly coming to an end and Nancy thought that Jake was right about its resembling life. She was sharply aware that her own life had barely begun, and she was hungry for what it would bring.

Jake said, 'Devil asked me if I would lend him some money to keep the Palmyra open.'

'I thought he might.'

'I'm afraid that I had to say no. I don't have the means, even though this house indicates that I might. It's only rented. But even if I were in a position to offer your father a loan, I don't think I would. Music hall and magic tricks aren't right for these times, Nancy. The pleasure of being deceived and distracted is a tease that relies on innocence, and the war has changed all that. People know all too well what's real, and their imaginations are haunted. They look for enlightenment, or comfort, and if they can't have those they want oblivion.'

'I see.'

She did, almost too clearly.

'I'm sorry for your sake and your brothers' that the theatre is in trouble. If you ever need me, personally that is, if I can help you in any way, a line sent here to Whistlehalt will always reach me.'

'Thank you,' Nancy said.

'Goodnight, then.'

She retreated along the corridor to her bedroom. The room was chilly and she undressed quickly, shivering at the kiss of cold air on her bare skin. Finding her nightdress she scrambled into it, then lay down quickly and drew the sheet up to her chin in the hope that the bed would soon warm up. Somewhere close at hand a door creaked open and shut, and pipes shuddered as water ran in a distant bathroom. At last the house seemed to settle for the night. The heat of Nancy's body slowly thawed the bedclothes and she sank towards sleep.

The click of the door latch jerked her back to full consciousness. She sat upright, her heart pounding, and saw the door swing open. A black figure moved against the deeper darkness of the room. Remembering the demonic swerves of the planchette and – from long ago – a glimpse of a silver locket engraved with Helena Clare's initials, she called out in a high voice cracking with alarm, 'Who's there?'

The figure came closer. She flung back the covers and scrambled to her feet.

'What do you want?'

It stopped.

'Darling, what do you think?'

'Lion?'

'Who were you expecting?'

'Nobody at all. You scared me. That's the second time tonight.'

'I'm so sorry. Come here. You look like a ghost yourself in that long white thing.'

His arms circled her and his mouth found hers as one hand moved over her body.

'Take it off, won't you?' he whispered.

'No.'

She struggled out of his grasp, caught between the residue of fear and a disconcerting flare of physical longing. He hesitated, his confusion evident even in the pitch darkness.

'What?'

'Why are you here?'

He chuckled. 'To make love to you, Nancy. Don't you want me to?'

'No.'

Perhaps she meant yes. She did want to be made love to. She yearned for it, and had done ever since the night of the rain and a single hour of talk in a Fleet Street pub. Only she didn't want it like this, under Jake Jones's roof at Whistlehalt, with this particular man.

'I misunderstood. I apologise.' Lion was offended but she couldn't see how this awkwardness was her fault. He added stiffly, 'You seem pretty modern, but perhaps you aren't at all.'

Jake had said at the beginning of the evening that his own appearance was an illusion, as she knew hers to be. At the end of it he had told her that the war had put paid to everyone's innocence. Including her own, she understood. If you couldn't have the man you wanted – obviously not – should you settle for a man you could have? The question was too big for her to answer now, when she was tired and a little drunk.

'I don't know what I am,' Nancy said sadly. 'I'm sorry, I didn't mean anything wrong or hurtful. I enjoyed tonight so much.'

Lion was slightly appeased.

'All right. I'm sorry too, I think we should both go to sleep now, in our own beds of course. Goodnight.' He spoke lightly and a second later the door closed behind him.

Nancy flung herself down and cried, from a mixture of exhaustion and gin and disappointment, as well as from longing to be as ordinary as she feared she was not. As soon as she had cried herself to sleep, it seemed that it was daylight and time to get dressed again. Devil had insisted they must leave first thing because he had business to do in town.

When she crept downstairs she found the house deserted and chaotic with the detritus of the party. The drawing room was littered with ashtrays and discarded clothing and empty and broken glasses. Miserably she picked her way to the kitchen and there she found her father, leaning against a sink crammed with dirty pots and eating bread and jam. There were grey patches beneath his eyes and he was unshaven, but otherwise he looked as usual. He offered her a slice of bread but she refused it and drank a cup of water instead.

'No one will be up here for hours. I'll write a line to Jake. You should do the same,' he said.

'Of course I will.'

The morning was sparkling. Turning the starting handle of the Ford gave Devil trouble and he sweated and cursed, but at length the engine spluttered and the little car shuddered into life. Soon they were spinning under the arch of beech trees.

Devil glanced at her. He was in one of his comic moods and she knew he wouldn't try to talk about money, or welcome any conversation.

'Now you know what fun is, eh? Jazz and cocktails and kissing? What do you think of it?'

Nancy looked through the tiny windscreen at fields of lambs.

'I'm in favour,' she replied.

# CHAPTER NINE

The glamour of Whistlehalt and the pleasurable *frisson* of being found desirable soon faded from her memory. It was as difficult to find another job as Nancy had feared it might be. Every day she hunted through the advertisements, but she was not well qualified for the print even though in their years at Lennox & Ringland Jinny Main had taught her everything she knew. For every one of the handful of vacancies Nancy applied for, she found a line of determined men ahead of her.

Devil and Eliza didn't speak of it to their children, but the crisis at the Palmyra deepened. Following the begging expedition to Whistlehalt Devil's once unshakeable confidence seemed to have faded. There were layers of debt that he hadn't even acknowledged and once they understood that the Palmyra had permanently closed his creditors homed in on him. He became even more evasive, until a knock at the door was a thing to be dreaded. He sat close up to the kitchen range in his shirtsleeves, making urgent calculations in notebooks, or pulled on his coat and left the house for unexplained hours at a time.

Arthur's return to France was hard for all of them to bear. Once he had gone gloom settled on the Islington house like an extra layer of city grime. Nancy didn't even ask if there was money to pay for painting the kitchen because she knew there was not, and this certainty made her even more aware of the faded curtains and worn drugget in the tall rooms. Eliza drifted through the house in her layers of scarves. Her moods were erratic. Sometimes she was wildly energetic, as when Lizzie sent a sack of Seville oranges from the fruit warehouse and she embarked on a project to make pounds of marmalade. Cornelius advised against it but she wouldn't hear him. The marmalade turned out over-boiled and bitter, and set so hard that it wouldn't yield to a spoon.

'It's only marmalade,' Eliza snapped. She threw the filled jars away.

At other times she sank into languor. She sat in the window overlooking the canal, childishly pleased by the rare sight of a horse-drawn barge gliding past with its cargo of timber protected from the rain by a shroud of tarpaulin. Sometimes she was possessed by irreconcilable anger. Nancy felt that most of her mother's rage was directed at her. She did her best to smooth all the moods, or to deflect them as gently as she could.

And at last she did find work. She was offered a post as a counter assistant at the same draper's shop in the Essex Road where Eliza had once been a valued customer.

Eliza was horrified.

'I didn't bring you up to be a shop assistant.'

'I don't know what you did bring me up to be.'

'A success in life,' Eliza snapped.

Nancy hesitated, looking into her mother's blazing eyes. 'I will do my best.'

Eliza had wanted so much and she had schemed and

fought to achieve her aims, and it was not her fault that her lack of physical strength had destroyed her hopes.

Cornelius followed his sister out of the room.

'Don't blame her. She doesn't mean what she says.'

'I know that, Neelie.'

He pushed his spectacles back up to the bridge of his nose, the same gesture that he had made as a little boy. It told her that he was more than usually troubled.

'I'm the son of the house. I should really go and ask for my old job back. I was quite good at it, you know.'

He squared his shoulders as he spoke but Nancy knew the effort of will that it cost even to voice the suggestion. Lately Cornelius had seemed comfortable at home, close to Eliza and soothed by his experiments in the kitchen. He made simple excursions to the nearest shops but never went any further afield. As they talked she could see the silvering in his eyes that meant he was close to tears. Her brother's suffering was harder to bear than anything else.

'Neelie, you don't have to do that. Ma needs you here, and you are much better at looking after her than I am. This job's only temporary anyway, until we think of something else.'

'Pa will work one of his tricks.'

'I expect so.'

They didn't laugh.

The draper's shop was a friendly place and the manageress had been an early suffragist. As spring turned into early summer Nancy grew to respect her colleagues, and felt at home amongst the bolts of cloth and spools of satin and velvet ribbons. She was a good enough saleswoman, but she came to the conclusion that Eliza had given her the best advice years ago. Her likeliest prospect was to become a personal assistant to a businessman, so she enrolled in evening shorthand typing and language classes at the City Institute. Her typing improved quite quickly although she struggled with the strokes and hooks of Pitman's shorthand. It was difficult to study at the end of a day's work and she had little time in which to practise, let alone to try to recover any of her forgotten French.

Eliza seemed confused. In one of her dreamy, abstracted moods she asked, 'Aren't all these classes you go to very expensive, darling?'

'Not really. I can manage.'

In fact it was Lizzie who paid for the lessons.

She said to Nancy, 'Go on, you might as well have a bash. I liked secretarial work when I did it. God, but that time of my life seems so long ago. I had nothing to worry about beyond my clothes and who admired me most.'

'It's just a loan, then,' Nancy insisted.

The cousins saw each other frequently in Islington or at Bavaria and Lizzie had also drifted back into the loose group of WSPU friends they held in common, including Jinny Main. Lizzie's son was growing into a solemn child who closely resembled his grandfather. Matthew and Faith both adored Tommy, and they looked after him while Lizzie spent her days telephoning or directing the shippers and the recalcitrant warehousemen and carriers who imported and packed and distributed her exotic produce.

'It's an uphill bloody struggle, darling. If I had only women to deal with it would be a different business.'

Lizzie hadn't yet made her fortune, but she insisted that she would in the end. She spent money on her appearance, she smoked and drank like a man, and she was good fun in a brittle way. Lizzie had a series of shadowy boyfriends, none of whom seemed to interest her particularly.

'I like the sex, you see,' she said to Nancy. 'Otherwise, what is there?'

'I'm not sure,' Nancy admitted. Lizzie made her feel like a nun. She wished she hadn't rebuffed Lion Stone at Whistlehalt.

It seemed, though, that that wasn't to be the end of the story. One day, six weeks after the party when the memory of it had almost faded from her mind, a letter came.

Lion wrote that he hoped she didn't mind his asking Jake Jones for her father's address. He apologised for not having written earlier and explained that he had been marooned in the country with no prospect of escape. However, the good news was that he now had a job in London.

Lion wondered if it might be jolly to meet up one evening.

Thinking it over, she realised that she did want to see him. He didn't inhabit her consciousness in the pervasive way Gil Maitland still did, but she had liked him. She wrote back to tell Lion that most of her evenings were taken up with efforts to master shorthand and French, but she was quite often free at weekends.

They met one Saturday in a coffee shop near Fleet Street and ate their dinner together. Afterwards Lion took her hand as they strolled along the Embankment. The Houses of Parliament and Big Ben turned dark against a sunset fleeced with cloud before Lion kissed her on the corner of Westminster Bridge. Then he pressed his hands on either side of her face and looked down into her eyes.

'Was that all right?'

'Definitely.'

'Oh, good. I wondered, you know, after the night at Jake's place.'

'That night was too soon.'

'And tonight wasn't quite soon enough,' he laughed.

He kissed her again and they wandered across the bridge to lean over the smooth stone parapet. They watched the khaki swirl of the river as Lion told her about his new job in an advertising agency. He wrote paragraphs of copy in praise of fountain pens and laxatives.

She said in surprise, 'You went to Eton and you'll inherit a big house some day. I have to earn my living, but surely it's different for you?'

'Not a bit. Stadling is mortgaged and falling down, and it sucks up money the way an electric vacuum cleaner sucks up dust. "It beats . . . as it sweeps . . . as it cleans." Don't you *love* that for a slogan? I wish I'd come up with it. No, my father's at his wits' end because no one wants to work on the land any more, or in the house, and he can't afford to pay the same as the factories in Reading and Swindon, and there's no money in agriculture nowadays anyway. He rattles around in one draughty wing of the place and asks me what we won the war for if this is how it has turned out for us all.'

Lion had been in France, like Cornelius and Arthur, and like them he didn't speak of it.

He said cheerfully, 'I'll probably have to sell Stadling in the end. Can't see how to keep it going and there are no decent pictures or anything of much value to flog so as to put off the day until my own sons have to deal with it. I don't want my old man to be around to see it go, though. So in the meantime, it's sweating over slogans for me. Which is much easier and more fun than many things, I'm sure. I mean I couldn't learn shorthand, for a start. I was always useless at lessons. The school beaks gave up on me.'

'I don't believe you.'

Lion seemed to Nancy to have a sharp mind.

'Perfectly true. I was nearly sacked. It's quite lucky the

army gave me something to do because I was never going to get into Oxford or anything useful like that. Come on, it's getting cold.'

They linked arms and walked back the way they had come. Nancy said she would take the bus the short distance to Islington and Lion held her tightly as it trundled towards them, before asking if he might see her again.

'Yes,' she said, feeling shy in a way she hadn't done all evening.

They met again a week later, and the following week too, and each time she saw him Nancy liked him better.

Jinny Main also had a new friend, a young woman called Ann Gillespie. Ann was Scottish, striking with her red-gold hair, and she was as round and soft as Jinny was angular. Appearances were deceptive, though. Ann was a communist, Jinny explained, with serious views about the future of the nation.

Both girls were interested in bicycling, and they were pioneering members of the new London Women's Cycling Club. This organisation ran club rides on summer evenings, and weekend excursions into the Kent countryside, renting out machines to those who didn't have one of their own. Under Jinny and Ann's tuition Nancy made her first attempts at learning to ride on two wheels. She wobbled up and down the paths in London Fields while Jinny held the bicycle saddle and shouted at her to steer or to pedal harder. It was a proud hour when Jinny finally let go and Nancy careered the whole width of the park without once falling off or veering into a flowerbed. Her riding abilities improved and she began to accompany Ann and Jinny to club meetings. Once or twice Lizzie came too, although she complained afterwards that she couldn't see the real point of any club that had no men in it. The other two only laughed at her.

In July Arthur wrote with the good news that he expected to be returning home with his regiment before winter came. The grim work in Flanders would be over before too long. The Wixes were all delighted, and Nancy was especially happy when Arthur confided in a separate letter to her that he was longing to come home not only to see his family but because he had fallen in love. She was the sister of his school and army friend Harry Bolton, and her name was Isabella.

*She is the most beautiful creature in the world and I will be the luckiest fellow if she will even think of me. I do believe she might, though. Am I foolish? There's a ton of practical problems to solve, but when was there ever not? I look forward to the day when I can introduce her to you, Nancy darling. I know you will love each other.*

She smiled at his exuberance, although she was sure there would be problems if Arthur was hoping for the daughter of a family like the Boltons. She didn't know them, or Harry, but most of the friends from Arthur's separate world were grand and these people were unlikely to be the exception.

Financial anxieties apart, it was a happy interval for Nancy. She was still troubled by the spectre of the small, soaking child who appeared in odd corners of the house, and by more frequent occurrences of the Uncanny, but for the time being there seemed to be no threat in these manifestations. The places she saw were benign and empty landscapes, quite unlike the premonitory battlefields. There were lanes garlanded with dog roses and poles twined with hop bines, and the smells that heralded her immersions were the thick waft of mown hay or the fecund stink of farm animals. In one vision, as vivid as any she had ever had, she saw a lane rising between hedges whitened with summer dust and a gate leading into a broad empty field shaded by elm trees. She was sorry when the picture faded, as if it was a place she might be happy in. She supposed these rural associations had been triggered by the drive to Whistlehalt, and that time had twisted again in one of its inexplicable and porous loops.

Jinny and Ann proposed a cycling excursion for the imminent August Bank Holiday.

'Come with us – it will be two whole heavenly days out of London. We are going to camp. You can borrow Beryl's cycle. Ann has already asked her for you and she has said yes.'

Nancy laughed. 'I've never camped out in my life, and I can hardly ride. I'll hold you up, won't I?'

Ann had a ripe, suggestive laugh. 'Not a bit. You can cook, which gives you a distinct advantage over Jinny as a campfire companion. In fact we might leave Jinny behind, eh?'

Nancy rather enjoyed the way she flirted with her because she knew there was no meaning in it. It was Ann's way, to be franker than the world expected her to be, and it was also a part of her teasing of Jinny. Nancy didn't try to fathom the relationship between the two of them, not believing that it was any of her business, but she couldn't help noticing it hummed with sex. She felt jealous.

'If it's just you two and me I'll feel like a sad chaperone.'

Ann snorted. 'A *chaperone*? For Jin and me? That's a comic notion.'

'No, I mean it. So can I bring someone?'

Ann stared. 'Who? Who is she?'

'It's a he. My boyfriend.'

Jinny looked up. She had been squatting beside her bicycle, with spanners and an oilcan neatly laid on the ground as she performed some maintenance task on her Sturmey-Archer gears. She wiped her hands on her overalls.

'Your *boyfriend*? You are a dark horse, Nancy Wix, I must say. He isn't one of your figments, is he?'

Nancy reddened. 'Of course not. You'll see. His name is Lycett Stone but everyone calls him Lion.'

The idea had come to her as the solution to a problem. She was beginning to tire of the way another man's face and voice defined her dreams, and she told herself that she should put Gil Maitland out of her head and concentrate instead on a flesh-and-blood individual. Lion was certainly that, she reflected, reddening at the private admission. He had implored her to come to his lodgings but she had resisted. If she were to go as far as to cement their relation-ship, a tent beneath a hedge, perhaps with the sound of a brook trickling close at hand, would be a safe and innocent shelter.

'Of course he can come. Does he ride?' Jinny asked.

'I expect so. He went to Eton. Chaps like that can do anything, can't they?'

'He *what*?' Ann's eyes popped. 'Is he an English bloody lord or something?'

'Of course not. He's not like that at all. He joined in the ranks and came back a sergeant.'

She had found out these details almost by accident. When they were together they had other things than war and politics to occupy their thoughts but Lion's beliefs were in their own way almost as radical as Ann Gillespie's.

'My old man's world is finished,' he had shrugged. 'I don't want to acknowledge it to him, because it breaks his heart as it is, but it's the truth. And anyway I would like to bring up my children under a more equitable system. Wouldn't you?'

Ann said, 'He sounds all right, I suppose. Bring him if you want.'

Lion agreed to the plan immediately. Nancy had to work on the Saturday morning so the four of them arranged to meet at two o'clock at the ticket barrier at Charing Cross station. As she hurried from the underground Nancy looked along the Strand towards the Palmyra. The cupola was just visible between the rooftops. There had been constant talk at home of selling the theatre to pay off the debts, with Eliza strongly in favour and Devil furiously insisting that there was no need to let it go. He had plans, he said. Their raised voices were often audible behind closed doors. Once Nancy and Cornelius heard their mother throwing the scent bottles off her dressing table, one after the other. Devil must have ducked because a missile hit the door panel and the crash was followed by the sound of breaking glass.

Nancy turned away from the distant glimpse of the theatre and dashed towards the platform for the Folkestone train. Jinny and Ann were waiting for her with three bicycles between them, all with loaded panniers. Lion was there too, leaning on the handlebars of his own cycle. Damn and blast. She had meant to get there before him, to make the introductions, but Mrs Lloyd had kept her back to tidy shelves.

'At last, Wix. C'mon, we'll have to skedaddle,' Ann cried. They raced to the guard's van to load the cycles and then tumbled into the nearest carriage. The whistle blew and a thick pall of steam and smoke poured in through the open window. Lion hauled on the leather strap and secured it shut.

'This is Lion Stone,' Nancy puffed. The train clattered over the river.

'Thanks for asking me to join you,' Lion meekly said to the two girls. 'I'll make myself suitably inconspicuous.'

Nancy knew at once there was nothing to worry about. The three of them had already made friends. Lion had the knack of fitting in here as seamlessly as he had done at Whistlehalt. Social ease was one of the gifts of a highly privileged upbringing, she thought, although she knew she was being unfair to him.

He hefted his khaki rucksack on to the luggage rack, suggesting by a faint lift of the eyebrow that he would be ready in the unlikely event that the three women couldn't handle their own. His nose and forearms were sunburned and he was wearing corduroy breeches and a tweed cap pulled down over his thatch of curls. He looked as if he had been working in a hayfield all week rather than at a desk in an advertising agency.

Before they reached Croydon Jinny had the map spread out on the seat and she and Lion were studying it together. She said the campsite was in a field belonging to a farmer who offered it for club use, but it wasn't easy to find. Everyone was laughing, in anticipation of the challenge and the ride and the little holiday, even though Nancy still felt slightly put out that Lion had made himself already so much a part of everything when she had imagined how she would be the one to draw him in. Lion glanced up and winked at her. Remembering the way this day might conceivably end, Nancy forgot everything else in a shiver of anticipation.

'Did you bring those sandwiches?' Ann demanded. 'I'm famished.'

Dazedly Nancy said that she had them somewhere. She fished in her bag for a greaseproof-wrapped package.

Jinny peered from Nancy to Lion. 'Look at you two,' she smiled.

They left the train at a deserted halt amidst apple orchards. They slung their bags on their backs, secured the panniers and set off down a rutted lane. Jinny led the way and Lion meekly pedalled at the rear. It was a sultry afternoon, the sky shawled with haze and the shadows of trees no more than a faint dapple on the dried earth. The crimped leaves of the roadside oaks already showed ochre rims, and the hawthorn hedges were subdued with dust. Today was the first day when high summer admitted the certainty of autumn, and so the glory of it was intensified.

They passed beyond the orchards into open cornfields. The bicycles crunched over loose stones or a twig snapped in someone's spokes. Occasionally a skylark twirled over their heads, but otherwise there was silence. After struggling at first Nancy found a rhythm in the steady effort of pedalling and she fell into a trance as the miles went by. They stopped at a tiny crossroads with a slanting fingerpost and again Nancy recalled the drive to Whistlehalt. Jinny studied her map and Ann gulped water from a metal flask.

'Is this right?' Ann asked, wiping her mouth with the back of her hand.

Lion mopped his forehead with a red handkerchief. 'Hot work, eh?'

Jinny folded the map and pointed. 'This way.'

As they cycled onwards Nancy felt an ease and lightness that were new to her. The countryside as it unrolled seemed as perfectly recognisable as if she had grown up surrounded by golden fields of corn. Each corner seemed to reveal a homely view, lovely in its known contours. There was no thought of getting lost, no fear of loneliness, no anxiety for the future. Now, and this world, were all that mattered.

She was startled out of her reverie when Jinny braked

again. She pushed her cap to the back of her head and scratched her damp hair.

'Sorry. I think we should have turned back there. There's a stream alongside the field so climbing this hill can't be right.' She spread the map on her handlebars and Ann and Lion dropped their cycles into the grass and nettles of the verge to examine it with her.

Nancy shaded her eyes and looked west. The air was clouded with gnats.

'This is the way,' she heard herself saying. 'The lane goes up this hill for about a mile and turns a corner, where there is a gate on the left into a field. There is a line of elm trees.'

'You can't know. You haven'a so much as glanced at this map.' Impatience sharpened Ann's Scots accent.

They were all staring at her. Understanding flickered in Jinny's eyes.

'Nancy's right. She knows.' The other two looked startled but Jinny hurried on to cover the moment. 'Let's go. I need a cup of tea.'

She wheeled her machine aside to let Nancy take the lead. Nancy pedalled up the hill, through the soft and welcoming landscape, until she reached the gate in the hedge. Here were the shady elms, and a long slope of grass leading to a flat expanse on the bank of a stream. It was an exquisite spot. She gave a long sigh of happy satisfaction.

'I'll be blowed,' Ann Gillespie muttered.

They charged down the slope to the bank. Lion hit a rabbit hole and pitched off his cycle, rolling downhill amidst thistles, tumbled bags and hoots of laughter.

Two small green canvas tents were quickly erected with a wide expanse of rough grass between them.

'May I?' Lion called once this was done, and at a nod from Jinny he set to work with the Primus. A billycan was boiled and tea spooned into it. Jinny pulled off her boots and perched on the bank to soak her hot feet in the stream. She drank the tea Nancy gave her.

'I think this is the very best campsite I have ever seen, on the best cycle trip, and the best mug of tea I have ever tasted.'

'I know,' Nancy agreed. Happiness and eagerness ran through her veins like quicksilver.

The haze disappeared as evening approached and the clear sky turned lavender and then deep indigo. Nancy and Lion waded the stream and rambled uphill to collect wood for a fire. They kissed in the shelter of a tiny copse.

When they eventually made their way back to the camp Jinny and Ann had returned from the village with bread, and bottles of beer that were cooling in the stream. Twilight gathered under the elms sheltering Jinny and Ann's tent. Lion made a fire and Nancy fried sausages and bacon on the Primus. Ann lay watching them, her head resting in Jinny's lap, the two women still for once. Jinny absently stroked the red-gold hair and stared into the flames.

Nancy handed out the two tin plates of food and she and Lion shared the frying pan. Ann mopped her plate with a chunk of bread and Lion raised his beer bottle.

'Friends,' he toasted them.

'Friends,' they responded.

It was dark now. A fingernail moon hovered at the crest of the hill.

'What was that about?' Ann suddenly asked. 'That business earlier, about knowing the way?'

Nancy reclined against Lion who was propped up by his khaki rucksack. His shoulder and thigh were warm and solid.

'Annie,' Jinny warned.

But the darkness felt safe, and her friends' faces in the coppery firelight showed no hint of judgement.

Nancy said, 'It's all right. I see things sometimes. I don't know how or why. Jinny knows about it because I talked to her during the war, when we were on LAC duty.'

A bat sheered through the darkness and vanished over their heads.

'Things?' Ann doubtfully echoed. The imagined world was not her natural territory. Lion said nothing, but his protective arm tightened around Nancy and she believed that all would be well.

'People, and places. I had seen this spot before, inside my head, and so I knew how to get here. I felt it was good and I was right, wasn't I?'

'It was described in the club newsletter,' Ann pointed out.

Nancy smiled. She had never seen the newsletter. 'I don't know what my Uncanny is. That's what I call it. I don't know how to explain it. When I was younger it used to disturb me, but lately I don't mind. Today's the first time it's been useful, I must say. Long ago somebody told me that I am a seer.'

Lion stirred.

'Who was that?'

'Your godfather,' she admitted.

'Yes, it sounds like him.'

Ann's scepticism was unalloyed. 'A seer? What on earth do you mean?'

A branch fell into the heart of the fire and a plume of sparks flew upwards.

'I suppose . . . I mean that there are more dimensions than are commonly acknowledged or measured. We can't understand everything that balances this world, let alone what lies beyond it.'

Nancy didn't want to sound like Mrs Bullock Dodd. She

could feel Lion listening with delicate attention while Jinny squinted at the fire through the glass prism of her empty beer bottle. Only Ann was combative, and Nancy wanted at least to shake her friend's disbelief. The sky was spread with a veil of stars and she felt a moment's unison with an infinity she couldn't quite comprehend. Each of them owned their separate truths. On this important night in her life she didn't feel it was her place to deny the ghost of the little girl, or the animation of the planchette at Whistlehalt, or even Lawrence Feather's conviction that had so troubled her adolescence. Mrs Bullock Dodd probably had her role too.

Ann persisted, '*Why* assume we can't understand everything? Certainly we don't yet, but science makes progress. Take Darwin or Edison, or think of aspirin or vaccination. Mumbling about the great unknowable is deliberately wrapping yourself in a cloak of primitive ignorance.'

Her indignation was partly for effect. Jinny propped herself on one elbow.

'Ann Gillespie, I do love you.'

Nancy sat upright.

'All right. Hold my hands. Let's try something.'

They shifted to one side of the embers and sat in a circle with their hands linked. It seemed to Nancy that energy raced between them, even as she remembered one of her father's stage illusions that had turned on the creation of an electrical circuit.

'Are you sure?' Lion asked.

Nancy was compelled now.

'Yes. Close your eyes.'

Lion's hand seemed very large, Ann's was smooth and cool. Nancy let her mind float free.

'Is there anyone there?'

Soft air with the scent of mist in it drifted off the stream.

There was no sound except running water and the rustle of leaves.

'Is anyone there?'

A small voice spoke to her. 'I am here.'

No one else moved. It seemed they didn't hear it.

'What is your name?'

On either side of her Lion and Ann shifted a little.

'Martin,' the voice said.

'Who do you want to speak to, Martin?'

Ann's hand jerked and then gripped Nancy's so tightly that the finger bones cracked.

'My sister,' the voice said.

'Who is your sister?'

Ann snatched her hand away. She drew up her knees and circled them with her arms. She was visibly shivering.

'Stop it. That's enough.'

Nancy felt her certainty drain away, to be replaced by bewilderment and the clasp of nausea. The night was chilly. Jinny put her arm around Ann's shoulders.

Nancy whispered, 'What's happened? Who is Martin?'

Ann almost spat. 'Don't be cheap. You got the effect you wanted, all right?'

'Hush, darling,' Jinny implored.

'I don't understand', Nancy said humbly. 'I heard a voice. It might have been a young woman's or a child's.'

A silence followed. Ann rose on to her knees and stared into Nancy's eyes, then cupped her chin and twisted her face towards the firelight in an attempt to read her expression. At last she seemed mollified.

'Martin was my twin brother. He died of rheumatic fever when we were six years old. I was very ill too, but I recovered. My mother blamed me for being the survivor.'

'She didn't. You just think that,' Jinny murmured.

'How do you know about him?' Ann demanded. 'Did Jinny tell you?'

'*No*,' the two women said together.

'It's just how it is,' Nancy said. 'I've never summoned it up quite so deliberately. I'm so sorry. I didn't mean to upset you. I would never have prepared such a revelation on purpose. Please believe me.'

Lion stirred the ashes to a brighter glow and piled on some dry twigs. There was a cheerful snapping as yellow flames licked up. Then he rummaged in his rucksack and produced a battered pewter flask.

'Look what I've got. Whisky.'

Ann put out her hand and took a long gulp. She wiped the neck of the flask and passed it to Nancy.

'Sorry,' she said.

'I am sorry too. I was piqued that you didn't believe me, and the night was so beautiful after a perfect day, and I suppose I felt confident.'

Was that the supernatural ingredient? *Confidence?*

Ann's laugh sounded harsh. 'I still don't believe you. There is always a rational explanation.'

'Or maybe an irrational one?' Lion suggested.

The moment was past, although Nancy still heard the echo of a small voice.

*Martinmartinmartinmartin*

Lion drawled, 'If it is all the same to everyone, I think I shall propose bed. It's not too early, is it?'

They withdrew across the field and only when they lay down together under the green canvas shelter did he put his mouth to Nancy's ear.

'What the dickens?'

She had done nothing wrong although she was sorry to have upset her friend. She knew that the Uncanny did not always control her because she had been able to control it, but she had learned something new – in future she would have to be more guarded about what she saw or heard.

'We can't know everything,' she said simply.

Lion seemed ready to abandon the subject.

'I know one thing.' It was too dark to see anything but she felt his mouth against her cheek.

'What's that?'

'You are beautiful. And I want to make love to you.'

'That's two things.'

'So it is.'

Until this moment she had been unsure whether she would really let him or not. To want to be modern, as free and passionate as her friends and her cousin, was one thing but the memory of Gil Maitland interposed itself, crystalline as if it was etched on glass, minutely separating her from Lion.

He ran his hand over her hip to her breast. At once her skin seemed thinner, her limbs alive with electrical impulses. The perfume of damp canvas and crushed grass swept through her, but she didn't fear the return of the Uncanny. Everything on both sides was hers to explore, and the awareness of that was suddenly more intoxicating than a dozen of Freddie's gin martinis. Involuntarily she lifted her hips and Lion continued his explorations.

She yielded and slowly the glass misted and dissolved. Gil Maitland's shadow was dispelled by Lion's warmth and urgency. To her surprise Nancy discovered the same urgency. They undid each other's buttons and laces, alternately laughing and groaning at the obstructions.

Nancy was astonished to discover the heat of another body with its unfamiliar contours of skin and curling hair and bunched muscle under her fingertips.

There was no going back now. She didn't want to go back.

'Hold me,' Lion ordered. 'Like this.'

She did as she was told, with pleasure.

'And now like this, with you.'

'Ah. *Oh.*'

'Do you like it?'

As with the gin martini.

'Yes.'

'More?'

'Please. Yes.'

It felt wonderful to find no impediment to their hands and mouths.

'Move your legs, so. You could wrap them around me.'

In some corner of her mind she was thinking, *at last.* This was sex. It wasn't ethereal or transcendent, as she had innocently assumed it would be. Under Lion's tutelage it was – comically – more like a form of calisthenics directed by a good-humoured gym master. Their wriggles and gasps were broken up by surges of laughter, yet the urgency always returned. The conclusion for Nancy when it came was startling.

'Was that all right?' he enquired, politely. When she told him it was very much all right she caught the glimmer of his triumphant male smile.

'Good. Now me.'

She liked this almost as much, even though he retreated as it was happening into some realm of his own. Quite soon he groaned, and withdrew in the nick of time. She held him in her arms and knotted her fingers in his tangled hair, and she was swept by a feeling of sweetness and intimacy that she was sure must be close to love. She smiled at herself. There was no need to equivocate, surely. It *was* love.

Today and over the past weeks Lion had crept into her heart, and looking back it seemed that she had been wrong and wilful to deny him that place in order to nourish a fantasy. Now she had given herself to him, to a good man who wanted her, and he had given himself in return, it seemed there was nothing else to wish for. It had been easy, after all. She smiled again, with her head resting against his chest. She could hear the steady drumming of his heart.

'There,' he murmured. 'Are you happy? Because I am, you know.'

Two more idyllic summer days passed. They cycled miles of lanes buried deep in the Weald, filling their water bottles at village pumps or stopping at pubs to drink beer and eat ham sandwiches. Some of the people they met stared at Jinny in her breeches, but no one said anything.

'Is this the way, Nancy?' Ann joked when they reached a crossroads, but there was no further mention of the impromptu seance.

On Monday evening they returned in a wide circle to the halt in the apple orchards, and contentedly waited on the deserted platform for the train. Its approach was heralded by a banner of white smoke trailing over the laden trees on the horizon.

The two couples parted at Charing Cross. Jinny and Ann were going home to the pair of rooms they had taken in a red-brick block close to Shaftesbury Avenue. After the others had wheeled away the third bike, Nancy and Lion stepped into each other's arms.

'I wish we could go home together too,' she sighed. She didn't want to relinquish him, even for a moment.

'I know.' He kissed her forehead. 'Letting you go is a bit

of a wrench, I must say. It was a splendid weekend, Nancy. Thank you.'

They made arrangements to meet again, and went their separate ways.

As soon as she was alone Nancy realised that her arms were sunburned and her long hair was a tangled mass. She hadn't given her appearance a thought for two whole days and now women in hats were looking askance at her. Reflecting on how hot and grimy the city was after the fresh Kentish lanes, she hoisted her bag and began to walk. Progress on foot was plodding after the freedom of spinning along on two wheels and in the end she queued for a bus. There were plenty of holidaymakers spilling out of the pubs at the end of a day's drinking, and many of them were boisterous and ready to pick a fight. She was tired after the experiences of the weekend so she stood quietly and kept her eyes on the floor. It was a relief to reach the Angel and walk to the mouth of the tunnel where the canal emerged as a tongue of black water.

Looking towards the house she was shocked to see that the steps were piled with haphazard towers of loaded crates. From a box at the top protruded a blackened saucepan and the favourite doll that resembled Suzette.

She ran the last few yards, her bag thumping against her hip.

'Pa? Ma? Are you here?'

There was evidence of further upheaval in the hallway. Books teetered in uneven heaps and rows of old shoes marched up the stairs like an invisible army.

Eliza was in the drawing room. Furniture had been pushed aside and shelves ransacked.

'Ma, what's happening?'

Her mother stared at her. Her hair hung in disordered

186

hanks and her pupils had shrunk to pinpoints. Her face shivered and then crumpled as sobs overcame her. Between the convulsions she gasped, 'The house. Your father has sold our home from under our feet.'

Nancy supported her in her arms, her mother's body pathetically fragile after Lion's breadth and weight. She knew at once what must have happened. The choice had come down at last to the theatre or the house, and Devil had inevitably chosen to save the Palmyra.

'Where is he?'

'I don't know. I never want to see him again.'

'Neelie?'

'Upstairs. What can we do?' Her mother grasped her hands.

'We'll think of something. Come here, sit down.' Eliza's legs seemed on the point of giving way. Limp as a puppet she flopped into a chair that Nancy set for her. They sat knee to knee until the sobs died into ragged gulps and slowly subsided.

'Thank God you've come home,' she hiccoughed.

Guilt twisted in Nancy. 'I'm so sorry, Ma, I should have been here. Will you be all right for a minute if I go downstairs and make you a cup of tea?'

Nancy hurried down to the kitchen where she found Devil. A bottle of beer stood on the table in front of him but he seemed sober.

She tried to speak evenly, but she was furious to think that he would put her mother and brother out into the street in order to save the Palmyra.

'What's going on? You can't sell our house. Why are you doing this to Ma?'

Devil's black glare sliced like a knife blade. 'There's no choice. She took the news badly, of course. Started tearing down pictures and screaming. I had to call Vassilis to her in the end. He's just gone.'

'It's true?'

'I am afraid so. I'll rent another house for us, Zenobia. It won't be too bad. The theatre has to go on, don't you see?'

She was boiling with anger. 'No, I don't see. This is our *home.*'

Devil dropped his head into his hands. Grey hair stuck out in tufts between his fingers.

'The Palmyra has been the work of my life. Devising new illusions and building the apparatus. Rehearsing and performing. Carlo and me, your mother, the stage and the audiences . . .' He broke off. Devil almost never spoke of the dwarf who had once been his partner. She softened a little and took a step forward, placing her hand on her father's shoulder. She could smell the glue and sawdust of the workshops, and the greasepaint and heated dust and human sweat of the theatre itself. Nancy recognised how powerfully the memories of the past and the desire to maintain the theatre's life ran in her father.

'But we have Neelie to think of, as well as Ma.'

A floorboard creaked before Eliza appeared in the doorway. Half-blinded by tears she stumbled on a trailing scarf but even in this anguish some of her magnificence remained, like the memory of a fine portrait glimpsed long ago or a fading waft of perfume.

Devil leapt to his feet.

'Eliza,' he implored.

Nancy was thrust aside as Eliza ran at him and pounded his chest with her clenched fists.

'What else will you do?' she howled. 'Why not just shoot us?'

'Be rational. A house is just a house,' Devil murmured, unwisely. Eliza's frenzy increased to the point where they had to pinion her arms and wait until the rage exhausted her. Finally she sank against him, crying bitterly. Devil cradled her head and rocked her, still looking into the distance. He was making mental calculations, even now.

Nancy edged past. There was no role for her in the drama that endlessly played out between her parents. She filled the kettle at the sink, lit the gas with its popping flare and placed it on the burner. It seemed a long time since she had shared a pork pie and tomatoes for tea with Lion and Ann and Jinny. How much easier it would be, she thought, to come home to her own place instead of returning to arguments and anxiety and illness. Guilt at this disloyalty swelled in her. Her emotions jarred as she warmed the teapot and spooned tea from the Victoria Jubilee caddy. The old tin had stood in its place on the shelf for as long as she could remember.

Eliza hunted amongst the pots and bottles on the table for the familiar brown phial.

'I don't want tea. Where's my medicine? Vassilis brought it.'

'You've already had some,' Devil warned.

She glared at him, dismay followed by cunning chasing across her face.

'I haven't. I can't have done. My back is so painful.'

'Here, Ma,' Nancy said. She gave her mother a cup of heavily sweetened tea and Devil coaxed her to take a sip.

Nancy found Cornelius sitting in his bedside chair, his hands hanging between his knees, as he used to do when he first came home. She saw that he was shaking. To be taken out of this house and deposited in a strange place would terrify him. She tried to offer what reassurance she

189

could muster, but he answered only in monosyllables. In the end she kissed him and told him to try to sleep.

In the refuge of her own room Nancy stared at the wall and thought about what was to be done. The refrain *Martinmartinmartinmartin* softly sounded and she shook her head to try to silence it. An odd impulse made her get to her feet and search the top of her dressing table, but there was nothing unusual there.

It was Lion who came up with the idea.

Nancy described to him the dismal business of packing and emptying the Islington house before the move into a much smaller one that Devil had discovered for rent, in the network of seamy streets to the south of the canal.

Lion listened with her hands folded between his.

'I've got a suggestion to make,' he said in the end.

Nancy sighed. Whatever the idea, it had come too late. Devil was not to be deflected from his purpose, and the old house had already been sold.

'What is it?'

'My godfather.'

She hesitated.

'What about him?'

Lion told her that Lawrence Feather's seances had become enormously popular. Bereaved women flocked to him in the hope of a word or a sign from the men they had lost, and Mr Feather was now in need of bigger halls to play in and new voices to help him deliver the stream of messages from the other side.

Nancy raised her head. The clatter of the café was stilled.

'*You* could help him, couldn't you?' Lion said gently. 'You wouldn't even be a fraud.'

She didn't immediately dismiss the idea, as she would definitely have done only a month earlier.

Instead she considered the implications.

'Does he make money?' she asked at length.

'A whole heap, believe me. Everyone has lost someone, haven't they?'

Nancy was no longer a frightened child. She was a grown woman, with the ability to steer her own course, and with a family who needed her support. Automatically she felt in her pocket, although she had long ago thrown away the card Mr Feather had once given her.

She summoned up her resolve.

'Will you arrange for me to meet him?'

# CHAPTER TEN

A few days later Lion strolled with Nancy to Gower Street where he rang the bell at a grand, gloomy house. They were shown upstairs to the first floor and Lawrence Feather emerged through double doors to greet them. Nancy saw that the man looked much the same. His long dark coat still made him resemble a Nonconformist preacher although the cloth and cut were finer now and there were glints of gold from a signet ring and an opulent pair of cufflinks.

Lion greeted his godfather affectionately and then said he would retire to a handy pub so Lawrence and Nancy could talk in peace. He named a place nearby and went on his way.

Feather seized Nancy's hands and led her into his rooms. The roar of Gower Street traffic was subdued by heavy brocade curtains. The room was crammed with mahogany and velvet-padded furniture, a breakfront bookcase stuffed with heavy books loomed to one side and on a table stood a spherical item draped in a paisley shawl. This object was quite possibly a crystal ball. The set-up was somehow so reminiscent of one of her father's most stagy and old-fashioned tricks that she had to swallow a laugh.

The medium studied her face.

'You have grown so like your mother. How is she?'

'She is fairly well, thank you,' Nancy lied.

The truth was that the Wixes' forced removal to the small dark house in a cul-de-sac called Waterloo Street had precipitated a serious crisis. Eliza seemed deranged by the loss of her home and refused to settle in the new one. She had retreated to her sister and brother-in-law's house while Devil ranged through the disordered rooms of the rented place like a shabby tiger.

'And how are *you*, child?'

Nancy extricated her hands. 'I'm not really a child any longer. And I am at a crossroads, I think. It was Lycett who suggested I might come and talk to you about choosing a direction.'

'Of course, of course. I am so pleased you felt you could come to me. How may I help you? Do you wish to consult the spirits for guidance? Or perhaps –' his glance slid keenly over her face – 'the time has come to discuss your own gift? I was always convinced it could be remarkable, if allowed to develop. But you know that, of course.' He smiled, without warmth. 'It was your mother who was not in favour of our connection.'

Almost ten years ago Eliza's hostility had been rooted in instinctive mistrust, whereas Nancy had recoiled from the man for a deeper reason. Now she was able to judge for herself, and she marshalled her thoughts from the new perspective. Mr Feather no longer seemed particularly alarming, although she didn't care for the way he assumed a familiarity that he hadn't earned. But she was here today for her family's sake, so she would have to overcome her misgivings.

'Mothers are always protective.'

Feather nodded and waited.

'I have begun to understand that I can't deny my gift, if that's what it is,' Nancy continued. 'So I would like to explore it and try to find out what it means. With your help, perhaps?'

Her eyes travelled across Chinese silk rugs, over the solid, expensive furniture and upwards to the high cornices of the room.

'Please go on.'

'Lion – Lycett – tells me that you are the best and most sought-after medium in London.'

It was true. She had looked into it, and Lawrence Feather was famous in Spiritualist circles. Aristocrats, politicians and artists consulted him, as well as the women longing for a sign from their lost husbands and sons. Pushing out his lips in a deprecating shrug, Feather couldn't disguise his pleasure at the compliment.

She went on. 'I . . . find myself in difficult circumstances. My family does, I mean. I need to earn a living, perhaps a better one than I could hope for as a saleswoman or a secretary.'

'I understand.' There was a flash of malicious satisfaction. 'I have heard that your father is insolvent, and has had to close down his music hall.'

'Yes.'

'It is many years since our last unfortunate meeting, Nancy. If I understand you, you propose yourself now as my protégée? Do you look for tutelage as a fledgling medium, spreading your wings under the banner of my reputation?'

His voice was silky.

Nancy had known that it would be awkward to offer her gift, or her affliction, whichever it was, as a commercial

194

proposition. But she believed in the Uncanny; furthermore it was all she had and there was no point in trying to pretend the situation was anything other. She needed Feather's help and she hoped she could be useful to him in return.

She said honestly, 'If I set out alone, to offer private and public seances, I believe I could do it. Based on what I know and have already experienced, that is. But you did acknowledge my ability, and you once said to me if I should need anything . . .'

Her eyes met his.

She could see him turning her proposition over in his mind. He could either launch a new voice that might capture public attention in association with his own, or suffer the threat of competition if he chose not to.

'I see.'

There were heavy blinds at the windows, at present raised.

Looking towards them she asked, 'Do you hold your seances here?'

'For individual clients or small family groups, yes. Of course for bigger events I need a hall.'

'Do you have the use of one?'

A corner of Feather's mouth tucked inwards. 'Not permanently.'

A French clock on the mantel struck sweetly seven times. Lion would be sitting in the pub with a half-pint of bitter, the evening newspaper folded on the table and his cigarette tin and match case beside it. She would have liked to be there with him. The medium let another minute tick by before he stood up. He moved to lower the blinds against the evening light and beckoned her.

'Shall we close the spirit circle together, Nancy?'

He raised her to her feet and guided her to two upright

chairs separated by a small table. They faced each other over their interlocked fingers. His were solid male fists with a tiny whorl of black hair on each knuckle. She could hear the man's breathing, see the bobbing of his Adam's apple above his starched collar.

Nancy cleared her throat.

'Is anyone there?' she asked.

She felt none of the energy that had raced through her beside the Kentish campfire, and none of the certainty.

It wasn't going to be as easy as she had hoped.

'Speak to us,' Lawrence Feather urged.

She wondered if she should utter a name or make some interesting claim, but inspiration entirely failed her. If Feather was hearing a clamour of spirit voices he didn't volunteer to be their mouthpiece. She was the one who was being auditioned, not vice versa.

'This is a safe place,' he murmured, either to encourage her or the invisible others, she wasn't quite sure which.

Some time passed in silence.

Nancy concentrated so hard that blood roared in her ears but she realised they might sit here until midnight and nothing would happen. The seance was a miserable failure. She had been over-confident in expecting the Uncanny to favour Lawrence Feather's polished rooms, and she was quite unable to fake it.

'I'm sorry,' she faltered.

His pale face remained impassive.

'There is no need for apology, Nancy. You mentioned experience, so you will know already that there is not invariably a successful connection.'

Feather left the table and raised the blinds. A shaft of light fell across the rugs as she confided, 'I can't control what I see or hear, Mr Feather. I hoped that you might be able to teach me. Perhaps you would say, to harness my abilities?'

He drifted from the covered crystal ball to the bookcase, running his fingertips over their surfaces as if to emphasise the breadth of his resources. There was more theatre than substance in him. Her confidence began to creep back as he talked at her.

'I don't know about that. You see, Nancy, I have an obligation to my sitters. They bring me their trust and they look for – yes – messages of hope and reassurance. They have lost their beloved and they want to believe in survival after death. It's my privilege to assist that belief, and it *is* a privilege to see the joy and tears, the relief and hope that come springing from a word or a name from beyond. But by the very nature of what we do, the channels are not always reliably open.'

His voice shook a little.

'My own poor sister's voice has never been audible to me.'

Nancy listened intently, hearing the whisper of truth beneath the smooth skin of words.

'The supplicants on this side are always with us, and always waiting, and so my work – ours, if you will – involves an element of performance. Not every time of course, not even often, but sometimes I have to speak on my own authority. I offer sitters nothing but what I know to be there in essence and to be true in outline, you understand.'

She noted the predatory glint beneath the priestly earnestness.

So Lawrence Feather was a showman just like her father, which was more or less what she had always assumed. The difference was that Devil was an entertainer with no ambitions but to give pleasure – 'to create wonder' as he often said – while Feather played deliberately on the anguish of human loss. Yet Feather's grasp of the paranormal had allowed him to recognise Nancy's ability and therefore, she judged, he couldn't be entirely cynical about what he did. Quite likely he made use of what talents he possessed, and supplied the rest from his imagination. In doing so he brought comfort to those who were in need of it.

Was that helpful or otherwise?

She hesitated, caught between conflicting impulses.

Then she remembered Cornelius waiting for her at Waterloo Street and Eliza angry and wounded in her sister's house.

'I would like to learn from you,' she said.

Feather looked as pleased as a stroked cat. He crossed to the window and looped back the curtains in order to gaze down into Gower Street, conscious theatricality in every movement he made.

At last he sighed.

'I am flattered, but I'm afraid I can't undertake to sponsor you professionally. These business matters are always ticklish, as your father well knows. If there is another way I can help you?'

Nancy hadn't anticipated that Feather would reject her proposal out of hand. This was a real blow. Eliza's brutal dismissal of him so long ago must have seriously punctured his pride. Silenced by disappointment she could only nod and begin to gather her coat and bag. Feather made some small talk about Lion, saying how pleased he was that the young people had struck up a friendship.

'Poor John Stone, Lycett's father and my old friend, was quite a theosophist in his younger days, you know. He's grown frail lately. Within the framework of our beliefs he made me godfather to his boy, and I have done my best to pass on the knowledge.' Feather pursed his lips. 'I am afraid

Lycett is not one of us, my dear, in talent or inclination, although he is a fine young man. He was only a boy at the time but I will never forget his kindness to me after our beloved Helena passed across.'

Already halfway to the door, Nancy saw the flash of stark grief in his face. A channel to his drowned sister was what the medium had craved all along.

Impulsively she said, 'Please, may I tell you something?'

He heard the change in her voice.

'Why, yes. Anything you wish.'

'I saw a locket lying on my dressing table that day, just after you came to visit my mother in Islington.'

He seized her arm, the fingers digging into her flesh.

'A locket?'

'It was a silver locket, with a pretty design of leaves engraved on the front. On the back there was a monogram.'

His grip tightened until she almost winced.

'The initials were HMF.'

She could see it as clearly as if she were back in her old bedroom with the trinket cupped in the palm of her hand.

'Tell me what was inside the locket, Nancy.'

She came closer and whispered, 'Two locks of hair, formed into a ring bound up with scarlet thread.'

Feather threw back his head. He gave a cry that was more animal than human.

'I gave that locket to Helena on her sixteenth birthday. And when I buried her it was fastened round her throat.'

Nancy waited.

'And then?' he begged.

'There was some disturbance outside the room. My younger brother. When I turned back to the dressing table the locket was gone. Only my hairbrush and comb were there, lying in their usual places.'

Feather gave another cry, this time with a raw edge in it that made Nancy shiver. His eyes glittered with tears.

'Thank you', he gasped. 'Thank you. It's the sign from her I have longed for. She survives in another place.'

'I am sorry', Nancy whispered, wishing she had not kept the sign from him for so long.

'No, no. Never say you are sorry for having given me such joy.'

He lifted her hand and kissed it.

'I can't explain to you how I saw the locket', she murmured. All she knew was that it had been there and then it had vanished. Even stranger was the way Helena's presence somehow flooded into her whilst evading her brother's supplication. Rowland and Edwin had never appeared amongst the scores of soldiers who populated her Uncanny, perhaps because she had been too close to them. Quite possibly, Nancy thought, there was a blankness about her that made her a ready mouthpiece. She felt cloudy inside her head when she tried to work it all out, and the suspicion that there was something unhealthy about Feather's relationship with his sister made her shrink from their history.

Feather stepped closer still and almost reverently brushed his lips against her forehead. Her antipathy to him dissolved a little at his touch. She was left with an odd fellow feeling, as if the two of them had walked a great distance together.

'No one could have known I placed the locket around her poor lifeless throat. You were such a striking child, Nancy. You need not question your power, now or in the future. You must simply relate what you see, or speak as the voices direct you.'

He was right, she thought. What else was there to do?

She felt exhausted, as if it was an age rather than a few hours since she had hurried up Essex Road to open the shop for that day's business.

'Yes. All right. Thank you.'

He stood back again and studied her face. His cheeks were wet but he glowed with joy.

'You have given me great happiness this evening. I'm sorry to have rebuffed you earlier. I shall be happy to work with you, my dear. I will teach you everything I know, and encourage your gifts to the very best of my ability.'

She gratefully agreed to his proposals. To earn money was the important thing, and somehow she would manage to yoke the Uncanny with the pressures of performance. Lawrence Feather promised her that he would prepare her for her first public sitting as soon as possible.

They shook hands on the agreement.

Nancy stepped out into the city dusk and her tiredness lifted. It was a beautiful evening. Perhaps she would soon follow Feather into the ranks of professional mediums, and then she could make life at Waterloo Street more bearable for everyone. Her plans extended to the Palmyra too. As she hurried to join Lion the paving stones under her feet seemed to shift, as if they formed a vast grid on which she might perform her next moves. She skipped over the joins like an eight-year-old playing hopscotch.

The pub in which she had agreed to meet Lion was called the Old Cinque Ports. She found the gaunt old place to the north of New Oxford Street. Under a tobacco-brown ceiling there was a long, curved bar of polished mahogany with a series of bevelled mirrors multiplying into infinity the reflections of a few morose drinkers. Lion was reading his newspaper next to a sign for '*Worthington on Draught*'.

He looked up as she approached and his face split into a broad grin.

'Here you are at last. I was ready to give you up for lost. What happened? Hang on a tick, let me get you a drink before you tell all.'

He returned with two glasses.

'Mr Feather was very kind in the end. He said he will teach me.'

Lion pursed his lips in a low, soundless whistle.

'I say. Madame Blavatsky.'

'Hardly.'

Lion was so good-humoured and tolerant, but his response to everything was a joke or a tease. Nancy found it slightly irritating that he could never be serious. She took a sip of beer and licked her top lip to remove the froth.

'Li, do you think I am peculiar?'

'Eh? Of course not. I think you are completely divine. Kiss me?'

He hadn't probed any further about Ann's brother. Lion simply noted what happened, made a connection between his godfather's success in his field and Nancy's unusual abilities, and cheerfully brought them together. He might as well have been introducing a strawberry picker to a jam maker. Of course I am peculiar, Nancy thought. What else did *Martinmartinmartinmartin* indicate, or a drowned woman's locket, or the soaking girl who had recently made her appearance in Waterloo Street as if to reassure Nancy that she was still there?

'I mean, you will certainly make your fortune mumbling to lost grannies, just like Lawrence does. In this harsh modern age we all have to make compromises, darling. Look at me. I have spent the whole day thinking up ways to persuade people to buy Goodenough's tonic, which has quite probably got arsenic in it. "It Perks You Up" isn't quite punchy enough, is it?'

Nancy laughed in spite of herself.

'How about "It Knocks You for Six"?'

'Damn. I wish I'd thought of that.' He clasped his hands and screwed his eyes shut. 'Is anyone there? Speak, I say.' He cracked open one eye and grinned at her. 'See? Not a dicky. You could do my job but I'd be clueless at yours.'

'It isn't my job yet. And you'll just have to keep on taking the tonic.'

'Ha ha. I say, do you fancy the pictures? We're in time for the last of Charlie Chaplin at the Empire. If you're hungry we could pick up a bag of chips.'

'Why not?' In his avoidance of anything complicated, Lion was easy-going company. 'Yes, please. That sounds lovely.'

'Drink up then.'

They made their way to the cinema, digging in turn into a newspaper cone of hot chips while they waited in the queue for tickets. Lion probed the corners for the last salty scraps before crumpling the empty bag.

'Why not come back with me after the picture? If your ma is still at her sister's?'

Lion's idea of economical living was a flat in a Georgian house just off Shepherd's Market in Mayfair. It was an attic, perched over a series of rooms occupied by women who always greeted him with friendly enthusiasm.

'Well, of course they are tarts,' he had told her when asked about this. 'But they don't mind my gramophone and I don't mind their visitors. A good arrangement, don't you think?'

Nancy thought this was funny. The flat was small and the neighbours were unusual, but it was fashionably bohemian and private and Mayfair was still Mayfair. Lion inhabited a different realm from Waterloo Street.

'I must go home tonight.'

He raked his curls with chip-greased fingers, but he didn't bother to argue.

'What a shame.'

A couple strolled down the central avenue of a suburban park. They passed through a tunnel of plane trees with leaves browned by the previous night's frost, the first of the approaching winter, before making a single circuit of the display of scarlet and lemon dahlias in the central flower-bed. The man seemed to be pleading with his companion, who kept her face averted.

At the far end of the avenue they came to a twiggy arbour sheltering a bench. Pausing to look at the rustic shelter the woman said bitterly, 'It's not as pretty as the one we had in the old garden.'

The man took the opportunity to slide his arm around her waist.

'Let's sit down anyway.'

They settled themselves on the bench and the woman huddled inside her violet wool coat which was layered over an embroidered crimson skirt and woollen stockings. She made a patch of colour almost as bright as the municipal bedding. Breathing out as if she expected to see it clouding in the damp air, she sighed.

'Look, this is what we have come to.'

'The park?'

'Cast out to a public bench. After all the years, after all we have done and all we have been through.'

They were both remembering a long-ago walk in Hyde Park, and another day when they had taken a train journey to a quiet country churchyard. Even with these memories in common they were separated by antagonism. They fell into a sombre silence.

The man said at length, 'We do have a place to live. A home, with two of our children safely in it. We aren't obliged to take refuge on a bench, or at least we only have to do so because I prefer not to discuss our private difficulties in front of Faith and Matthew.'

'I miss our house. The house you sold from under my feet and our children's.'

This discussion was so dulled by repetition that neither of them could summon the energy to follow it through. Silence resumed while they watched a row of swallows assembling on a telegraph wire.

'I suppose you have been to see Vassilis?' Devil asked at last.

She shook her head.

'No.'

At that he turned to look at her.

'Is this the truth? Is it, Eliza?'

'Yes. I won't go to him any more.'

He stared. 'If you don't take any more of that vile stuff I can manage everything else. I'll get the theatre open again and I'll buy you a house in Park Lane, if that's what you want. The only thing *I* miss in the whole bloody world is you, and you've been gone far too long.'

The words were painful for him to utter, and hearing them caused her as much pain. A floodgate seemed to open in her. She leaned forward briefly and pressed her mouth to his.

'I know. I am so sorry, Devil.'

'My darling, I'll help you. I'll be with you every minute you need me.'

'I'm sorry,' she repeated. 'I should say it to you and Cornelius and Nancy as well. Especially Nancy. Thank God Arthur isn't here.'

'He will be. You don't want to be this way for him, do you? Promise me now, you won't see Vassilis again.'

'I won't. He doesn't want me to take the medicine any more either.'

'Say it, Eliza.'

'I won't see Vassilis again.'

Her free hand curled inside the pocket of her purple coat where the brown bottle safely lay. The last time she visited him she had implored the doctor, alternately pleading and weeping in his dilapidated surgery, but Vassilis had flatly denied her need.

'I am a *doctor*, Mrs Wix. You have got quite well and your situation no longer is critical. We must make another way to manage the discomfort from your condition. Let me give you the examination again next week.'

But to Eliza a week might as well have been a decade.

Her only hope had been to find another source of supply, and this she had been able to do by recognising on the street a frail-looking man she had seen twice before, each time seated in Vassilis's waiting room. With the cunning of desperation she had followed this person to a shop selling prosthetic limbs made of tin or alarmingly pink ceramic material, and the harnesses of webbing and leather that attached the devices to damaged bodies.

'Yes, miss?' the man had asked from behind his wooden counter.

She had mumbled her request, and submitted to the prurient scrutiny that followed.

'You don't look the type, if you don't mind me saying.'

'Is there a type?'

'Oh, yes. Yes, indeed there is.'

He had looked her over even more baldly, pricing her shoes and her eccentric clothing and her emphatic but mostly valueless jewellery. At last he scribbled an address on a scrap of paper and thrust it at her.

'Here. Don't say who told you, and don't come here again.'

The place was down an alley, off a low street almost directly beneath the skeletal cranes of the docks. Eliza crept there and found a foetid room in which cats and small children scrabbled amongst debris on the bare floorboards, all of them ignored by a woman with blackened teeth who sold her what she needed without once looking her in the face. That suited Eliza well enough.

The price was high. Eliza had only a tiny sum of money put away and it didn't call for any elaborate calculations to work out that this would very soon be used up. She thought Faith might lend her some more, perhaps, when the time came.

There was no point in worrying about it in any case. For now, she had what she needed.

'Good girl. I'm proud of you,' Devil whispered.

She kissed her husband again to stop the unwelcome words. Then she stood up and wrapped her arms around herself.

'Let's walk back. Faith will be wondering where we are.'

Devil grinned. 'She will not. Your sister will be relieved that we are behaving like a married couple for a change.'

They set off towards the gates. These had once been elaborate wrought ironwork, raised by public subscription to commemorate the Golden Jubilee, but the metal had been torn away and melted down to support the war effort. The iron hinges left behind bled rust into the stone gateposts and the replacement wooden gates had a ramshackle, splintery quality. An hour ago Devil would have regarded this as an emblem of the blighted and despairing condition of the city, even of the whole country, but Eliza's promise had changed his view.

His wife would come back to him, Arthur would soon be home, Cornelius would surely recover, given time. And Nancy had told him of her intriguing idea.

He tipped his soft hat to a sharper angle and began to whistle a tune.

Lawrence Feather kept his promise. Weeks turned into months as he painstakingly schooled Nancy in the Spiritualist principles. She read the books he handed down from the Gower Street bookcase, absorbing the high-flown theories derived from shakily conducted 'experiments' in Beyond. She attended dozens of seances, sitting thoughtfully at the back of hushed rooms as wildly differing messages flooded over from the other side. Florid rappings and ectoplasmic manifestations and hovering presences did not convince her at all – she knew those tricks of the illusionists' trade too well – but a few of the spoken channels did. She noted that the most convincing and affecting performances were the simplest. The medium should be no more than a mouthpiece, working without distracting props or costume, offering a few words that could be taken as comfort or reassurance by those left behind. She judged that some of the connections at one or two of the seances – not all of them, by any means, but some – must be genuine. The belief lay within her, in her own experience, and as the conviction grew her confidence in what she was learning developed with it.

Whatever his real powers might be, Mr Feather was the best performer of all of them. He had the ability to be still, to be a commanding presence without one histrionic gesture, and above all he knew how to look and listen. She noticed right away how he could take a question and turn it inside out to provide an answer. He could read a sitter's clothes and facial expressions and the language of her gestures, and weave a dense narrative from these thin shreds. He was inventive and authoritative, and at the same time he could be kindly and reassuring. Almost invariably he was able to send his clients home in the belief that reunion with their loved one lay somewhere ahead. It's not wrong, Nancy thought. Time's coils mysteriously furled and looped around them all.

They did not always get on well – Feather could be unctuous, and she prickled under his presumptions and the forced intimacy of their strange situation. He behaved properly enough, even though she had been afraid at the beginning that she would have to deal with kisses and fumblings. Probably she was protected from the man's inclinations by her relationship with Lion. As the time passed she came to respect her mentor, although not to like him any better.

Within a few more weeks, under Feather's tutelage, she was conducting private sittings of her own. Although he was never again as explicit as he had been in their first conversation at Gower Street, the understanding remained clear. Sometimes, if the Uncanny forsook her, she would have to use her own voice. She must not be cruel or give pain – the objective should always be to comfort and console. Imagination, generalisation, tact and human sympathy were to be her tools.

And the Uncanny did not often forsake her. She learned how to open herself to it, by neither resisting nor over-reaching. She began to gather a small reputation, until the day came when her tutor judged she was ready to hold her first public seance. Nancy immediately thought of the Palmyra stage, but quickly realised that the green-and-gold theatre was far too big, and the association with tongue-in-cheek music-hall magic too close. Lawrence Feather booked a hall. It was the very same one that Nancy had known before the war, from accompanying Lizzie and then Jinny to WSPU meetings. It was large enough to seat sixty or so people in reasonable comfort, but not too big for one inexperienced speaker to fill with a voice that might well falter.

On the night of the seance she arrived an hour early, alone, at her own insistence. A thick smell of mackintoshes, damp woollen clothes and London fog seemed embedded in the walls. Nancy was shaking with nerves, but she was also buoyed up by excited anticipation. Almost all the tickets were sold. Devil and Eliza and her friends would be in the audience. Her parents were sceptical of the theory and suspicious of the set-up, but they were deeply interested in the commercial potential. Tonight, Nancy thought, perhaps she might even do something that would make her mother proud of her. She took a last look round the hall and retreated into the little room backstage to prepare.

The seating was arranged in a horseshoe facing a single straight-backed chair. Devil and Eliza chose to sit at the back of one of the arms of the horseshoe, deliberately out of what would be Nancy's line of sight. In the corresponding position across the room Devil spotted Nancy's friend Jinny Main. He smiled when he caught her eye and she gave him a nod. With Jinny was a rounded, pretty girl whose red curls spiralled out from beneath her knitted cap, and a young man who looked vaguely familiar although for the moment Devil couldn't place him. These three were clearly saving a place for a fourth who had not yet arrived.

Silence gathered under the beams of the hall and spread until it held everyone in expectant stillness. There was a brief scramble as a last-minute arrival slipped into her seat beside Jinny Main. It was Lizzie Shaw. Eliza and Devil waved to her. Eliza slipped her hand into her husband's and he squeezed her chill fingers.

A minute later Lawrence Feather emerged from a door at the side of the hall. He spoke a few words of introduction, telling them that tonight's spirit channel was gifted with the most startling talent he had ever encountered. He had developed her skill, personally working with her to enlarge her range. He was proud of his young protégée, he confided, pushing out his lips in his deprecating pout.

'Zenobia Wix,' he announced.

He took his seat at the front centre of the horseshoe. To her family, waiting in the tense seconds before her appearance, it was as if Nancy was already not quite daughter or cousin, but something that was both less and more – a public property.

Nancy came out and closed the door behind her. She crossed to the straight-backed chair and moved it a few inches to the left across the bare floorboards. Devil tried to exchange a knowing wink with Eliza, signalling *no wires, no electrical contacts*, but his wife stared straight ahead as if she were made of stone. She was very pale and even the tremor in her hands that had lately become habitual seemed to have frozen.

Nancy sat down. She was wearing a plain grey dress they hadn't seen her in before, black stockings and solid shoes. She had recently cut her hair short and her small head and slender neck were as fragile as a flower on its stalk.

'My name is Zenobia Wix,' she said, and closed her eyes.

The silence was intense. Beside Devil a nervous woman

211

touched her fingers to her lips. She jumped when Nancy spoke.

'Is anyone there?'

Nancy turned her head a fraction, listening. No one in the room could have doubted that she strained to catch a sound that came from beyond these walls. The slow seconds ticked away.

'Come to us,' she implored.

When she did begin to speak properly it was in a low, hesitant voice. The woman next to Devil craned forwards now to catch what she said.

'Elizabeth? Elizabeth . . . yes. Is your Thomas here? The cup and the old cupboard? What do you mean by that?'

A man stood up. 'I am Thomas.'

Nancy's face was a pale oval. Her wide eyes fixed on Thomas's face.

'Please sit down. Yes. Elizabeth is here with us. There is a key to the cupboard. Inside the cupboard you will find a china cup with a gold rim. Do you understand, Thomas?'

The man turned crimson. 'My grandma. Lost her mind at the end. She never said nothing to us about a cup.'

'Is it a real cup, Elizabeth? Or does it stand for something? What did it hold?'

These questions and answers didn't lead anywhere, nor did the next subject.

The tension leaked away. The audience settled, creaking and shuffling in their seats, shoe leather scraping the floor. It was the same fare that was served up at any spirit circle. Zenobia Wix was nothing new, after all.

Eliza seemed lost in a place of her own. Devil folded his arms. He had recognised the boy seated opposite as Nancy's dancing parter at Whistlehalt.

The seance proceeded.

Some subjects were grateful for messages delivered in the voice of this novice medium; one woman burst into uncontrollable weeping and had to be led away by her husband. The few who were flippant or obstructive, Nancy headed off. Lizzie whispered behind her hand to Jinny.

Then without warning came a change. Nancy covered her mouth and nose as if overcome by a nauseating smell. She threw herself backwards and the chair rocked alarmingly.

A damp chill seemed to gather in the hall. One or two people even turned up their collars or pulled scarves about their necks.

Nancy swayed upright. Her eyes focused on the empty space in front of her. She extended a hand, more to fend off what she saw than to beckon to it. She murmured, 'You are here?'

The silence seemed heavy enough to press into their skulls. They waited it out, watching the small tense figure before them.

Nancy gathered herself and spoke out in a clear voice quite unlike her earlier tentative tone.

'Sarah Doherty. I am here to speak for Mrs Sarah Doherty. Is there anyone in the room who knows her?'

A woman in the centre of the hall audibly gasped and nudged the man beside her. He hadn't removed the thick, flat labourer's cap he wore pulled down over his forehead. The exposed half of his drunkard's face was dark red and heavily veined. He flinched and sank deeper into his chair.

Nancy said, 'There is sawdust on the floor. The woman who was here has left us.'

The man's companion stumbled to her feet. Every pair of eyes fastened on her, a heavy woman in a shapeless grey coat. No one would have looked twice at her in another place but now her anguish marked her out.

'Sarah's ours. She's been missing these ten months. Left three little ones, she did. Tell us what she says.'

'There are drops of blood in the sawdust.' Nancy's pale fingers fluttered to her mouth. 'Fresh meat . . . The smell of it.'

'That's right. My brother's a butcher. Tell him.'

Nancy was absolutely white. She was struggling for words.

'*Tell him*,' the woman screamed.

Jinny and Ann exchanged shocked glances. All Lion's smiles had faded, leaving his face blank. Devil scanned the room for the apparatus of trickery and Eliza sat with the life seemingly drained out of her.

'Sarah is gone. I mean that she is dead.' A long pause followed before Nancy murmured, 'I am sorry. I see the violence that was done to her.'

'What are you saying?'

The woman's voice shook so much that she could hardly get out the question.

'Sarah lies in woodland, a lovely place. She is at peace now. It is best to leave her where she is. There is nothing we can do to help her.' Nancy picked her words as precisely as type from the case, although the horror of the vision was evident.

The brother staggered to his feet. He broke out of the row of seats with the woman frantically catching at the tail of his coat. He shoved her aside and flung himself at Nancy.

Jinny shouted, 'Stop him.'

From opposite sides of the hall Devil and Lion were forcing their way to the front. Lawrence Feather remained impassive except for two blots of colour showing high on his cheekbones. The butcher seized Nancy by the collar of her dress and gave her a vicious shake.

'My Sarah ain't dead. She's run off, that's what. When I find her and bring her home I'll give her what for, leaving us like this.'

His sister reached him and caught his arm.

'Sam, listen to what she says,' she implored.

The man rounded on her, his red face suffused with guilt and pain. He was like a bull at the doors of the abbatoir, sensing what lay ahead.

'I'm not listening to no one. I only come here tonight with you because of what you done for us, and because you wouldn't bloody shut up.'

Devil and Lion reached Nancy's side but she raised a hand to warn them to stay back. She was deathly pale, but in command of herself and of the packed hall.

'Sam, you know what happened to your wife. Tell us the truth,' Nancy whispered.

They might have been the only two people in the room.

He roared, 'You see nothing, you lying bitch.'

He swung round to the horrified audience. 'Don't you listen to these lies. I never touched her. What does she know, doing this for money?'

The people shifted and murmured.

'She wears a wedding ring with a little red stone. Beneath her chin, just here –' Nancy indicated her own throat – 'I see a small brown mark. A birthmark.'

The sister began to sob.

'It's her. Where is she?' she begged.

Nancy answered, 'I don't know. There are trees, close together. It is woodland.'

'Shut your mouth.'

The butcher gave a final bellow and swung his fist. He was unsteady on his feet and the blow glanced off the side of Nancy's head. Amidst cries of alarm Devil and Lion

215

dived at the man to pin his arms to his sides. Nancy didn't flinch.

'Listen to me. *There is no more hurting, Sam.* That's what she says. Did you hurt her? Did you kill her?'

The clamour of the audience swelled. Their support seemed mostly for Nancy, but some were protesting that it wasn't right to say such things to a fellow who had lost his wife. Shouting and disputes broke out as Jinny and Ann struggled through with Lizzie to form a protective circle around Nancy.

Sam somehow broke free of Lion and Devil. When he raised his huge fists everyone except his sister took a step backwards.

'You don't know nothing,' he hissed at Nancy. 'It's a fucking lie.'

Then he whirled away, trampling through the fringes of the audience and kicking aside chairs as he bolted. He broke out of the door and disappeared into the darkness. His sister bunched her grey coat to her hips and reeled after him.

Nancy pressed her hand to the side of her head.

Jinny held her. 'Are you hurt?'

'No. I'll be all right in a moment.'

The women tried to lead her towards the side room but Nancy still craned round to the empty spot just in front of her chair. When she was sure there was nothing there she let herself be taken out of the hall.

A few handclaps trailed her and some insistent voices called for more, but most of the witnesses were too stunned by what they had seen to make further demands. When it became clear that Zenobia Wix was not going to reappear the noise dropped to an excited buzz. People prepared to leave.

'He did away with his wife, that feller, did he?' one astonished woman asked another as they filed past Lawrence Feather on their way to the door.

Her friend wagged her head. 'It seems that's what she was saying. It's not like any sitting I've been to before. I'm not sure it's what we want to hear, that sort of thing, is it? My Stanley wouldn't have cared for it.'

'Your Stanley wouldn't have come in the first place, Dora. It would have been too strange for him.'

Nancy sat in the chair they had placed for her. She looked as if she might pass out. Jinny spotted a bottle of sal volatile on a shelf, uncorked it and waved it under her nose. Nancy sniffed and gagged, but it revived her. Unwillingly she allowed Jinny to take her pulse.

'Dear bloody hell,' Lizzie cried. 'Was that an act, Nancy?'

Ann Gillespie hushed her.

Slightly chastened, Lizzie crossed to the sink in the corner of the room and ran cold water on the spider trapped in it. She filled a glass of water and took it to her cousin.

Lion moved protectively to Nancy's side.

'There,' he told her. 'You'll be fine in a few minutes.'

The nature of their friendship was obvious, and it was equally clear that her parents didn't know it existed. Ann and Jinny saw the two of them attempting to absorb this further development. Devil Wix looked a powerful man although there was a touch of dissolution in his handsome face. His wife was a wild-haired, emaciated but striking figure whose eyes seemed far too large. For all the drama of the evening, Devil and Eliza appeared to be confused rather than deeply shaken. They were theatre people, and perhaps they had seen even stranger and more disturbing things.

Nancy rested her cheek against Lion's.

'Thank you,' she whispered.

She looked up at Devil and Eliza, knowing that she must try to explain herself.

'Don't worry. Sometimes I do see things I can't explain. I always have done.'

Eliza swept forward.

'Why didn't you tell me?'

It seemed to Jinny and Ann that Nancy and her mother were the twin pivots of all the passion in this room. The rest of them, even Devil Wix, were peripheral.

Nancy shrugged, made cruel by the exhaustion that always came in the wake of the Uncanny, and by a headache that threatened to crush her skull.

'I never felt that I could *tell* you. It wouldn't have been what you wanted for me.'

Eliza flinched. Turning aside she groped for and found her husband's supporting arm.

'What did you *see*, Nancy?' It was Devil who put the question.

She ran her tongue over dry lips and swallowed before she spoke. 'I saw a dead woman in a forest. She had been hacked to pieces with a meat cleaver.'

Lawrence Feather walked into the silence. Ignoring all the others, he spoke quietly to Nancy.

'You were magnificent,' he said.

'Is that what you'd call it?'

He took her hand and kissed it.

'I would. You have a great career ahead of you, Nancy.'

Feather was smiling. For a man who was usually sombre he was almost animated.

'My boy.' He embraced his godson as Eliza stared at them.

'I remember now,' she whispered.

'This is my friend Lycett Stone,' Nancy said to her parents.

Devil moved forward to confront Feather. He held himself very straight, except for one thumb hooked into the pocket of his waistcoat where he kept his old-fashioned fob watch.

'I am Devil Wix,' he said. His voice was like a dripping icicle. 'Nancy's father.'

'Lawrence Feather.'

The two men were the same height, and over Nancy's head a look passed between them. There was a depth of recognition in it, as well as mutual antipathy.

Jinny and Ann exchanged a glance and Lizzie stared. Lion's good-humoured face was clouded with discomfort. Eliza's hands were shaking.

'Mr and Mrs Wix,' Feather said pleasantly. He could afford to be polite. 'I think you should take your daughter home and let her rest.'

Devil seethed. He didn't possess Feather's self-control, and his fists bunched.

'Pa,' Nancy warned.

'I can take care of my own family without the benefit of your advice, you trickster. Voices of the spirits? The cheapest of stale old tricks.' He laughed in the man's face.

Feather cocked his head.

'You would know, Wix.'

Nancy stood up. The authority she had acquired in the hall stayed with her. In a level voice she said, 'I am not a commodity. I will make my decisions about where I go and with whom.'

It was Lion she reached out for, and he took her arm at once.

The three young women closed ranks behind them and Devil and Eliza were left with Feather.

Eliza followed her daughter with her eyes.

# PART THREE

# CHAPTER ELEVEN

*London, 1921*

Nancy and Lion were at a party. Surveying tonight's scene from the threshold Nancy remembered what Jake Jones had told her. Parties were like life, consisting of the predictable spiked with moments of high drama.

Night after night they all went to parties, as if every single person they had ever met had taken the decision to live without remembering yesterday or thinking of tomorrow. This hectic pace suited gregarious Lion, who was careless about having to go to work the next day with a headache, but Nancy had begun to find so much studied frivolity tiresome. It was hard to believe that only two years ago the Whistlehalt party had seemed so exotic. As Lion Stone's girlfriend she had long ago lost count of its gaudy successors. Lion never seemed to want anything more out of life than fun. She wondered how other people progressed from cocktails to being serious, and when she asked herself what serious might mean she admitted that it was getting married and having children.

With Lion there was never any discussion of the future,

and when she tried to introduce the subject he laughed it off.

Sometimes, in quiet moments, she still thought of Gil Maitland.

At parties, she searched the crowd for a glimpse, but he was never there.

Small gatherings tended to take place in cramped upstairs flats in Earl's Court. The bigger ones happened in empty warehouses near the river, or in galleries with brand new avant-garde art decorating the walls. The smartest affairs were in the Mayfair town houses of friends of friends, usually when their parents were away. There was always loud music, from a gramophone or even a real band with a singer who tried out the latest hit tunes. Suzette and Dorothy were usually present, showing off their tango moves together or partnering one of the black dancers from a fashionable African troupe. The girls would be with Caspar and Freddie, and the lesbian who wore a monocle and a duke's younger son who was known to take quantities of drugs. Surrounding them would be a throng of jockeys and publishers and the children of landowners, thrilled debutantes and beady social climbers, actors without any roles and aspiring artists, all of them dancing and shouting and trying to attract each other's attention. The din always made talking difficult but the tide of drink meant that no one cared what anyone else said in any case.

Nancy did not possess Lion's stamina or his casual attitude to the demands of work, and the rackety existence they led would have been impossible to combine with her job at the draper's shop at the top of Essex Road. Luckily she had been able to give that up, because slowly at first and lately more steadily she had been gaining a reputation.

Zenobia Wix was the fashionable new medium and spirit

channel, and the bereaved and the lonely and needy had begun to seek her out. Lawrence Feather managed her appearances and even after the takings had been split between them there was enough money for Nancy to feel, for the very first time in her life, that she had some actual freedom of choice.

Following her debut in the chapel hall, a few paragraphs in the newspapers announced the arrest of a butcher from Bethnal Green, east London, detained on suspicion of murder after the disappearance of his wife. Most of the papers reported the story, but only the *Daily Sketch* ran an inside-page headline about the sensational paranormal seance that had indicated the woman's probable fate, after which the butcher's own sister had reported him to the police. No further details came to light and by the next day the story had been forgotten by most of the world.

In the depths of the winter, a police search turned up a grave in Epping Forest and an excavation brought up the body of the missing woman. The butcher confessed to the murder, and was committed to trial. Nancy did not read the lurid newspaper accounts. She knew what she had seen, she grieved for the misery that must lie behind such a crime and its concealment, but she understood the importance of detachment and of husbanding her energy.

In the circles linking Lawrence Feather and his followers to other spiritualists, the events at the seance caused a more lasting stir. The first invitations for Nancy to appear at open and private sittings began to arrive at Gower Street, and almost from the beginning she was able to pick the most promising engagements.

In spite of the difficulty of it all, she discovered satisfaction in weaving the fragments brought up by her clairvoyance with the coarser yarn of observations and deduction. Nancy liked watching people and listening to their stories. The questions she was asked did often betray the desired answers, as she had learned from Mr Feather, and soon the processions of faces, all marked with lines of grief or anxiety mingled with hope, began to seem almost as legible as a headline set up in bold type. The people listened to what she had to say, and they went away comforted. Even the children of the butcher from Bethnal Green, she thought, would be better in the end from knowing their mother's real fate and the justice that had been done on her behalf.

Working as a stage medium made a real performer of her. As well as the ability to detach from the worst of the sorrows, she was acquiring the skills of timing and delivery. Learning from the mistakes she made at her own early seances, and by watching the success of those who were better at it – in particular Jake Jones, as an actor – she was discovering how to hold an audience captive. Just to see if she could do it she would wait, and listen, and let the silence extend until her sitters drew in a breath and held it.

It felt like cradling a bird's egg, warm in the palm of her hand.

Eliza and Devil's stagecraft had been all about speed and glamour and forms of deception that were visual rather than abstract, but she was sure that the concentration required was the same. Public performance absorbed more energy than Nancy had ever known she possessed. She understood her parents better for this discovery. Once she experienced the terror and the answering thrill of the stage for herself, her mother's longing for her lost days seemed natural. So too did Devil's passion for keeping the Palmyra alive at any cost. They hadn't been attentive to their children, but the reasons for their benign neglect were much clearer now. For many years the Palmyra had been a challenge and they had risen to it. They made it a success, until the war came and changed the world.

She admired them for what they had done. Now, with her growing success, she felt the old theatre drawing her back.

*Wix and Family*, she thought.

Devil had spent the money from the sale of the Islington house on paying off the theatre debts. He was preparing to launch a new show, with tricks of his own devising accompanied by music for the modern age. He was sceptical when she suggested that the week's programme might include a performance by her, although the money flowing in from her outside work impressed him. And he had always hated the way that Lawrence Feather claimed half of everything she earned.

'I'll talk to your mother,' Devil said.

Eliza had finally been persuaded to come and live at Waterloo Street. She loathed the house and its cramped rooms and the rowdy neighbours, but Devil wooed her and in the end she wearily gave way. She made no effort to arrange the smaller pieces of their old furniture that would fit through the meanly proportioned doors, and she spent a good deal of her time sitting in the little front room she dismissively referred to as the parlour. Surprisingly, Cornelius took to the place far better than the rest of them and he settled in like a snail drawing into its shell. He occupied the bedroom under the eaves, building a set of shelves for his architecture books and boxes of butterflies. At the back of the house was a very long, thin strip of garden and although the ground was more soot and brickdust than soil he began patiently to cultivate it. A man and a cart arrived with a huge mound of rotted horse manure and Cornelius dug it in and planted vegetables. Eliza watched him through the back kitchen window. She missed her old garden with its elegant pale blooms and arches of greenery.

Arthur had returned with his regiment from France, and was now stationed at regimental headquarters in Surrey, although there were rumours of imminent deployment to Palestine. He didn't need to make his home at Waterloo Street, but even so the house was much too small. As Cornelius was not likely to move out Nancy decided that she should be the one to go.

'Move in here with me,' Lion murmured as he undid the buttons of her blouse in the attic above Shepherd's Market. Over his shoulder she regarded the detritus of Lion's haphazard life and the views from the smeared windows that consisted mainly of pigeons perched on sloping roofs.

'We aren't married.'

A merry smile lit his face as he kissed her.

'Are we to be governed by such bourgeois pre-war constraints, my darling? Is all the discussion with Jinny and the others about equality and women's freedom mere talk?'

'No. I do believe we should be equal,' Nancy said.

'Good. So, I love you and you love me. You *do* love me, don't you?'

'Yes,' she answered, because she did. She liked him too, and there was no point in speculating on what might have been with another man.

Yet, and yet.

This would have been the moment for Lion to ask her to marry him. It was disconcerting to have to acknowledge that it was secretly what she hoped for. Perhaps the carefree version of herself she presented to Jinny and Ann and their friends was just that, a version.

It was confusing.

Lion only smiled again. 'Well then, what's the problem?'

She tapped his lips with the tip of her finger, echoing his lightness.

'I wouldn't be an independent woman, would I, if I moved in with you?'

She found herself a tiny place to rent, just one-and-a-half rooms with a windowless cave of a shared bathroom, near the vegetable market in Covent Garden. It was noisy at all hours but there was a side view of the Actors' Church of St Paul's, and she loved it from the very beginning. To be alone in her home seemed the greatest of all luxuries. She splashed white paint over the dark Victorian wallpaper and pinned a cheap print of Dürer's *Adam and Eve* above the bed.

Eliza and Devil didn't try to stand in her way. She would still be contributing money to the Waterloo Street household – she had insisted on that – and the balance between parents and daughter had subtly shifted as a result. She was allowed her freedom, within reason. Eliza was interested to hear about the new place, although when Nancy pressed her to come and see it she only smiled vaguely and said, 'Covent Garden? I think long ago Jakey Jones had a room there, right beside the market. Sylvia Aynscoe and I went to visit. In those days he was such a starved little waif and now look at him, on stage at the Haymarket.' She lifted a hand in acknowledgement of Jakey's rise in the world and gave a shiver of a laugh. 'I remember the stink of rotten tomatoes and squashed plums. In a week or two, yes, I'll come and see you there. I'd like that.'

Eliza liked to talk about how Nancy was following in her footsteps. When she was a girl she had left her father's house, and the stepmother she disliked, to live for a little while with Faith and Matthew. After Edwin was born she moved to a room in a ladies' boarding house in Bayswater, financing herself with a small legacy from her mother and her infamous job as an artists' model. Sylvia Aynscoe was her upstairs neighbour and Eliza persuaded her to leave her job in a dressmaker's atelier to become the wardrobe mistress at the Palmyra.

'When I left that house it was to get married to your father. When is that boy of yours ever going to propose?'

Eliza approved of Lion. He was an old Etonian and he had a respectable job, even though it was in a dubious trade like advertising. She had found out that one day he would inherit Stadling. She continued to insist that Nancy must do well for herself; if it was not to be as a personal assistant to a businessman then a good marriage was preferable to continuing in her present peculiar occupation.

Nancy said, 'I am not expecting him to propose, Ma. Why don't you tell me the story about the beginning of the Palmyra?'

When she was in one of her euphoric moods Eliza loved to reminisce about the old days. She laughed and sparkled and Nancy could see the lovely girl she had once been.

They were all in love with her, Faith had said.

Lion had plunged into the depths of the party but Nancy still lingered in the doorway. She felt tired and out of sorts, and not in the least like dancing. She and Lion had quarrelled earlier, although they had made it up under the Dürer engraving before they came out. The day before, a mother who had lost her only son in France had come to a sitting and almost as soon as Nancy closed her eyes the boy was there. He was stark pale, seemingly unhurt, posed with his cap under his arm against a background of bare fields as if for a photograph.

Through colourless lips he murmured, 'Mum, I am sorry you have to be without me. I broke my promise, didn't I?'

The woman wept when she relayed the words.

'He wrote in his last letter that he would be coming home to take care of me. Tell him I understand. Tell him I love him.'

A whole day later Nancy was still shaken and listless from the after-effects of the Uncanny.

Lion was irritated.

'Why do all your insights have to be concerned with death and decay, Nance? Why can't you tell someone that Grandpa wants them to know there's a thousand gold sovereigns buried in the back garden and you are going to draw them a map of where to start digging?'

'I suppose it is the time we are living in. So many boys died.'

'Do you think I don't know that?'

It was rare for Lion to allude to the war.

Humbly she said, 'No. I'm sorry for being rotten company sometimes. I'd adore it if there were gold sovereigns but I can only see what I can see. Maybe it won't always be like this.'

She meant that as time passed the memories might soften into history and the losses become easier to bear for those who were left behind.

Lion sighed.

'Poor old Nancy.'

She said carefully, 'No, there's nothing to complain about.'

Lion was looking over his shoulder to see why she hadn't followed him into the thick of the crowd. Instead of leaving her to her own devices he threaded his way back through the jigging bodies and took her arm.

He pleaded, 'Nancy, we're at a party. I like this tune. Have a drink and a dance with me and then I promise we'll go home, eh?'

The room's heat prickled in her hair. They were doing a new dance called the Bon Bonbon, which involved sticking out the bottom and shaking the hips. It was ridiculous but everyone loved it.

A hand shot out from the fused mass of people and clamped her wrist.

'I say, aren't you Zenobia Wix?'

The woman's lips were painted purple and the thick kohl rimming her eyes emphasised their blackness.

'I hear you are the most marvellous spirit voice. I really have to come to you right away. Tomorrow if possible. But must I do it through that terrible Feather person?'

'At present, yes. Perhaps soon I'll be at a new venue. The Palmyra theatre.'

'Darling, really?'

The black eyebrows shot up. The woman, whoever she was, wanted an immediate private hearing.

At that moment Nancy felt another person's gaze locked on her. It was magnetic, almost burning on her skin, and it dragged her attention away from the insistent woman.

She turned her head. And met Gil Maitland's eyes.

He was standing motionless, less than a yard away. He must have heard everything because he repeated with the slightest of smiles, 'Zenobia Wix?'

The room was stilled. Nancy's lips parted but she couldn't speak. Blood pounded in her throat, and the breath locked in her chest as astonishment followed by hope and longing crashed though her. Every instinct told her to reach out and seize this man's hands and then run with him, as fast as they could, away from the din and the people and all the constraints of her life. But her legs had turned to jelly, and she stood transfixed.

'Excuse us,' Lion said.

He removed Nancy from the woman's grasp, circled her waist with a proprietorial arm and steered her away. Nancy sensed Gil's eyes on her shoulder blades, the back of her head, on the bare nape of her neck.

'Wait . . .' she stammered.

'What for? You needed rescuing,' Lion laughed.

When she was able to look back again, Gil had gone. The crowd had swallowed him up and it was as if he had never been there at all.

Was he real or had she summoned him from her subconscious? Nancy felt giddy with shock and disappointment. In desperation she scanned the room but there was no sign of him.

'Look who I've found,' Lion crowed.

She spun round, and saw Lizzie.

Her cousin was Bonbon-ing with a cigarette holder tilted between her crimson lips. She did sometimes pop up where the various segments of London nightlife intersected, accompanied by her latest beau who was a racing driver called Raymond Kane. He held the record for the fastest lap of the Brooklands racetrack. Lizzie seemed no more taken with him than any of his predecessors. Her main interest was still in building up her business and making herself rich.

'Showing the world what's what' was how she put it nowadays. Nancy and Lion agreed that by the world she meant men. Her absconding husband must have hurt her more than she would admit to any of them.

Lizzie flung her arms around her cousin and blew a kiss to Lion.

She yelled into Nancy's ear, 'Have you seen who's here?'

Yes. In the entire crowd there was only one person, the only one she wanted to see.

Nancy stared in the direction of the brandished cigarette holder, to the back of a man's head. The fair hair was shaved to the nape with military precision.

'Arthur?'

It was weeks since she had seen him. He very rarely came to Waterloo Street. The army gave him far too little time off, he claimed. Arthur was commanding some special training units bound for the Middle East and he would not enlarge on what he did, but the family understood that it was something to do with military camouflage against the latest threat of attack from the air. Devil proudly nodded.

'Of course. The craft is in his blood. Disguise, distraction, misdirection, remember?'

Lizzie beamed at Nancy and Lion. 'This shindig is turning into a family gathering. D'you think my ma and pa will be the next to show up?'

Raymond loomed beside her.

'Hullo there, Nancy. Do tell your cousin to pay some attention to me, won't you?'

'Say something interesting, and I might,' Lizzie retorted.

'Come and meet my brother,' Nancy said to Lion. They didn't mingle with each other's families, and he hadn't yet met either of the Wix brothers. But the evening had already spiralled so far beyond her grasp that she didn't care about any of the social import.

Lion raised an eyebrow. 'Really? From the sound of him I didn't think this would be Cornelius's sort of show. Will he teach me to Bonbon?'

'Not Cornelius. I mean Arthur.'

When they reached him, they were astonished to see that Arthur now had a girl in his arms. He was the handsomest person in the room, as evidenced by several of the most notorious old predators of both sexes who hovered nearby and shot hostile glances at each other. Arthur and the girl hastily separated. She was very young and slender, with a cloud of soft hair and the small chin and round eyes of some shy woodland creature.

Arthur reddened.

'Nancy?' He turned to his companion. 'You didn't tell me my cousin *and* my sister would be here.'

The girl scanned the crowd. 'How could I have known? I only came because Brian insisted. I hardly recognise another soul. Won't you introduce me?'

She was wearing a jersey dress and a single strand of pearls, obviously judging the party to be the bohemian sort one didn't dress for. This must be Isabella Bolton. Arthur hadn't mentioned her for months and Nancy had quietly assumed that peacetime had changed his feelings, or hers, along with so much else. Clearly she had been wrong – it was obvious they were together.

Arthur made the introductions. Another young man stepped forward and shook hands with them. This was Harry Bolton, Bella's brother and Arthur's old school friend with whom he had been through the war. Harry was dark and sturdy, with an athlete's muscular poise. His frank smile made Nancy like him at once.

Arthur told Lion that he was glad to meet him because Nancy had so often spoken of him. She had also mentioned the day of the Eton–Harrow match, he said.

'Despair,' Arthur added and Lion grinned back.

'Rotten luck for you.'

Lion pondered, 'Isabella Bolton, eh? Didn't I go to Miss

Wicklow's dancing classes with your big sister? I probably trampled on her patent-leather shoes.'

He mimed two steps of a clumsy waltz.

'Probably. I went to Miss Wicklow's too. It was hellish, wasn't it? Maudie's an old married creature now and has hatched a proper brood.'

'I got chucked out of Miss Wicklow's after one lesson,' Harry said. 'Never did learn to dance.'

Further conversation wasn't easy. The floor vibrated with the noise and there was a loud crash of breaking glass followed by some shrieking.

Arthur put a finger to his stiff collar. A bead of sweat shone at his hairline.

'God, this is a terrible racket. Have you two had supper? There's a little place round the corner that's not too bad. Bella likes it anyway and Harry'll come along too, if it's not just me and his sister. Won't you, old boy?'

'You make me sound a perfect clod,' Harry complained.

Lion was always glad of an opportunity to eat. They crunched awkwardly over shards of glass on the way to the door. Lizzie was nowhere to be seen but the black-eyebrowed woman darted at Nancy.

She shrieked, 'Zenobia Wix! You can't leave, I have to talk to you. Somewhere quiet.'

Nancy had no wish to engage with her. Backing away from the woman and holding up her hands like a shield, she scanned the room one last time. Gil wasn't there.

'Are you all right?' Arthur murmured in her ear. Lion was deep in laughing talk with the Boltons.

'Yes,' she managed to answer. They escaped from the party.

The restaurant was tiny, with red-shaded lamps on the tables and ambitious murals of mountain scenery. The tablecloths weren't too clean but the proprietor flicked a napkin over the best one and gave them a warm welcome. His accent was a thicker, heavier version of Dr Vassilis's.

'Ladies, what is your pleasure? Come, have a cocktail. I make for you myself.'

Bella wasn't too girlish to order gin. The drinks came quickly and the food soon followed. It was unusual in that it consisted mainly of highly spiced minced meat wrapped in stewed leaves and served with bowls of rice and olives. Lion ate eagerly, licking his fingers and nodding approval.

'Decent little joint.'

'Bella and I come here when I'm broke. Which is more often than not,' Arthur sighed.

Bella couldn't be as ethereal as she looked, Nancy decided. And as if she had spoken out loud, the girl pushed aside the dinner she had barely touched and leaned across the table to confide.

'I can't tell you how bucked I am we've met at last. Arthur is so secretive about his family, I'd more or less given up on ever seeing any of you in the flesh. Unless I bought a ticket to the music hall or turned up to a seance, perhaps.'

There was a silence. Laughing uncertainly Bella put her head on one side and Nancy became aware that she had probably had quite a lot to drink.

'I mean, I wondered if there was something wrong. A terrible family secret or something of that sort, you know?'

'Bella.' Arthur looked imploringly at her.

Harry put in, 'My sister always leaps in with both feet. You'll have to forgive her, Miss Wix. She means well.'

'Please call me Nancy,' she said vaguely. There were two

refrains running in her head, the talk and laughter at the table, and the sound of Gil Maitland's low voice.

*Zenobia Wix?*

Bella protested, 'Well, what? I mean, Arthur and I have been in love for what feels like centuries, ever since he was away in France and writing me heavenly letters, and I thought when he came home we would announce our engagement like everyone else. But it turns out that there are about a million obstacles. Money, and my parents, and expectations, and all that sort of stupidness. I don't care about any of it. I love Arthur, you know. And that's the only thing that matters, isn't it?'

Arthur put his hand over hers.

'I have to do the caring for both of us, darling. And I will, I promise.'

He said to Nancy and Lion, 'Bella and I met at her debutante dance. Harry said it would be the usual insipid affair of fruit cup and girls who talked about their dearest ponies, and he begged me to keep him company.'

'I was right, wasn't I?' Harry sighed.

'No, old chap, you were quite wrong. As soon as I saw Bella I knew there would never be another girl for me. It was perfectly simple. I was going to marry her.'

Arthur's certainty was touching. Naturally Isabella Bolton would return his feelings. His spectacular physical beauty didn't narrowly define him, as it did many handsome people. He managed to be both kind and good, and he was of Bella's world because he had been to Harrow and Sandhurst and held a commission in a good regiment.

Nancy's thoughts scattered as she found herself staring across the table at Harry. The litter of dishes and glasses between them shimmered with strange prisms of light. Instead of smiling at his sister, Harry's face contorted in a spasm of agony. Nancy heard a hubbub of shouting, and saw his body huddled on a gritty road. She clenched her fists and stared hard at the tablecloth, willing the image to disappear. After a second the Uncanny faded and the ordinary bustle of the restaurant swelled around her. Harry looked the same as before and Nancy was left wondering if she had glimpsed the past or the future. She made herself concentrate on the here and now.

Bella's eyes were glittering with tears. The girl blinked them away.

'Darling, light up a cig for me?'

Arthur took out the gold case that had been his twenty-first birthday present from Devil and Eliza, lit a cigarette and placed it between her lips.

He said, 'We have to wait, you see. Bella's father is a soldier and I intend to be as distinguished as he is some day.'

'General Sir Reginald Bolton,' Lion murmured, because he knew such things.

Arthur said, 'Is it all right to talk about this, Harry?'

His friend nodded through a curl of cigarette smoke.

'Bella will inherit a substantial fortune through her mother, who is an American manufacturing heiress. There are conditions attached to the inheritance involving a suitable marriage and parental consent and so on.'

Lion's mouth humorously curled. 'How quaint.'

'I don't care about the money,' Bella protested.

But you would, Nancy thought, if you didn't have any.

Bella knew nothing about being poor, and Arthur was wise to put off asking her formally until he had established himself. He would throw all his energy into soldiering and he would certainly succeed at it, and the process would remove him even further from his background. By giving him the best of everything Devil and Eliza had cut themselves off from their beloved boy.

'You and Nancy know each other's families, I'm sure?' Bella asked Lion.

He looked surprised. 'I have met Mr and Mrs Wix, yes. Just the one time. The circumstances were a little unusual because it was after the first of Nancy's public sittings and there was a huge clamour to do with a murderous butcher. Apart from that, not at all. This is 1921, my dear. Nancy and I are individuals, a man and a woman in the greatest city in the world, living the way we want to live. We don't care a damn for what has been, or who was second cousin to whom, or about the shackles of inheritance and entails and wills. That's pre-war. Last century. History. I believe in who *I* am, and what I can achieve in my own right. That's right, Nancy, isn't it?'

She gave a non-committal answer, wondering as she often did how Lion combined these radical ideas with his casual attitude to actual work.

Harry Bolton looked sceptical but Bella wanted to be convinced. She said doubtfully, 'You will have Stadling, won't you?'

She knew these things, just as Lion did.

He shrugged. 'Some day. I'll probably have to knock the place down. I can't afford to keep it going on what I earn as a copywriter, can I?'

Nancy and Arthur glanced at each other. It was only possible to dismiss the prospect of coming into a fortune if you were an heiress, and to talk wildly about demolishing a crumbling old house if you were the last descendant of a landed family. Their own position offered a different perspective.

'There you are,' Bella cried triumphantly to Arthur.

Forlornly, Nancy recalled her own speculations about marrying a man with a chauffeur and a Daimler and all the assurance that wealth bestowed.

How pointless, when she had just seen him and he hadn't tried even to speak to her.

Arthur took Bella's left hand and kissed the ringless third finger.

'Trust me,' he said.

Lion was restless.

'Shall we go on somewhere else?'

'Definitely not,' Arthur groaned. 'That party was quite enough for one night. Who was the fellow with Lizzie, by the way?'

'Raymond Kane. He is a racing driver,' Nancy said.

Bella raised her eyebrows. 'Is he? I thought he must be a bookie.'

Arthur signalled for the bill and when it came he paid it, dismissing Harry's ready offer. Lion tried half-heartedly to hand over a pound note but he waved that away too.

On their way out Arthur said privately to Nancy, 'How is Ma?'

'She isn't so good. Will you come and see her?'

'Of course I will. Just as soon as I can.'

'I am so proud of you, Arthur.'

He paused. 'Are you? Really?'

Out in the late-night street clamour Bella kissed Nancy on both cheeks. 'We'll be friends, won't we? Can you arrange for me to be introduced to your mother and father? Arthur came to tea with my aged P's. It was quite sweet – Daddy and he talked about the army for two whole hours.'

Nancy was pleased.

She said, 'I'd like you to come. I'll see what I can arrange. You will have to take us as you find us, you know.'

The girl's eyes innocently widened. 'Of course.'

'Good night, Nancy,' Harry Bolton said, warmly shaking her hand.

Having escorted Nancy home to Covent Garden, Lion followed her inside without waiting for an invitation. There was a huge damp patch on the landing wall and a clump of fungus sprouting from behind the skirting. Lion prodded it with his shoe while Nancy searched for her door key.

'Could we harvest this and sell it in the market, do you think?'

'I might just pick it and have it fried for my breakfast.'

She pushed the door open and Lion fell inside.

'Your breakfast? Don't I get any?'

'Have I asked you to stay the night?'

Lion kicked off one shoe and hopped towards the bed as he tried to pull off the other. He collapsed on the mattress and the springs squealed.

'Oh, please. I am too drunk to go home.'

Nancy was a little drunk too. Lion held out his arms.

She lay down with her chin in the hollow of his shoulder and ran her hand from his hip up over his belly and waist, feeling the slabs of solid flesh under the smoothness of his skin. With the tips of her fingers she traced his wide lips and touched the springy curls. She was safe here. Not excited or enthralled, but safe.

It had been a long, strange and very uncomfortable evening.

Firmly she closed her mind to Gil Maitland. She wouldn't think about him any more, because it hurt her to do so.

'I think Bella is very pretty, don't you?'

Lion answered drowsily, 'Not really. Her big sister is more interesting, if you happen to like those saucer-eyed English-rose types. This one is a little too marsupial for my

242

taste. In any case I care for no one but you, my bad-eyed Madame Blavatsky.'

'Shh. Do you think she and Arthur will make each other happy?'

'What kind of a question is that? I haven't the foggiest idea.'

'I am going to make sure she meets Ma and Pa. She should know them, at least.

A long sigh told her that Lion was asleep.


After months of preparation, Devil opened his new show at the Palmyra.

Nancy went to the first night alone and she was surprised to encounter Jake Jones, also alone. They had met a handful of times since the Whistlehalt party and she had been to see him in every stage role he had taken. Once or twice she had even ventured backstage, where she was affection-ately welcomed by Freddie and by Jake himself. They drank what she learned was Jake's invariable after-show reviver, champagne with the bubbles swizzled out.

'What do you think?' she asked the actor after Devil's show.

For all the popular music and dance routines that show-cased it, Devil's magic employed electrical circuits, mirrors and wires and black velvet drapes, handcuffs and locked boxes. It was Victorian music hall in the age of airships and cinema, Nancy feared.

'Telling the truth? I'm sorry to say it all creaks louder than a fishmonger's cart. As a birthday matinee treat for children and grannies, maybe. But as a fashionable night out in the West End, for men and women who have lived through the past seven years and must face up to the next? Perhaps not.'

'I know,' she sighed. It was painful to realise that her father might be losing his touch.

Jake looked keenly at her. 'The stuff *you* are doing. The spirit voices. *That's* fashionable. Why aren't you onstage here at the Palmyra?'

'It's rather complicated. I have an arrangement with Mr Feather, an informal one, and Pa doesn't think much of the Spiritualists.'

'He likes money at the box office.'

Nancy smiled and Jake took her arm.

He said, 'Come on, let's go backstage and talk to him.'

The stage doorman let them in and they shouldered their way between downcast artistes hurrying in the opposite direction, along the mouse-scented passageways and stairways that Jake evidently knew far better than Nancy did. Devil was in his shirtsleeves, drinking brandy. He glared at Jake.

'So, Mr Jake Jones. As an actor, tell me what went wrong this evening?'

Jake put his hand on her father's shoulder.

'Does it matter what I think?'

Devil regarded him.

'Yes.'

'All right. Are you living in 1921 or 1891?'

Devil stared, and then he grinned.

'1921, I'm sorry to say. My God, Jakey, what wouldn't I give to be the man I was back then.'

'Quite frankly, tonight's show belongs there too.'

'Rubbish. I've got Tanner Bracewell on the piano and music by Sonny Gooder.'

'You could put every negro hoofer in the world on that stage, dress them up in the latest from Paris and have them dance the Bonbon all night in front of every flapper in

London, and what you'd have would still be old-fashioned music hall. People want different things these days, Devil.'

Devil drank brandy and frowned into the glass.

'What should I be putting on my stage?'

Silently, Jake pointed to Nancy.

Devil mused, 'A fat man called Jacko Grady used to do a spirit voices show, do you remember? It was at Haggerston Hall, and Miss Someone-or-Other sat on a chaise longue with an electric circuit under her backside, tapping out the letters engraved on the case of my old watch here, as spied out by her accomplice in the audience.'

He took the watch from his waistcoat pocket and swung it through a lazy arc.

Nancy thought of the initials on Helena Clare's locket.

'You were at the first public sitting I ever did, Pa. I wasn't putting on an act, you know that.'

Devil frowned.

'I don't want to think about ghosts. This theatre is haunted, did you know that? I used to see a boy, a poor creature I knew when I was only a boy myself. He died, but he was *here*, I tell you.'

'When I was young I used to be afraid of seeing. I could never talk to you or Ma about it, or even to Neelie. Lawrence Feather knew without my having said a word. I'm not scared any longer, because I have learned what to do when it comes, and how to use it. Some of that he taught me, and I'm grateful to him.'

'Feather is a charlatan, no better than Jacko Grady.'

'Mr Feather believes in what he does. And I believe in what I do.'

There were infinite shades beyond the solid hues of normality, so diaphanous that she could not define them even for her father.

Grudgingly, Devil admitted, 'There may be some sense in what you say, Zenobia. Do you really want to do this? *Can* you do it?'

Nancy was thinking that the Palmyra was in her bones as much as Devil's. She had always shrunk from it, for its sinister backstage smells and darkness and the gaudy blister of the auditorium that lay on the other side of the footlights, but it seemed now that everything that had happened in her life had been leading her to the empty stage. She shaded her eyes with her hand, as if dazzled by the spotlight.

Jake nodded his approval.

There was a long silence. At last Devil snapped upright. 'Very well. Let's give it a try.'

He could always be decisive when the situation called for it.

Nancy went to speak to Lawrence Feather.

He was enraged. Nancy had never seen him like this before, all the man's unctuousness burned up like oil consumed by a flame. His shoulders uncontrollably twitched in the black coat.

'You have used me,' he spat.

She forced herself to meet his eyes, her old fear of him reawakened and sharpened by guilt.

'I'm so sorry. It's natural that in the end I'd want to work with my father at the family theatre, isn't it?'

'Natural? To betray my faith in you? It is the most unnatural and vindictive act. In my most precious link to Helena it is no less than wickedness.'

Feather continually begged her for a word or a sign from his sister. These days there was a lasciviousness in his grief, and he clung to it as passionately as if it were Helena herself. Nancy had come to hate the mention of her name.

He fixed her with his eyes. 'I have made a fine medium of you. My followers have become yours.'

This was true. Zenobia Wix was now a bigger public draw than Lawrence Feather.

'I am not wicked. My father needs me.'

'Your father.' Feather's voice splintered with contempt. 'A penny-in-the-hat magician, a card sharper, a drunk.'

Nancy stood taller. 'My *father.*'

Gower Street murmured beyond the thick curtains.

Feather tried a different tack. 'Nancy, I beg you. Don't withdraw from our partnership. We have worked so successfully together.'

'I'm truly sorry to make you angry. I did everything I said I would do about the money and learning from you. I will always be grateful for your guidance. Circumstances change, and I must look after my father and the theatre. From now on I will be appearing at the Palmyra.'

'What about Helena?'

'If there is anything, the smallest sign, I will come straight to you. I swear on my mother's life.'

His glance shifted. His dismay was not even about Helena, or not principally. Lawrence Feather was just another showman and he was more interested in his protégée's earning potential.

Knowing as much made it easier for Nancy to break from him.

'I'm sorry,' she repeated.

'And my godson?'

'I'll tell him, of course. I haven't spoken about it yet because I wanted to see you first.'

Feather went to the window. He drew aside the curtain to peer out, as if he expected there to be watchers in the street. When he turned back the anger had indelibly set in his face.

247

'You make a mistake in crossing me,' he said. 'Because I shall retaliate.'

She determined not to flinch.

'I hope we'll meet again when you feel less upset.'

Nancy gathered her gloves and bag and left the muffled room for the last time.

# CHAPTER TWELVE

By the summer of 1922, after more than a year of regular seances at the Palmyra, Nancy had developed a ritual that preceded every performance. When she arrived at the theatre her dresser, Sylvia Aynscoe, made a pot of tea. They drank a cup together and talked about trivial things while Nancy flattened her hair and powdered her face. The dresser helped her into one of the sombre wool or plain crêpe de Chine outfits she had adopted for the stage.

'No shawls, feathers, turbans, painted screens or mumbo-jumbo of any kind,' Devil decreed, and he was right.

The nightly repetition was soothing. At the ten-minute call Sylvia walked with her from the dressing room to the wings. Nancy spoke quietly to the backstage workers, glanced up into the flies to reassure herself that there was nothing untoward up there, checked the positioning of her mirrors and then squeezed Sylvia's hand for luck. The dresser left her and Nancy slipped to the chink in the curtain that gave her a view of the house. The audience would be shuffling and coughing, or sending up puffs of laughter, but a moment always came when silence gathered and spread.

No matter how impervious they believed themselves to be, however cynical they might have been up to that second, every single person from the cheap seats to the front-row *fauteuils* was experiencing a tremor and wondering, '*What if there turns out to be something in it?*'

Nancy knew this, and she used it.

As the silence collected she studied the faces suspended like so many pale moons, picking out the likeliest targets for the night. Women were in the majority because they had lost sons and husbands and brothers, but sometimes there was a nervous-looking young man, or a much older one who didn't know how to live in the world without his wife at his side. People came to the Palmyra to be entertained, but Nancy understood that many of them longed for something more.

Sometimes she was able to give them what they wanted.

This evening she saw the face immediately. The young woman was seated in the second row from the front, in one of the paired armchairs with a little table and a silk shaded lamp between them. She wore a fur that billowed like a cloud under her chin, her painted lips were slightly parted, jewels glinted in her hair. Longing pulsed in her like a second heartbeat. Her husband or her beau, whoever he was, sat in the shadows beside her. Nancy didn't even glance at him.

The silence reached its deepest point. Nancy nodded to the boy who operated the tabs and took her mark at centre stage, where the tight spot would fall on her. A single long note was drawn from the cello in the musicians' pit, and the curtain lifted.

There were some familiar faces dotted further back in the stalls. She had her regulars and she had constructed a series of voices for them. She swept into her practised introduction, choosing the easy targets to begin with and deliberately allowing a ripple of humour to lighten their exchanges. These people were the ones who told her in as many words what they wanted to hear, so she only had to turn it round and repeat it back to them.

Letting her subconscious guide her she tried the name Stella on a useful-looking man in the front of the gallery, but he shook his head. A woman seated behind him bobbed up at once, crying out that it was the name of her sister who had died as a child. One person's blank could be another's seam of gold. The second spot operator smoothly swung the beam on to the woman's face.

Ignoring an inner whisper of *Martinmartinmartinmartin* Nancy said, 'I hear her voice. She's with your mother, the two of them together. There is a beautiful garden.'

Stella's sister looked to be in her late sixties. It wasn't a reckless gamble that her mother would be dead. But she stuttered in amazement, 'My . . . Ma loved her garden. So do I.'

'They want you to think of them when you are with your flowers. That's when they are closest to you.'

The woman pressed a handkerchief to her face and her voice caught on a sob as she tried to answer. Tactfully the lighting man slid the beam away. There was a murmur of appreciation as the alert audience relaxed. The atmosphere was building well.

This was what Nancy had learned from Lawrence Feather – to allow information unspoken as well as spoken to build a picture in her head. While the face was held in the spotlight she tried to see into and beyond it, using her wits to dance ahead of the words. It was Jakey who had coached her to be physically still, to pitch her voice, above all to command the theatre and never be intimidated by it. She

251

was good, and getting steadily better. She had no need for props or any fakery of visible manifestations, other than the mirrors Devil had taught her to position in the wings. In these she could observe her subjects' responses while seeming to look elsewhere. During the Stella exchange, Nancy observed the girl in the second row. She was clutching her sable and drawing it closer about her throat, unaware that she was cold because the piped heating was closed off and one of the front-of-house hands had inched open the street doors. A satisfactory chill crept along the aisles as the lighting boy faded out the golden tones to leave a blueish cast.

Nancy sat down in an upright chair, the only piece of furniture on the stage. The audience craned forwards, understanding that the seance was properly beginning. She met the young woman's eyes.

Seeming to speak only to her, although her words could be heard in every corner of the theatre, she said, 'There is someone here for you. A man. A very young man.'

Nancy could see how the longing surged through her. Her head turned fractionally and a diamond earring flashed in the beams of light.

Nancy whispered, 'I am right, aren't I?'

The girl nodded, anticipation leaping in her face.

'I have the initial R.'

Nancy could have picked any letter of the alphabet. As with 'Stella', her instinct was her only guide.

The woman's fur fell to her shoulders, revealing her white throat. She was wearing a necklace to match her earrings. Her lips moved, framing a name.

'Richard,' Nancy repeated. It was so easy.

The woman gasped.

On another night at a different show Nancy would have

moved smoothly forwards, from question to answer, building up a story. Tonight she found she had to grasp the frame of the chair where the folds of her skirt fell over her knuckles. The faces were staring at her.

The smell had come on her so quickly and it was so strong that she almost flung up her hands to ward it off. It was putrefaction, the old stench from the long-ago morning on the Kentish beach.

She managed to say, 'Richard. He was killed, wasn't he?'

The woman's eyes were enormous pools in her white face.

'Please, tell me, what does he say?'

'He is here,' Nancy repeated. And he was, but not in any way she could describe, not to tie up with a ribbon bow to comfort the bereaved in the way she had done for Stella's sister. By now the Uncanny was all around her. She looked from side to side and the clutter of the wings had vanished. The mirrors were populated with the remnants of men. In a scoop of slippery filth lay a young boy. His rifle rested across his chest and from beneath his twisted body another man's legs protruded. Just legs, with boots and gaiters and knees in crusted khaki. There were no thighs or hips. Beyond the hollow more men, blackened, dragged a gun carriage through the mud.

In his agony the soldier looked straight at her.

'Help me,' he begged. 'Help me.'

Nancy was shivering. The woman in the second row stared and it was as if the two of them were submerged together in the Uncanny. All Nancy could hear was the boom of guns.

She ran her tongue over dry lips.

'He . . . he was with his men. He was very brave. It was quick. He didn't suffer.'

The boy's face loomed out of the mirror's mist. Even on the point of death the resemblance was striking. They were brother and sister.

Nancy lurched to her feet. She had to get offstage for a moment even though it meant running towards the mirrors. The woman jumped up too. 'Wait,' she called.

In a stronger voice Nancy told her, 'It's over. Passchendaele is gone and the war is in the past. You have to look ahead now. Have children,' she added, a little wildly. 'That is how your brother will live on. Do you hear me?'

The soldier was horribly dead now, she could see his body in the mirror.

There were no soothing words or messages of hope from the other side – those she had to supply herself. The spirit voices were a sham and there was only death and decay. She felt sickened by the theatre, and this work, and the Uncanny itself. She stumbled offstage, past the images caught in the glass that shimmered and pulsed as in a migraine. A pair of arms supported her. Sylvia held up a tin basin and she vomited.

'There you are. My poor love.'

Sylvia gave her a damp cloth to wipe her mouth and another to cool her forehead. The stench drifted away and the roar of the guns with it, leaving the disturbed murmurs of the audience. Nancy couldn't stay off for too long in the middle of a show. She sipped some water. The Uncanny was fading.

'Warm up the house,' she told Desmond the stage manager. 'Lights and heat.'

She walked back onstage to a ripple of uncertain applause. The two armchairs in the second row were empty. The rest of the performance was dull, but no one asked for their money back.

Afterwards in the dressing room Sylvia helped her out of her dress and wrapped her in the red Chinese robe that had once belonged to Eliza. Her mother had given it to her, wondering why Nancy would want such a shabby old thing.

There was some privacy backstage these days because Nancy had insisted to Devil that she must have a corner of her own to dress in, and he had grudgingly cleared a space not much bigger than a cupboard. At least the room had a door that could be closed. She and Sylvia had furnished their retreat with a miniature fender placed in front of the gas fire, and a cooking ring. The old piping from the days of gas lighting still ran through the theatre.

Nancy put her feet on the fender and rested her head against the chair cushion. She needed to sit quietly to recover herself.

'How's your tummy, dear?'

'It's settled, thank you.'

'Would you like your drink?'

She had copied Jake's pleasant custom. Nancy was in a position nowadays to drink a glass of champagne if she wanted to. She took the glass.

'What about a nice poached egg?' Sylvia asked.

There was a knock at the door. Desmond would be wanting to know if tomorrow's show might be threatened following Nancy's sickness. The stage manager preferred Devil's music-hall nights, with the acrobats and magicians and dancers who did not act either mystic or artistic, as he put it.

'Tell him I'm fine,' she said hurriedly to Sylvia.

The dresser cracked open the door.

'Miss Wix . . .' Desmond began.

'Thank you. That will do,' a man's voice broke in from behind him.

Every nerve in Nancy's body shrilled. She looked up to

see the woman from the second row, and presumably her shadowy escort.

He was Gil Maitland.

The woman was deathly pale except for two patches of colour high on her cheekbones, yet the pair of them still looked as glossy as a picture in a society magazine. Money gave people that burnished sheen. The woman's diamonds were obviously real.

'It's all right, Sylvia.' To her unexpected guests Nancy managed to say, 'Please come in. Won't you sit down? Perhaps you would like a glass of champagne?'

Without as much as a glance in his direction, she was aware of Gil's attention. She held herself rigid, forcing herself not to meet his eyes.

The only seating other than Nancy's armchair and the stool at the dressing table was a narrow bench with shiny leather padding that had spent long years pushed against the wall in Devil's office. The couple sat down on it, their gleam incongruous as they perched on the narrow slope.

'Miss Zenobia Wix?' the man said. He lingered over the syllables.

Sylvia found two more glasses and dusted them with the corner of her apron.

'Gil,' the woman murmured, touching his arm. Nancy noticed her wedding band and the oversized ruby of her engagement ring.

This must be Mrs Gil Maitland. It was funny that she had imagined herself in the role.

'Yes, darling.' He spoke gently, as if he were soothing a nervous colt. 'Miss Wix, may I introduce my wife, Lady Celia Maitland?'

He neglected to introduce himself. Lady Celia didn't notice the omission.

They shook hands. Nancy still didn't meet his eyes. She was struggling not to betray any sign of recognition, or any quiver of dismay. Gil was turning the stem of the glass in his fingers as he examined the clutter of brushes and jars of cold cream, the glass propped against the wall, and the wilting bouquet sent a few days ago by Nancy's stage-door admirer, Alfie Egan.

'How may I help you?' Nancy asked them.

'I want to speak to my brother,' Lady Celia said in a rush. 'I know you can help me.'

Nancy had seen such pitiful eagerness before. Lawrence Feather had been only the first of many.

'It's not quite so straightforward. It's not like using the telephone. I'm sorry . . .'

'I didn't imagine it was. But you saw him. You weren't putting on a show, I know that. You *saw*. I want to know more. Everything. I need to, Miss Wix. You'll help me, won't you? Please?'

There was a troubling intensity in her manner. In the sickening depths of the Uncanny Nancy had the sense that the woman had followed her. Somehow Lady Celia had distinguished the real thing from the performance. Perhaps untapped grief thinned her skin and heightened her perceptions beyond normal limits.

'I don't think I can.'

Her husband crossed his legs. 'Why is that? Can Miss Zenobia Wix's Spirit Voices be a mere act?'

Nancy disliked the show's vulgar title too, but Devil insisted on it. She felt the prickle of challenge, and the current of his interest in her.

Sylvia indicated her disapproval of all this by clattering the plates and frying pan.

'Gilbert.'

'I'm sorry, Celia. Please, Miss Wix.'

'Obviously, Mr Maitland, my performance is an act. It would be pointless to argue otherwise, since we both know that you paid ten-and-sixpence for the best seats from which to watch it. But what I do in the course of the performance is attempt to channel what I hear and see on the other side. That is my talent. Or my gift, if you like.'

Gilbert Maitland slid out a gold cigarette case and offered it. Nancy shook her head.

'My wife believes that you can help her to contact her late brother. Richard was only nineteen when he was killed.'

Nancy turned to his wife.

'Lady Celia . . .'

'Please, won't you just call me Celia?'

She was two or three years older than Nancy. She wanted to make friends, perhaps believing that this was her quickest route to Richard.

'I'm trying to explain. It's not like asking the operator to put you through to Kensington. Sometimes I can hear clearly, at other times there is just noise. Or silence.'

Essentially, that was the truth. Gilbert Maitland watched Nancy. She felt it keenly.

Celia said breathlessly, 'I understand. I don't ask for any guarantees. But perhaps you might come to our house, for a private sitting? If I could have just a single word, a sign, the smallest thing? After that I believe I could bear what seems so hard.' She was twisting her beautiful gloves into a rope. 'I love him, *loved* him, more than anything in the world. Until I married Gilbert, that is. When we were children, the two of us, we were allies. Conspirators against a harsh world.' She smiled with her lips pressed together.

Nancy could imagine it. She felt sorry for her. She felt sorry for Faith and Lizzie too, and all the other women whose men had died.

The high colour in Celia's cheeks intensified to two circles of dark red.

'I'd pay you well, of course. I'm sorry to mention it if it's not a matter of money.'

'It's not, really.'

Nancy was thinking that it would take a lot more money than she was ever likely to earn to buy just one of the diamonds from Celia's necklace. The woman's accent and her manner brought Bella Bolton into her mind, although they were hardly similar. It was as if Celia somehow provided a photographic negative of Bella's upper-class innocence.

The fire dully glowed. Staring into it, it occurred to Nancy that if Gil Maitland and his wife were here, in her dressing room, it was because he had – at the least – agreed to come. Perhaps he had even suggested it. Did he want to see her, after the brief glimpse at the party? After overhearing what the painted woman had said?

It was possible. Yet this woman was his wife. Of course he would be married – how could she have imagined he would not be?

She felt a turmoil of longing and disappointment and self-dislike as she tried to work out what she should do. Almost certainly she should refuse to see either of them again, even professionally. Yet through all the clamour of her thoughts she knew that however hard she might try, she couldn't – physically, mentally, abjectly – turn her back on the opportunity to see Gil again.

As if he read her thoughts, he shifted his position on the uncomfortable seat.

She said to Celia, 'I will give you a private sitting. But you may learn nothing at all. It often happens.'

Celia sat up.

'Thank you, thank you.'

As soon as she had extracted a promise the ugly flush faded and she grew listless. They discussed money, with Nancy naming a healthy sum and Celia agreeing to it without a murmur. She seemed exhausted now.

Sylvia said, 'Your egg is almost ready.' She speared a slice of bread with the prongs of a toasting fork and held it to the fire.

The Maitlands politely stood up and Celia passed across an engraved card. The two women agreed on a date and a time for the seance.

'Thank you, Miss Wix,' Gil bowed.

The dresser firmly closed the door.

'Well, really,' Sylvia exclaimed.

'I liked them. They're used to getting their own way, but people of that sort always are, aren't they?' She tried to speak normally.

Even Lion was the same, for all his egalitarian notions.

Nancy finished her glass of champagne and meekly ate the egg on toast. Her mother's old friend was aged and her tiny frame was bent and as brittle as a dried leaf, but at the theatre she had taken on a maternal role. Nancy had long ago learned not to look for mothering, but she let the faithful dresser fuss over her. Sylvia was washing up the pan and plate and Nancy was changing out of the scarlet wrap when they heard a footstep creaking on the old boards outside.

Devil's head poked round the door.

'Pa? What are you doing here?'

'Eh? This is my theatre, isn't it? Evening, Sylvia.'

Desmond was Devil's lieutenant and informer nowadays. He would certainly have let Devil know that Nancy had been ill during the performance.

'I thought I would come down and motor you home, Nancy. How was the show?'

'It went all right. It wasn't the easiest of nights. But a couple came back afterwards, wanting a private sitting.'

'Ha.'

Devil had come to terms with his daughter's success. He much preferred Nancy's act to be just that, and to take place only on the stage under the lights where it could be contained. He understood that tonight's performance must have called up other voices, and as always he shied away from acknowledging anything further.

'They'll be paying, will they?'

'Yes, they will. Sylvia, don't wait for us, unless you'd like a lift?'

Sylvia put on her coat, tying a scarf over her white hair before placing her hat on top. Nancy went to kiss her but Sylvia brushed her off. She never liked to be the focus of attention, especially when Devil was present.

'I'd rather go on the underground, just as usual. You are a good girl,' she murmured.

After she had gone Devil looked at the champagne glasses, two empty and the third full. Lady Celia had not touched hers. He knocked it back before picking up her card from the arm of the chair. Then he pursed his lips in a silent whistle.

'I know,' Nancy smiled.

Parked in the alley with its nose towards the river, Devil's latest car was another Ford, a little less crumpled and beaten than the wartime messenger vehicle. He handed Nancy to the passenger seat and swung the starting handle.

As they chugged eastwards along the Strand Devil said, 'You should have seen what was outside the front tonight. A brand new three-and-a-half-litre Bentley, no less, with the Flying B shining on the front. Cream bodywork, with dark red outlining. Perhaps a little flashy, but still gorgeous. There was no chauffeur to be seen, just a couple of men who looked as if they'd been paid to mind it for an hour. So the lucky fellow must have been driving it himself. Wait until I tell old Gibb about it.'

'How do you know the Bentley owner was a man?'

Devil looked shocked for a moment, but then he obligingly chuckled.

'Where do you get these notions, my girl? Do they all come from Jinny Main?'

'Not all of them.'

The house in Bruton Street, Mayfair, was five storeys tall. The facade was an intimidating expanse of white-painted lintels and glittering windows, with a fanlight arching over an immense front door set with polished brasswork. Nancy thought how much Cornelius would like to make an architectural drawing of this fine terrace, only to remember that Cornelius hadn't done any drawing for years. She climbed six immaculate steps, past a pair of lead lions couchant that guarded the area railings, and rang the bell.

The door was opened immediately by a wax-faced man wearing a white tie and a short black coat with silver buttons. He was the first footman she had ever encountered in a private house.

'Good morning, miss. Lady Celia is expecting you.'

There were silver trays for cards, a floor waxed to the point of hazard, and a tiered chandelier suspended over the curve of a grand stairway. The portraits lining the walls were clearly ancestors. They must be hers, she thought. They didn't look as if they had anything to do with cotton mills.

Celia Maitland jumped up as soon as she was shown into the room. She rushed forward to shake hands and Nancy felt how thin and cold the other woman's were.

'I'm so glad you have come. Will this room suit you? I mean, it might be too small. Or too big, I don't know.' Her voice tailed off.

This would be Celia's private sitting room, Nancy supposed. It was pretty and feminine with silk-covered walls and upholstery in pale grey and rose pink.

'It's perfect.'

'I have lowered the blinds a little. But we could have them raised, if you prefer?'

She answered that the light was just right, and refused the offers of tea or a cocktail. They sat down together.

'Well, then.' Celia chewed the corner of her lip. 'Shall we begin?'

Nancy said gently, 'Yes, if you are ready. Won't you tell me about Richard?'

Celia's eyes slid at once to a silver-framed studio portrait of the two of them angled on the table beside her.

They had no other siblings and their childhood had been lonely, she said. Their parents seldom appeared and the nanny they shared had been unkind. Nancy could imagine the two forlorn little creatures set apart by privilege in a vast, echoing old house. After her father's death, Celia explained, the title and estate would now pass to a cousin.

'If I had been a boy . . .' she said.

Her smile was so weak it was more like a shiver. Nancy suppressed what she had seen in the Uncanny and concentrated on the two young faces in the photograph.

Celia went on, 'I am quite useless, aren't I? You said at

the seance I should have a child. My husband is a very kind man and he is patient with me, but that no longer seems likely to happen.'

'There is time.'

'Yes. Gilbert sends his regards, by the way. He has some business to see to today.'

'Of course.'

Disappointment stretched stubborn black wings inside her.

Nancy let stillness gather around them as they listened to the tiny ticking of the Sèvres clock on the mantel. There were avenues she could have gone down, gentle clichés and generalised assurances she could have offered, but she did not. None of the medium's repertoire of devices seemed appropriate here. The walls of the room pressed inwards as they waited. At last Celia raised her head.

'You said it wasn't like making a telephone call.'

'No.'

The girl's damp lashes were faint crescents against the papery skin. Her whisper was almost inaudible.

'I was so feeble when he died. I should have been brave instead, for my mother and father's sake.'

Nancy didn't ask whether her mother and father had been able to look after her when she needed them. She assumed not.

'You know, I must have been quite, quite mad for a while. I tried to kill myself but I couldn't manage even that. There were all kinds of doctors and treatments. I think poor Gilbert married me to keep me alive. We had only been engaged for a few weeks before the news about Richard came.'

'I'm sure that's not true.'

'Well. It doesn't matter. Thank you, Nancy. Will you come again? I would like it so much if you would.'

Nancy shook her head. She regretted the misplaced longing that had impelled her to come here. It had been wrong of her and she felt ashamed.

'No. I don't think I can help you.'

'Oh, no! I have put you off. This is too terrible. I am not always such a miserable specimen, you know. Sometimes I can be the most tremendous fun, honestly.'

Celia became agitated. She fidgeted on her sofa and then jumped up, her eyes flicking restlessly across the room. Nancy felt a subconscious twitch of alarm, rooted in some association that she couldn't quite place.

Celia pounced on a thick creamy envelope that lay among the new novels and glossy magazines on her writing desk.

'Please do take this. It's the least thing, when you have been so kind to come here and listen to me talking nonsense.'

Nancy drew back.

'I really can't take your money. I don't have the right to tell you what to do or think, but I'm not surprised you are suffering. You have been through a terrible time. I don't think reaching out to your brother through someone like me, a stage entertainer, will heal anything. Couldn't you forgive yourself instead for a tragedy that wasn't your fault, and let yourself begin to recover?'

She expressed herself clumsily, but it was what she felt.

Celia sank down on to the sofa.

'Dear God. Recover? I don't know. I wish I could.'

She covered her face with her hands and began to sob. Appalled, Nancy hovered beside her.

'I am so sorry to have upset you. Is there someone I can call?' she whispered.

The girl fended her off. 'No. Thank you for your kindness. Please leave me alone now.'

There was nothing she could do. Nancy found her way to the head of the stairs and looked down at the footman standing with folded hands in the hallway.

'I'm sorry, miss. I didn't hear her ladyship's bell.'

'I found my own way, thank you.'

It was a relief to step out into the street where cabs rattled past and news vendors were crying the late edition. The looming house reminded her of the wooden display boxes for Cornelius's butterflies, with Celia the single fragile butterfly in a huge, polished case.

Nancy's tactic for subduing her feelings was to absorb herself in work and in the unending problems of Waterloo Street. She trod numbly through the days until another ordinary night at the Palmyra and a show for an unremarkable audience. She came offstage afterwards and sat in Eliza's red wrap with her feet up on the fender. Sylvia was humming as she tidied the room and the footsteps of stage-hands sounded along the passageways.

There was a knock at the door. Gilbert Maitland stood framed by the dim corridor light.

'May I come in? Your stage-door manager sent me up.'

The dresser stepped aside. Nancy gasped and instinctively hid her bare feet under the folds of silk.

Gil refused a drink. He said, 'Thank you for seeing Celia last week. She said you gave her a great deal to think about.'

'I'm afraid I didn't help.'

He glanced in Sylvia's direction. The dresser had turned aside. He said formally to Nancy, 'I wondered if I might take you out to supper? If you are not already committed, that is? There is something I would like to discuss with you.'

The unspoken silently clamoured between them.

'I'm not committed.'

*No,* she warned herself. *Yes,* every fibre of her being insisted.

Gilbert said, 'Then I'll wait for you outside in my car. Please don't hurry.'

As soon as he was gone Sylvia protested, 'He can't just walk in here, cool as a spring evening. What does he want?'

'I have no idea.' Seeing her expression Nancy tried to laugh. 'There's nothing to worry about, Sylvia. I can look after myself.'

Sylvia pursed her lips. 'What about your young man?'

Lion. In the rush of the moment Nancy had all but forgotten him. She flushed.

'It's nothing like that, Sylvia. For goodness' sake. It will be some sort of business proposal, I expect.'

Nancy drew on her stockings, careful with the seams, and clipped the suspenders. Sylvia's expression conveyed dismay as well as the suggestion that Nancy was not being quite candid. But Nancy only shook her head to loosen her hair, leaned towards the mirror to redden her lips and finally slid her arms into the sleeves of the coat Sylvia held for her.

She said lightly, as if nothing was happening, 'Goodnight. You will lock up, won't you, if Desmond and the others have gone home?'

If she stayed late and Devil was not there Nancy liked to secure the theatre herself. She would walk back to the stage and take a moment to look into the confection of green and gold and thick velvet. She was her parents' child after all, the daughter of the house.

'I can slide a few bolts and lock the doors, yes,' the dresser said.

Sylvia was rarely disapproving. Nancy didn't stay to

placate her. The only car parked at the theatre front was a cream-and-red Bentley with the winged B tipping the bonnet. Gilbert Maitland stepped down and opened the passenger door for her.

Nancy laughed. 'My father saw this car the other evening. He described it to me rather as if he'd seen a film star. What happened to the Daimler?'

'Higgs insisted on the new Bentley. I do like the sound of your father. Are you comfortable?'

She was embraced by an acre of cream leather upholstery.

'Quite comfortable, thank you.'

They drove westwards along the Strand, the evening flood of buses and taxicabs seeming to part like the Red Sea ahead of the car's huge headlamps. Nancy stared out at the windows and street signs and raucous West End dazzle as if she had never seen these familiar sights before. She was hardly aware of drawing up in front of the Ritz.

'Do you have any objection to this?' he asked.

Women in silver shimmer and furs and dancing shoes were passing under the arches of the facade. The hotel's name blazed out in electric lights. Gilbert extended his arm to her.

She was in a plain frock and her ordinary coat.

'I'm not dressed for it.'

'Dressed? You needn't give a damn about what you are wearing, now or ever. Clothes are superficial and you are nothing of the kind.'

She would have liked to believe him. She accepted the arm he extended, held up her head, and the doorman bowed as they passed into the scented warmth of the hotel.

'Good evening, Mr Maitland. Good evening, madam.'

They were met by banks of flowers, music, and crowds of people in evening clothes. They processed through the throng to the doors of the dining room where the head waiter led them to a table. Nancy surveyed the room and all the edges of her prejudice melted. It was absurdly glamorous and it was beautiful. Panels of mirrors reflected the drapes at the windows facing over the darkened park and a dozen chandeliers were linked by swags of bronze. Through an opulent haze of gold and rosy light waiters bore domed dishes, diners talked and laughed over silver and crystal, music played and on the small dance floor dancers swayed in each other's arms.

She breathed, 'My goodness. What a wonderful sight.'

If anyone was to be here, in this room tonight, Nancy was pleased that it happened to be her.

Gil Maitland smiled. Her unaffected delight in the Ritz dining room pleased him.

A glass was placed next to her hand. In this place, it seemed nothing had to be fought for. A wish had only to be half-formed and it was granted.

'Miss Wix. Oh, for God's sake. May I call you Nancy? That's how I have thought of you since we first met, all that time ago. I'm afraid I draw the line at Zenobia.'

*Since we first met? I have thought of you?* The words hammered in her head.

'Zenobia is my stage name. Nancy will do very well.'

'Thank you. I'm Gil. You know that.'

She drank some champagne before looking at him over the rim of the glass.

'Where is Lady Celia tonight?'

He nodded. 'Celia is at home with her family, in Northamptonshire. She has been unwell the last week, so her formidable mother has stepped in where it seems I can't manage.'

'I'm sorry. I hope it wasn't anything to do with our failed

seance. I tried to convince her that most probably nothing would happen. It doesn't always. I could have made up something to satisfy her, I suppose, but I like your wife and I didn't want to embark on a deception.'

Gil didn't answer directly. They were circling each other, Nancy knew that much. He held his sleek head on one side and his light-coloured eyes ran over her face. Beneath his left cheekbone was the indentation, not quite a dimple, flickering in place of a smile. She remembered it very well.

'I would do anything, anything at all, to make Celia feel happier,' he said at length.

Nancy waited. Of course he would. He was her husband.

He went on, still studying her. 'I overheard what the woman said at that dreadful party last year, and I remembered that Celia had spoken about your work. I was quite startled to recognise you as the girl from Fleet Street.'

'If you recognised me, why didn't you speak to me?'

His gaze steadied. 'Did you want me to?'

'Yes.'

'You were with your young man. I felt very old and dull and out of place.'

Even though her throat felt constricted Nancy couldn't help but laugh.

'*You?*'

He sighed. 'Ah, Nancy. We don't know the first thing about each other, do we? Celia wanted to come to your seance at the Palmyra, so I accompanied her. I was interested to see what you might do, and I imagined that the whole business would be easily dismissed. Then that . . . strange event occurred. I admit that it shocked me. It was my idea to come backstage afterwards, thinking there might be a way you could help Celia.' There was a pause before he added, 'I should say, I also wanted very much to see you again.'

'I know.' She spoke so softly that the music almost drowned her words.

Gold-rimmed plates were placed in front of them.

While they ate, Gil wanted to know how she had been transformed from a print-shop worker into a stage medium. In this most worldly of settings it was difficult to explain any of it, but she did her best.

'When I was a young girl I met another medium, a very strange man, who said I had a gift.' She described how that had come about, and what had happened after the war. 'It was very haphazard to begin with. We had family troubles and I needed to earn some money.'

Gil Maitland was remarkably easy to talk to. She had never told anyone so much so quickly, not even Lion or Jinny.

'Where is this person now, this Mr Feather?'

She hesitated. 'I sometimes catch sight of him.'

Once in a while she would look out into her audience and meet his disturbing stare. At other times she would catch a glimpse of him in the street, turning a corner ahead or watching her from a doorway.

She was aware that Feather always kept her in his sights, either as his link to Helena or for other reasons she was even less eager to imagine.

Gil said at last, 'Forgive me, Nancy. I'd assumed these seances were usually faked.'

'That's understandable. I don't mind you saying it. Sometimes – usually, in fact – I *am* a fake.'

'But you did see Richard, didn't you?'

Her eyes were on the tablecloth. 'Yes.'

He prompted gently. 'And?'

'I couldn't describe to Celia what I actually saw.'

'I imagine you sometimes witness painful sights.'

'My boyfriend complains. He wonders why I can't see buried treasure in people's back gardens. I would if I could, honestly.'

'Ah yes, your boyfriend. Will you marry him?'

'No,' she said.

Their plates were removed, the spotless cloth covered with another.

'May I smoke?'

She accepted one. It was oval with a gold tip, densely packed and fragrant, quite unlike any cigarette she had ever smoked. They leaned back in their chairs, openly studying each other.

'How do you explain your gift?' Gil asked.

'I can't. It's possible that time doesn't move in one direction but in two, or twenty, or even a million. Or perhaps it's an illness. A tiny brain seizure, or a *petit mal.*'

He raised an eyebrow, giving the theories proper consideration.

'I think some mathematicians might be interested in your first proposition.'

Nancy watched the dancers stepping with their bodies closely locked. She would have liked very much to dance with Gil Maitland, and she forced herself to recall why he had brought her here.

'How do you think I might help Lady Celia?'

She had the distinct sense that he also had forgotten the reason. He rotated his gold cigarette case on the tablecloth, tapping the long edge with his forefinger.

At last he leaned forward.

'My wife is a morphine addict.'

The music stopped and there was a brief patter of

applause. Couples passed on their way back to their tables in a ripple of chatter and perfume.

There was pain and weariness in his face. There were conjectures she would readily have made about him, if this had been a sitting.

'I am sorry. That must be very difficult.' An uncomfortable association stirred in her, as if she almost recognised someone or something else. She tried, but she couldn't grasp what it was. 'What can I do?'

'Perhaps you could let her talk about Richard, in the way her parents are too buttoned up to allow? I've done my best, but repetition and familiarity have dulled my effectiveness. I am not asking you to invent some golden afterlife for him to inhabit, but a single word might make a difference. It might offer her some hope.'

Nancy both wanted and didn't want to do what he suggested.

She said, 'I would find it difficult to deceive her.'

Involuntarily Gil reached out. Their hands hovered for an instant, separated by a sliver of air that was alive with electricity. Then they touched.

'My dear girl,' he said.

*I wish.* The longing to be Gil's dear girl shot through Nancy like a bolt of lightning. She withdrew her hand and hid it in her lap.

All around them was a busy surge of diners, greeting and kissing and exchanging one table of friends for another.

Gil said, 'I want to talk to you. Shall we get out of this zoo and have a drink somewhere?'

'No.'

She said it quickly, because if she had waited a second longer it would have been impossible to get the word out.

He exhaled, slowly, and then he slipped his cigarette case into his pocket.

'I understand.' The dimple showed, briefly. 'Let me find you a taxi.'

Out in Piccadilly the doorman flagged one down. Gil handed her inside and stood back, one hand raised.

'Until next time, Nancy.'

She didn't echo the words.

As she sat in the speeding taxi, she thought that if she had spent a moment longer with him she would have been physically unable to tear herself away. Leaving him was the hardest thing she had ever done.

# CHAPTER THIRTEEN

At last Arthur gave way to Bella's entreaties and Nancy's persuasion. He invited Bella home to Waterloo Street to meet the rest of his family.

'Is there an engagement?' Eliza cried when Nancy suggested a tea party.

'No, no. It's too soon for that. They are friends, that's all.'

Nancy did her best to reassure him but Cornelius looked unsettled when he first heard about the visit.

'I don't like crowds, I hate loud noises, and talking to strangers makes me anxious. I've already got everything I want under this roof.'

It was true that he seemed happy so long as he could plant vegetables and read his books. The damage he had suffered in France would never be fully repaired, although he didn't seem to be suffering any longer. He moved deliberately through his uneventful days.

'You don't have to do anything you don't want to, Con.'

He tilted his head and peered at her through the thicker lenses he now wore. His fingernails were ingrained with garden dirt.

'Whereas you have to carry the burdens for all of us,' he said sadly.

Nancy was surprised. It wasn't what she felt.

'Actually, I go to parties and drink too many cocktails.'

'Well and good. If that's what you like to do, of course. Personally I would rather pull my own teeth.'

Eliza insisted that she must bake a cake for Bella's visit.

On the day she got up early, not long after Devil had gone out to the theatre, and enveloped her skeletal frame in an apron that had once belonged to Mrs Frost. While she swept the hall and stairs and dusted the dado rails Nancy heard cupboard doors banging in the kitchen. Spoons clattered in the sink. She concentrated on rearranging the mats to hide the worst gaps in the floorboards, determined not to interfere. The parlour was not an inviting place, but she did what she could to make it look homely. When she was straightening the cushion on her mother's chair her fingers encountered something smooth tucked out of sight between the seat and the arm. It was a small brown phial, empty, of the sort that had held Eliza's medicine long ago when she was recovering from influenza. Nancy stared at it, wondering why an empty bottle had found its way from Islington to Waterloo Street. She put it in her skirt pocket.

'Nancy? Where are you?'

Eliza was calling from the kitchen. Nancy saw that her mother hadn't cleared the table before starting her preparations, and the breakfast crusts and Devil's fried-egg plate lay in a jumble of flour bags and smears of butter. Small pancakes of dark yellowish sponge mix had appeared in two baking pans.

Nancy ran her finger inside the mixing bowl and licked up the sweet residue, recalling how she had helped Mrs Frost to make birthday cakes amidst the appetising smells of the Islington kitchen. It had been a place where scoured pans hung from hooks in descending size order and jars of jam and chutney winked on the shelves.

'Into the oven with them,' Eliza cried. 'How long, do you think?'

Nancy tested the heat of the oven door with the flat of her hand. Baking didn't happen much at Waterloo Street although Cornelius always lit the fire as soon as he got up and the oven seemed good and hot now.

'Half an hour?'

Eliza slid the pans into the oven. The second the door clanged shut she whirled to the store cupboard and began to rummage through the packets and boxes.

'We must have icing, of course. White icing with coloured piping, don't you think? I know Cook used to have a piping bag, it must be here somewhere. Pink sugar rosebuds would be pretty and I shall do an inscription in the centre, *Arthur and Isabella.*'

'Ma, I don't think there will be time for that. The cake will have to cool, and icing needs to set . . .'

Eliza ignored her. 'Icing sugar, let me see. Cornflour, no. Tapioca, no. Arrowroot, no . . . why would anyone need such a thing?'

Nancy turned to the sink. It was half-full of washing-up and an inch of grey water with eggshells and tea leaves floating in it. She began methodically to stack the pans on the wooden drainer, glancing out at Cornelius in the garden as she did so. It was a grey day of early winter with damp glimmering on slates and beading the humps of sacking he pegged over the beds to keep the earth warm for early planting. Cornelius was working in his shirtsleeves and braces, sweeping up the last of the dead leaves with slow strokes. He shovelled the resulting pile into a wheelbarrow and trundled it to the compost heap. He was absorbed in his work, bending and stretching his broad hips and meaty arms in a steady rhythm that showed contentment.

The kitchen filled with the scent of baking and Nancy relaxed with her hands in hot soapy water.

'Oh, *hell.*'

Eliza screeched as a bag of icing sugar slipped out of her hands. The bag burst open as it hit the floor and a fat plume of sugar rose into the air. At the same moment the back door flew open and a gust of wind blew the sugar everywhere. It stuck to the layer of greasy dust coating walls and shelves and in seconds the room looked as if it was silvered by a heavy frost. Eliza seized a brush and began to jab at the broken bag and its contents, sending secondary clouds of sugar into the air. Nancy rushed to close the door.

'Ma, stop. Let me do that.'

Eliza faltered and sank down into the old chair next to the range. She gripped the arms and glared but she couldn't hold back the tears.

'I can't do anything,' she sobbed.

Nancy cradled her head, feeling the shock waves of her mother's despair.

'Hush. You can do everything. You always have done. For my whole life, as long as I can remember, you have been the star in the sky. No one else ever came close to you.'

Eliza lifted her ravaged face to meet her daughter's eyes. Icing sugared her grey hair as if she were powdered up to play an ancient crone.

'If that is what you think . . .'

'It is what I *know.*'

'My precious daughter, I don't deserve your admiration or your love. I am a feeble old fraud.'

Nancy made her sit back in the chair. She dried the tears

for her and said, 'I won't listen to any more of this. Let me clear up the worst of the mess before Arthur and his girl arrive.'

Eliza fretted, 'Where *is* your father?'

'I'm sure he'll be here soon.'

Nancy busied herself with a broom and a bucket of warm water until she became aware of smoke and a smell of burning. Eliza must have dozed off but she woke up now and screamed, 'The cake.'

The tops were blackened. Nancy prayed the cake was not completely beyond rescue.

'We've still got half an hour. Look, we can just slice these bits off and hide the rest with decoration.'

So it was that Nancy was still wearing her old skirt sticky with sugar when she opened the front door to Arthur and Bella Bolton.

'Welcome, Bella,' she said.

She led them into the parlour where Eliza waited tensely beside the tiny black-leaded grate. Her hair spiralled in damp grey twists out of a hasty bun and her eyes burned far more brightly than the sluggish fire. In a bold but last-minute attempt at style she had dashed upstairs and come down again wound in a cocoon of knit and crochet shawls and scarves, a swathe of clashing colours that made her look like a pirate-prophet, magnificent but mad. Nancy's eyes slid to Arthur, combed and handsome and upright in his uniform, and from her brother to Bella. Today Bella wore a little belted suit in soft lavender tweed, grey kid shoes, and a tiny hat perched on the side of her head.

Nancy instantly saw the room, and her ailing mother and herself, as if through Bella's wide eyes.

There were darker patches on the walls where someone else's pictures had once hung. The lace curtains at the window were slightly torn. On a low table a tea tray was laid with forget-me-not patterned china. A chipped cake stand displayed a cake piled with strips of luridly green angelica and halved glacé cherries thumbed into a bed of butter icing coloured salmon pink. Bella's gaze fixed on the cake.

Eliza said, 'How do you do? I made it myself, you know. We don't have a cook nowadays, of course.'

'It looks beautiful. How do you do, Mrs Wix?'

Arthur embraced her. 'Ma, dearest Ma.'

He hadn't seen her for a month, and the endearment didn't hide his shock at the sight of her. 'Where is Pa? And Cornelius?'

Bella sat down at one end of the chaise longue.

'What a . . . what a sweet house. How long have you lived here?'

Eliza's arm swept in a jerky arc, almost hitting the teapot. 'Not long. Too long, that is. I don't know where my husband is, I'm afraid, at this moment. He is not a predictable person, except in his unpredictability. My son Cornelius will join us in a moment. Are you out this Season, Miss Bolton? You look very young.'

'Please, won't you call me Bella? I came out absolutely ages ago. I help out now with some of my mother's work, raising funds for war disabled and so on. My sister was a VAD – there was a convalescent unit at our house in the country and I would have loved to do the same but I was still in the schoolroom. Maudie is married now, of course. Two little boys.'

Her chatter ran on, fluent and friendly, easing the atmosphere. Bella was like Arthur and possessed of the same skills. They were well matched. Nancy poured tea and sliced cake. Eliza was doing her best but she floundered.

'My sister Faith lost her two sons.'

A line appeared in Bella's smooth forehead. 'I know. How sad for you all,' she said gently.

Cornelius appeared and silently shook hands. The only place left for him was next to Bella, so he plumped himself down without looking at her, perching with his big earthy fingers splayed on his thighs. He accepted the cup and saucer Nancy gave him and the china rattled, betraying his anxiety, until he placed it on the floor next to his feet.

Arthur asked, 'How is the garden, Con?'

'It's December,' Cornelius answered patiently. 'When are you going to Palestine, Arthur?'

'Delicious cake,' Bella murmured.

The front door slammed. Devil shouted, 'Arthur? Where are you, my boy? Let's have a look at you.'

He burst into the room, grey hair ruffled from the removal of his hat, waistcoat loosened and watch chain glinting, electric with energy, wreathed in smiles.

'Eliza, forgive me. I am overcome with shame. Miss Bolton, delighted to meet you. Theatre people, you know, we are theatre people. There was mayhem in the flies and in the orchestra pit. A stagehand dropped one of the heavy mirrors and smashed it.' He took Bella's hands and kissed the knuckles. 'The worst of accidents in our world. Did you know that? Superstitious nonsense, of course. You look very beautiful, if I am allowed to say such a thing. Arthur, I see you don't spend all your time hiding tanks under haystacks. Excellent.'

'Call me Bella, please.' She smiled at him, a little uncertain but on the brink of being charmed. Devil's children exchanged glances. He had been drinking but was not yet drunk.

'What's this? Tea? Doesn't the occasion call for a cocktail, at the very least?'

'Pa, no. Take this, won't you?'

281

Nancy passed a cup and Devil took up a position on the hearthrug.

'When may I welcome you to the Palmyra, Bella?' He bowed, with more than a touch of the master of ceremonies.

Eliza stood up in a ripple of scarves. A line of bracelets clanked on her forearm and her head was held erect.

'Cocktails. Yes.'

Before they could stop her she had darted from the room, bright as a bird of paradise. A second later there was a sharp scream and the thud of a tumbling body. Cornelius was the first to his feet, overturning his cup and sending tea splashing over Bella's shoes. They found Eliza in a heap at the bottom of the short flight of stairs that led down to the kitchen. She was moaning in agony.

'I forgot. I thought I was in the old house.'

Cornelius bent over her, authoritative while the rest of them hovered in dismay.

'Where are you hurt, Ma? Here? Or here?'

'Ankle.'

Bella stooped beside her and took a handkerchief from her bag. She tipped eau de cologne from a crystal phial and pressed the cloth to Eliza's temples. Nancy was impressed.

'It's not broken,' Cornelius said after a careful examination. 'A nasty sprain, though. I'm going to lift you up. Ready?'

He hoisted Eliza easily in his arms and carried her back to the parlour. Arthur held one hand and Devil supported her while Nancy fetched a bandage and bound up her ankle. White to the lips, her pupils dilated, Eliza looked up at Bella at last.

'What must you think of us?'

'I think Arthur is lucky to have such an affectionate family.'

Arthur rewarded her with a smile so filled with love that Nancy had to look away. Envy of other people's happiness was an unpleasant sensation. She tried to dispel it by re-arranging cups and offering more tea and cake.

The rest of the visit occupied a more conventional hour, in which Arthur and Bella and Nancy did most of the talking. Devil was clearly sobered by anxiety about Eliza. He watched her closely, his expression dark.

At the end Arthur said, 'Bella, I think we should leave Ma to rest her leg now.'

Bella stroked her gloves over her small fingers and buttoned the cuffs.

'May I call and see how you are recovering, Mrs Wix?' she asked.

Eliza was growing agitated, but she nodded.

After the young couple had gone, Devil followed Nancy into the kitchen when she took out the tray.

'What do you think of Miss Bolton?'

'I like her,' Nancy said unhesitatingly.

'Yes,' he agreed. 'So do I.'

There were raised voices in the parlour. When they hurried back they found Eliza struggling to rise from her chair and Cornelius doing his best to restrain her.

'I must be able to walk,' she hissed.

'Ma, you have to keep your foot up to rest the sprain. You won't be able to get about for a few days at the very least, maybe longer.'

'He's right,' Nancy insisted, putting her hands on her mother's shoulders and trying to make her sit down. Eliza writhed out of her grasp, surprising her with the sudden strength in her frail body.

'I must *walk*.'

'No,' Devil said coldly. She turned to face him, catching her lower lip between her teeth like a guilty child.

'I want to see Vassilis, then. Call him for me.'

'No,' he repeated.

'I want to see him.'

'Why can't she?' Nancy asked. 'Vassilis is her doctor, isn't he?'

In the silence that followed her heart lurched.

She didn't want to hear the answer to her question and she couldn't stop it coming. She looked to Cornelius for support but he was staring numbly at the floor. His spilt tea made a dark stain on the mat.

Devil clenched and flexed his fingers, magician's fingers that were beginning to stiffen with arthritis.

'If she can't go out to buy it for herself, she will want Vassilis to give her more of that filthy stuff.'

Nancy looked from one to the other. Patches of colour burned in Eliza's parchment-white face.

'What? What stuff?'

'Your mother is addicted to morphine,' he said.

Nancy's hand crept to the pocket of her skirt, where the empty brown bottle lay like a poison capsule.

Here was the resemblance that had troubled her and which she had not been able to confront.

The feverish agitation, the bright-eyed lassitude – the fugitive sense of familiarity Celia Maitland had stirred in her belonged to her mother.

Eliza was quietly weeping. Between them Cornelius and Devil carried her upstairs to her bed and regardless of her father Nancy sent for Dr Vassilis. That night, after the muttering doctor had taken himself off, they made the decision that Eliza must have professional treatment and nursing care if she was ever to get better.

Lion took the news of what afflicted Eliza without a flicker of surprise, and he had a practical suggestion to make. He knew of a suitable nursing home.

He explained, 'My aunt Frances is a sort of patron. It's all very discreet and quite fascinating, in a way. There have been some rather prominent inmates, I gather.'

'Not *inmates*,' Nancy cried in horror.

The establishment was in a large house close to London, in a slice of countryside between the villages of Mill Hill and Stanmore. It was run by an order of nuns. Devil at first refused even to consider Nancy and Cornelius's pleas to place Eliza there, but in the end she had grown so weak and wretched that he was forced to agree to the plan. A week before Christmas they lifted her into the Ford, propped up the ankle that stubbornly refused to heal, and Devil drove her out of London. She was so ill that she didn't even try to protest.

On the day before Christmas Eve Lion came to see Nancy in her room at Covent Garden. They exchanged their presents before going out to a pub.

'How is your ma?'

'Devil says the doctor and the nuns are satisfied with her. We'll be able to visit her on Christmas Day.'

Lion was going home to his father at Stadling and Nancy would spend the holiday with Devil and Cornelius at Waterloo Street. Arthur had not been granted Christmas leave this year.

The bar was noisy and crowded with festive drinkers. A man stumbled against their table and spilled Nancy's drink.

'Oopsy. I'm sorry, darling. Let me fill you up. What'll it be?'

She thanked him and told him she didn't need another.

He patted her on the shoulder. 'Cheer up, my love, it's Christmas.'

Through the windows she could see lazy flakes of snow

spiralling through shafts of lamplight. Nancy rested her head against Lion's shoulder, feeling a weight of sadness that she didn't know how to dispel.

'D'you want to have dinner? I could get the later train,' he suggested.

Nancy knew she was poor company. 'I'm not very hungry.'

'All right. Walk with me to the station, then?'

Over the chorus of carol singing at Charing Cross he drew the collar of her coat up to her chin and kissed the tip of her nose.

'Happy Christmas, Nancy.'

'Happy Christmas, Lion.'

He had already turned away before she called after him. 'Lion?'

'What is it?'

She didn't know, except that she wished matters could be made right between them. It shouldn't matter that their backgrounds were so different. She didn't care about marriage, did she? She might yearn for children, but there was time for that. She found a smile and deliberately stretched it.

'Next year is going to be happy.'

'I know that.'

He winked and waved, and she set off for Covent Garden with a lighter heart. Her key was in the lock before the prospect of the empty room and an evening alone lost its appeal. On impulse she walked quickly through the powdering of snow towards Shaftesbury Avenue.

Jinny and Ann were at home. As soon as she rang their bell Jinny's head poked out of an upstairs window.

'Come on up.'

They were laughing on either side of a tiny fir tree fixed in a bucket swathed with shiny red paper. Ann wound strands of tinsel through the resiny branches and Jinny held up two baubles.

'Fairy or star for the top?'

'Star,' Nancy said firmly. Jinny fixed it with a twist of wire and stood back to admire the effect.

'Omadood barm,' she murmured. 'Omadood barm, each and every one.'

Ann slipped an arm around her waist. 'Christmas turns you all soppy, doesn't it?'

'Christmas with you is all I've ever wanted.' They were both slightly drunk. They kissed before pulling apart when Jinny saw Nancy's expression.

'There's beer, nice and cold on the windowsill. You'll have some, Nancy, won't you?'

'Yes. Thanks.'

Cramming between them on the sofa in front of the gas fire Nancy kicked off her shoes and settled down. Discovering that she was hungry after all she ate sausages and drank bottled beer as the tree twinkled and the room grew hot. Her sadness floated away. She was lucky to have such friends.

'Jinny's news from work is pretty dismal,' Ann said.

'Why's that?'

Jinny sighed. 'I think my New Year's treat will be the sack. I'm told the print isn't suitable work for women in peacetime. The union's getting ready for a battle at L and R, not that they aren't right and I'd support them every step of the way myself, including coming out on strike, but they don't offer membership to women because that's taking a man's job.'

'What will you do if it does happen?'

'Find a job somewhere else, doing something else.'

Ann insisted that they would be fine, because she could support them both. Nursing was women's work, at least.

'If we had a garden, Annie, I could keep some chickens and grow vegetables. Perhaps we should move to Kent?'

'Please don't do that,' Nancy begged. 'I'm selfish and I don't want you to move away. Couldn't you get an allotment? Or – I know – ask Cornelius if you can share the garden at Waterloo Street? You could start a cooperative. Your runner beans in exchange for his onions.'

They laughed, and divided the last sausage into three bites. It was late when Nancy finally headed home, leaving dark footprints in a thin veil of snow.

On Christmas morning Devil and Cornelius and Nancy drove up to the nursing home. A plain wooden crucifix hung on the wall above Eliza's bed. She lay against white pillows under a white coverlet, her grey hair combed to one side and tied with a red grosgrain ribbon. It was the only spot of colour in the bleached surroundings until Nancy unwrapped Lizzie's gift of a basket of tangerines and purple hothouse grapes. Eliza slowly ate a tangerine, pressing the segments against the roof of her mouth and smiling at each burst of sweetness. The festive scent of citrus peel dispelled the hospital taint of Lysol and waxed linoleum and the clamour of nearby church bells brought Christmas into the room. Devil and Cornelius sat on either side of the bed and held Eliza's hands. She was animated, although she had developed a troubling cough. She described how the Honourable Mrs Templeton, patron of the nursing home, had paid an early Christmas-morning call on each of the patients.

'*So* grand, my dears. She swept in with a retinue of nuns behind her and wished me a Merry Christmas exactly as if she was the Queen on a tour of the unfortunate poor in the East End. She was handing out a little booklet that I expected to be about God, but no – it's called *Women and the Future*.'

'Good,' Nancy smiled, because that was what was expected of her.

'Remind me, what relation is the great lady?'

'She is Lion's late mother's sister.'

'So she will be your aunt by marriage?'

Eliza hitched the sheets in a pretend curtsey and they all laughed.

'Ma, I don't think Lion and I will marry.'

Nancy unpacked the clean linen she had brought and tidied her mother's belongings, and when there was nothing else to occupy her she looked out at a view of grey trees and rimed grass. The window stood open six inches at the top even though the panes were spangled with frost flowers. Fresh air was deemed to be good for Eliza's chest.

The nuns were caring for her with calm attention as the allowance of morphine was steadily reduced. Soon it would be nothing. Sometimes Eliza wept and raged at them, begging and pleading to be given more.

'Jesus Christ is not my Saviour,' she stormed. 'I want my medicine.'

'He is if you will allow Him to be. I will pray with you,' one of the sisters said. Eliza writhed, but there was no mercy.

Cornelius found it hardest of all of them to witness her suffering, but he insisted to Devil and Nancy that this treatment was her best hope of recovery.

At one o'clock precisely a nun brought in a bowl of soup. Her starched coif nodded as she straightened the already smooth bedcovers. She told them the short visiting hour was over and Nancy begged for a few more minutes. She fed her mother the soup, spoonful by spoonful as though Eliza were her child, and afterwards Eliza turned her face up to be kissed.

'My dearest girl,' she said. Exhaling made her cough.

Cornelius stooped over her in turn and then the two of them went out into the corridor to allow their parents a few moments alone together. When Devil rejoined them he was jaunty.

'She'll soon be herself again. I've got to lick the stage show into better shape before she comes in to see it.'

The magic and illusions continued at the Palmyra while Nancy's spirit evenings brought in the money. There was some talk of Jake Jones putting on occasional evenings of poetry and Shakespeare readings.

They drove back to Waterloo Street in the spluttering Ford. Nancy and Cornelius companionably cooked their Christmas dinner while Devil dozed in his old chair beside the range.

The next day came the news that Eliza's cough was much worse and she had developed a high fever. By the day after that she was gravely ill. Eliza was weak and her few reserves were already depleted. She died from double pneumonia in the early hours of New Year's Day, 1923.

All four of them as well as Faith were with her, but Christmas morning was the last time she knew them.


Devil insisted that she be buried in Stanmore churchyard, close to the cottage where he had lived as a small boy and where his father had been the village schoolmaster. With Arthur and Cornelius and Matthew Shaw he shouldered his wife's coffin from the church to the graveside. Nancy stood with her arms linked in Faith's and Lizzie's. The bitter wind dragged at the vicar's surplice beneath the hem of his cloak and stung the mourners' cheeks and noses. Nancy was too numb even to shiver. Faith silently wept and Lizzie stared straight ahead of her.

Eliza's children each scooped a handful of earth and let

it fall on to the coffin lid before Devil dropped in a loop of golden cord with a tarnished tassel from the Palmyra curtain. They turned away to allow the gravediggers to finish their work. Devil had shrunk overnight into a frail old man. He shuffled off in the wrong direction, seeming disorientated by grief.

'Pa, wait for me,' Nancy called. She tried to take his arm but he pressed forward between headstones until they reached a flat tablet with two names carved on it.

*CHARLIE MORRIS*, she read, and beneath it *CARLO BOLDONI*. It was the dwarf's grave. Devil squatted on his haunches and traced the handsome square-cut letters.

'My old friend Jasper Button found the stonemason. We didn't know Carlo's birth date for certain so we left off the – the end date as well.'

'Where is Jasper now?'

Nancy had heard this name mentioned, but she knew nothing about him.

'I don't know. I wish I did. He emigrated to Canada with his wife. I didn't put enough value on my friends, did I? I never considered them. I thought your mother was all I needed.'

She couldn't contradict him. She tried to steer him back to the small group of mourners whose black clothes twitched in the wind like crows' feathers, but he still resisted. Nearby there was a boulder against a dark hedge and he stopped next to it. Here was an iron plaque, bearing a name she was certain had never been spoken in her hearing: *GABRIEL GRIGG, 1870.*

'So, Gabe,' Devil muttered.

'Who was he?'

'A boy. I killed him.'

'No, you didn't. Don't ever say such a thing.'

Shock made her voice shrill and she dragged him away from the memorial. Her brothers were coming towards them, one upright and handsome in uniform and the other slightly shambling, his heavy head on rounded shoulders. Cornelius's collar looked suddenly too large for his neck.

Back at Waterloo Street Jinny Main and Ann Gillespie waited for them. They had made sandwiches and laid out drinks for the mourners. Familiar faces from the Palmyra included Sylvia Aynscoe, tiny as a bird, and two boys from the third generation of the Crabbe family that had been employed by Devil since the beginning of his ownership. Jake Jones was there too. Sylvia was too much in awe of him to catch his eye until he drew up a chair and sat down next to her.

'I remember Jasper and Hannah Button's wedding day,' Jake murmured, although he had not spoken of the long-ago occasion to anyone else.

Sylvia had been among the guests that day too, at Islington, when Devil and Eliza were riding high in their fine new house and all their fortunes were still to be made. Cornelius had been no more than a baby and there had seemed every chance that Eliza would fully recover from his birth.

'You've done so well, Mr Jones,' Sylvia murmured. 'I saw your Hamlet, you know. I had a seat up in the gods. It was a magnificent performance.' She coloured up again.

'I'm Jake, not Mr Jones. Thank you. I wish I'd known. I like to think of you being there. What about you, Sylvia?'

'There have been some hard times at the theatre lately. You know that.'

They looked to Devil on the far side of the room. While there were people in the house to be greeted and entertained he was managing to hold his show together.

'There will always be work for a good theatrical dresser. You would ask me, Sylvia, wouldn't you?'

She said quickly, 'Oh, I couldn't leave the Palmyra. For Eliza's sake now, as much as his and Nancy's.'

'I understand. But don't forget what I said.'

Jake watched Devil touching a shoulder here and shaking a hand there. 'Devil is a lucky man to have such fine and loyal children, but I wonder how he will be without Eliza? He couldn't stay faithful to her for as long as a month yet she was his sun and moon and all the stars besides.'

'Those of us who remember her as she was can understand why.'

'Yes. She was a remarkable woman.'

Cornelius had retreated into the garden. He stood with his back to the door, tears silently running down his face. Jinny went out and gently walked him up and down between the vegetable beds.

Lizzie Shaw and Ann Gillespie collected plates and washed up at the old stone sink, providing fresh pots of tea for those who couldn't drink spirits at Devil's pace. Nancy and Arthur moved between the groups accepting condolences and exchanging memories as Lizzie's son Tommy ranged between the adults, quite used to being the only child present. Faith and Matthew sat in a corner and kept an eye on him. Neither was in good health and Eliza's death had been a terrible blow. Lizzie had recently learned to drive and she had brought them from Bavaria to the funeral and then on to Waterloo Street in her own car. She had also acquired an emerald-green van, employing a uniformed driver to deliver her imported produce from the refrigerated warehouse to expensive greengrocers and smart private addresses in the West End. '*Shaw's Exotics*' was sign-painted in gold letters on each side.

'Palmyra colours,' Eliza had remarked, the only time she saw the vehicle.

'Of course, Aunt Eliza, what else?' Lizzie agreed.

There was a late ring at the doorbell and Nancy went to answer it. She found Bella and Harry Bolton on the doorstep. Both siblings embraced her.

Bella said, 'I didn't think we should come to the church because I only met Mrs Wix that one time. But Harry and I wanted to pay our respects and to tell you and your father and Cornelius how sorry we are for your loss.'

Nancy was touched. She clasped them both by the hand. 'Thank you. Come in.'

Arthur hurried towards them. 'Bella, my darling. And Harry, old chap.'

His pleasure at seeing Bella almost rubbed the grief out of his face. She stood on tiptoe as he kissed her, visibly filled with warmth and concern for him.

'My poor boy,' Bella murmured. Nancy was heartened. With Bella beside him, Arthur would do well.

After he had accepted their condolences Devil took the brother and sister by the arm and led them off.

'Miss Bolton, Mr Bolton, do you know Mr Jones?' Even today, his lips curled with satisfaction at being able to effect this introduction.

Bella gave a gasp. 'Jake Jones? But I saw you in the film *Sweet September*. You were wonderful, really. My mother will be madly jealous to hear I've actually met you in person.'

Nancy knew Jake well enough by now to see him as he really was, but Bella's admiration brought his fame into the room with them as if a further unexpected guest had arrived.

The time came for Devil to speak. He stood up, shaky and bowed, just managing to thank everyone in a few choking words before having to turn aside. He hid his face in his hands, unable when the moment came on this day of all days to deliver the curtain speech. Cornelius shook his head so it was left to Arthur to speak a short tribute. Jake responded for all of them with a toast to Eliza's memory.

Afterwards Nancy found a quiet moment in a corner of the kitchen to take her younger brother aside.

'I'm so glad Bella and Harry are here,' she said.

Harry was deep in conversation with the two Crabbe boys. They were lively in the warmth of his attention.

'I know. Bella makes everything possible for me. She is magnificent, isn't she? And Harry is a good fellow.'

'Arthur, listen to me. Why don't you and Bella just run off and get married? You love each other, you'll make each other happy, so why waste any more time?'

'You know why we can't, Nancy. The bloody inheritance. Parental approval and all that rot.'

She seized his arms. They were as solid as teak.

'What does Harry think? Does he care about your pedigree?'

Bella's brother wasn't imaginative, or unconventional by as much as a hair's breadth, but Nancy instinctively knew that his opinions were to be relied upon.

'Ah, I'm pretty sure Harry would give us his blessing. We went through a lot together and he'd say I'm a decent enough chap even though we're only theatre people.'

'So, does the damned money matter? Couldn't the two of you just live on your army pay, in some ordinary little house, have some children and grow old together? The Boltons should be grateful to have you to father their grandsons anyway. There isn't a man in the world braver or more decent than you.'

His handsome face fell. 'I don't know about that. I do know I'd gladly live in a hut and eat nothing but potatoes if that's what it would take, but I don't want Bella to have to do the same. What is all this, Nancy?'

It was wanting to see her brother happy. Lion wasn't here today – he was still at Stadling because old Mr Stone was unwell. He had written her a thoughtful letter as soon as he heard about Eliza, and she had to acknowledge to herself that she didn't mind all that much about him not being present. Lion didn't have a sombre dimension, at least as far as she was concerned. Their existence together was only concerned with pleasure.

'I met a woman. She came to a seance, you know,' she hastily added to Arthur. 'She is rich, titled, and married to a good man who cares for her.'

What had Gil said at the Ritz?

*I would do anything, anything at all, to make Celia feel happier.*

How would it be, she wondered, to have a man say the same about her? Arthur had Bella, and Jinny had Ann. Devil had loved Eliza in a way their children couldn't even fathom and the loss of her was turning him before their eyes into an old man. If she was not to experience it for herself, it seemed more important than anything in the world that Arthur shouldn't miss the chance of happiness.

'This woman is like Ma. Addicted to morphine.'

Arthur listened, leaning against the sink with his arms folded.

'Poor creature,' he said at the end. 'I am sorry for her, but what's your point?'

The point was about money and captivity, the divide that existed between Arthur and herself and people like the Boltons and the Stones, and the troubling dimensions of privilege, but she didn't try to explain how Celia loomed in her mind as the dark obverse of Bella's light.

Nancy only begged him, 'Please, Arthur. Marry her as soon as you can, won't you? Don't let anything stand in your way, least of all a name and an inheritance.'

It was late in the evening before the house finally emptied.

Jinny and Ann and Lizzie between them had left everything clean and tidy so there was no work to do. The Boltons had gone, and Nancy noted how tenderly Bella said goodbye to Arthur. Jake was the last to leave. Devil was drunk and he stumbled as Arthur took him upstairs and saw him to bed. Arthur would share the attic bedroom with Cornelius, as they had done when they were boys, before returning to his regiment in the morning.

Nancy knew she would not sleep.

As soon as the house lay dark and silent she let herself out into the garden to watch icy stars pricking the patches of sky between black roofs and chimneys. She listened and waited, and after a moment a solid waft of soot-impregnated earth, dense with cats and crumbling city bricks, rose into her mouth and nose.

She breathed in the sour waft, allowing the Uncanny to creep up on her. She did not dare even to formulate the thought, but perhaps Eliza was near. She bent her head, studying the shape of her shoes against the cinder path, and caught a movement out of the corner of her eye. The London reek was strong enough to make her gag, ancient layers of shards and dirt compounded with manure and smoke and rotted vegetable peelings, pressing like a mask against her face.

The soaking girl was standing beside a vegetable bed. Her hair streamed over her shoulders and her eyes were dark holes in her white face. Nancy heard the drips from her clothing pattering on the earth.

'What do you want?'

There was no answer. The apparition never spoke. This time the little thing sadly raised her arm and pointed towards the house. The dripping grew louder.

Nancy looked to see what she was indicating. There was a gust of wind, and the clothes prop supporting the washing line jerked free and fell sideways.

The house burst into a sheet of flames.

Within seconds the kitchen was roaring like a furnace and ravenous tongues of fire flickered out of the attic windows, painting the sky with a lurid crimson wash. Plumes of sparks shot upwards. Nancy began to run, reaching out with her hands until the furious heat singed her hair and the palms of her hands. This was a foreshadowing of something that had not yet come about. She must save whoever was in the heart of the fire.

The soaking girl stood aside as she stumbled past her. Now Nancy could barely move. Her feet seemed to be sucked down by heavy mud, hot over her ankles. She struggled for a forward step and to draw a scorching breath into her lungs.

She must get inside, into the fire. Someone she loved was burning, helpless, burning, burning.

A black figure was outlined against the blaze.

For long seconds it seemed to hang motionless and then it broke free and barrelled towards her, surrounded by a corolla of flame. The figure spun in an agonised circle before it crumpled and collapsed in a flaming heap.

A few steps nearer. Now close enough to smell the charred reek of skin and hair.

It took all her strength, another step. Fall to her knees beside the burning body.

Reach out, trembling fingers.

Not burning any longer, just a dark huddled shape. Damp, solid, not hot at all. A sob caught in Nancy's mouth as she ran her hands over it. It wasn't a human body, not a living thing, merely a bundle of sacks.

She raised her head.

The Uncanny receded, leaving her breathless. The sockets of her eyes were painted with flames, her lungs and throat were choked with soot, but the house wasn't on fire. The dark windows reflected only the night sky, the back door stood open on a slice of deeper blackness.

Slowly, painfully, Nancy got to her feet.

She wasn't sure now if she had glimpsed what had been, or what was still to come.

She was terrified of fire, and she hadn't even known it until this moment.

# CHAPTER FOURTEEN

Late one evening in the icy depths of February, Nancy came back from the theatre to Waterloo Street and found a letter waiting for her. The Palmyra was an engine that had to be kept ticking over; there was no question that either she or her father had been able to take any time off after Eliza's death. She studied the envelope for a moment in the dim light of the hallway before carrying it through to the kitchen.

The rest of the house was already in darkness. Nancy had the electricity of performance jerking in her as well as a headache that clamped her temples. She settled by the warm ashes of the fire, telling herself that she would put it out properly before she went up to bed.

She hadn't yet given up her whitewashed room in Covent Garden, but she would soon have to. Cornelius tried to insist that he and Devil could manage the house on their own but it was clear that they could do no such thing. Devil had never been domestically inclined. Without Eliza at its centre the house grew cold and dismal, the haphazard cooking stopped and Cornelius began to withdraw into silence. If she lived at home again, Nancy thought, she could at least be company for her brother and do her share of the housework. It would mean a big change in the freewheeling way she and Lion coexisted. Devil was broadminded enough not to ask questions if she were sometimes absent overnight, but there would be no question of Lion sleeping at Waterloo Street.

Nancy was still Lion's girl, yet an antiphonal vagueness about their future had developed between them. She thought too often about Gil, although she tried to contain her longing for him.

She raked the embers in the range to stir up a flame before noticing the jam jar on the kitchen table. Nancy smiled to see it. It held an arrangement of the last frosted leaves and shoots from the feverfew bush in the garden, placed next to a scribbled note that simply read '*Omadood, darling*'. As predicted, Jinny had lost her job. As a stopgap she was working as a van driver for Shaw's Exotics, but this only occupied her mornings. She had taking to coming over and spending the empty afternoons with Cornelius in the garden.

Nancy picked off the leaves one by one and placed them on her tongue. She bit and then chewed, letting the rankness flood her mouth. Jinny knew that feverfew calmed her friend's headaches.

She sat down in her father's old chair and used his penknife to slit open the envelope. The card inside it was square and heavy, cream-coloured and embossed with a business address she didn't recognise. The handwriting in black ink was fluent and decisive.

Gil Maitland wrote that he had seen the announcement of her mother's death in *The Times* – once he had recovered himself a little, Devil had insisted on placing it – and he sent his deepest sympathy. He added that he very much hoped Nancy would agree to see him again.

He thought of her constantly, he said. He signed it 'GM'.

She let her head fall back. The letter contained barely a hundred words, but the few lines set up a storm of conflicting emotions. She wanted to meet Gil more than she had ever wanted anything, and to know that he felt something similar only intensified the urgency.

Wheedling half-reasons for allowing herself to accept Gil's invitation circled inside her head. What about Celia? A sick woman, with an illness that was so close to Nancy that it felt almost like her own. Perhaps she could after all do something to help her, where she had not been alert enough to do it for Eliza? The intention seeded itself and sprang up, fertilised by her seething desire to see Gil.

*Would* it be so very wrong?

Lion only ever did what he wanted to do, and the routines of her own life seemed suddenly lonely as well as hard. Nancy rarely felt sorry for herself, but as she sat there by the fire and remembered the glorious dinner at the Ritz she was assailed by a longing for ease and security. Just for an evening – perhaps – it would be wonderful to let go of the Palmyra and her family's needs and the shadow of the Uncanny, and do what she wanted.

Without giving herself time to consider further she found a sheet of paper in a drawer and wrote a reply. Yes, she said. She rummaged deeper for a stamp and an envelope and so as not to leave room for second thoughts in the morning she put her coat on once more and ran to the postbox in the next street.

When she came back, panting from the dash through the

darkness, she raked the ashes in the range to make sure that not a single ember glowed.

Gil's reply came by return. He suggested a time and a place for them to meet, and she agreed.

Piccadilly was crowded with well-dressed people hurrying to theatres and restaurants. A legless man with a chalked placard reading '*Help Me*' leaned against a pillar and Nancy stopped in her tracks. Gil dropped a coin into his hand.

'God bless you,' the soldier muttered.

Without saying a word Gil took her arm and they passed into the web of streets to the north of the thoroughfare, reaching an alley that led in turn to a silent cul-de-sac. Gil rang the bell of an anonymous-looking house and they were admitted to a drawing room. Groups of well-dressed men and a handful of women sat talking in armchairs as a pianist played softly. It was a long way from the rowdy parties Nancy was used to frequenting with Lion.

'What is this place?'

'It's called Fifteen. If I don't want to stay at home I come here to play cards, or to talk or read. It is the antithesis of a Pall Mall club and nothing that takes place here goes beyond these four walls. What will you have to drink?'

'I'd like a whisky.'

'What an excellent woman you are.'

They sat side by side in an alcove at one side of the room. A decanter was brought on a silver tray and placed on the low table. Nancy curled her fingers round her glass.

'Tell me a little about your mother? If that wouldn't be too painful for you?'

Nancy began uncertainly.

'I . . . didn't know until almost the end, but Eliza was a

morphine addict too. Pneumonia was the cause of death, although she was already so weak I think almost anything would have been too much for her to withstand.'

'I am sorry you had to bear that, Nancy. It's a rather cruel coincidence, don't you think?' After a moment he added, 'Will you tell me some more? I wish I'd had a chance to meet her. She sounds remarkable.'

For almost the first time in her life Nancy began to talk without first considering what she was going to say.

'Yes, she was remarkable but she was unlucky. My older brother's birth was a difficult one.'

It was like opening her heart and letting the words and the pain flood out. She found herself talking and talking, about the burden of the Uncanny and about Cornelius and Arthur, Devil and the Palmyra and Feather and Jinny and the suffragists, and about Eliza – most of all about Eliza. Her mother was always inside her and it made her sadder to think that they had never been truthful with each other, not in the way she seemed able to be with this man who was a stranger.

Gil listened, taking it all in, drinking his whisky and sometimes asking a question.

'I can't describe to you how much I miss her,' Nancy said at last. 'Or how sorry I am for what didn't happen between us, and should have done. And now never can happen.'

She was pleating the folds of her skirt and suddenly the smells of sea salt and sun-bleached wood swept over her. Gil reached out and very lightly stroked her hair.

'I am afraid this is probably a very vulgar question. Couldn't you use your gift to reach her? On the other side, isn't that the phrase?'

Barely moving in case he withdrew his hand she whispered, 'I am clairvoyant and precognisant, but I can't control what reaches me. What does come through is often very dark. My voices don't chat about happy times, and I never see buried treasure. It's a pity, isn't it? I sometimes hear words and phrases, but they are often iterations of what I already know or have heard elsewhere. I think I am only a mouthpiece. Those people I knew or cared for don't speak to me. Or I don't hear them.' She raised her head. 'I do hope you won't use this information to destroy my stage career. I told you, I need the money.'

'Nothing within these four walls.'

The salt-air smell faded.

She said, 'This has been a rather one-sided conversation so far. Am I allowed to ask you an even more vulgar question?'

'Go ahead.'

She thought for a moment. 'Have I imagined that there is a connection between us? I don't know how else to describe it.'

He lifted a strand of her hair. 'No, Nancy. You haven't imagined it.'

'But we're also separated, aren't we? By Bruton Street, and the Bentley, and this.' She gestured at the room. 'I really mean by money, I suppose. I think of wealth like the ramparts of a fort, rearing up to the sky. Have you always been rich or did you earn it? Or marry it?'

He gave his rare laugh, genuinely amused now. He had all the easiness the rich possessed, Nancy thought. It was only small people like herself and Arthur and Jinny Main who took note of its presence and absence.

'I certainly didn't marry it. Celia's family, the de Laurys, can trace their history back to the Conquest but her father, the Earl, is in straitened circumstances these days. I inherited a new Victorian fortune, based on cotton manufacturing, as I told you that night in Fleet Street.'

He remembered their conversation even though it was four years ago.

'I still have the handkerchief you gave me,' she told him. It lay in the drawer of her bureau.

'You don't have chilblains any longer.'

They looked at each other. A moment crept by while the import of what was happening dawned on them both.

'Celia and I were judged to be an appropriate match by both sides, which is the way such things happen. We aren't very much alike. The Bentley is flashy because I chose it. The de Laurys owned the London house and they made it over to us on our marriage. The arrangement of it is much more Celia's province than mine.'

'She's so young.'

Nancy meant to be the mistress of such an establishment. He said quietly, 'It's what she was born to do.'

At some point this evening, Nancy understood, Gil Maitland and she had crossed an invisible line. She couldn't work out precisely where it had been, but her breath became tight in her chest while her limbs felt loose as a puppet's. It wasn't the whisky. It was something much more dangerous because they stood on the same side now. Everyone and everything else – Lion, Celia, their families – was left on the far side.

She asked, 'Why did you come backstage with Celia that first time?'

'I'm ashamed to tell you. I thought that if I passed you some information you couldn't otherwise know, between us we might be able to work out a convincing message from Richard. And if you delivered that message, because Celia believes in you she might think she really will meet him again. I know how much that would mean, and it might make her feel better. And therefore make my life a little easier. You wouldn't countenance it, remember? I told you, I *am* ashamed.'

'I see. I understand. It wasn't a wicked idea.'

'I did love her, you know. There was a shadow in her, even before he was killed, but she shone all the more brightly for that. Then Richard died and Celia was destroyed by grief, and the doctors got hold of her with their medicines. She always has the little silver syringe with her these days. But I don't have to tell you about that.'

'You could have broken off the engagement, I suppose?'

Their eyes met again. 'No, I couldn't have done such a thing. I am trying to be as truthful as I can, Nancy.'

He reached into an inner pocket and took out a photograph.

Two young people in period costume were framed by a painted proscenium arch. Richard wore a crown and a doublet and Celia a smaller crown with a long flowing veil.

'When they were children they liked to put on little stage performances. They loved theatre. This was the last one they did, just before Richard went to France. It was the wooing scene from *Henry the Fifth*.'

Nancy knew the play although she had read very little Shakespeare. She had seen Jake Jones play Henry.

'"I will kiss your lips, Kate,"' she said.

Gil's smile was painful. 'Precisely. If you said only that much to her, she would know it came from Richard.'

'I'm sorry. I can't do it.'

'I know. I realised it was wrong to approach you as soon as we sat down at the Ritz. You aren't a charlatan, not in the least. You are remarkable, just like your mother.'

There was a rushing noise like waves within Nancy's skull. She turned to him and her eyes travelled over his features.

Then she leaned slowly forward and kissed him full on the mouth. Gil didn't draw back. There was a moment of stillness before he caught her face between his warm hands, and kissed her in return.

A long moment later they separated. They were both shocked into silence.

At last he stammered, 'Truly I didn't mean this to happen. I thought I could see you and talk to you and somehow keep it at bay.'

'I know. I felt the same.'

He laced her fingers in his, raised their joined hands to his mouth.

'But it seems that it *has* happened.'

A bubble seemed to swell inside Nancy.

It's you, she thought. You are the one I was meant for. Here you are, at last. *Here.*

'I am glad,' she said clearly.

'God help us. Do you know what you are doing?'

'No. Yes. I don't care, I want you.'

'You want *me*?'

She looked past the walls of Fifteen, past Gil's well-cut coat and the cream Bentley and his suave manners, and recognised loneliness as deeply entrenched as her own.

'I do.'

They studied each other for another moment, like starving people gazing at a banquet. Then Gil abruptly stood up and helped her to her feet.

'I'll let you consider that in a cooler light. In the meantime I'll see you home, if I may?'

She said fiercely, 'Send me home if you like but I don't believe I shall change my mind.'

It was the truth and she wanted to acknowledge it. The line was well and truly crossed now.

He touched her cheek and the gesture was more intimate than a kiss.

'No. I don't really think either of us is likely to do that.'

Nancy didn't want the Bentley drawing up anywhere near the house, so when they reached Piccadilly Gil hailed a cab and paid the driver.

'Twenty Waterloo Street, Clerkenwell,' she told the man.

Gil stood back from the kerb.

All the way home, through the late-night streets, the iridescent bubble lifted within her.

It was happiness, she realised.

Harry Bolton was about to sail with his regiment to India. Bella and Arthur had invited him with Nancy and Lion to dine again at Arthur's favourite Greek restaurant, the one with the eager proprietor and the less-than-pristine table-cloths. Harry pretended to balk at the plates of rice and *dolmades*.

'Couldn't we have gone to the Café Royal?'

'Come on, old chap,' Arthur laughed. 'You'll be eating dinners more far-fetched than this out in 'Pindi.'

'I imagine the mess cooks will be able to manage consommé and roast beef exactly as they do in Pirbright,' Harry answered.

'Darling Harry, you are such a pompous old stick. I so wish you weren't going away again. I shall miss you like mad,' Bella told him. She patted her brother's hand and sighed.

'What about you, Arthur? Damn shame to miss out on Palestine. It's to be Mesopotamia for you fellows, I hear,' Harry winked.

'Is that what you hear? It's news to me,' Arthur said. He chewed steadily and swallowed.

Arthur was now commanding a special operations unit for the development of camouflage techniques. That was as much as any of them knew. He joked that given a few yards of muslin and a tin of paint his men could conceal an entire army under a lady's parasol. Devil loved to hear these stories and he could listen for hours, even though Arthur did not possess the gift for embellishing a tale.

Harry prodded his kleftiko.

'Ah, I know it's deeply hush-hush. The RAF chaps are in charge of seeing off the rebels, I believe. But they'll need you hide-and-seek wallahs on the ground in Sulaymaniyah. Can't get anything done without army assistance, the crabs, can they?'

Bella shook her head at him. 'Arthur won't tell you anything, you know.'

'He will if I take him off to my club after dinner. No man could withstand my subtle line of questioning. We'll put you girls in a taxi first. Eh, Nancy?'

Nancy and Lion hadn't joined in any of the army banter. Lion ate quickly, not looking as amused as he usually did. They had been seeing each other less frequently since Nancy had given up her Covent Garden room and moved back to Waterloo Street. Earlier in the evening, as they walked to the restaurant, she had begun to say that perhaps they should think of calling themselves just friends from now on. Lion irritably silenced her before she got anywhere.

'I don't want to hear gloom and doom. Can't we just have a jolly evening for once?'

One more evening, she told herself. She wanted to be fair to Lion. Gil was always in her head, his voice in her ears and his hand on her cheek, even though they had made no attempt as yet to contact each other.

310

'You will do nothing of the kind,' Bella crisply told her brother. '*We* won't be banished, Nancy, will we?'

The restaurant owner came over with the bill and Arthur quickly paid it, as usual.

The five of them made their way down towards Oxford Street. Bella walked between Harry and Arthur, her arms linked though theirs. Nancy and Lion followed a little behind, isolated in their discomfort with each other.

They reached the corner near Oxford Circus and at first they didn't pay any attention to a closing-time skirmish that was developing in a bus queue a few yards ahead. A man's hat was snatched off and sent bowling into the street. He dived after it and a speeding motor bus knocked him down.

Thrown backwards, the man fell in a heap across the kerb. At the same instant there was a screech of brakes and a volley of cursing greeted a second bus approaching from the opposite direction. The driver braked and slewed his vehicle to block the road. Two women were roughly hustled off before this bus rapidly reversed and swung to face the same way as the first.

'What the hell's going on?' Arthur said.

'Pirates,' Lion called.

The bus wars were the latest London difficulty. The first bus was a licensed vehicle and the second was a pirate, driving faster so as to scoop up the queues ahead of its competitor. It didn't matter to the second driver that he already had passengers, including the two women, who had paid to travel in the opposite direction – there were more fares to be collected by going back the way he had come.

'Bastard,' one of the women yelled. 'Bloody crooked bastards.'

No one in the crowd was paying any attention to the

man who had been knocked down. He sprawled on the pavement, trying to prop himself up on his elbows.

Harry was the first of their little group to reach his side. 'Are you hurt, old chap?'

Three young men were playing at hauling the official conductor off his bus. Others pushed past in order to clamber aboard the pirate vehicle. The rogue services were popular because the fares were a penny cheaper. There was a strong smell of drink in the air and the jostling became less playful.

'We've already paid to Holborn,' the second ejected woman squawked.

'Change of route, love.' The pirate conductor barred her way.

'Form a proper queue,' the official conductor vainly insisted, trying to defend himself from attack. He was a hollow-chested fellow whose ticket board hung loose on its leather strap. All his potential passengers were already swarming aboard the rival bus.

A stone flew from the back of the crowd and pinged off the dark red livery of the official bus. It must have hit someone as it rebounded because there was an oath, and in that instant the mood of the mob swung from merry impatience to fury. A shower of stones whizzed through the darkness. A fist smashed into a face, mouths opened in a black roar of anger. Both buses were engulfed by furious people and the vehicles rocked dangerously as the crowd shoved at them. Jeering men attempted to haul both drivers out of their cabs. Lion stood looking on, and Nancy knew he was enjoying this demonstration of mass choice in the face of imposed regulation.

Arthur hustled Bella and Nancy into the shelter of a shop doorway. Harry was half-kneeling beside the man who had fallen. He stuck out an arm to shield him and in the melee someone stumbled over it. A flicker of memory fleetingly troubled Nancy but everything happened too quickly for her to skewer it.

'Mind your feet. This man is injured,' Harry shouted.

A couple of drunken labourers swayed on the platform of the pirate bus. '*Bleddy hell*,' they catcalled in a parody of an officer's commanding tones. '*This men is hart.*'

One of them flicked his wrist in an obscene gesture and another spat in Harry's direction.

'Fuckin' toff,' a voice bawled.

In an instant Harry became the focus of the mob's rage.

'What you want with a bus anyway? Why don't yer get a fuckin' cab? Or get yer batman to carry yer? *Sir?*'

The spindly conductor's ticket board was torn off and tossed into the crowd.

'Free rides, lads,' its captor bawled.

Harry sprang up and launched himself into the fray.

'Run to Great Marlborough Street and fetch a constable,' Arthur ordered an open-mouthed urchin. 'Stay here,' he told Bella and Nancy.

He sprinted after Harry. Lion finally took his hands out of his pockets and loped in his wake.

The pirate driver was out of his seat and a burly man leapt into his place, tooting the horn and madly revving the bus engine. Harry leapt on to the platform beside its conductor and there was a roar as he tried to help the man back down to the street. Before he could do so and before Arthur could break through the mob to reach him, the new driver engaged gear and the bus jerked forward. It zigzagged wildly through the traffic that had built up. The handful of people who had managed to get aboard were flung sideways into the aisle.

Harry had both hands on the conductor's shoulders and they swayed together like drunken dance partners before they lost their balance. Nancy saw in agonising detail what was about to happen.

Harry's body flew in a vicious arc.

He would have tumbled into the gutter and perhaps have been only slightly injured but his waistcoat, undone at the bottom buttons, caught on one of two projecting brass hooks at the rear entrance. The conductor would suspend a webbing strap between them to prevent unwelcome passengers from boarding. So Harry's fall was arrested with a jerk that punched the breath out of him. His torso was hooked like a salmon on a line as his legs helplessly trailed in the road. The bus accelerated away, its driver unaware of what was happening behind him and thinking that the onlookers only cheered him on.

Harry gave one choking cry. His feet raked the dirt like a puppet's as he tried to scramble to safety. Twenty yards away, Bella pressed her hands to her mouth in a silent scream. Arthur flung himself in the wake of the bus.

The bus cleared the queue of vehicles by making a last violent swerve. Harry's feet and ankles were crushed between its wheels and the kerb. It began to gather speed.

Panting for breath, Lion had to stop but Arthur sprinted even faster. His arms and legs pumped and the street lamps flashed on his blonde head. Nancy saw him launch himself into a giant leap and with one hand catch the pole at the rear of the platform. By rights his arm should have been torn from its socket but somehow he clung on. He hoisted himself on board and curled his free arm around Harry's chest. With a colossal effort he dragged his friend's hips and legs clear of the wheels and on to the bucking platform.

'Hold him,' he howled to the horrified conductor and

two of the involuntary passengers. He dived the length of the bus but the joyrider only yielded the wheel when Arthur struck him a blow to the jaw. He wrenched the bus into the kerb and it crunched to a standstill. There was a grinding shudder before it stalled, followed by a silence that lasted for three or four seconds.

The only sound was the injured man's gasp of agony.

'Oh, God,' Bella moaned. Nancy tried to turn her aside but she broke out of her grasp.

With a blast on their whistles two police constables dashed round the corner. The crowd immediately melted into the side streets, leaving only the grim-faced bus crews, licensed and pirate, and a handful of witnesses.

'I fetched the rozzers, didn't I, like the gent told me?' the urchin said.

Arthur had already folded his coat under Harry's head. He was exploring his injuries as Bella and Lion and Nancy reached them. The girls had been hampered by their high-heeled shoes so they kicked them off and ran the last few yards in their silk stockings.

They stared at the mess of crushed leather, torn socks and bloody flesh shockingly spiked with bone that had been Harry's ankles. It seemed impossible that such a disaster could have unfolded in the brief moments since they had left the Greek restaurant. Bella dazedly sank down beside Harry on the bus platform and cradled his head in her lap.

'Darling, you have hurt your feet. I know it hurts but you will be all right, Arthur and I will take care of you. Just lie still for me.'

'Thank you,' Harry murmured.

A trickle of blood ran from the corner of his mouth and Bella touched it with her handkerchief. Nancy groped for Lion's hand.

The police acted with speed. The burly man had been seized as he tried to run off and handcuffs were sprung about his wrists. Two more officers sprinted up and restrained the opposing crews. The women who had been expelled from the pirate bus were excitedly shouting their accounts of what had happened, and the man whose lost hat had triggered it all sat on the kerbstone with his head in his hands.

One policeman bent down beside Harry and Arthur and Bella and Lion. His helmet was pushed back from his forehead, making him look as if he was in fancy dress.

'There'll be an ambulance along directly. I won't take a statement from you now, but I'll need all your names and addresses.'

'My friend saved me,' Harry murmured. 'He risked himself for me. I'd have been dragged under the wheels otherwise.'

'He did.' Bella was fierce.

'Anyone would have done the same,' Arthur said.

An ambulance bell was shrilling in the distance. Harry struggled to sit upright, propping himself against Bella's knees so that he could peer down at his injuries. His mouth twisted at the sight.

'I say, how strange. That one should live through everything we did, Arthur old chap, only for this to happen on the pavement in Oxford Street.' He had gone very white. 'Be a brick and light up for me before the stretcher bearers get here, would you?'

Arthur took out his case, tapped the tobacco and clicked his lighter, drawing in the smoke himself before placing the cigarette between Harry's lips. Nancy thought that Cornelius must have performed the same small service countless times.

Bella went off in the ambulance with Harry. Arthur

assured her he would telephone General Bolton and break the news. The man who had been knocked down was taken away too and Nancy and Arthur were left with Lion as the last spectators drifted away.

Lion rubbed his eyes. 'This is horrible,' he muttered.

Nancy would have welcomed his comforting, but with the props of comedy and ironic detachment removed he didn't seem to know what to do. Would Gil, she thought?

Yes, he would.

She held on to Arthur's arm instead, although he was anxious to telephone Harry's father before following Bella and his friend to the hospital.

'I'll take Nancy home,' he told Lion and there was no further discussion. Lion trudged away towards Shepherd's Market without looking back.

At home in Waterloo Street Devil had returned from the theatre and Cornelius was still up. They listened in shock as Nancy told them what had happened. Arthur went away to telephone, and came in again to tell them that the General was on his way and the hospital reported that Harry was already with the surgeon. He sank down at the kitchen table and accepted the brandy poured by Devil.

'Bella insists there's nothing I can do there. She's waiting for her father to arrive. Did you see how calm she was, and how she looked after Harry? She is amazing.'

'She is,' Nancy said gently.

The glass rattled as Arthur drank the brandy and she exchanged a glance with Cornelius.

Devil shook his grey head. 'What a cruel accident to happen to a fine, fit young soldier. Will he walk again, do you think?'

Unlike her brothers, Nancy had never seen such an injury. She thought of the beggar she had seen with Gil in Piccadilly, and the other ex-servicemen who limped and hobbled through London.

Arthur said, 'Doctors can work miracles nowadays. And it could have been worse. He could easily have been killed, you know.'

'Arthur saved his life,' she told them and Devil reached out to grasp his son's hand.

'My boy.'

She thought the Boltons owed their son's life to Arthur's bravery. *I want to be a brave man*, he had said, on the day of the *Queen Mab*. There was no doubt that was what he had become.

Then next afternoon Jinny came. Dressed in brown overalls and with her hair tied up in an old handkerchief she worked alongside Cornelius in the garden and when the weak afternoon light faded into twilight she took off her boots in the scullery and followed him into the kitchen.

Cornelius said, 'I'll do these last spuds for Nancy's tea before she goes out to the theatre. If she'll have anything at all, that is. You never know, nowadays.'

'Your dad will probably eat them. You could cook him a mutton chop, maybe.'

Jinny was at the sink, soaping the garden dirt off her strong forearms. She turned to dry her hands on the tea towel and found that Cornelius had placed a glass of water for her.

'Ta,' she said, draining the glass. 'Thirsty work, eh?'

He reached out and tucked a lock of hair behind her ear for her, letting his touch linger for a second. There was a scatter of freckles on her nose and cheeks.

'Do I look a mess?'

'No. You look as if you have been working hard.'

Jinny sighed, 'It's what we do in life, isn't it?'

She did not often admit to low sprits but the devastation of Harry's accident had affected them all.

They heard Nancy's step on the stairs and turned together. She was ready for the theatre, her face strained with yesterday's anxiety and with anticipation of the evening's performance.

'Have you got time to eat anything before you go? I've brought in potatoes and there's some tinned ham and the end of the tomato pickle if you'd like.'

Tomatoes were Cornelius's speciality. Last summer he had positioned sloping panes of glass against the back wall to form a makeshift greenhouse where the plants flourished. Jinny rinsed out her glass and placed it on the wooden drainer.

'Maybe I'll have something later, Neelie. But thank you.'

Nancy saw and felt somehow excluded by their joint concern. She had the sense that she stood all alone on the brink of a precipice, with Lion shrinking behind her and only Gil Maitland to steer by. Either she could turn away from him and back to plain safety, or she could step forwards.

'Where is Pa this afternoon?'

She only asked to preserve the illusion of normality and she could tell that Cornelius was surprised by the question.

'He's with old Gibb in his workshop. He told you this morning. They're building apparatus.'

'Oh, yes. I'd forgotten.'

The old man was now Devil's most regular companion. They tinkered together in one of the stables buildings that had once housed the barge horses, and Devil muttered about the sensational new Egyptian trick that he was engineering with Gibb's help.

'How is Harry today?' Jinny asked.

'The surgeon has done what he can to repair the damage. Harry will be in hospital for a few weeks. After that, who knows?'

'It sounds like no more soldiering,' Jinny said at length.

'Not for Harry, no,' Nancy agreed.

The old clock ticked steadily and Nancy found herself staring at the heel of a loaf and scattered crumbs on the breadboard, the orangey residue of soap left on the enamel dish beside the sink and the copper water pipes rimmed with verdigris. In another moment her throat would flood with saliva and thick odours would rush at her. Delayed shock from yesterday brought the Uncanny dangerously close.

'I really must be off. I don't want to be late at the theatre.'

Cornelius nodded and Jinny gave her a brief hug. After she had gone the two of them sat at the kitchen table and shared the work of peeling potatoes.

Nancy walked to Blackfriars. The reek of freshly laid tar on the road skirting Smithfield and the thick waft from the meat market clogged her head and when she boarded a tram the press of tired people emanated gusts of sweat and cigarette smoke. In the dressing room Sylvia helped her off with her damp blouse.

'Are you fit to go on?'

It was too early yet for most of the audience to be arriving, but Nancy imagined she could hear a murmur from the packed seats. It sounded like waves breaking.

'Yes, I think so. May I have some tea?'

There was the pop of gas followed by a rising whistle when the kettle boiled.

'Has Desmond been in? What's the house tonight?'

'Full,' Sylvia told her.

More and more people were discovering the Palmyra

seances and swelling the regular audience. Nancy had to hold dozens of stories and a cacophony of voices in her mind, recalling the webs she had already created and holding them in place as she spun new filaments. She was no longer playing to the old music-hall crowd, Devil and Eliza's audiences, who could be happily entertained with a few crude effects sandwiched between the conjuror and the acrobats. The current audiences were austere by comparison, demanding of the medium, and they came from all walks of life. There were rumours that even the new Duchess of York followed Spiritualism.

Sylvia worried that it was too much for her. The party-going with Lion Stone had been one concern, although lately that had almost stopped. Sylvia was observant enough to note the change that had come over Nancy but she didn't know the reason for it.

The call boy tapped on the door. The Palmyra was still a theatre, with its backstage rituals.

'Ten minutes, Miss Wix.'

Nancy jumped. She must have fallen into a doze over her cup of tea. She hurried out of Eliza's red silk wrap and into her stage dress, draping a towel over her shoulders before powdering her face at the mirror. She liked to blot out her physical features as far as possible, leaving a blank oval for others to inhabit. Once she was ready Sylvia faithfully shadowed her to the wings. She squeezed her hand before releasing her into the performance.

Here was the expectant silence. The curtains parted and the spot fell on her.

She saw him almost at once, sitting towards the rear of the stalls.

Lawrence Feather's hair had grown long and now fell to his shoulders in grey hanks like a dishevelled prophet's, and

321

his once-neat clerical clothing was rusty and crumpled. There were two people with him, an almost hunchbacked man and a tiny woman, set apart from the rest of the audience by their unkempt looks. They leaned forwards in their seats, fixing their eyes on her. The scrutiny was disturbing.

As calmly as she could Nancy sat down in front of her audience.

To begin with, the seance followed its usual course.

There were the regular postulants and some hesitant new ones. She concentrated on the latter, drawing out their halting questions and listening with all her faculties. The concentration required was intense and she briefly forgot about Lawrence Feather although the shimmer of the Uncanny blurred the edges of the stage and clouded the mirrors in the wings.

It was half an hour before Feather suddenly stood up. He shouted over the rows of heads, 'Why don't you acknowledge the channel, Miss Wix? I know it's open.'

The lighting man swung the following spot to him, as he was supposed to do.

'I hear other voices tonight,' she answered. She pointed to someone at random. 'You, sir. There is someone here. Who is it wanting to speak to you?'

The man sat woodenly. She had picked a dud, and the spot obstinately held Feather in its beam.

'The channel,' Feather repeated. 'She is here, isn't she? Helena is here.'

There was a crash of water so violent it was as if the wave broke over Nancy's head. Salt wrack and engine oil gusted through her and Helena Clare spoke in a low voice.

*'He did what he shouldn't have done.'*

Nancy moistened her dry lips. 'No, she is not here this evening. I'm sorry, and I'm sorry for your loss.'

Nancy tried to fend off Feather and the Uncanny together but the audience was rapt. There was nowhere she could steer the seance except where Feather wanted it to go. The low murmur persisted within the plates of her skull.

*'He shouldn't have done it. I knew no better. I was hardly more than a girl.'*

Suddenly, with a tremor of nausea, clear understanding dawned on her. They had been lovers. There had been inklings before, but it was only now that Nancy knew for sure why the brother and sister's relationship had been so troubling. With the nasty truth laid bare to her it didn't seem strange that poor Mr Clare had seemed little more than a shadow, and that Eliza had instinctively recoiled from the medium. Nancy's reaction now was as intense as her mother's.

*'Ask him about the boathouse.'*

Feather shouted, 'Tell the room about the locket. My sister's locket, which I buried with her. It was a sign, the clearest and most certain sign I have ever witnessed. This medium is gifted, we all know that.'

His blazing eyes raked the stalls before he tilted his head to gaze into the wings of the gallery and the boxes.

'See? She won't speak. Miss Zenobia Wix will not share my sister's presence with me. After all I have done for her.'

The man was clearly out of his senses. His companions nodded and shuffled closer as the people seated around them tried to edge away. All three of them were on their feet.

*'Ask him,'* Helena Clare begged.

Nancy tried to breathe evenly but the close air seemed to catch in her chest. Except for Feather and the two strangers the audience waited in rapt silence.

She raised her head, although she could hardly bear to

look in the man's direction. 'Very well. Mr Feather, your sister directs me to ask you about the boathouse.'

It was as if she had darted an electric current through him. His body painfully jerked, but a wild grin stretched his mouth to expose the teeth like a skull's.

He crooned, 'Our boathouse? Yes. I remember every plank of it and I remember what happened there. Helena, my beloved, I'll come to you soon enough.'

Without warning the voice faded. There was no sound, not even the vacuum of an absent sound.

'Speak,' Feather roared. 'Tell me what she says.'

'Nothing more,' Nancy whispered.

The man spun on his heel and seemed to beckon something from the rear of the auditorium.

A small figure raced down the aisle towards the stage. No one else saw it but they instinctively drew their sleeves and collars closer because of the chill. The soaking girl ran past the orchestra pit and up the little flight of steps at the side of the stage. She dashed straight at Nancy, but there was no impact. She was gone, leaving a trail of dark spots on the boards. Even as Nancy stared they faded and vanished.

'You see?' Feather called, with his death's-head smile.

So that was it. He controlled the soaking girl.

He must have sent her, all the times in the past that she had made an appearance. Nancy shuddered. The little thing was harmless; it was the notion of Feather and his manipulations that was terrifying. It seemed that he owned a spyhole that looked directly into her life.

Lawrence Feather grandly gestured to his friends. They left their seats and marched out, the woman of the couple keeping her eyes on Nancy until her head almost twisted off. Shocked murmurs began to spread through the theatre. Nancy looked into the mirrors and saw they reflected nothing but the oblique view of surprised faces. There was no shimmer, and the smells were of backstage apparatus and the faint drift of ladies' perfumes from the front *fauteuils*. She uncurled her fingers one by one and raised an imperious hand.

'Quiet, please. Now. I see an Italian city. Is it Rome?'

This time the spotlight obligingly swung and the performance resumed, and somehow she worked her way through to the end of it.

Sylvia was waiting to catch her as she stumbled offstage.

'My poor girl. It's all right, dear, it's all over for today.'

The dresser led her through the wings, past stagehands who pressed against the walls to let them pass. Even Desmond was silenced. In the dressing room Sylvia helped her to a chair.

'Shall I call Mr Wix?'

'No, please don't do that.'

'Your young man, then? Wouldn't you like him to come and keep you company?'

Nancy shook her head.

'Just you, Sylvia. I only want you.'

That wasn't true. Her yearning for Gil was breaking though all the stretched tissues of her life.

Sylvia drew Nancy's head against her thin chest and rocked her.

'I'm here, love. Don't you worry.'

# CHAPTER FIFTEEN

Another week crept by. There were two more routine performances, with no hint of the Uncanny and nothing else that was untoward. After the third she had been back in the dressing room only just long enough to change out of her stage clothes and do up the Chinese robe before there was a knock at the door.

Nancy's head jerked up. Was it Gil?

Sylvia opened the door to Bella and Arthur. They bundled into the room in evening clothes, flushed and bright-eyed with cocktails. Arthur caught Nancy by the lapels of the robe and kissed her on both cheeks. The ends of his clipped moustache tickled her nose.

'Goodness, this red thing makes me think of Ma.'

'Me too,' Nancy said.

Bella put aside her velvet coat and evening bag, gaily chatting to Sylvia as she perched in Celia Maitland's place on the slippery seat. This was the first time they had come backstage together to see Nancy. The two of them looked far too happy to be bearing bad news about Harry, at least.

'No, no, he's doing well,' Bella assured her. 'He's a magnificent patient.'

Ann Gillespie told them the same thing. She was a nurse in a different ward at the hospital and she looked in on him whenever she could.

Before anything more could be said there was another knock and two more arrivals came crowding in. Lion and Jake Jones had been to a first-night party and Lion had decided he must scoop up Nancy and take her back there. There were extravagant greetings and kisses. The room was too small to hold six people and Sylvia looked displeased on Nancy's behalf, but she said nothing and only searched for more glasses. Lion hugged Nancy briefly.

'Hullo, old thing. How was your show? The nonsense we saw won't run for a month, but why don't you get dressed and come with me to the wake? Freddie is there, and Dorothy and Brian, it'll be quite like old times.'

'A new play and half an hour of its players afterwards was more than enough for me. I'm for Whistlehalt and bed,' Jake said.

He took a sip of the swizzled champagne before nodding his approval. Nancy smiled across at him. Perched in a chair at the mirror, dark-suited, his elbow resting in the clutter of make-up and brushes, he looked nowadays less like an unassuming undergraduate than a senior bank employee or perhaps a prosperous dentist.

'A party?' she said vaguely. 'I'm not sure I'm in the mood either.'

'You are never in the mood,' Lion retorted.

Arthur reached for Nancy's nail file and tapped it against his glass.

'Excuse *me*, ladies and gentlemen.'

Lion lifted a lazy eyebrow in Nancy's direction.

'Bella and I have some news. We wanted my sister to be the first to hear it but you are as good as family, Jake, and Lion too, as well as Sylvia of course.'

Bella slipped her hand into his as Arthur cleared his throat.

'General Bolton has given his consent to our engagement. Bella has agreed to be my wife.'

Nancy leapt up and swept them into her arms.

'Oh, that is wonderful. I am so happy for you both. Congratulations, my darlings.'

She could see how it was. Arthur was no exchange for Harry – how could he be? – yet the General surely would be pleased to see his daughter safely settled, after the blow to his only son. The old man might even recognise a debt of gratitude. Again she remembered Arthur's fear on the day of the *Queen Mab*, that he might not own the courage he had assumed to be his by right. She had never felt so proud of him as she did at this minute. Eliza and Devil had been right after all to push him so hard, even out of their own orbit. Love constricted her heart and she was lost for words.

Grinning, Lion raised his glass. 'I say, what about a toast to the happy couple?'

'There is no happier life but in a wife,' Jake gravely quoted. It seemed that he meant it.

They drank and Sylvia added her shy congratulations.

'I am the luckiest fellow,' Arthur beamed at them all.

Bella said to Nancy, 'I love Arthur so much, and now I shall have you for a sister.'

'When and where will the wedding be?' Nancy asked.

Arthur said, 'As soon as possible. I had an early word with the CO and he says if we can fix a date before the summer he could wangle a later Mesopotamia posting for me. Or wherever we are going,' he hastily added.

Lion discreetly yawned behind his fingers. It was as if he had to demonstrate his boredom with this marriage talk. Nancy was annoyed.

Bella didn't notice. 'Arthur would like a town wedding, but I think my mother and father will insist on Henbury.'

This was the Boltons' house in the country.

'Very suitable,' Sylvia nodded.

Harry said, 'I would happily get married in the tomb of Tutankhamun, so long as Bella will have me. What are you doing now, Nancy? I thought Bella and I might come home with you to tell Pa and Cornelius our news.'

'But she's coming to a party with me,' Lion cried.

'I am not, Lion. Arthur, Cornelius will have been in bed for an hour and Pa might or might not be there.'

His movements were unpredictable these days. Sometimes Devil stayed at the stables workshop until the small hours, tinkering with his latest illusion.

'If we come tomorrow afternoon you won't breathe a word beforehand?'

'Cross my heart,' Nancy promised.

The room was too cramped to encourage further lingering and the happy couple departed. As she said goodnight to the others Nancy became sharply aware of Lion, dressed in his invariable jersey and flannels, the collar of his shirt poking up from the neckline of the jersey. He was large and physically at ease with himself, impatient to be somewhere where the fun might start again, always agreeable but – she reflected – in his inner core, absolutely and implacably selfish.

An answering point of determination, hard and bright as a diamond, crystallised within her.

'I'll come with you,' she told him.

'Good show. Let's get moving.'

Sylvia and Jake went in opposite directions and Lion and Nancy were alone. He tipped his head in the direction of the Strand.

'It's not far. We can easily walk.'

'Lion,' she began. 'I don't want to go to the party. I thought we might talk.'

He laughed. 'Ah, it's the engagement, isn't it? I'm afraid there will be a flood of business between now and the wedding. Dresses and favours, honeymoon and hymns and attendants and bouquets, tra la.'

He saw Nancy's face.

'Wait a minute. You don't mind about it, do you? Are you envious of Bella? It's not you, Nancy darling, all that conventional frippery. You are far bolder and more original than she is.'

'No, I'm not jealous of Bella.'

The night air was still and cold, tasting of acrid city dust. She linked her arm through Lion's and he made no objection as she led the way up a spiral of dipping stone steps to Waterloo Bridge. They reached the central span and leaned on the granite coping to peer down into the water. The current swirled around the pillars, catching and reflecting the lights from the bridge. Behind them two open carloads of rowdy young people roared past, reminding her of their early days of scavenger hunts and midnight excursions upriver to swim in the Thames at Maidenhead. Lion flicked a halfpenny in the air and watched it spin into the water.

'Make a wish?' he suggested. When she didn't answer he said, 'This *is* about Arthur and Bella's wedding, isn't it?'

She paused, but didn't give herself time to change her mind.

'No, it's about you and me. I want to end it.'

'I see.' She saw surprise and displeasure darkening his face. 'Why? We have a happy time, don't we?'

'We do. We have done ever since the bicycling weekend.'

'What's wrong, then?' His hurt pride was turning to the sulks. She was disrupting his natural ease and self-satisfaction.

Nancy hesitated.

Happiness – or Lion's superficial definition of it – wasn't precisely what was at stake. Gil Maitland was both wrong and terrifyingly right, although she hadn't seen or heard from him since the evening at Fifteen when he had advised her to consider matters in a cooler light. All she had learned from the intervening weeks was that she couldn't begin to contemplate the future – any future, whether Gil was somehow to be part of it or not – without first setting the present straight. She had to break off from Lion, whatever else happened.

'We're good at *now*, most of the time. But what about when we get older?'

She kept any plaintive note out of her voice.

Lion scowled, 'I haven't the faintest. I am interested in now. The war was only a beginning, you know. There is far worse to come, in Russia and in Europe as well as here. Live for today, Nancy, that's my motto.'

'I know that. But I would like to think I might marry and have a child some day. I am twenty-six.'

Lion's frowning profile and the curly mane of hair were outlined against the sky. He seemed to be intent on the flow of the river.

At length he shrugged.

'I'm sorry. I never thought of marrying you.'

She had been a fool ever to hope otherwise. It was cruel of him to say it so baldly, but now she knew. She

331

had to pinch her bottom lip between her teeth to hide the quivering.

'I see. All right, then. We can still be friends, I hope?'

'I'll miss all the splendid fun we've had,' he answered.

It was probably what was always said in these circumstances.

'So will I.'

This was the truth. She might also come to miss Lion himself, but Gil Maitland filled her landscape so entirely that she couldn't envisage where or how.

They walked up to the Strand as they had so often done before, and Nancy climbed aboard an eastbound bus without saying anything except goodbye. She looked back at Lion standing with his hands in his pockets. Briefly she let herself imagine that he felt sad, and was sorry to have let her go.

At home Nancy quickly wrote a letter to the City address, marked it '*Personal*' and sealed it in an envelope, ready for the post.

In his reply Gil invited her to meet him at an address in a Bloomsbury square not far from Gower Street. If she was sure, and if it was convenient, he had written. If it was not, they could perhaps make a different arrangement.

Yes, it was quite convenient, she inwardly laughed as she scribbled the answer. She would find it convenient to swim the Atlantic or fly to the moon, if she was sure Gil would be waiting at the journey's end.

On the doorstep, with her hand raised to the white ceramic button in the centre of a polished brass surround, she found her heart thumping and all her senses heightened in a way that was nothing to do with the Uncanny. She was on the brink of something momentous, and there would be no stepping back once the move was made. At the same time she recalled the steps up to the much bigger doors at Bruton Street, and the way Celia had reminded her of one of Cornelius's butterflies pinned in a polished box.

Nancy squared her shoulders. Right and wrong, she was thinking. She was doing wrong, but all the pin-sharp impressions of the hour and the urgency of her senses cried *right*. She put her finger to the bell push.

Gil opened the door himself. Inside was an inner door that let them into a small windowless hallway tiled like a chessboard in black-and-white marble.

'This way,' he said.

As soon as the second door closed behind them Nancy had a sense of privacy and security. The walls were solid, and the ceiling overhead. No sounds of traffic penetrated from the square.

He took her by the hand and led her through the rooms. The drawing room was empty, and the view from the windows into the plane trees at the front was hidden behind closed blinds. Next to this room were a simple kitchen and a bathroom, and at the rear a bedroom opened through French doors into a secluded garden flooded with pale sunlight. A table and wrought-iron bench stood under the bare branches of a tree.

The rooms were minimally furnished and there was not a single ornament or personal possession to be seen. The space seemed almost insistently neutral, as if it had been scrutinised in advance and swept clean of any traces of previous occupation.

'Whose flat is this?' Nancy asked.

'I bought it some years ago. It seems a shame that it's never used.'

He lifted her hand and placed a set of keys in it.

'It's yours now.'

'*Mine?*'

'Why not? I never want to take you to a hotel. I can hardly bring you to Bruton Street, nor will you want to see me at Waterloo Street. This is a place to which you may safely invite me, if that's your inclination. Those are the only keys, by the way.'

The dimple beneath his left eye appeared in advance of a smile.

'But . . .' Nancy protested. Her mind raced through the implications. 'If you install me in a flat like this, it makes me your *mistress*.'

'Is that a moral objection? Or is it the term itself you dislike?'

She began to laugh. 'It's rather old-fashioned, yes.'

'You haven't committed yourself. There's still time to come up with another word or to change your mind altogether.'

'I'm not going to do that.'

In a low voice he asked her, 'So, would you care to become my mistress?'

She took a step towards him, and then another, until barely an inch of air separated their bodies.

She remembered the electricity that had passed between their hands, poised over the table at the Ritz. The current was so powerful now that it almost stunned her.

'*Lover* is a better word,' she said.

'Lover, then.'

Gil Maitland was almost certainly practised in these matters. He had probably practised them in this very room. Yet he said now in a rush, 'I don't care what we call it. Nancy Wix, I want you. I want you more than I have ever wanted anything in my life until this moment.'

She dismissed her final quiver of misgiving. Whatever had happened to them separately before this, all she cared about was now and the future. She knew that his longing for her matched hers for him, and that physical urgency was only the shell of it. She could hear his heart speaking.

His hand touched the small of her back, the lightest of touches. She submitted to its pressure as he guided her. He kissed her as he undid the buttons of her dress and slid the straps of her underclothes down her shoulders. She arched herself against him, the weave of his coat coarse against her skin. Every piece of her was thirsty for him.

'May I?' he murmured, as his lips moved over her skin.

Yes. Yes, and yes. Don't ever stop.

She stroked his hair, finding it smooth after Lion's matted curls.

His fingers explored her and she gave herself up to him.

'Won't you take your clothes off too?' she murmured.

Obediently he removed links and undid buttons, until they were naked and facing each other.

The neutrality of the rooms lent the two of them a sort of equivalence. They could paint their own pictures on the walls, and furnish the shelves with happiness still to be created. Their faces moved closer until their mouths just touched.

'Now,' he said.

'Now,' she echoed.


Afterwards they lay for a long time in each other's arms, listening to the sound of one another's breathing. Nancy studied the intricate flecks of colour in his irises, the sheen of sweat at his temple, the taut skin where his razor had met the hairline. It was startling to be so easily and absolutely entwined with another human being. It was like finding that all the leaks and cracks in her awkward life had been quickly and deftly sealed.

Lion would have been laughing, propping himself on one elbow, talking unstoppably and coming up with ideas for what they might do with the rest of the day. Gil seemed content to lie and look at her, letting the moment extend for as long as they could remain in it.

Slowly, though, the angle of the light changed and the ordinary day gathered itself in the corners of the room. Nancy sat up, drawing her knees to her chest as she surveyed it. On the wall across from the bed was the place for her Dürer print.

She took a sharp inwards breath as reality descended.

She had just had the best physical experience of her life – better sex than she had ever imagined – but it had been with another woman's husband. And here she was, planning the arrangement of her possessions in the rooms that husband had prepared for her.

Guilt spread its black wings.

And this is what you must live with, she told herself. Don't forget for a moment what you are really doing. What you have done.

And then she made the silent vow. Don't let any damage come about. Nobody must ever know about this day and – whatever happens – Celia must never, *never* find out. The guilty fervour set up a tremor of perverse pleasure. She and Gil were yoked now, by the need for secrecy as well as by passion.

For some reason her cousin Lizzie Shaw came into her head with a ripple of involuntary amusement.

'What makes you smile?' He reached up to outline her lips with his forefinger. 'Don't stop, by the way. I want to lie here and look at your mouth forever.'

'I was thinking about my cousin. She says she adores sex, but she doesn't like men.'

'I hope you don't feel the same?'

'About men? I like you. I like you to an absolutely embarrassing degree. Didn't you notice, when you bought me a half-pint of beer in Fleet Street and drove me home through the rain?'

'Maybe a little. Myself, I felt quite thunderstruck. I wanted to boot Higgs out and drive off into the night with you. But what would a beautiful and unusual young woman – young suffragist, I beg your pardon – want with a dull old economist like me? I had to let you go. I wondered about you often enough after that night.'

He hesitated over the next question. 'Nancy, what about your boyfriend?'

She leaned over him, looking into his eyes.

'I told him that it was over. He was decent about it. I don't think I broke his heart, in any case.'

'I didn't even have the right to ask. But I'm glad. I'm a jealous man.'

'Gil, what about your wife?'

His eyes didn't leave her face.

'I married Celia. It is my responsibility to take care of her, and my promise was to love her. Both of those I will do, as far as I possibly can. I am her husband and that can't and won't change. But I will take care of you too, Nancy, if you will allow me to. And somehow our love will find its own level. Like mercury,' he added.

She stared.

'In a certain light, a puddle on the step at our old house used to look like mercury. I know because my father used it in one of his old illusions.'

Gil kissed her.

She added, 'I can't come to live here. I have responsibilities too. My father and brother need me at home.'

'I understand. Then we can make a small secret world for ourselves in these rooms, can't we? And live in our world when we are able?'

'Yes,' she agreed. This was a lovely prospect. She hoped that she was not drawn to Gil Maitland because he could make difficult things appear so easy. Not just because he was powerful. Not just because he sealed the leaks within her and melted her bones. He deserved to be loved simply for who he was.

'Excellent.' He pulled her down to him. 'Now I would like to make love to you again, please.'

It touched her that he made the request sound like a child asking for a treat.

# CHAPTER SIXTEEN

The day of the wedding came.

At Henbury church Nancy slipped down the aisle and unobtrusively took her place in the pew next to Devil. She would have loved to arrive at Arthur's wedding on Gil's arm, but she had already learned that relationships like theirs always stayed behind closed doors. They most definitely did not announce themselves before the eyes of an entire congregation. Arthur and Bella had invited Lion and he had waved to her as she came in. She felt Gil's absence particularly because Lion was here.

The church bells rang down one by one, the organ voluntary ended and the congregation shuffled to its feet. In the porch the bride's old nanny adjusted the train of the dress as General Sir Reginald Bolton held out his arm to his daughter. His bearing was upright even though his service history was heavy enough to weigh down a much younger man. Bella radiantly smiled through the folds of her great-grandmother's Honiton lace veil. She had never looked lovelier, and she knew it.

The sidesman was the son of a family that had

worked for the Boltons at Henbury Manor for generations. He signalled to the organist, a great chord broke the tense silence, and Bella and her father processed down the aisle to the music of Handel. The pews on the bride's side of the church were packed with Bolton cousins and aunts and godparents and a few of the most important family retainers squeezed in at the back. The pews on the groom's side held a less homogeneous crowd.

At the chancel steps Arthur gazed ahead, as if he feared that a wrong move even at this last moment might jeopardise everything. Every fold and crease and ribbon of his dress uniform was perfect and the stained glass cast dapples of colour on his straight back. Standing beside him as his best man, Cornelius was buttoned into a morning coat that was inevitably too small. The waistcoat strained and his neck bulged over the stiff collar. He was sweating with nerves and his garden-roughened hands shook on the order of service.

Devil's tailcoat and neatly parked topper made him look as if he had turned up for work and was about to go onstage. Enjoying the comedy as well as the triumph of their presence at this gathering of the upper classes he turned to Nancy, winked, and made a magician's pass over the upturned hat. In the pew behind them Faith and Matthew were with Lizzie who was with Raymond Kane, and behind them rows of Arthur's brother officers and army friends lined up with the more presentable of the Palmyra's artists and stagehands. Sylvia Aynscoe had sewn an afternoon dress for herself and a rather more chic outfit for Nancy, every stitch of each as tiny and perfect as if she had been locking the couple's future happiness into the bound seams. Jake Jones sat next to her, impeccably correct in his turnout too, to the extent that he had left Freddie behind.

Jinny Main and Ann Gillespie were just behind them, next to Lion who seemed to know half the congregation and whispered scandalous versions of their histories and inter-relationships to his companions.

'Ah, how lovely,' he murmured as Bella passed by and then leaned forward to wave to a girl seated on the opposite aisle.

Arthur dared to look over his shoulder. His bride in her lace and pearls came softly to his side and her small attendants spread her train over the chancel steps. There were no girl children on the groom's side, so seven-year-old Tommy Hooper was a page. He stuck out his tongue at the smallest bridesmaid and the little girl turned her back on him so sharply that her ringlets bounced.

The rector of Henbury came to the chancel rail.

'Dearly beloved,' he began.

A mossy scent drifted from the arrangements of paper narcissi and early white roses – Lady Bolton wanted lilies and hothouse blooms, but Bella had held out for simpler flowers – to mingle with the smell of mothballs and eau de cologne that Nancy always associated with such occasions.

Across the aisle the General sat beside his American wife. As far as Nancy could judge, Lady Bolton had become more English than anyone else in the church if a certain kind of Englishness could be measured by hauteur. A reflection on how the bride's mother might have reacted to Eliza's hair and scarves and clashing bangles made Nancy quiver with laughter, but her amusement was pricked by a stab of grief. Eliza was so absent, so entirely gone from them. As if sensing her sadness, Devil took her hand and patted it.

If only Eliza could have been here to see one of her

341

children following the route she had planned. She had given up her son to the unknown world of Harrow and then to the even less comprehensible army and today she would have judged the sacrifice well worth it.

Harry Bolton sat in his wheelchair to one side of the chancel steps. He sang the hymns without having to refer to the printed sheet and he followed the order of service with full attention.

Cornelius read the first lesson, only the slightest tremor in his voice betraying his terror in standing up in front of so many people. Harry was to read the second and when the time came Arthur stepped briefly from Bella's side to wheel his friend's chair to the centre of the aisle. There was a murmur of surprise as he helped Harry to rock to his feet. Balanced partly against Arthur's shoulder and partly on the casts that encased his feet and ankles, Harry read the verses with his family and friends looking on.

'I'm not going to damn well sit down to do it, am I?' he had insisted.

Behind the net veil of her smart hat his sister Maud dabbed her eyes with a handkerchief.

The newly-weds processed down the aisle and emerged into the sunshine beneath a guard of honour formed by soldiers of Arthur's regiment. The ancient churchyard was packed with villagers and estate workers eager to see Miss Bella's wedding. Children perched on the walls and old women pressed between the gravestones for the best view. Two or three of the young girls must have been cinemagoers because they nudged each other and pointed at Jake Jones. He raised his hat to them and they giggled.

Cornelius kept to the shelter of the church porch as the bride hitched up her skirts, seized her husband's hand and dashed through the showers of rice to their waiting landau.

The coachman flicked his whip and a pair of greys decked in ribbons and flower garlands trotted away from the lych gate. In twos and laughing groups the guests followed them down an avenue of chestnut trees to the manor house.

Maud's husband came to wheel Harry's chair, but Harry told him to accompany his wife and sons and let Cornelius do it instead. The two of them lingered in the porch.

'I think we did jolly well,' Harry remarked.

Cornelius's shaking hands were hidden in his pockets.

'I don't know about you. I almost couldn't manage it,' he muttered.

Harry settled his cumbersome casts on the chair's foot-rests. 'I felt the same. Speaking selfishly, I can't bear to be looked at with all the glow of people's sympathy. I don't blame 'em, I've done the same myself. You know, even though I saw all those poor chaps going through hell I never properly took account of how bloody lucky I was to be unhurt, until I wasn't.'

He flicked a glance at Cornelius and then gave a quick cough. He rummaged under the blanket that covered his knees and fished out a crumpled cigarette packet and a box of matches. He lit two cigarettes and passed one to Cornelius before sucking the smoke into his lungs.

'Those who don't know any better might call it bravery, eh? But to be brave you have to know fear, and I wasn't quite imaginative enough for that. You strike me as a different case, if I may say so.'

'I can imagine, all right,' Cornelius replied.

Harry took another deep pull on his cigarette before throwing it aside. He hoisted himself upright and gave Cornelius a full salute.

'Arthur told me what you did, and for how long.'

Cornelius didn't answer and in the following silence

Harry adjusted his lap rug and peered out into the grave-yard to see how many onlookers remained.

'Most of them have gone, in the wake of your friend the film star. I think I'm ready, if you are.'

Cornelius took the chair handles and started pushing. Over his shoulder Harry remarked, 'My ridiculous accident with the runaway motor bus did have the effect, as a result of your brother's bravery, of obliging my dear mother and father to see sense at last. Arthur has been my friend since our first day at Harrow. He's an excellent chap and he will make Bella very happy.'

'I think so too,' Cornelius said. 'And he is a lucky man to have her.'

'Stop pushing a minute, will you, and come round here?'

Cornelius did as he was told. Harry put out his hand and the two men gravely shook.

'I'm proud to call Arthur and you my brothers-in-law. Not that Maud's Hughie isn't a perfectly decent chap. Now, we'd better show ourselves at this wedding breakfast or Ma and Maud will be furious with me. It doesn't take much to have that effect, believe me, as I've unfortunately discovered since I've been living back at home. Never mind. I can give you my solemn promise that there will be more to drink than a single glass of champagne with the toasts because I have seen to it personally.'

'My father will be pleased to hear that,' Cornelius said as he propelled the wheelchair down the chestnut avenue.

The wedding breakfast was laid out at round tables in the great hall of the manor, under a beamed roof and overlooked by gloomy Bolton portraits. The room had been emptied for the occasion of a grand piano, several dog-dented chintz sofas and other ponderous family furniture. The receiving line was in the hall's anteroom, where Lady

Bolton had gone her own way with the flowers. The scent of lilies was overpowering.

Devil stood in the line with Arthur and Bella and the General and his lady. He had found a source of drink independent of Harry's supply because although he started meekly enough by shaking hands with county grandees and describing himself if asked as an impresario or a theatre owner, by the time the end of the line was in sight he had become an escapologist who was about to amaze the world with an impossible feat based on the Earl of Carnarvon's discovery in the Valley of the Kings.

'Come to my first performance at the Palmyra theatre. Prepare to be amazed,' he repeated.

One elderly lady wanted to know if he was acquainted with his lordship's grieving family.

'Not personally,' Devil grinned. 'Are you?'

'Why, yes. His widow is a cousin of mine,' she replied faintly.

Jake rejoined the line and firmly took him by the arm. 'That's enough.'

'I was just starting to enjoy myself,' Devil complained.

In the crowd Nancy found Lizzie with Raymond Kane. They had been quarrelling and Lizzie angrily pursed her full red lips. Her hair was arranged in a row of pin curls under a saucer-shaped hat.

'He's just a child,' she protested.

'He's a brat,' Raymond snapped.

'Tommy is overexcited,' she explained to Nancy. 'Ma and Pa have taken charge of him.'

The Shaws were uncomfortable in what they felt to be elevated company so they had withdrawn to a corner behind a pedestal flower arrangement. Tommy hopped up and down beside them, his satin stock askew.

'The boy needs a thick ear, if you ask me.'

'Nobody did ask you.' Lizzie gave Raymond a little shove. 'Go away and let me talk to my cousin.'

As soon as he was out of earshot she gave Nancy a shrewd look.

'So. Tell me everything.'

'What do you mean?'

'Come off it. Something has happened and I want to hear about it. Don't you dare be evasive with *me*, Nancy Wix.'

Nancy had to laugh. At that moment the crowd parted, and as if the little scene had been lit for her benefit she saw Lion Stone. He was at the other end of the room, whispering in the ear of a girl who reached up and provocatively tugged a handful of his curls.

'Do you miss him?' Lizzie demanded.

'I miss the idea of him.'

'Any new ideas?' Lizzie took a sip of her drink and mimed a splutter. 'My God, what is this? Fruit cordial?'

'Lady Bolton inclines to TT, according to Arthur.'

'To hell with that. Over here, please.' Lizzie crooked her finger to one of the hired staff and ordered him to bring them some real alcohol. 'Go on,' she ordered Nancy once their glasses were charged.

Nancy's happiness welled up, splashing the already delicious day with shards of iridescent light.

'There is someone.'

'*Aha.*'

'But he's not free, and I can't tell you a single thing so don't ask me.'

'Married?'

'I'm afraid so.'

Lizzie regarded her over the rim of her glass. 'You're a

346

grown woman. If you want my advice it would be to take what you want from life, don't be browbeaten just because you're a woman, and don't make excuses or look for any allowances for the same reason. Bear in mind that you rarely get a second chance. I won't pry any further, which is damned difficult for me, but – darling Nancy – I have never seen you look so bloody enchanted.'

It was true. In the space of six weeks Nancy's loneliness had dissolved and only through its absence did she understand how it had afflicted her. In the quiet Bloomsbury evenings she and Gil talked for hours at a time, unfolding their histories to each other. On the nights they were able to spend together she lay in his arms, almost unable to believe in her own happiness. If Celia was away in the country for a weekend they stayed in the flat, only emerging for decorous walks beside the boating pond in Regent's Park or for drives to sit beside log fires in country pubs. This must be how it was to be married, she thought. It was a matter of ease and intimacy, of being able to be silent or sad as well as foolish together. It was having a safe harbour. As for the future – she let herself wordlessly dream without even giving shape to the wishes.

Nancy smiled at her cousin. She was too protective of the magical state to say another word.

'What about you?' she parried.

Lizzie was always ready to talk about herself. 'I'm trying to make money. It's not easy.' This was what she always said. 'Otherwise, Ray's all right. He can be a bit of a boor but he's got what it takes, if you know what I mean. I wouldn't marry him though, even if he was asking, which he isn't. He doesn't hit it off too well with Tommy for a start, and the boy has to come first.'

They watched the child emerge from his corner and make

a dart at one of the crimped bridesmaids. Lizzie took more of an interest in her son these days, apparently valuing his company while offering him her own unimpressed view of the world.

'Don't pull the girl's hair. Oh dear, too late,' Lizzie cried. She grabbed her cousin's arm. 'Come on. Let's see who's here before the speechifying starts.'

Somewhat surprisingly General Bolton was deep in talk with Faith and Matthew. He left it to his wife to steer the Lord Lieutenant towards suitable county targets. The groups of country neighbours and Bolton cousins and Arthur's brother officers parted as the cousins passed. Powdered faces peered, soldiers stood an inch taller and gentleman farmers shook their crimson jowls. People looked at Nancy not because they recognised her from the stage – this was not a Spiritualist crowd – but because her brightness today drew the eye like a fine picture.

'See what I mean?' Lizzie Shaw murmured from the corner of her mouth.

The double doors to the hall were thrown open and the guests were invited to take their seats for the wedding breakfast. Nancy was delighted to find herself next to Jake. Jinny and Ann were also on their table although the two women had been tactfully partnered with a neighbour's shy son and one of Arthur's bachelor friends.

Jinny winked at Nancy and Jake. In theory the room contained everything she most disapproved of, but that didn't mean she wasn't going to enjoy herself.

Jake leaned back in his gilt chair to study the room.

'Eliza would be pleased.'

Unlike Whistlehalt, the only other sizeable establishment Nancy knew outside London, Henbury was defiantly a pre-war country house. It was a realm of dogs and stirrup cups and rhododendrons, of military service and medal ribbons, and county hierarchies that were minutely understood and observed. Eliza had aspired to this world for Arthur, but Jake and Nancy understood a little more about the subtle strata of English life and so they looked beyond. That was the definition of social advancement, Nancy decided, which was what her mother had ultimately believed in. She wondered what Eliza would have made of Gil, and his more elevated position in the world. She would have been interested in him as a man, she was certain of that.

Jake murmured in her ear, 'When will you come down for a weekend? Freddie told me to make sure of you because I shall have to go to America again quite soon. Movie work pays.'

Nancy hesitated to make plans. The chance of time with Gil doing the simple things they enjoyed together was too precious. It made her smile that for a sophisticated man he liked the most ordinary activities – to be alone with her, taking a stroll to the shops in Kingsway and carrying back groceries in a netting bag. They would sit at the little kitchen table to eat what she cooked and then retreat to the bedroom. He enjoyed the respite from being rich.

She demurred. 'I'm not quite sure when I can leave town, Jake.'

Jake raised an eyebrow. 'Bring him, whoever he is.'

She really hadn't known it was so obvious.

'I can't do that, but I promise I'll come soon. I need you, and Jinny and Ann.'

Pointedly he said, 'Yes, you do.'

He was so shrewd and feline, and the better she knew him the more dearly she loved him. They talked a little shop about the theatre. Jake was booked to do a short series of readings at the Palmyra and these were already sold out. Devil was enthusiastic about his long-threatened Tutankhamun escape trick.

'What do you know about it? Will he manage to bring it to the stage?' Jake asked her.

'It will be impossible to stop him. In the meantime it's giving him and Gibb a lot to work on. I don't know anything else, except that it's a tribute to the great Houdini.'

The first plates were being lifted and it was time for them to turn to their neighbours, but before they did so Jake nudged her. Sylvia Aynscoe, tiny as a wren, was placed between two large soldiers. In her old age she was becoming forthright and she was putting them both in their place.

Soon it was time for the speeches. General Bolton's in praise of his younger daughter was so gently affectionate it made Bella blush. Arthur thanked his new in-laws with modest grace. Nancy thought again that it was Arthur's gift to fit in anywhere, but he did it particularly well here at Henbury amongst myriad Boltons. He might have been bred specifically for the role. It was a good match – no one in the room, Lady Bolton included, could imagine otherwise.

Cornelius said he could not manage a best man's speech, so one of Arthur and Harry's brother officers gave a tribute to the groom. A modest buzz generated by an equally modest flow of champagne filled the room. The shy boy beside Ann was trying valiantly to flirt with her.

After the toast to the newlyweds Arthur and Bella prepared to cut their cake and Nancy went hunting for Devil. She found him at the table he had shared with the Boltons, his chin propped on his hand.

'I keep thinking I'm going to be asked to do my act for the gentry, and then be dismissed afterwards with a couple of guineas in an envelope.'

'I feel the same. A private sitting in the Blue Room, do

you think? How much should I charge? Jinny and Ann are joking about feeling so *déclassé*. Jinny said she might ask the head gardener if there's any greenhouse work going this winter. But you shouldn't be thinking like that, Pa. We're family now.'

He huffed. 'I prefer the family I've already made, thank you.'

Bella's hand with the wedding ring rested over her new husband's as they sliced the cake with Arthur's dress sword. After the applause and cheers the couple left to change and the older country neighbours and relatives began to say their goodbyes.

'You are a horrid boy and I hate you,' the ringleted bridesmaid hissed at Tommy Hooper.

The boy was seized by a dark idea. He ran behind the floral arrangement that had earlier sheltered his grand-parents, gathered his strength, and pushed. He wasn't tall, but he had his departed father's compact strength. The plaster pedestal rocked satisfyingly and he pushed harder until it gathered momentum. Finally the tipping point came. Flowers, vase and pedestal fell and smashed into a thousand pieces. A tidal surge of water rose in the air before gushing across the floor. An old lady screamed and the bridesmaid pointed a small finger.

'It was him. He did it on purpose.'

Devil sighed at the mess.

'If only I could do a pass and put it all back together. But I'm afraid that is beyond even me.'

Lizzie seized her boy by the arm, marched him to Lady Bolton and made him apologise. He didn't get much of a scolding because the bride and groom were ready to leave. The guests surged out into the damp twilight to wave the newly-weds off.

Arthur had borrowed a car. In the press of well-wishers surrounding it he hugged Nancy.

'You are the best sister a fellow could have. I'll be so happy when you get married too. Won't you and Lion think of it?'

For a conventional man on his wedding day the desire to draw her into the same favoured circle was understandable, but Nancy still felt a tremor.

'No, that's over now. Who knows what will happen next?'

She kissed his cheek and patted the spruce shoulder of his civilian coat.

'All the joy in the world to you and Bella.'

The bride's bouquet was caught by the girl who had tugged Lion's curls. Bella and Arthur motored away to their week's honeymoon with a selection of army boots bouncing from the rear bumper. Tommy Hooper liked this better than anything else about the long day.

The Shaws were setting off. Faith quietly wept into her handkerchief so Lizzie steered her into the back of her car and bundled the disgraced Tommy in beside her.

'Look after your granny until I'm ready,' she ordered. 'Don't you dare make any more mischief.'

Faith sniffed.

'He's no trouble, really. Are you, Tom?'

Matthew was telling everyone how the General had thanked him for Rowland and Edwin's sacrifice.

'I said to him, how proud I am of my sons. Faith sees it a different way. I suppose she's taking on now because we won't have a day like this one for either of our boys, and of course Lizzie's occasion was a wartime event. But we've seen Arthur wed, and that's a great pleasure. If only Eliza had been here with us, eh, Devil?'

He clasped the hand of his brother-in-law and Devil

patted him on the back. It was a rare display of affection between the two men.

The charabanc Devil had arranged to transport the Palmyra contingent was also ready, with Sylvia Aynscoe perched up at the front. There would be a sing-song, and they would stop somewhere along the road for beer and sandwiches. Devil said wistfully that he wished he could go with them.

Raymond Kane took the opportunity to give Nancy a very thorough embrace.

'What a family,' he said ambiguously, before jumping into his open tourer.

It was already dark beneath the copper beech trees bordering the lawns and the church tower at the end of the avenue was outlined against a deep purple sky. Through the windows of the house the hired staff could be glimpsed stacking glasses and dismantling tables. The Wixes went to find General and Lady Bolton.

The General shook hands with Devil and Cornelius, and he kissed Nancy's hand in a courtly way that touched her.

'God bless our children,' he said to Devil.

'I think it went off quite well, all things considered,' Lady Bolton added. 'Please don't concern yourselves any more about the floral arrangement. I'm sure the boy understands and regrets what he did.'

As they motored away from Henbury Devil wondered, 'Do you think the old chap would have liked to drink a quiet glass with us, Con? After all the clergymen and maiden aunts had taken themselves off?'

'She would never have allowed it,' Nancy said.

With two hands Cornelius outlined a monstrous brim and imposing crown.

Devil sighed. 'What do you expect from a woman who wears a hat exactly like a coal scuttle?'

When they reached London Nancy said she thought she would drop in on Jinny and Ann and talk over the day with them. Devil set her down at the corner of Shaftesbury Avenue and she walked quickly across New Oxford Street and up into Bloomsbury, to Gil and whatever lay ahead of them. The plane trees in the square were leafed in fresh green.

# CHAPTER SEVENTEEN

They were to share so many similar evenings over the years, but whenever Nancy thought over her life with Gil it was the evening of Arthur and Bella's wedding day that came back to her. Perhaps because it glowed with the happiness of the day, or perhaps for the way its intimacy contrasted with the clamour of the party, or perhaps it stayed with her because it was the first time she lied about her whereabouts to Devil and Cornelius.

It was also the first time Gil told her that he loved her.

She let herself into the Bloomsbury flat and its muffled seclusion closed around her. She had time to set out cutlery and glasses and lay a simple meal before Gil knocked at the door. He took her by the hand and kissed her, and she didn't mind that he hadn't been at Henbury or that he had never met any of the people who had shared the joyful day.

'Tell me all about it. I want to hear every single detail.'

'It was a perfect wedding.'

He took off his coat and sat at the table in his shirtsleeves, in the place that had already become his. Nancy had lit a pair of plain candles and their two minutely superimposed shadows lengthened on the wall behind him. After she had finished the stories of the day and they had laughed about Devil and the country ladies and Lady Bolton's coal-scuttle hat and Tommy's act of sabotage, he stood and drew her to her feet. He cradled her head against his shoulder, in the place where the double thump of his heart was amplified by his ribcage.

'Nancy, may I say something?'

The thudding of her heart matched his.

'Yes, always.'

'I want you always to remember that you deserve a better man than me, and you deserve far more from life than I am able to offer you. Wasn't there any young officer who took your eye at Henbury Manor?'

He was only partly joking. She thought he did perhaps fear losing her, incredible though it seemed.

'Such as Harry Bolton? No,' she said. 'Can you imagine me as a colonel's lady?'

'Perhaps not, but as a banker's wife? An actor's? A doctor's?'

She noticed that he only cited the professions.

'I don't think so. Do I have to be anyone's wife? Can't I just be myself?'

'Nancy, you don't know what you're saying. You are an exceptional creature. Even if it didn't happen that first night in Fleet Street, or when I saw you through the crowd at that abysmal party, I certainly fell half in love with you in your dressing room, you in your red wrap with your lovely bare feet up on the fender and your little dresser frowning at me. Plenty of more suitable men will feel the same and want to care for you. I'm no more than an adulterous husband and a liar.'

'I don't care about that. I am a liar too.'

Gil put a finger to her mouth.

'Hush. I am sorry my situation is what it is and to have put you in this position. If it's worth hearing in spite of my failings, I want to tell you that I love you.'

Her heartbeat was a quicker counterpoint to his.

'To hear you say it is enough. I'm not a child, or incapable of making my own choices. You gave me the opportunity to pull back, didn't you? I didn't do it and I've never had any doubt that this is what I want. I love you too.'

In that moment they seemed to know and understand each other perfectly and to look for nothing more.

Gil led her back to her chair. He poured two glasses of muscat to accompany the slice of wedding cake she had brought for him and sat down to regard her through the candlelight.

'Celia tells me that she plans to take a cure at a medical centre in Switzerland this summer. It's on her latest doctor's advice. She will travel with her mother and a cousin, and they will be away for perhaps as long as a month.'

'Does that mean you'll be mine to do what I want with, for all that time?'

He nodded and she saw the dimple at closer quarters, as when they lay in bed together.

'I will be yours. But a man has to do business. I must visit some of our manufacturing partners near Paris, and after that perhaps take the opportunity to look up an old friend. He is a diplomat, at present based in Rome. Would you like to come with me, Nancy?'

As recently as yesterday she would have said no. She had the Palmyra to think of, and her booked seances, and Devil and Cornelius and the never-ending drain of Waterloo Street. Today her responsibilities were exactly the same but the wedding seemed to have lightened them. She didn't hesitate.

'I would adore to come with you. Will I be your secretary? Your personal cook, perhaps?'

He laughed at that. 'Of course not. You travel as my friend, Nancy. It won't be until the summer but with your permission I'll put the arrangements in hand.'

She felt slightly dazed. 'How wonderful. But you know, I'd be just as happy to stay here.'

They looked round at the simple room.

Gil said, 'Me too. Should we go to bed now, do you think?'


When the time came, Nancy told Devil that she was taking a holiday. The Palmyra was closing for a month in any case, while Devil prepared a show called *Dreams of Ancient Egypt* to showcase his long-awaited illusion.

She had never asked for even a week off before, and he was astonished and not at all pleased by the request.

'A holiday? For a *month*? What an idea. With whom, may I ask?'

'With a friend.'

Devil glowered. 'Is this the same "friend" who seems to take up half your life nowadays, as if your brothers and I have ceased to exist?'

Nancy had already stopped making up stories about where she was going and with whom. The complications only multiplied and tripped her up until she felt mired in deceit. She explained that she had met a man she cared for and whose circumstances were not straightforward. He made her happy, she added, and if that was enough for her it should also be enough for her family and friends. She refused absolutely to be drawn any further, and her brothers and Jinny and the others accepted her decision and left her in peace. It was only Devil who made any real difficulties.

'Who is this person? I demand to know. I'll give him a horsewhipping.'

'Pa, you haven't got a horsewhip. Do you mean that thing you cracked to set the balls spinning in the old show opener?'

'Be careful. You're not too old to be put over my knee, my girl.'

She circled his shoulders with her arm. Devil seemed frail these days, for all his noise and bluster.

'I am, actually. Don't make me want to leave you and Neelie and this house, just so I can live my own life.'

Devil buckled at once. He shut his eyes and pressed his head against her arm.

'Don't do that, Zenobia. Please don't.'

She kissed the top of his head.

'I won't. Just let me be.'

In this way her life came to be lived in separate compartments. In one box she kept her family and the Palmyra, and Jinny and Ann and Jake and all her friends; and in the other was the Bloomsbury flat with the newly installed telephone that she willed to ring, and there was waiting for Gil to come, and sometimes there was Gil – which made up for everything.

Nancy had never been abroad. They took the boat train from Victoria and embarked on the Channel ferry at Dover. She insisted that Gil come up with her on deck to watch England sliding away behind the churning wake.

'Look, Gil. Look at the white cliffs.'

'Very picturesque, darling. Almost as appealing as the tables laid for lunch in the dining room.'

She leaned in to him, loving the salt wind in her face. She didn't even think of the *Queen Mab*.

'All right. Let's have lunch. My first ever meal outside England.'

Gil travelled efficiently, but with every comfort. There were always first-class tickets and porters flocking for the luggage and bowing managers showing the way to the best suites. Nancy was shocked by the extravagance, to the point that the collision between his profligacy and her parsimony became a joke between them. Yet such luxury was alluring when he laid it before her. She didn't think even Ann Gillespie would have turned her back on it.

At the Paris hotel Gil immediately established himself at the desk in their suite. She was intrigued to overhear him making telephone calls and issuing terse directions to contractors and engineers. On their second morning a sheaf of letters was delivered for his signature from the hotel's commercial bureau and he frowned over the typing errors. Nancy looked over his shoulder.

'I could do better than that.'

'Can you?'

'Just don't ask me to take shorthand dictation.'

A typewriter was carried into the room and she sat down at the corner of the desk. Gil was impressed that she knew some French, and her years in the print and the secretarial course Lizzie had paid for stood her in good stead now.

He raised an eyebrow when she handed him the finished work.

'I may reconsider what I said about you being my secretary,' he said.

She was amused by the strangeness of life. Here she was, exactly as Eliza had wished, a personal assistant to a businessman. She was also the businessman's mistress – undoubtedly she was – which fell more into Lizzie's area of expertise.

360

'What are you laughing at, Miss Wix?'

'Time. Destiny. That sort of thing.'

'Eh? Please explain yourself properly over dinner. I have to go out now for my meeting with Monsieur Emanuel of Matériels Duchamp.'

When Gil was occupied Nancy strolled out to the Champs-Élysées and admired the elegant shops and fashionably dressed women, or lingered over coffee at one of the mirrored cafés. She walked in the Tuileries and explored the cobbled avenues that bordered the Seine, and even found her way as far as Notre Dame. One afternoon Gil took her to the Louvre and introduced her to his favourite pictures, another night they went to the opera to hear *Don Giovanni*. In a succession of shimmering restaurants she ate delicate *quenelles* of pike in a silky cream sauce, or sampled *cuisses de grenouilles* or sole *bonne femme* or *crêpes Suzette*. She was startled on the last evening when Gil abruptly took away her fork and squeezed her hands in his until the bones almost cracked.

'Thank you,' he murmured, with an odd light in his face.

'For what?'

'For your splendid appetites and your energy and for taking so much pleasure in life.'

He pushed his plate away and lit one of his black-and-gold cigarettes. Gil rarely spoke about Celia and he had never uttered a word of criticism, but Nancy understood from his words that Celia did not have the same traits.

'I have never enjoyed anyone's company so much,' he told her.

Nancy glowed. She loved to think that he was finding equivalent pleasure in what felt like pure magic to her.

That night, after they had made love, she lay curled amongst the piles of pillows and gazed at the shadows of gilt furniture and swirls of rococo plasterwork. The heaviness and grime and uproar of London, and the drudgery and plodding routines of her own life – even the queasy swell of the Uncanny – had been consigned to another universe. She listened to Gil's breathing. He was contained and quiet in sleep, unlike Lion who had thrashed and muttered and snored. She moved her hand stealthily under the starched sheet and let it rest on his warm flank.

In the morning they drank coffee in bed as Gil frowned over the foreign financial news.

'I think I am in heaven. I adore Paris,' she sighed. 'Thank you for bringing me here.'

He folded a broadsheet page.

'Ah, wait until you see Rome.'

She felt apprehensive about it. In Paris they had been anonymous in the opulent and discreet cocoon of their hotel, whereas in Rome they were to be guests in the apartment of Gil's diplomat friend.

When they arrived after the long train journey it was blindingly hot and Nancy did not have the right lightweight clothes. She sweated and itched while Gil was cool in a linen suit and a panama hat. She thought irritably, Well. This is where the differences between us will really start to show. I am a badly dressed girl from the lower classes, I don't know a word of Italian and I haven't a clue how to make diplomatic small talk. How will he deal with *that*, I wonder? She stared gloomily out of the taxi window as they whirled past fountains and through dazzling baroque squares.

Francis Lowell's apartment was huge, with high arched ceilings and cool marble floors. She was shown to a bedroom with faded lemon-coloured shutters folded against the blinding sunlight. The walls were painted with a frieze of cheeky *putti*. In the pier glass in the little dressing room she caught sight of her red-faced reflection and stuck her tongue out at it. Beyond the dressing room she discovered a tiny bathroom furnished with a sit-bath and a bidet. She ran water into the bidet and defiantly soaked her feet.

Gil's bedroom was discreetly nearby and his head soon appeared round her door.

'Are you ready to come and meet everyone?'

'No. Look at me.'

'I'm always eager to look at you. Any particular bit?'

She was almost in tears. He didn't understand what it was like to feel out of one's depth.

'Gil, what am I to wear? What am I to say to your friends?'

'Why? My friends will love you. It's not like you to be in a funk, Nancy. I've seen you onstage, remember, holding two hundred people captive with ten words. And you are dressed perfectly, by the way.'

He held out his arm, and after a moment she took it.

He wouldn't have brought her here if he didn't think she could survive.

They emerged on to a shaded terrace lined with lemon trees in huge terracotta pots. Nancy glimpsed basket chairs with white cushions, a gramophone on a side table, and a number of willowy young people drinking cocktails. A man detached himself from the group and came towards them.

'Here you are. Was the journey frightful? Gil, my dear, what a pleasure to see you.'

Francis had greying hair and crinkly eyes and he wore a cornflower in the buttonhole of his beautiful jacket. When Gil introduced her he took Nancy's hand and kissed it.

'*Che bella*,' Francis murmured.

He drew her into the nearest group. The guests were a mixture of English and Italians, most of them young men. They all wore un-English clothes in shades like lavender and primrose, and the talk immediately switched out of Italian into English to include her. Francis Lowell spoke Italian perfectly, and Gil had told her his German and French were just as good. He was attached to the embassy in some cultural capacity although his role was not to be discussed in any detail. The two men could not have been more unlike, but the same vagueness surrounding her brother's precise occupation brought Arthur to mind.

'What a divine bag that is,' one of the chic women said to her. 'Don't let it out of your sight or I shall steal it.'

The bag was made of golden straw in the shape of a fish. Nancy had bought it on a whim in an antiques market on the Left Bank, so she told them how she had had to haggle for it in her abysmal French and had confused *poisson* with *poussin*. Everyone laughed, and at the edge of the group she saw Gil watching her and smiling.

On the way into dinner they followed two of the epicene young men. Gil murmured in her ear, 'You understand what sort of a household this is?'

'Yes. I told you about my good friend Jake Jones, didn't I?'

'Jake Jones the actor? Is *he* a . . .'

Gil's hand made a small arc and she had begun an answer before she realised he was teasing her. This Roman establishment did strangely remind her of Whistlehalt, and as a result if she didn't feel exactly at home she didn't feel lost either. The understanding was the same; you could be anyone, man or mistress or matriarch or hermaphrodite, from any walk of life, and there would be no judgements passed. The only obligation was to be interesting and if possible amusing.

It made her realise that she could and should take Gil to Whistlehalt and introduce him there.

At dinner she was placed beside Francis. Logically she knew that she had never been anywhere and couldn't contribute to the political or artistic talk, but Gil's old friend behaved as if she were the most sophisticated and intelligent woman he had ever met. He was the embodiment of charm and good manners and she liked him, as well as admiring his assurance. She was pleased to make him laugh with stories about working as a medium and her theatre background.

'Can't we persuade you to do a seance for us here, Nancy?'

'Oh please, no. I am on holiday.'

He nodded, his eyes crinkling. 'Everyone deserves a vacation. I'm happy to see my old friend thriving on his. Thanks to you, I believe.'

In Rome, Gil took her on the tourist circuit to the Coliseum and the Spanish Steps and St Peter's, and she was suitably awed. They also went shopping – although to Nancy it was quite unlike the harrowing business of searching for anything she liked and could afford in London. They looked into one or two shops and that afternoon a stack of white and pink and gold boxes was delivered to the apartment. Inside layers of tissue were crisp blouses and sundresses in melting shades, silk scarves and exquisite kid gloves. There was lingerie too, with ribbons and lace edgings and inserts. Her favourite of all the things was a hat with a brim that shaded her eyes, in exactly the same golden straw as the fish bag.

'I can't possibly accept all this,' she said. 'But I will keep the hat.'

He looked hurt. 'Why not? I am indulging myself far more than you.'

She understood that an argument was the last thing Gil wanted. In the end she accepted the wonderful clothes with some misgivings, but she wore them with elan.

After a week she was sorry to say goodbye to Francis and his friends.

'I liked him so much,' she said to Gil.

'And he you.'

Rome had been even better than Paris, but now they took a train to the Mediterranean coast where Gil had borrowed a villa belonging to another friend. The house stood alone on a headland, surrounded by sunny or shaded terraces and overlooking a bay that looked too sapphire blue to be real. An Italian *mamma* came in every morning to do the housework and prepare a dinner, but otherwise they were completely alone. In the mornings, while Gil wrote letters or telephoned, Nancy read and sunbathed and went for walks through the aromatic scrub that clothed the headland. In the afternoons they climbed down to a little beach to swim and dry off by baking in the sand. In the late afternoons they strolled to the village, where Nancy found in the tiny square all the shades of yellow-grey and green-black and faded sepia that were the heart of Italy. Her skin turned golden in the sun and her limbs loosened with the days of swimming and relaxing; even her sharp bones seemed to melt in the buttery heat. Gil studied her from under the brim of his panama and then pulled her to him as if he would never let her go.

The two weeks of their idyll came to an end, and an old grey taxi bumped up the headland to take them to the dusty railway station. All the way up the Ligurian coast Nancy sat with her face to the carriage window, fixing the last glimpses of blue Mediterranean in her head. Gil held her hand and watched the same view.

When they reached London he said that Celia would be returning tomorrow and he must go to Bruton Street at once.

'When will we see each other again?'

His face tautened. 'As soon as I can arrange it.'

She nodded quickly, wishing she hadn't asked.

She held the images of their holiday inside her like a series of lantern slides, reviewing them whenever she felt downcast. The Bloomsbury flat was airless from being closed up for the whole of July until she threw open the doors to the tiny garden. The telephone stood stubbornly silent on its table.

In Waterloo Street she admired Cornelius's crop of summer vegetables and set about scouring away the grime that had collected in the kitchen in her absence. She went joyfully to the pub and to the pictures with Jinny and Ann. ('Where did you get *those*?' Ann demanded, eyeing the hat and the fish bag. 'I'm not even going to ask,' Jinny said. 'But you look bloody marvellous.') She went to visit Faith and Matthew at Bavaria and to see Jake in a new play by Noël Coward. At last, reluctantly, she turned her thoughts inwards to her stage work. The Palmyra was about to reopen for the new season with the anticipated spectacle.

Devil's way of advertising a show had been honed over almost fifty years. *Dreams of Ancient Egypt* was only the latest in a long series. He liked to design posters in the old cluttered style and to pass out handbills to the crowds in the Strand. If he took out a press advertisement it was likely to be a quarter of a page in the *Stage*. Nancy tried to convince him to spend more money on teasing the public appetite, but he dismissed the idea.

'You're exactly like your mother, wanting to spend money

on puffery. Word of mouth, that's the best recommendation. When Carlo and I did *The Philosopher's Illusion* people came to see me because their friends told them it was the best spectacle in London. The Prince of Wales himself came one night. I mean the old one, of course, not this boy.'

'Yes, Pa.'

'The craze for King Tut and anything Egyptian is playing straight to the Palmyra. It's a great opportunity for us.'

'If people aren't tired of him?'

Devil retorted that the public was a fickle entity but he saw no serious decline in its enthusiasm for songs and fashions and cheap souvenirs based on the excavation of the boy king's tomb.

'Let him do it his own way,' Cornelius said privately to Nancy.

'When did he ever do anything else?'

Nancy and Cornelius went to the first night together. Cornelius seldom visited the theatre and never sat through a performance, but Devil insisted that he and old Gibb had done so much work on this trick that his children must be there to see the result. Arthur had already been posted abroad and there was a suggestion that Bella might be in an interesting condition, so she was staying at Henbury with her parents and Harry.

Desmond loyally reported that the rehearsals had gone smoothly, the various desert-themed support acts by singers and contortionists and magicians as well as Devil's centre-piece. Nancy and Cornelius were sitting towards the back of the house. The *fauteuils* had all been taken by paying customers, and in any case they were both superstitious about sitting too close to the stage. It was only once they were seated that Nancy made the ominous realisation that she was sitting in exactly the same place as Lawrence

Feather, the last time she had seen him. Since meeting Gil she had rarely even thought about the medium. To her relief his public presence seemed to have declined almost to nothing – she didn't think he was even working any longer. Certainly he made no appearances at any of the venues she knew and when she passed by she noticed that the rooms in Gower Street had a new occupant.

Cornelius shifted heavily in his seat and fanned himself with the programme. The house lights dimmed and the green-and-gold curtains swept up on a line of girl dancers in Cleopatra costumes with gilt snakes coiled up their supple arms.

When the time came for Devil's illusion a team of stage-hands wheeled on a tall wooden structure in the shape of a pyramid. It stood well clear of the boards. The front section swung open to reveal a replica of the famous sarcophagus with the gilded mask, its painted wide eyes gazing deep into the auditorium. There was a ripple of appreciative applause. At the same time a giant hopper with a funnel mouth was lowered from the flies.

Devil strode from the wings in a purple cloak with a golden key border. His eyes were painted to match the mask. He ran through his introduction with gleeful brio.

'I will be buried alive before your eyes, but I shall escape the tomb itself,' he promised.

Two of the Cleopatra girls came on and lifted his cloak from his shoulders. Beneath it he was wearing a white singlet and drawers. One of the girls chained his wrists and padlocked the chains, and a man was invited up from the front seats to make sure that the lock was secure. The second girl began to wind a thick bandage. She covered Devil's face and head and his crossed arms and chained hands while her companion began working up from his feet to his knees and hips. Within a minute Devil was a wrapped mummy with only a tiny slit left for his nostrils. The girls gently turned him in a circle to show his back and then two men came onstage and hoisted him to stand upright in the narrow confines of the sarcophagus. After demonstrating that the box stood free of the pyramid and was otherwise empty, they indicated a steel brace bolted to the interior, before locking that round the mummy's neck. The door of the sarcophagus was closed over him and the painted lid padlocked in the same way as his wrists and throat.

Now it was time for the burial.

The front of the pyramid was locked and chained but the tiny top section, too narrow for a man's shoulders to squeeze through, was neatly hinged. This cone tipped sideways now and a whispering cascade of sand immediately fell from the hopper to fill the space inside the pyramid. The stream didn't stop until the sand was overflowing on to the boards. The peak clicked back into place and locked, making the pyramid unassailable.

The four assistants stood aside and the theatre filled with the amplified ticking of a clock.

The seconds agonisingly stretched.

Nancy and Cornelius could not look at each other. There was a scrape of strings as one of the musicians shifted his position in the pit. Beads of sweat on the brow of one of the male assistants glittered in the lights. It seemed that several minutes passed.

The audience was transfixed.

The ticking suddenly stopped and Nancy gasped. The terror of a bad dream clung about her.

A great crash of music sounded as Devil staggered from behind the pyramid, dressed only in the sweat-soaked singlet and drawers. He held up his arms but his chest was visibly heaving as he gasped for breath. Slowly he sank to his knees. The Cleopatra girls quickly muffled him in the purple cloak, supporting him as they did so. The audience applauded in relief and Devil was dragged off the stage.

Horrified, Nancy was pinned in her seat. Cornelius rubbed his eyes with the back of his hand.

The programme indicated that Devil would perform another series of smaller sleights, but when the time came he did not appear. Without explanation the next artist came on in his place and the show continued.

As soon as they were able Nancy and Cornelius slipped out of their places and raced backstage. They found Devil slumped at his desk in the old office, his head buried in his hands. Sylvia hovered nearby, a small glass of brandy and water at the ready.

'Pa? What happened?'

He looked up, his face sagging. Cornelius took hold of his wrist to count his pulse.

'I dropped the hair grip.'

'What hair grip?'

'Eh?' He seemed not quite sure of what was happening. 'I dropped it, I tell you. There's no room in that bloody box.'

Desmond appeared in the doorway.

'It's all right, Mr Wix, we're covering. We've put in a longer dance number, I'll ask the girls to show an extra inch of bum, and the band can extend the playing in. Don't you move.'

Devil looked beseechingly at his children. 'Eh? What's he say?'

Cornelius waved everyone away.

'Give him some space. Tell me, Pa. Does anywhere hurt? Your chest? Your head?'

Devil massaged his ribs with a shaking hand. But the question seemed to revive him.

'You would be hurting everywhere, my boy, if you'd damn nearly suffocated. I dropped the hair grip, I tell you. I had it here.' He lifted his other hand, fist clenched. 'The bandages came off easily enough. But as I went to pick the wrist lock with the grip it fell between my feet. Lucky I'd already sprung the neck brace or I'd have garrotted myself trying to reach downwards. That sand is heavy, and hot. Speed is everything. I have to get out of the box as quick as I can, before the air's all used up.'

He shook his head.

'Not like tonight. I strained for the bloody hair grip but I could feel myself going. A big black hole yawning. I could hear your voice, Nancy, screaming like a little girl. *Papa, Papa.* That was what brought me back. Somehow I got the grip with the very tips of my fingers, freed my hands and pressed the box springs. Christ Almighty, what a relief. I just about got out of there, but I was more dead than alive when I took my bow.'

'You looked it,' Cornelius agreed.

Nancy tipped her father's chin, forcing him to look into her eyes.

'Pa, you'll do no more escapology. It's for young men. You are too old.'

Anxiety made her speak more sharply than she might have done.

Devil's mouth slackened and his eyes filmed over. Suddenly and shockingly he began to weep. She stooped over him and held his shoulders. He had become the child and she the protective parent.

He sobbed. 'Fifty years in the theatre. A man's life.'

'I know, Pa.'

She tried to soothe him but he was as inconsolable as an infant.

The next night Nancy and Gil were dining at Fifteen after seeing a new production of *The Seagull*. It was only the third time they had met since their return from Italy. Celia's health had improved following the cure and she had been almost continuously in London. It was only three days ago that she had left to spend a long weekend at home in the country with her mother. Gil had been eager to see the play but Nancy's head was too full of Devil and the Palmyra for Nina and Arkadina to have made much of an impression.

One of the soft-footed staff brought the late supper to their table and Gil refilled their glasses himself. Celia was to return to London in the morning and the Maitlands would be leaving almost immediately to stay with the de Laurys and some relatives in Scotland. Gil was expected to go shooting with his father-in-law.

Nancy was more than ever sharply aware that there would always be evenings like this, when separation loomed without any certainty as to when they would be able to see each other again. She told herself to be happy with what they did have and not to yearn for what was impossible.

As Gil reached across the table to touch her fingers she looked up to see the discreet head waiter threading his way towards their table.

Celia was following behind him.

Nancy snatched away her hand and the look on her face made Gil spin round. He was on his feet before his wife reached his side.

'My darling. How wonderful to see you. How was your stay?'

Celia's eyes were wide, only slightly dazed. She looked puzzled but she offered her cheek for her husband to kiss.

'Mummy wanted to look at some new tweeds for Scotland, so we came up to town this afternoon. They told me at home that you were probably here so I decided to come.'

She gave a little laugh but it trailed away in an uncertain cadence.

Gil said, 'How marvellous. You remember Miss Wix, don't you?'

'Oh, the medium? Yes, yes, of course. Hullo there.'

She stretched out her fingers, sheathed in pearl-white evening gloves. A chair was hurried to the table and Celia sat.

Gil seemed absolutely untroubled.

'Miss Wix and I were this moment talking about you.'

He glanced once, briefly, into Nancy's eyes. And then he said to his wife, 'Yes. Miss Wix has a message for you. She came to ask me what would be the best way to communicate it.'

Celia's lips parted in amazement. She whispered, 'A message for me? From Richard?'

Nancy's face flamed and the muscles of her throat clenched. The impending betrayal cut in every direction and she writhed inwardly. How could she escape? She felt like her father, stifling in the hot sand of the pyramid.

Celia urgently leaned forward. A diamond cuff flashed as she seized Nancy's wrist.

'Tell me.'

'Perhaps not here. I could . . . I could come to Bruton Street.'

The wrist grip tightened. Those fragile fingers were capable of startling pressure.

'Tell me *now*.'

Celia's voice was raised. Heads turned at the nearest tables and Nancy became aware of the clink of cutlery, even the rattle of ice in people's glasses. She had to do it. Gil had thought quickly and if she could do the same they were reprieved. The words she hadn't yet spoken tasted bitter on her tongue.

'*I need to know*,' Celia cried.

More heads were turning in their direction. The head waiter was poised at the side of the room. Gil adjusted the position of his cigarette case on the starched cloth.

Nancy slowly nodded. 'I do understand.'

Celia was absolutely intent. 'Go on.'

It was only like a seance. That was all. It was what she did. No more, no less of a deception. It would not be even as difficult to do as a Palmyra performance.

She spoke through the constriction in her throat.

'I heard your brother's voice.'

True.

Celia's lips parted. She seemed to have stopped breathing. There might have been no one else in the room for either of them. Even Gil had become a shadow.

Nancy's mind raced. What the hell were the words? Somehow they came to her. There was no going back. She recited in a low voice:

'*Fair Katherine, and most fair,*
*Will you vouchsafe to teach a soldier terms*
*Such as will enter at a lady's ear*
*And plead his love suit to her gentle heart?*'

The transformation in Celia was terrible for Nancy to see, because it was so immediate and so joyous.

Colour instantly warmed her white face and her eyes glittered with tears. She drew in a shivering breath, hardly daring to believe her ears at first, and then allowing the significance to sweep through her.

'Is that what you heard? He said that? It's Prince Hal, you know. King Henry. We performed that scene, almost the last thing we did together, before he left for France. Those lines come straight from his dear heart, I know that. He's *there*. After all, after so long, I feel him close. It's the most perfect message you could have brought me.'

This time the clasp of the hand was fervent and Nancy could feel that Celia was trembling.

'Thank you, thank you so much. You are truly, truly gifted.'

In spite of her guilt Nancy was stung. Naturally Celia Maitland wouldn't have thought that Nancy Wix might know the play, or any Shakespeare. Gil had chosen the message adroitly. Coming from a mere medium it was convincing and had it been planned it would have been suitable for the best of seances, worthy of Lawrence Feather himself. This chill knowledge filled Nancy with a deeper degree of dismay, of dislike for what she must do to earn her living, and of disgust with herself.

Gil attended to his wife. He drew her to him and she sobbed a little against his shoulder.

Over her head, his eyes urgently met Nancy's. He signalled his love and need for her and the intimacy revealed in that single glance was almost shocking to Nancy. They depended on each other now. They were locked into a bond that absolutely excluded Gil's wife and which seemed far more dangerous than mere adultery.

Gil murmured, 'Celia? If you are ready I think I should take you home now.'

She nodded, and let her husband help her to her feet. The way he picked up her little velvet bag for her indicated that he knew exactly what it contained. Nancy saw that clearly too.

They each took one of Celia's arms and they steered her gently between the tables. Heads were discreetly lowered now and no one stared at them.

The Bentley was at Bruton Street so a taxi was summoned. In answer to Gil's polite question Nancy said that she would easily make her own way home. He shook her hand, a quick and urgent grasp, and helped his wife into the taxi. She stood alone on the kerb as they drove away.

Now she and Gil were more than illicit lovers. They were conspirators and the landscape was darker and wider.

# PART FOUR

# CHAPTER EIGHTEEN

*December 1931*

As soon as she reached the flat Nancy lit a fire. She knelt on the hearth to put a match to a pyramid of coiled newspaper and kindling, then fed it with sticks until the flames leapt up. Once the fire was blazing she sat back on her heels and slowly warmed her fingers. The weather had been bitterly cold and her chilblains were troubling her again.

She found some red candles in a drawer and placed them in the silver candlesticks. She had picked a few tendrils of ivy in the square's gardens and now she twisted these between the candlesticks on the mantelpiece. They looked festive amongst the ornaments and framed photographs.

Over the eight years the quiet rooms had acquired the patina of occupation. The shelves overflowed with books, there were well-tended plants on the sills and pairs of Gil's spectacles lay unfolded on the arm of a chair and on the little bureau. She prepared a tray with some glasses and the whisky decanter and sat down to wait for him. He had already told her that he would have to return to Bruton Street for dinner because Celia was at home.

He came a little later than promised, driving his latest Bentley into the square and leaving it parked outside. It was not an unfamiliar sight there.

'Darling, I'm so sorry. What a day.'

He kissed her on the bridge of her nose and she let her head briefly rest against his shoulder while she breathed in his good scents of starch and cologne and male skin. She resisted the urge to cling to him.

'Drink?'

He made a face. 'God, yes, please. I've been shopping. I can't stand Christmas.'

His shopping would have included a well-chosen piece of jewellery for her, and although he was generous she thought in her heart how an extra hour or two with him would have been even more precious.

'And I adore it.'

They smiled at each other, acknowledging the familiarity of their differences. Nancy would spend Christmas as always with her father and brother, and this year Jinny and Ann were to join them. Bella and Arthur would be at Henbury with their three boys and the Boltons. Gil would leave with Celia in the morning for a week with her parents. He was always humorous about the clockwork inevitability of church on Christmas morning with the lesson read by the Earl, the King's speech, the Boxing Day shoot, but she suspected that he didn't mind any of it all that much.

'How is Celia?'

Their way of dealing with their old deception was to tiptoe around it. Celia was often mentioned, and Nancy knew about all the superficial social and domestic events of Gil's life with her, but she was never properly discussed.

'Not very well. But reasonably calm. When are you to see Jake?'

Nancy planned a pre-Christmas visit to Jake and Freddie. It would have been even more enjoyable if Gil could have come with her. Jake and Gil liked one another in spite of being different in every possible respect, and the particular limitations of Nancy and Gil's relationship were accepted without comment in the way that all human permutations were accepted at Whistlehalt.

'I wish you were coming. I think I'll go tomorrow. Freddie'll pick me up at the station, he said.'

They put their feet close to the fire and she told him about her week. There had been the usual crises to deal with at the Palmyra, and Devil grew more difficult with every year. These were the problems contained in one of her boxes, and in the other box the serenity of her half-life with Gil – idyllic except for its incompleteness – was unchanged.

This evening there wasn't time for them to go to bed, even for an hour, although she longed to feel Gil's arms around her as much as she wanted sex. They exchanged their Christmas presents instead. Nancy's was a necklace with a sapphire pendant in the shape of a heart, a lovely jewel with a point of blue fire leaping in its centre. She thought it was a little hard and cold, and then felt guilty for her own ingratitude.

Much too soon it was time for him to go. It would be more than a week before they could hope to see or even speak to each other. He took her in his arms and she felt better at once because love seemed to flow out of him.

'I'm sorry,' he murmured, gently rocking her.

'Don't be.'

'I love you.'

'I love you.'

After the door had closed she listened to the rich burble

of the Bentley's eight cylinders as Gil prepared to drive away. She thought absently of how Devil would admire the car and what a shame it was that he had never seen it.

Whistlehalt had always seemed to offer a sanctuary, although Nancy would have insisted that she had no need for such a thing.

She loved its isolated setting above the silvery curve of the river and the dense woodland that hid the house. A solitary walk before tea led her along paths snared with dead brambles and under canopies of leafless trees, and with the surface of her attention occupied by finding the way she let her deeper thoughts play over the business of the theatre and what needed to be done at Waterloo Street. Another year was coming, and the demands at the end of this particularly dismal one had never seemed more pressing.

Their Waterloo Street landlord was a rapacious man. In all the years they had occupied the little house he had done next to nothing to maintain his property. The slates were cracked and creeping loose and Nancy was tired of shuttling tin buckets placed to catch the drips. Draughts sliced between the damp bricks and the warped sash frames and Devil caught colds that descended to his chest until he was racked with coughing. But still the landlord insisted that they didn't pay enough rent to allow him to toss pound notes, as he put it, at the decaying bricks and mortar.

When they confronted him directly he told Nancy and Cornelius that they should make him an offer for the house. He would be glad if they would only take the damned place off his hands he said, before naming an outrageous sum. When they refused he gave them a glare from under the greasy brim of the hat that he never took off. They returned home and rolled up strips of newspaper to stuff into the chinks of the windows, and tried not to hear the irregular ricochets of dripping water. Devil wore two waistcoats under his coat, which made him look like a vagrant. The boys from up the road hooted at him as he shuffled by. Depending on his mood, Devil would either lunge at them with his stick, shouting imprecations until they scattered in alarm, or produce a halfpenny from the ear of the smallest child and drop it into his hand. As a result they would approach him with wary greed every time he left the house.

Devil worried much less about the practicalities of life than either of his children. He inhabited a world of memories, most of them relating to his past glories.

'I used to make 'em laugh', he said. 'And then scare them stiff, and send 'em out wondering and amazed.'

Chuckling, he would take out his handkerchief to wipe the corners of his streaming eyes. He still practised sleights and flexed his knobbly fingers in the least chilly corner of the kitchen, but he had long ago retired from the stage. *Dreams of Ancient Egypt* had been his last show. Whenever Nancy or Cornelius sighed too audibly over the theatre or domestic accounts he would thump his stick on the floor.

'The Palmyra is mine, remember. The deeds are in the safe. Worth a fortune, that place is. Not that I'll ever sell it.'

Nancy turned up the path that led towards Whistlehalt. Wet undergrowth slapped against her corduroy trousers and she dug the balls of her fists deeper into her pockets as she tackled the slope. The clean scents of mud and leaf decay and country rain lifted her out of the circle of anxiety.

Takings were down, but somehow the Palmyra survived. Her own shows still drew decent audiences, and the Society for Psychic Research had adopted the theatre for their demonstrations and public lectures. Jakey's occasional one-man readings were an important mainstay because they always sold out, and for the rest of the time the stage was given over to a hybrid of music hall and magic variety acts. As the owner-manager Devil stubbornly clung to the traditions of the house and Desmond, who did the bookings and all the rest of the work, invariably supported him. It was Desmond who had booked Gracie Fields for a few nights, and although they couldn't afford her any longer Nancy made sure that the star's name always appeared in their publicity with her praise for the Palmyra quoted in bold type:

### A grand little theatre with a great big heart.

Nancy didn't need Jinny or Ann to remind her that she was fortunate, at least compared with many. This year three thousand hunger marchers had converged on London, bearing a petition with a million signatures. The Depression was no longer a notion associated only with America and its stock market. It had taken shape, like a vast hooded crow, and it flapped over all of Europe as well as England. Only that morning Nancy had flicked through a magazine left behind by one of Jake's guests and come across a cheerily inclusive article in which the writer spoke of 'profiteers, dole-drawers, music-hall artistes – in fact the only people who have money today'.

She gave a hollow laugh before chucking the magazine at the wall.

A wicket led from the woods into the Whistlehalt garden. It was the still point of a winter afternoon, when the light had drained away but it was not yet fully dark. When Nancy glanced across the lawns to the golden squares of the house windows and afterwards looked down, she could no longer pick out the delicate thorny margins of the holly leaves. The bushes themselves stood out as dark clumps lining the paler gravel. She was approaching the house, thinking ahead to anchovy toast and the possibility of a slice of Dundee cake, when she noticed a car drawn up by the front door. She had been envisaging a cosy, shoes-off tea with Jake and Freddie and so the prospect of visitors wasn't particularly pleasing, especially as there were several more people already expected for dinner.

She slipped round by the terrace, intending to take off her muddy boots outside the kitchen door. As she passed the drawing room she looked in and saw a grey-haired woman seated with her back to the French doors. She was moving on down a path that led between rhododendrons to the side entrance when something caught her eye, just before she stepped into the tunnel of evergreens. A small figure was standing motionless at the far side of the terrace, a child with long hair falling over a face as pale as the moon.

It was Feather's soaking girl.

It was years since Nancy had last seen her.

She called in a low voice, 'What do you want?'

The apparition turned on its heels and ran away over the pewter grass. Nancy stood staring after it. Lawrence Feather had sent the little creature back to her, she was certain of it. Fear crept through her at the thought of his return.

'What do you *want*?'

Her voice quavered in the wet air. Nothing else stirred and her heart slowed to something like its normal rhythm. She continued on her way into the house.

Freddie was in the back kitchen, half-buried in the branches of a giant fir tree that he had dragged in from the back step. Needles strewn over the lino indicated the route he had taken.

'Isn't this a beauty?' he called.

The house was full of its primitive forest scent.

'It's very big.'

'I told them to send the biggest they had. Let's go to town, I said to Jake. Christmas comes but once a year.'

'Who's the visitor?'

'Oh, that's Mrs Templeton. I came in here looking for tea, or preferably someone to make it, and found the delivery boy with this.'

No one had real servants any longer, except for people like the Maitlands. The hospitable tradition at Whistlehalt was nowadays supported by a series of migrants, young men who were theatrical or musical or still in the process of choosing which of the arts to adopt. Drawn into the circle that revolved around Jake, they were invariably eager to stay and pay for their keep with cooking or housework. Some were better at the work than others but the atmosphere of high culture and bohemian manners suited them all.

Freddie said that the pansy bowl, as he called the household, bloomed beautifully so long as Mrs Gubbins came up from the village every day to do the real slog. Nancy wasn't even sure if this was her real name. She was a well-padded woman never seen without her wrap-around apron, except in the few seconds before she bundled herself into her overcoat and pedalled off down the drive. She pretended to be ignorant of the exact nature of her employers' lives but she liked nothing better than stage-door gossip, and the jokes of the snake-hipped young men who called her Mrs G as they ran in and out of the kitchen. The current mainstay of these was a dancer called Guillaume who had had a career with the Ballets Russes. He was an excellent cook but he wasn't good at clearing up. This afternoon the sink was full of pans and dishes and Guillaume was nowhere to be seen.

As she rolled up her sleeves a memory came back to Nancy of Devil leaning against this sink, on the morning after the first party of her adult life. There were fewer parties these days, even at Whistlehalt. Dorothy and Suzette and the others had stopped whirling, or else they had spun off the merry-go-round and disappeared altogether.

She told Freddie, 'Go on. I'll make the tea and bring it in.'

'Darling, that would be angelic. Where do you think that lovely tub can be, the one pretending to be a squat little Grecian urn that we put the tree in last year?'

'No idea. Does the Honourable Mrs Frances Templeton like anchovy toast?'

Freddie raised a plucked eyebrow. 'I'd forgotten you know her. Of course, she's a relation of Lion's, isn't she?'

'An aunt. I met her even before I knew Lion, through the suffragists.'

'Lord,' Freddie sighed. 'I'm going on a hunt for the balls to hang on the tree. They'll be wrapped in cotton wool somewhere.'

Nancy laid a butler's tray with the best china and napkins, with dishes of anchovy paste and honey in the comb and farm butter, and made tea in the silver teapot. She swaddled the toast in a clean teacloth to keep it warm and hurried the whole lot through to the drawing room.

Jake leapt up, looking relieved to see her. He took the heavy tray while she unfolded the frame beside the fire. Logs blazed in the hearth.

'You know my neighbour, Mrs Templeton, don't you?'

The lady held out her hand, appraising Nancy as she did so.

'Zenobia Wix?' Her memory was formidable. 'Are you still a Spiritualist?'

389

'I never was one, really. I am just a stage medium.'

Mrs Templeton patted the seat beside her to indicate where Nancy was to sit.

She said, 'I believe Mrs Bullock Dodd has sadly passed to the other side. Do you ever hear from her there?'

'I'm afraid not. She probably has more interesting people to converse with.'

Mrs Templeton looked amused. She hadn't in the end followed Lady Astor and successive women into Parliament, although she remained a pillar of the Liberal party and a campaigner for women's rights. Nancy reflected that it was thanks to the efforts of women like Frances Templeton that even she had gained the vote.

She had used hers in support of Ramsay MacDonald.

Jake held up the silver teapot. 'Frances, may I pour you some tea? We're just talking about some odd people who have set up a camp in one of the fields, Nancy. It looks a thoroughly miserable place, but if that's where they want to be I can't see any harm in it.'

'I am inclined to agree with you,' Mrs Templeton said. 'My husband has some reservations to do with precedents and property, but as a lawyer as well as the owner of the land it would be surprising if he did not. However, if you have no objections, Jake, I think we'll let the poor creatures stay where they are for the time being.'

The business was briskly concluded. The corners of Jake's mouth twitched and he took care not to look at Nancy. Even Mr Everard Templeton KC would have little say where his wife's wishes were concerned. She was another Englishwoman of the emergent breed who took on the male universe without a tremor, and Nancy admired her for it – as she had done ever since her first suffragist meeting in the old chapel hall. Mrs Templeton had turned her high privilege to better use than Countess de Laury or Lady Bolton.

Lady Bolton was widowed and now occupied the dowager's wing at Henbury while Sir Harry and his new wife occupied the main house. Harry walked with two sticks and had exchanged the army for life as a farmer. There was no direct heir to the baronetcy as yet but Bella and Arthur had produced three boys in rapid succession.

'I've no idea how it happened,' Bella always laughed, meaning that Arthur spent so much of his time overseas. The three Wix infants were sturdy children. The first and second had Rowland and Edwin added to their Bolton Christian names, to Faith and Matthew's great satisfaction.

The world seemed to be repopulating itself with boy children to replace the lost fathers and uncles. Even Lion Stone had two sons. He was married to the girl Nancy had seen him with at Arthur's wedding, a vivacious creature whose brothers had been in the same house as Lion at Eton.

Mrs Templeton drank her tea and ate her toast. Nancy was being shrewdly evaluated, and the realisation made her feel even more set apart than she did already.

If she had been asked to define herself, what would she have said?

She had learned to control the Uncanny and to profit from it, a little. But it was not enough to make her. She was a daughter, a sister and a friend. What else? She would have liked to be a mother, but it seemed that was not going to happen. She was thirty-four.

'You are an old friend of my nephew's, of course.'

'Yes. How is he, and the family?'

This was no more than a polite exchange. Nancy knew they were flourishing. She heard from Lion from time to time and she was still fond of him. Nancy tried not to think about it, but she had to assume that he hadn't after all been opposed to the institution of marriage itself – he just hadn't wanted to marry *her*. She wasn't the right type.

Frances Templeton would know all this. She probably also knew that Nancy had been Gil Maitland's mistress for years. They were careful always to be discreet, for Celia's sake, but Nancy was aware that her situation was not particularly unusual. Even the Prince of Wales lived by the same double standard. Lady Celia Maitland spent her time in sanatoria, or secluded at home in the country if she was well enough for that. She appeared only occasionally in London, always ethereally pale in her sable and her Vionnet gowns. Gil was known to be a modern husband, the conventions were observed, and there was no need for anyone ever to discuss where the boundaries of his loyalty actually lay.

'It doesn't matter,' he would insist. 'There's the outside world and its circumstances and there is here, with you and me, and that is what I care about. You are the real world to me, Nancy.'

Gil was generous; she loved him and was loved in return. Yet now, in the firelight at Whistlehalt with Guillaume cosily drawing the curtains and Jake lounging in his velvet slippers, she felt an almost irresistible urge to draw up her knees and give way to noisy tears.

She bit the corner of her lip to hold it firm as she stared into the fire. The vivid pictures of her life with Gil leapt up within the flames. They had shared so much, she thought, considering their circumstances. Gil's work took up much of his time and a proportion of what was left necessarily had to be devoted to Celia, so the remaining hours were often brutally short. But from the time when they came back from their first holiday onwards, Gil convinced her to make the very best of what they did have. While they were alone in the Bloomsbury flat they concentrated absolutely on each other and Nancy discovered how sweet and soothing it was to be open and at ease with another human being. She told Gil about every facet of her life, even the inner realms of the Uncanny, and she accepted his corresponding admissions without criticism.

As she had guessed, she was not the first woman he had installed in the Bloomsbury flat.

'But you are the last,' he promised her.

As their years passed, slowly at first and then gathering the momentum of happy routine, this proved to be the truth.

Nancy might have looked for more of what she already had, yet she didn't remotely yearn for anything different. They went out quietly together in London, to dine at favourite restaurants – although he never took her to the Ritz again or to Fifteen. They went regularly to concerts and the theatre, as well as the opera. Celia had developed claustrophobia and would never go with him into enclosed places, and Gil loved music. He taught Nancy to appreciate his favourite composers and he bought her a gramophone and piles of records.

After that first holiday there were others, usually business trips abroad on which Nancy accompanied him in the half-ironic role of personal assistant. She toured factories in Germany and Belgium at his side and typed letters in hotel suites in Berlin and Milan and even New York. For the rest of her life she would remember their Atlantic crossings aboard the *Ile de France*. The outward journey had coincided with her thirtieth birthday and there had been nights of dancing and strolls on deck under the ocean stars.

On these journeys she altogether forgot the questions

about class and status and even morality. She was with her life companion, and that was all.

They even developed a small circle of trusted friends. They saw Francis Lowell whenever he was in England, and others from Francis's indefinable cadre of diplomats and travellers. She knew some of Gil's business associates and even occasionally met their wives, although the women tended to be more reserved. In time Nancy introduced him to Jinny and Ann. The girls never properly warmed to him and Nancy thought it was because he took her away from them, rather than because they mistrusted his wealth or standing or took a moral view. Cornelius was the same. She never even tried to bring Gil together with Devil, or Lizzie Shaw. She didn't think Lizzie would be capable of keeping their secret and Devil in his old age was increasingly combustible.

The two of them were most comfortable at Whistlehalt in Jake and Freddie's worldly circle.

'Of course Lion has a connection to our friends who are camping out in the fields,' Mrs Templeton was saying.

The tears no longer threatened and Nancy dragged her gaze away from the fire.

'He does?'

'Yes, it's one of the reasons why I'm giving them the benefit of the doubt.'

Freddie appeared bearing a box of gaudy glass baubles. Nancy longed for the talk to shift to him and the tree and the tinselly rustle of approaching Christmas, or even the beef that Guillaume was proposing to roast for dinner. She most definitely did not want to hear what Lion's aunt was about to say.

But there was no way to stop her.

'I understand they are an odd cult of extreme parapsychics. Their leader is your friend Mr Feather, Lion's godfather.'

Lawrence Feather, Lawrence Feather. The name roared like surf in her head.

He never disappeared, never. He dipped below the surface of her life until she believed he was really gone, and then each time he re-emerged it seemed that he had only been watching her and biding his time.

'He's not my friend,' Nancy protested.

At last Mrs Templeton drove away in her little car. Guillaume was wobbling on a stepladder in the panelled hallway, two other boys were helping to secure the immense tree and Jake and Freddie competed with each other in the bossiness of their instructions. Nancy went up to her room to change. It was the bedroom she had been given on the first visit, overlooking the river that she hadn't recognised as the Thames. She quickly drew the curtains on the spectre of who or what might be outside looking in. She didn't feel sociable but nor did she want to be alone. She changed into a dress and ran downstairs again.

The tea tray had been replaced with cocktails. There was dance music on the gramophone, the fire had been built up and Jake's guests were gathering for another evening.

A man she didn't know, older than the others but still not out of place in the pansy bowl, held out a hand.

'How do you do? You must be Eliza Dunlop's girl, from the look of you?'

He was wearing a plum velvet smoking jacket with cigar ash powdering the lapels. Nancy acknowledged that she was her mother's daughter after which the man dropped a heavy arm over her shoulders and steered her to a sofa. They sat down and he stuck out his short legs. He had a plump man's small feet and he was clearly vain about them because his shoes were handmade, and exquisite.

'George Gardiner,' he introduced himself.

She didn't recognise the name, although it seemed that she was meant to.

He explained that he was here to begin work on a portrait of Jake, and she recalled then that he was a painter best known for his pictures of Edwardian society beauties, hourglass figures in court dresses with ostrich feathers nodding in their hair.

'Long ago I painted a prize portrait of Devil Wix,' he told her, as if to deny this pigeonholing. He puffed out his broad chest. 'It was rather fine. He was in his costume for some magic illusion, a cloak and a sword as I recall. I wonder what became of it?'

There had been a portrait, Nancy remembered, hanging in their long-ago house by the water in Islington. She couldn't recall seeing it after the day she had come home to find Eliza piling up their belongings on the step and raging because Devil had sold their home to save the Palmyra.

The image was coming back to her – the heavy chiaroscuro, Devil's scowling features made lasciviously handsome in a way she comprehended a little better now. The picture had been mysteriously damaged and restored, although the savage slashes in the canvas could never be fully repaired.

The portrait had not reappeared at Waterloo Street, but nor had Eliza arranged any of their other belongings in the cramped rooms. She had lost heart.

It made Nancy sad to think of it.

'Were you a friend of my mother's?' she politely asked.

Mr Gardiner crossed and re-crossed his ankles, admiring the twinkle of lamplight on glacé shoe leather.

'Ah, Eliza, yes. What a vision. Half the students at the Rawlinson School were in love with her. All the fellows who were susceptible to the ladies, that is. She was a life model as well as a student, you know. I hope I'm not telling you anything too terribly *shocking*?'

'My mother loved to talk about it. Her life-modelling career was one of her very favourite topics.'

George Gardiner rumbled with laughter and folded his hands over the draped velvet.

'You know young Alfie Egan, I think?'

Nancy did, in a way. Alfie became one of her admirers when she first took to the stage. He was a reedy young man with a fine, fair moustache who sent her flowers and shyly invited her to take supper with him. She had never encouraged him and he had long ago taken his mild devotion elsewhere.

'Not very well.'

'His late father, Charlie Egan, was my good friend.'

Sir Charles Egan RA was a more celebrated painter who had held out against the Cubist and Surrealist tides with large canvases titled *The Emperor Hadrian's Feast* or *Cleopatra Bathing with her Handmaidens*.

'Charlie bequeathed me a folder of his early work in memory of our student days. A gesture combining generosity and a certain vanity, which rather neatly conveys the man himself. Did you ever meet him?'

He was chuckling again, setting up a wobbling of his chin and jowls. Nancy relaxed a little. Guests at Whistlehalt were usually interesting or likeable, and Mr Gardiner was both.

'No.'

'Then let me tell you how I recognised you. In Charlie's folder of sketches and doodles there is a life drawing of your mother, rather better executed than the others, which indicates that his attention might have been engaged.'

The painter's hands outlined rounded shapes in the air.

'Your resemblance to her is striking, even though you are . . .'

'Dressed?'

He patted her knee.

'We must meet up in town, and I will show it to you. Your father would like to see it, I'm sure. Do give him my regards, won't you?'

She promised that she would, without adding that the message wouldn't mean much to Devil.

After the drawn-out cocktail hour Guillaume and his friend called the guests to dinner. Nancy sat near the centre of the table and looked up and down at the gesticulating, smoking, gossiping actors and artists, catching the shreds of talk and teasing. Tonight Whistlehalt felt particularly like one of her multiplying series of compartments, separate from the Palmyra stage and the quietly opulent restaurants of Mayfair, cut off from the creaking house in Waterloo Street and equally removed from the two rooms in Bloomsbury that she thought of as the heart of her existence.

She wondered if she was the only one to live this way, moving alone and endlessly from set to set like an actor always preparing for the big speech but never quite delivering it. She glanced up to find Jake gravely looking at her. She flicked him a smile and turned to beg a cigarette from Guillaume, making a point of talking and laughing as she smoked.

In the morning she felt thick-headed and lethargic. She had drunk too much in trying to dispel the feeling that something bad was about to happen. It wasn't the Uncanny, but it was still a premonition that she couldn't shake off.

Jake suggested a walk. Freddie rarely appeared before midday, and the house was quiet.

Nancy didn't like the idea of the camp in the fields, nor did she want any glimpse of the soaking girl drifting at the margins of the woodland. But the landscape surrounding Whistlehalt was precious and she couldn't allow the proximity of Lawrence Feather to cut her off from it. She set out with Jake, leaving footprints in the rime that powdered the terrace and making a dark trail across the frosted lawn. It was a white-skied morning, bitterly cold, without even a bird stirring. Their breath rose in plumes ahead of them.

Instead of dropping down through the trees Jake took the path that led along the ridge. There were fields broken up with copses and brambly coverts. A mile or two to the west the Templetons' huge house lay in a grid of formal gardens.

'Where are we going?' Her voice was sharpened by apprehension.

Jake was surprised. 'Nowhere in particular. Just a circuit.'

They climbed a stile and walked a diagonal path across a field.

'Is something wrong? Are you thinking about the cult and Lion's godfather?'

'Not really.'

Jake knew she was lying. She shrugged off his concern with a few offhand words about the bad feeling that had never dispersed after she had left Feather's management for the Palmyra, and about their professional rivalry. To mention Helena Clare and what her brother had done to her, or the childish apparition that Feather stirred up, went too deep into her bone marrow. She was a thing of secrets, she thought sadly. She tried comforting herself with the belief that most people were. More was unknown than ever would be admitted. Did she even know Gil through and through?

'What else?' Jake prompted.

They reached a five-barred gate. From the opposite corner of a rough field a thin plume of smoke wobbled in the still air.

She stopped and leaned on the gate. The timber was old and seamed and lichens grew in the cracks. She rubbed at the surface with a gloved thumb, grinding the surface into an ochre powder. She tried not to look across the field but she couldn't help herself.

The camp was quite well established. There was an old green caravan at the centre of it, roofed in corrugated iron and with a tin chimney sticking up at an angle, and several rough tents and tarpaulins slung over timber frames were gathered around it in a loose circle. Smoke was rising from a brisk fire, and an old horse was tethered near the shelter of the hedge. She heard the tap-tap of a hammer on metal as if some machinery was being repaired.

She said quickly, 'It's nothing. Money worries, mostly. The Palmyra, Waterloo Street, Pa and Cornelius. I used to feel well off but I don't any more. Does anyone these days?'

Across the field a man ducked from a tent and stooped over the fire. He wasn't Feather but still she turned her back to the camp and pretended to study the view in the opposite direction.

'Is there anything I can do to help?'

There were wrinkles fanning from the corners of his eyes and his hair was more grey than brown, yet it was part of Jake's chameleon quality that he never seemed to age – he could play an old man or a young lover or anything in between. His unobtrusive kindness was undiminished.

'You're a good friend. Honestly, Jake, it's nothing. I just need to get the damned roof repaired at home and persuade you to read at the Palmyra a few more times.'

'I'm going off to America again.'

'Good. Make another film and become even more famous, then come back as quickly as you can. Shall we turn back now?'

It was important to get as far as possible from this eerie camp. She stuck her arm through Jake's and steered him back the way that they had come. Later that afternoon he drove her to the station for the London train.

Jinny's Christmas present to each of them was a yo-yo. Devil and Cornelius adored theirs from the moment they were unwrapped. Devil was naturally adroit, and in minutes he could make his spin horizontally and loop up in the air. Cornelius was far clumsier but he was fascinated by the play of forces on the wooden puck. Nancy had to prise the toys out of their hands to make them come to the table she had laid in the parlour for Christmas dinner. There was a tiny tree on the table in the window and ivy and holly tacked all round the picture rail. With a red tablecloth and a thick blast of heat from the fire the room was quite inviting.

Cornelius had recently assembled the components of a wireless set. He coaxed the dials until the King's voice suddenly boomed out. Nancy imagined Gil at this exact moment, listening to the same words and being waited on in some cavernous drawing room filled with intimidating furniture.

Devil wore a red paper crown that slipped down over one eye. He carved the bird with sweeps of the knife, pressing Jinny and Ann to second and third helpings and ordering Cornelius to top up their glasses. He loved the company of the two women, flirting with them indiscriminately and kissing Ann's flushed cheek whenever she leaned within range. Ann was exhausted from working a month of night shifts and when the time came to clear the table Jinny ordered her to sit still and let someone else do the work.

Ann didn't argue, for once. She sat back against a cushion and beamed.

'Three whole days off from the hospital, and no washing-up? What bliss.'

There was a basket of Shaw's Exotics to finish with. The scent of tangerines clung to their fingers and Nancy recalled the Christmas morning in the nursing home. Luckily Devil didn't seem to think of it. He proposed toasts to the King and Queen and to absent friends, and insisted on rounds of Consequences and Pelmanism before singing the old songs. At the end of the evening Cornelius found some dance music on the wireless and they pushed back the rug and swayed in a tipsy confusion of arms and backsides. It was a happy day. When the time came for Jinny and Ann to leave Devil protested.

'Don't go. People are always going. Eliza, tell them to stay and keep us company.'

'Pa, they need to go to bed and so do I. You've got another visitor tomorrow, remember?'

'Who? Who is it?'

George Gardiner had said he would be visiting some friends who lived not far away and she had already told her father of the painter's plan to drop in on Boxing Day. Devil shook his head when she reminded him.

'I don't know what you're talking about.'

Cornelius found the yo-yos and settled his father in his chair beside the kitchen range.

Nancy walked to the end of the road with Jinny and Ann. It was raining, with reflections of the street lamps breaking into circlets in the puddles and the wet air dense with coal smoke. The curtains of some of the houses they passed were torn or hanging loose, letting out chinks and ellipses of thin lamplight. They were all a little drunk and at the tipping point between finding everything hilarious and descending into melancholy.

'We've had such a lovely time,' Ann sighed as she put her arms around Nancy's neck. 'I do love you. Don't we, Jinny?'

'Of course we do. Come on, girl. We've still got skating to look forward to, the day after tomorrow.'

Ice skating was Jinny and Ann's new passion, taken up as eagerly as cycling, and they were proud of how good they were becoming at it. A big new rink had opened at Bethnal Green and they were taking Nancy for a Christmas treat even though she could hardly slither two yards on the ice. There was talk of a fish supper to follow.

The two women linked arms and set off for Shaftesbury Avenue, turning at the corner to wave. Once they were out of sight Nancy went back to join Devil and Cornelius. Her yo-yo kept stopping at the bottom of its descent and twirling on the dead string.

'Nancy? Jolly good. I wasn't sure this was the place. Just let me pay the cabbie.'

If George Gardiner was surprised by the neighbourhood and the state of the house, he did his best not to show it. Nancy tried not to mind about being discovered to be poorer than expected. At Whistlehalt she had been wearing an expensive dress chosen by Gil and her earrings had been another present from him, so the painter had assessed her on the basis of her outward appearance. To do him credit he quickly adjusted to the Wixes' circumstances, squeezing down the hallway and bustling into the kitchen on his twinkling feet as if he felt perfectly at home.

Devil was in his usual place. He was treating his headache with a glass of Guinness and the bottle stood at his elbow. Cornelius hadn't wanted to encounter a stranger so he had taken the wireless upstairs to his bedroom.

Gardiner held out his hand.

'Devil, old man. It's been a long time, eh? Getting on for forty years.'

After a moment's bewilderment, Devil shook.

Nancy said, 'It's Mr George Gardiner, Pa. The painter, you remember? He's brought something to show you.'

Instead of answering Devil leaned forward in his chair and fumbled in the pocket of his trousers. He brought out the toy and winked at Gardiner.

'I bet you've never tried one of these.'

Cornelius had done well to make himself scarce, Nancy thought a little grimly, because it wasn't going to be an easy visit. Devil's memory was better on some days than others although Nancy suspected that he chose to make himself more opaque when he couldn't be bothered to talk.

'A yo-yo?'

The painter reached for it but Devil feinted. The puck spun upwards, he seemed to release the string and the object vanished. Devil spread his hands wide and wheezed with laughter.

'Very good,' Gardiner chuckled. 'Just like old times. You used to do something similar with my brushes when you sat for me.'

'Sat? Where did I sit? Nancy, bring the man a chair.'

She placed one for him and hung up the visitor's handsome overcoat. He kept his leather-bound portfolio close

404

beside him. She offered him a drink and he politely insisted that he would like nothing better than a Guinness. Luckily there was one bottle left on the pantry shelf.

'What can I do for you?' Devil asked.

The painter reminded him of the portrait of Devil in costume for *The Philosopher's Illusion*.

He concluded, 'I'd adore to see it again. I won a student prize with it, you know. The Founder's Medal at the Rawlinson School.'

'I know. I was there. Eliza was wearing a new green dress.'

Devil drew in a deep breath, and his eyelids fluttered as if he were inhaling the scent of her hair mingling with the long-ago rose he had worn in his buttonhole. Nancy smiled inwardly. It was typical. He could also remember the exact sequence of a trick that he hadn't performed since before she was born.

Gardiner took the opportunity. 'Speaking of Eliza, I thought you might like to see this?'

He reached into the portfolio, brought out a sheet of drawing paper and placed it in front of Devil.

It was a long time before Devil spoke. And then all he said was, 'Yes.'

Nancy looked over his shoulder. The drawing was of a ripe and lovely young woman with rounded limbs and breasts. She was absorbed in her own thoughts and her nakedness seemed incidental.

'Old Charlie Egan left it to me when he died,' Gardiner said.

Very firmly Devil removed it from the painter's grasp.

'It's for me, I suppose?'

The other man hesitated. 'W-e-e-ll. I thought a fair exchange might be in order.'

He had come in the hope of retrieving his own lost

prize-winner. Nowadays his thoughts would continually return to the past, as old men's did.

Devil indicated the kitchen walls, bare except for a manufacturer's calendar. Gardiner's gaze passed over the newspaper coils plugging the gaps in the sash frames.

'Eliza took against it,' Devil explained. 'She took against a lot of things.'

Gardiner sighed. He could hardly snatch the drawing back again.

'I'd like you to have it,' he said in the end, to Nancy.

She was touched. They had a few photographs of her mother, but they didn't capture her in the way these deft pencil lines did. She was ten years older now than Eliza had been then, and not nearly as beautiful, but she could see how the drawing defined their resemblance.

'Thank you.'

Gardiner smoothed the front of his yellow-checked waistcoat and placed his feet together. His round cheeks shone with the satisfaction of at least having done a good deed, even if he was leaving empty-handed.

'Well, I won't keep you any longer. You have a splendid daughter to comfort your old age, Devil. I am quite stricken with envy. I'm sorry not to have met your sons this time.'

A footstep creaked overhead and they all ignored it.

When Nancy came back from showing the visitor out Devil quickly lowered the drawing and she had the impression he had touched his lips to it. He poured himself the remainder of Gardiner's stout.

'That fellow always was the biggest molly in London,' he said.

The ice was crowded with holiday skaters in pairs and zigzagging chains and the seats surrounding it were thronged with spectators. The new rink was hardly more than a barn with a roof over arched trusses and a waist-high wooden partition enclosing the ice, but the walls were painted in bold colours and decorated with huge photographs of the club's star skaters caught in mid-leap or pirouette. There was a little stage at the far end where a band played in the evenings and on weekend afternoons.

Jinny and Ann held one of Nancy's hands apiece as she struck out on her wobbling blades. With the two of them to support her she gained confidence and soon she broke free to balance with outstretched arms. Sliding in a long arc she finally crashed into the wooden barrier, knowing no other way to stop. Her ears filled with the rasp of steel, the laughing calls of the other skaters and the brassy oompahs of the music.

'Watch and learn,' Jinny called to her as she sped by. She carved a supple figure-of-eight and twirled to skim backwards, perfectly repeating the figure. Her ankles swiftly crossed and recrossed as she drew sharp crystalline furrows and Ann battled to keep up, her red-gold hair turned orange by the globe lights suspended overhead. Jinny held out one teasing hand and Ann just managed to catch her fingers. They raced away, speeding past the slower pairs, all the way up to the bandstand and the lively saxophonist who tilted his instrument and sent the notes glissading through the busy air before they turned back again.

Afterwards Nancy remembered their faces, looking for her through the swirling crowd, Ann's with a shadow already in it.

They set off across the ice and it seemed suddenly that Ann was holding back, shaking her head and with her eyes widening in alarm. She was panting as if she was out of breath. Jinny half-turned to see what was wrong as Ann's free hand came up to her ribs and she folded in pain. Her knees buckled and Jinny leapt to support her. They swayed for a second in each other's arms and somehow crept to the barrier. Ann leaned on it for support but her body slumped as her legs gave way beneath her. The nearest skaters swerved or stumbled as she collapsed.

Jinny knelt over her. She didn't speak aloud but Nancy heard her heart crying out, '*Ann? Annie, come back.*'

Ann lay staring with her left cheek compressed against the ice. Her jaw sagged horribly. Threads of her hair fanned out like a sparse pillow with melting crystals shining in it.

A circle of people jostled around her toppled body, their faces looming and their mouths opening and closing on a tide of meaningless words. Jinny lifted her love's head and tried to cradle it in her lap until two of the people took Ann's limp shoulders and heaved her up. Two more men seized her feet. Together they hauled her off the ice as if she were a sack of coal. A blanket was placed on the soaking walkway next to the ice and they laid Ann down on it. Her head was lolling and her unseeing eyes still stared.

Nancy struggled towards them. 'Help us. Oh, help us.'

A man knelt down and began to administer artificial respiration.

Jinny tore off her gloves and cupped Ann's temples between her hands. She was looking up at the people.

'She's a nurse,' she kept saying. 'She's a nurse, she knows what to do.'

Nancy stood by, wobbling on the blades because her trembling fingers couldn't undo the stiff bootlaces. Time crept by, full of voices and flurry. The music stopped and the ice was cleared, more faces turning to stare as the skaters silently slid by. A second man took over the work of pumping at Ann's chest.

'Keep going,' Jinny ordered. She was white to the lips.

A doctor pushed his way through to them. He held Ann's wrist and shone a light into her extinguished eyes.

It was obvious to Nancy that Ann Gillespie was dead.

# CHAPTER NINETEEN

Ann's funeral took place on the first day of 1932. The cause of death was a ruptured aortic valve, the weakness in her heart probably present since the childhood bout of rheumatic fever from which her twin had died.

Her aged mother and father travelled down from Dunfermline. The sudden death of their only surviving child had shrunk them to cobwebs in their black clothes. They stood alone in the front pew, bewildered by grief and the strangeness of being in London. Standing directly behind her, Nancy saw that under her hat Mrs Gillespie's grey hair held the faint remnants of her daughter's bright colour.

*Martinmartinmartinmartin.* She was thinking of the Kentish bicycling weekend, the brisk scepticism that had been so characteristic of Ann, and the child's voice she had heard. She half-glanced over her shoulder to see if the soaking girl was there, but there were only the rows of mourners.

At Jinny's insistence they were gathered in a crematorium chapel, recently constructed from raw red bricks on lines not dissimilar to the ice rink. She said that Ann was not going be laid in the ground and there would be no religious obfuscation over her body before the disposal, because she wouldn't have wanted either of these things.

'Annie's gone and there's nothing else. I am being practical.'

She didn't look at Nancy as she said it.

Cornelius sat next to Jinny, protective of her even though she held herself so tightly as to appear invulnerable. He explained to Nancy and Devil that the gas-fired ovens used in the new crematoria were hygienic and efficient and in his opinion Jinny was quite right to make this modern choice. Mr and Mrs Gillespie quietly accepted the decisions Ann's friends made, apparently relieved not to be called on to deal with the formalities themselves.

The vicar read out a short address. He said that sadly Ann had never married, but her life had been rich in friendships.

Jinny sat listening to him, her white face stiff.

The vicar's neutral words were accurate. Ann did have many friends.

Gil was amongst them. Just before the ceremony began he slipped quietly into the chapel and stood at the back with his narrow head bowed. Nancy didn't have to turn round; she sensed that he was there and his presence comforted her.

He had told her, 'I want to pay my respects to Ann and to be there for Jinny's sake. I won't stay afterwards because you will be with your family.'

They couldn't be seen together at their friend's wake because it would raise questions. So the boxes stacked up beside each other, year upon year. They were never opened at the same time and the contents never spilled over.

Lion had arrived too, correct in a black tie. In contrast to Gil he came over to clasp Nancy's hand and murmured,

'It's bloody awful. Ann, of all people, who was of value in this vile world. Couldn't someone else have died in her place?'

'I know. I feel the same.'

'How is Jinny?'

'Brave.'

Lizzie came with Tommy, now a lanky boy of fourteen. Matthew was suffering a bad attack of rheumatism and Faith stayed at home to look after him. Jake was in America so Freddie had come in his place, even though he had barely known Ann. The remaining seats were packed with her nursing friends and hospital colleagues, and more from the two women's trades unionist and political circles.

After the curtains closed on the coffin, Jinny stood up in front of the mourners.

'Ann's parents and I would like you to join us at the Thistle, the pub on the corner of this street.'

With a smile for the appropriate name she held out her arms to them all before leading the way out into the cold new year.

They crammed into the back room of the public house. There was tea and sandwiches, beer and whisky. A murmur of exchanged condolences soon swelled into a loud babble. In the distance Nancy could see Devil, gesticulating to an audience of nurses in the flow of one of his stories. His remaining hair was almost entirely white but his thick eyebrows were still dark. He was a magnetic figure even now.

Lizzie took her arm. 'I said to Jinny, give up the driving, there's a job with me in the office at Shaw's Exotics for as long as she wants it. And I told her to have some paid time off first, before coming back.'

'That's good of you.'

Lizzie compressed her lips into a dark red line. 'It's not an act of generosity. You know me better than that.'

Nancy was irritated. Lizzie didn't always have to pretend to be so hard-boiled. But her cousin went on, 'In a few months' time I'm going need to someone I can trust. I might have to hand over some of my work.'

'Why is that?'

A hairline crack seemed to be appearing in Lizzie's enamel.

'For the usual reason, I suppose. I'm forty-two and I've just found out I'm in the family way.'

'*Lizzie?* But that's good news, surely? Raymond must be pleased.'

Lizzie nodded.

'He is, as a matter of fact. He's delighted, and he's insisting that as I'm divorced there's no reason not to get married. Quietly, you know. I've had to agree. It wasn't my plan at all, not in the least, but I thought at my age . . .' She twisted her thin shoulders in a smartly tailored black serge coat. 'I must say, you seem to have managed better than I have. Never a slip. I take my hat off.'

Nancy was used to Lizzie but she was embarrassed. The compliment was misplaced, apart from anything else. With Lion, and at the beginning with Gil, she had taken every possible precaution. In the last years she had let herself become careless. She had not even pursued the idea to any conclusion, thinking only *oh well, if it did happen, there would be a way to deal with it.*

It had not happened, and she didn't suppose now that it would.

She kissed her cousin's cheek.

'I hope you'll be very happy.'

'Oh, I'm not sure that's in my contract,' Lizzie smartly

retorted. Nancy could see that she *was* happy though, and it might have been because for once she was not in control of everything that touched her.

Jinny was drinking hard. The mask that had stayed in place since the terrible hour at the skating rink was beginning to slip. She passed from one friend to the next, letting herself be supported. Her eyes swam with tears and she wobbled as she held on to Nancy's arm.

'I need to get drunk. Will you see Ann's parents to their train for me? I can't deal with them any more. I'm not Ann's bloody *flatmate*, I'm her husband. Her lover for more than ten years. Why can't they let us be what we are?'

Nancy thought briefly and bitterly that Jinny and Ann's relationship was more openly acknowledged than hers with Gil. Her lover had already quietly gone on his way, after they had exchanged only the briefest of words outside the crematorium. She kept her sadness to herself.

'Hush, darling. They don't understand what you and Ann meant to each other. Of course I'll take them to the station.'

Nancy begged Cornelius to stay close by Jinny and to see her home safely to Shaftesbury Avenue. His face turned dark red and he frowned at her.

'You don't need to ask me. As if I would leave her.'

The funeral and the wake were an ordeal for him but he would stay with Jinny as long as she needed him.

The Gillespies were waiting like a pair of small shadows against the wall. Nancy could feel their contained grief, tight and chill as a Scottish Sunday. They would have done better to get as drunk as Jinny, she thought.

Mr Gillespie kneaded the brim of his hat as they sat in a row on the bus.

'Look at all these folk. However did Annie manage in such a place?'

They gaped at the dark crowds that came flooding out of shops and offices only to be gobbled up again by the underground or the groaning trams.

'She loved her work. And her friends loved her,' Nancy offered.

'Aye,' the old man grimly said.

So children move out of their parents' orbit, she reflected. Work and war and love take them away from you.

At King's Cross she led the way to the platform for the Edinburgh train. Smoke collected under the vast roof and the stink of smuts and steam and the din of engines made the station seem a foggy and mundane version of hell. Nancy found two second-class seats, wishing that the old people didn't have to sit upright all night. She imagined them with their heads lolling in exhaustion as the train shuddered north through the darkness.

She said goodbye and shook hands, but Mrs Gillespie crept after her to the carriage door. As Nancy stepped down she whispered, 'Tell that girl, your friend, I'm sorry for her loss.'

'I will,' Nancy promised.

The year that had begun in such a sombre way gathered its own dim momentum. The people who came to Nancy's seances were looking back less than they were peering into an uncertain future.

'Is he there? Ask him, what shall I do?' they begged from the Palmyra gallery.

The Uncanny tugged at her. She felt physically jostled by it, her elbows and hips jarred by the pressure of multitudes, her brain seething with the unspoken and the effort of articulating it for public consumption.

'I can't advise you. I can only tell you what I am hearing,' she answered.

She had to fall back on the anodyne.

'He is here. He wants you to be brave.'

'You can't eat bravery,' a woman shrieked at her.

'I'm sorry,' Nancy whispered. Two or three seats banged as people left the auditorium.

The Palmyra also pressed on her, a physical weight composed of fraying velvet curtains and mouldering floorboards. She thought more often that her job was becoming impossible and sometimes she wondered if she might be going mad.

Well. Mad or not, she told herself in the wake of the visions of bombs and burning that had started to trouble her as they had when she was a girl, there was nothing to be done except keep on doing it.

At Shaw's Exotics Jinny tried to anaesthetise herself with work although business was slack.

'If you are feeling short of readies, the first thing you don't buy is a pineapple,' Lizzie said. 'Unfortunately.'

It was too early for Jinny to seek the extra balm of physical work in the garden at Waterloo Street. The vegetable beds were still shrouded in their thermal layers of sacking and the cold frames contained only brittle twigs. Even so, she came regularly to the house to play chess with Cornelius or to listen to the wireless.

'I don't like being at home on my own,' she confessed. 'I suppose Ann would tell me to pull myself together, wouldn't she?'

'Who?' Devil asked.

'Ann,' Jinny repeated.

Devil's wits were increasingly scattered, although he was usually benign in his confusion. Most of his time was spent pottering with old Gibb. Cornelius had framed Charlie Egan's drawing of Eliza behind glass for him and his eyes often turned to it.

'Do you know my daughter Zenobia?' he asked Jinny suddenly one evening when Nancy was out at a performance. Cornelius took off his spectacles and polished them with a handkerchief.

'Yes, she is my friend,' Jinny said gently.

'*Is* she? Is Nancy a lesbian nowadays?'

All three of them laughed.

The Uncanny came closer. As always the stinks affected her. The drains at Waterloo Street gave up a reek of rotting cabbage stalks and bad meat, the Palmyra was foul with damp and on the underground she could hardly endure the stench of unwashed clothing and mothballs and human breath. She lost her appetite to the point that Sylvia Aynscoe tried to bully her.

'You must eat,' she said, when Nancy put aside untouched the poached eggs she prepared for her after the evening show.

'I'm all right,' Nancy insisted. Until she blinked it away, the London skyline blazed with inexplicable fire.

Sylvia should have retired long ago on the small pension Nancy and Desmond had guaranteed for her, but she insisted that she would rather stay at the theatre.

'What would I do if I didn't come to the Palmyra?' she shrugged. Sometimes she even slept there, on a truckle bed in an alcove off the stage-door passageway. She was the guardian spirit of the old place, overseeing its hours of darkness as Jake Jones had done decades ago.

Gil worried that Nancy seemed tired. She insisted that she was fine, putting on her most cheerful face for him because that was what he looked for. Celia's afflictions were enough to absorb any man's stock of sympathy, and for her own part she wanted always to offer him strength, happiness and no cause for concern. She didn't mention the increasingly powerful swirl of the Uncanny, even though once she had hurried to confide all its nuances to him because she loved his reassuring acceptance. Although he never claimed to understand her gift he had developed his own interpretation over the years. Once, at a recital of Messiaen organ music he sat rapt and motionless as a marble statue. When they emerged from the concert hall he was blinking and disorientated.

'I know there are ways in which the human spirit can be transported. If it happens to a dull economist like me through listening to a piece of music, what must it be like to experience another realm through senses as fine as yours, Nancy?'

He had kissed her hand, and she had seen that it was with a kind of awe. He made her feel invincible, and not remotely flawed.

Yet lately, from being the one person in the world she could most easily confide in, he had somehow become the opposite. She couldn't define exactly when the change had come about but it had begun, almost imperceptibly, after they had faked the Uncanny to deceive Celia at Fifteen. They hadn't acknowledged the bad turn and it had become scarred by the ordinary accretions of life. The buried damage left them shy of exposure, and so their old honesty around the Uncanny had infinitely decayed.

Perhaps that was the way of human relationships. Perhaps the deepest intimacy always contains its own destruction, she sadly thought.

In the end it was Freddie, possibly at Sylvia's instigation, who turned up backstage one evening and insisted on taking Nancy back to Whistlehalt for three days before her next performance.

'I'm not leaving here without you. You can have a rest and let Guillaume feed you up and you'll be doing me the biggest favour at the same time. I get quite blue when Jake's away for months like this.'

Sylvia told her, 'Go on. Your pa's got Jinny and Cornelius to look out for him and the Palmyra's got me and Desmond.'

'We're not too bad at the box office,' Desmond put in. 'They like Norah Vaughan. I think we should offer her another two weeks.'

Miss Vaughan was a singer and comedienne who resembled Gracie Fields just closely enough.

'All right,' Nancy said in the end, putting too many concerns aside. Gil was in Manchester dealing with a threatened strike at the Maitlands mill. 'I'll be at Whistlehalt if you need me.'

Freddie drove along the familiar route out of London. The traffic dwindled and the ribbons of street lamps fell behind them until at last they were winding up the dark lanes to the house. The lights were blazing and a couple of windows stood open. As she stepped out of the car the sweetness of the air and the faint ripple of music fell on her.

She tilted her head to gaze up at the arch of stars.

'Thanks, Freddie. You were right.'

She slept more soundly that night than she had done for weeks and in the morning Guillaume brought up a breakfast tray. Wearing a blue kimono and the remains of last night's eye paint he plumped himself against the pillows to flip through the gossip columns in the morning's paper.

'People, people, people,' he muttered restlessly as they sipped their tea. 'Endless people. Look, Elvira Steele is engaged to be married.'

'Who's she?'

'*Exactement*,' he crowed.

That afternoon Nancy was reading in the drawing room when she heard someone at the door. A moment later one of the other young men looked in on her.

'There's a person to see you,' he said.

'Me? Who is it?'

Although she already knew.

Freddie had gone out to lunch. Mrs G would have bicycled away an hour ago. Nancy could smell a savoury waft of cooking which meant that Guillaume was busy in the kitchen. She couldn't remember who had been invited for dinner.

Lawrence Feather's hair and beard flowed over his shoulders and down almost to his chest. His layers of clothes were quite possibly the greenish and decaying relics of the priestly black he had once worn. He stepped forward with an extended hand. She hesitated before brushing the tips of his fingers.

'I heard you were here. I have called in the hope of persuading you to visit us, Nancy.'

'Us?'

He smiled at her. 'My friends and I live simply in the fields, but we follow the true path. We acknowledge no barriers between this world and the next.'

'Ah.'

He smiled again. 'Our last encounter was not a happy one, Nancy, and that troubles me. Of course I felt for many years that you wilfully interposed yourself between Helena and me, although mercifully that is in the past now.' His smile broadened, beatifically. 'She is with me, you know. I believe that your denial opened a direct channel between us, so it may even be that I owe you thanks. Even so, my dear, you accepted my guidance and then you took my followers and turned your back on me. Yet I bear no grudge. I have my group of disciples these days and I look for no others. We have shared much, you and I, so I would like to show you what we are doing in our little circle. You will be interested.'

He was mad, she realised.

'No, thank you.'

Still faintly smiling he studied her with the knowing insinuation she had always hated.

'I hope you are not afraid to pay us a visit, Nancy? After all we have experienced together?'

She thought of the handful of tents and the dilapidated caravan, and the forlorn waft of smoke. It was a sad place and the memory of it did make her fearful. Anger like a crisp curl of flame suddenly energised her. The man had sidled at the margins of her life for too many years and she wanted him gone, mad or otherwise. She wouldn't allow his proximity to affect her happiness at Whistlehalt.

'Afraid? Not in the least.'

Feather sensed the angry energy and he slyly seized on it.

'Shall we go, then?'

He held out an arm in its rusty sleeve.

He wanted to rekindle his influence over her. He was as vain and self-regarding as always. I despise you, she thought. You are a psychic first and a faker second, just like me, but I am the better at our game.

He cut into her thoughts. 'That's the attitude. You have your mother in you.'

'Please leave my mother out of this.'

He only smiled more broadly, showing his ruined teeth.

Defiance held the upper hand in her as she followed him along the ridge path to the camp. She would confront whatever it was he wanted her to see, because if she did not it would be allowing him to subdue her. They walked in silence and soon the column of smoke smudged the sky as the caravan and tents came into view. Feather bowed as he opened the five-barred gate and beckoned her through.

From beside the fire half a dozen pairs of eyes watched them approach over hummocks of dead grass. Behind the tarpaulin shelter a row of dead creatures hung on the wire fence. There were two pheasants, a rabbit and some smaller birds.

'Mr Templeton's man turns a blind eye if we help ourselves to something for the pot,' Feather murmured.

The members of his cult perched on logs or makeshift tripod stools. There were five men and a woman, their faces blackened with soot, sacks draped over hunched shoulders for warmth. Four of the company were wretched creatures, tramps or derelicts with drinkers' beaten features and hopeless, averted eyes. The other two were a couple, wizened and emaciated but far more alert than their fellows. They fixed her at once with greedy stares and she knew she had seen them before.

They had accompanied Feather on his last visit to the Palmyra.

Where was the soaking girl? These two were somehow connected with her. Instinctively Nancy searched along the hedge for a sight of the ghost child.

'As some of you already know, this is Miss Zenobia Wix, the medium. Make room for her to sit down.'

Feather spoke with curt authority. There was a rustle as the followers shifted to stare at her. Their sullen hostility was uncomfortable but Nancy stood her ground.

At last the man of the couple shuffled up from his seat.

Unwillingly she took his place, folding her skirt out of the way of the mud. An old black kettle was suspended over a smouldering log and a thin tongue of steam curled from its spout. The Uncanny was gathering.

The man who had given up his stool now hovered beyond the fire. Her eye went to something dangling from his fingers and she saw it was the leather sling of a catapult.

'That's Lenny. No one knows how to set a trap for a rabbit or bring a bird down better than Lenny does. You recognise him and Peg, Nancy, don't you?'

She could smell tar and salt water, the very reek of the *Queen Mab*. A cold finger of dread pressed into the nape of her neck.

She demanded, 'Why have you brought me here?'

The camp was a horrible, sinister place. These followers of Feather's were more pathetic than they were threatening, but she was uncomfortably conscious of the hundreds of yards of empty countryside that lay between her and Whistlehalt. In the fading light rooks were coming to roost in the tall trees at the lip of the ridge.

Lenny stepped closer with his catapult and his little wife moved at his side.

'Don't you know us?' Peg whispered. Her head was wrapped in a torn scarf and her eyes were like sloes in her walnut face. She turned from Nancy to Feather.

'Where is she? You told me this woman sees her. You promised me she would come to us if this woman was here.'

Her voice was wheedling, hoarse with desperation.

One of the derelicts produced an apple from his torn pocket, rubbed it on the corner of his coat and bit into it. Juice and pulp smeared his chin and he sniggered. These poor men enabled Feather to imagine he had a retinue, but in reality they were only here for the meagre shelter and whatever food he might offer.

'Stop that,' Feather snapped at him.

Lenny and Peg were different. They hungrily waited.

Feather stood tall, a black scarecrow at the heart of the circle.

'I have told you that my poor powers are limited and my links to the spirits are weakening. Our guest is a far more powerful channel and Emmy has always been drawn to her through my shallow mediation. Now I have brought Nancy to you, and we must open the channel directly. Shall we join hands and begin? Who will give me a message for you, Nancy? Your mother? Or perhaps your friend Ann Gillespie?'

She clenched her fists in the pocket of her coat. He would know about Ann's death because it was his business to do so. The man was ridiculous, but he was a stage medium and he had taught her the identical tricks.

'Do you remember the beach, Nancy? The day the *Queen Mab* went down?'

'Of course.'

'I unleashed your gift, didn't I?'

The Uncanny pulsed around her, but it was hers. Never his. Without warning the campfire became a roaring pillar of flame, twenty or thirty feet high. Nancy lurched backwards, arms flying up to shield her face from the threat of searing heat. When there was no burning sensation she looked through her fingers, to see that the fire was only a few red embers and Lenny and his wife had drawn still closer.

Feather murmured in his insinuating way, 'What's there? Who do you see, Nancy? Not Helena, because she is with me. Perhaps you have a message for one of us?' His gaze slid over his meagre audience. 'We have a powerful conduit here, as I told you.'

Feather needed his followers and he must have retained Lenny and Peg's allegiance by making claims and promises about their drowned daughter. Nancy had always known, in the recesses of the Uncanny, that the poor little wraith was the child with the posy basket from the *Queen Mab*. She could only guess at how Feather summoned her, or by what means he had controlled her parents. Now it seemed that they had challenged his influence and forced him to bring her here.

The rooks clamoured as daylight died.

'I have no message,' Nancy insisted. 'I thought you said you knew no barriers here. What could I offer, if all is clear already?'

He stooped to rest his hand on her shoulder.

'Not one word?'

The couple edged closer still.

Beyond them, where the field ended and the trees began, she saw the little figure.

It was Feather's ability to draw the apparition from her subconscious, as he had always done.

As it had been hers to hear Helena's confession and know of her brother's abuse.

Lenny stood less than a yard away now. Twilight and the fire's glow hollowed his face. His wife crept with him, her hands outstretched to clutch at Nancy's clothing.

'Where is she?' she whispered.

Nancy gazed towards the soaking girl, and her mother and father craned in the same direction. From their stricken faces it was plain they could see nothing.

'He promised us,' Lenny murmured.

'Give her to me. Give her to me,' the wife begged.

She was crazed with hardship and Feather's fantasies, and so was her husband in his ratcatcher's coat with the catapult dangling from a pocket. Their need was menacing.

These people were all deranged. She must get away from their camp or she would lose her own grip on reason.

'I can't give her to you. She is not mine to command.'

Somehow she broke free of Feather and lurched to her feet.

Lenny and Peg blocked the way, with the lumpen others ranged behind them. It was a hundred yards to the gate and beyond that the path was in darkness, bordering a steep drop to the river bank. The smell of weed and water flowed over her. The little figure stood motionless, almost melting into the murk gathered under the trees.

Nancy pointed her finger.

'She is *his*.'

In this isolated place Feather manipulated them all. Her head spun with the Uncanny, and a sickening new conviction. Feather still yearned to pay her back for rejecting him in favour of the Palmyra. He had brought her here with the intention of doing her harm.

Her mind reeled. The layers of subterfuge, the seances and the spirit voices, the tricks and confidences they had both employed obscured everything. Even gravity itself deserted her. She swayed as the ground tilted under her feet.

Peg snatched at her arm.

'Let my girl go.'

Lenny hissed, 'We've watched you, we have. With Mr Feather, since he came to tell us who you are, we've known you held our Emmy.'

Poor creatures, under his spell. Her skin crawled.

'I haven't held her. *He* did.'

She took a step, and another, trying to push past them and at the same time willing herself not to break into a run. Her heart was thudding. The accomplices converged, closing off her escape.

The soaking girl was drifting towards them. The sockets of her eyes were black.

The mother and father sensed she was close at hand at last. The mother moaned and opened her arms, staring around in hope and horror.

The apparition was holding up something Nancy had never seen her with before. It was the posy basket, her proud possession aboard the *Queen Mab*, from which Devil had produced the cricket ball. The child smiled at her through a hank of dripping hair and then she said, 'I am going now.'

Nancy had never heard her speak. It was a child's high innocent voice.

She tried to smile back at her.

'Yes, it's time to go.'

She felt rather than heard Lenny's wild bellow. He was as desperate as the butcher at her first public seance.

'No, darling. Let me see you. Emmy, stay here with me.'

Peg screeched in agony.

'Go to sleep, my baby. Rest now.'

The soaking girl seemed to hesitate between the two of them. Then she placed a finger to her lips. In a sudden rush of flying hair and scattered droplets she swept straight at Nancy. Nancy made to sidestep and there came a confused movement, too fast for her eye to catch, as Lenny fitted a stone into the leather sling.

There was a whistle in the air before the darkness exploded.

427

Nancy's hands flew up to cover her face, too late. Her legs gave way and she pitched to the ground.

Pain was a reality. Pain was the only reality, pain and more pain.

She was being carried in a blanket slung between two poles. Rolled up like a corpse. Jolting and swaying, bloodshot branches overhead against a netted crimson sky. The swinging beams of torches, and urgent voices calling.

A bed, more voices. One of them belonged to Frances Templeton. A hand was placed on her forehead but she could see nothing. She was blinded and in agony.

Darkness deeper, and a kind of sleep.

When she woke up it was to the impression of a clean white place, although she could see nothing. She twisted in panic and cool fingers found her wrist.

'Are you awake, dear?'

The other hand was free and when she raised it to explore the source of her pain her fingers encountered layers of bandages.

'Can you hear me, Nancy?'

She had been in the grip of horrible dreams and the visions receded slowly. Her mouth was parched.

'Where?' she mumbled.

'You are in hospital. Quite safe. Here's the doctor now.'

Someone was beside her head and she flinched. There was the creak of a starched shirt.

'I am Dr Pennington. You have an eye injury, but please don't worry. You are not blind.'

Nancy lay in the hospital. The heavy bandages covering her face were removed and with her right eye she could just pick out the blurry outlines of the window and the bed curtains. A huge pad of dressings still covered the left. Cornelius and Devil sat beside her. Devil leaned forward into her narrow field of vision.

'That bastard Feather. I'll kill him, with these.' He waved his bare hands.

'No, Pa. That won't help anyone.'

Feather and his followers had struck their camp and vanished. A vagrant had knocked at the kitchen door at Whistlehalt and told Guillaume that the lady was hurt, and then he had run away. So they had found Nancy, lying amongst the half-dismantled tents.

Mrs Templeton came to see her, and in her presence even the senior nurses shrank against the walls. Devil went quiet.

'You will get the best treatment here, Nancy. Dr Pennington is the top man in the field. Everything that can be done will be, I assure you.'

She understood that it was Mrs Templeton who had chosen and arranged for her care.

'The police are searching for Mr Feather and his companions. I am so sorry this dreadful affair happened on our land. I shouldn't have agreed to let them stay.'

At last, after what seemed a long time but was really only two days, Gil came. He had identified a time when she had no other visitors. She tried to smile but it turned into a wince of pain.

'Hello. What about the mill strike?' she whispered.

He stroked her cheek with his finger. 'Nancy, the strike doesn't signify. What happened? Jinny told me what she could but it wasn't much. I need to know what I can do.'

She understood his need to do something. He was a powerful man, used to giving orders and having them carried out.

She described the incident but it was as if she was telling someone else's story. It had been an accident. There was a dismal gathering of itinerant cranks, a poacher with a catapult who had taken exception to a supposed intruder. It had been a careless warning that had misfired. No mention of the soaking girl, or of Lenny and Peg. No *Queen Mab*, not a breath of the Uncanny. That would have been to unravel too much and they didn't do that any longer. What had once united them now drove a wedge between them.

'My darling girl. My poor Nancy.'

She didn't want to be his poor girl. That was not her role.

Her sight in the undamaged eye was accommodating, but when she was tired a faint rainbow haloed everything she looked at. Gil was outlined now, as if he were a rather well-dressed saviour in a religious picture. She smiled in spite of herself, and winced again.

It was enough that he was here. She didn't want him to do anything more than sit beside her. She held on to his hand, drawing strength from its warmth.

Gil had brought her a basket of hothouse roses. They were perfectly shaped blooms but after he had gone, when she asked the youngest nurse to hold them closer, she found they had no scent.

'They are still gorgeous,' the little nurse breathed.

When Freddie came later he brought a bunch of bluebells from the Whistlehalt woods. They were so fresh and delicate with their sapphire bells curling to pale azure at the margins. Made breathless by the discovery that she could still see colours she traced one sappy stem with her fingertip.

A telegram came from Jake in California and there were dozens of other messages and cards and letters with good wishes. Nancy lay against her pillows, listening and watching as the sight in her right eye came back. The nurses' shoes squeaked on polished linoleum and their starched head-dresses lifted like flags of an unexpected truce. Squares of weak sunlight illuminated cream-painted walls, flowers opened and faded in their vases, chips in the enamel of water jugs and dressings cases revealed themselves in the shape of continents or crouching beasts. She drank the soup that was fed to her, sipped cocoa, pulled the crisp sheets against her chin and slept, woke again and found herself at peace.

She gave herself up to the daily routine of being cared for, and to the long nights that were disturbed only by the muttering and cries of the other women. Even the pain in her head was a finite thing, capable of management. The nurses began to praise her for being a model patient; she joked about their boyfriends or tiny rebellious infringements of uniform rules.

It was peculiar to discover serenity in such circumstances, but she did find it.

One day, Dr Pennington explained that the sharp stone had been fired with such force that it had shattered her left eyeball. He had done his best but it had been impossible to save the sight in that eye and he had taken the decision to remove it.

'I see,' she murmured automatically as she took in this information, and then laughed aloud. 'I *do* see, don't I? Even if it's only with the other eye.'

The doctors and nurses were surprised by her equanimity. She supposed that being partially blinded would have its impact on her before too long, but while she lay there in the ward she was preoccupied with a different realisation.

In this place she would have expected the reek of anti-septic, floor polish, sickness, boiled greens and a dozen other odours to flood through her. They would herald the warning flow of spit into her mouth, the rising gorge, and the shimmer of the Uncanny. But there was nothing. The hospital was functional, a place of repair, perfectly predictable.

She corrected herself: there were a few scents, she hadn't lost her sense of smell, but they were no more than wafts and they disappeared altogether as she grew accustomed to them.

Yet another day came when the last layer of padding was briefly lifted and she was allowed to study her face in a hand mirror. She took in the purple-and-yellow bruising and the weeping, scabbed lids welded over the crumpled and empty socket. It was ugly and sad, but it wasn't fearful.

She handed back the glass.

'I'll be needing a black eyepatch,' she said. 'Like a pirate's.'

After two weeks Dr Pennington told her that she had done so well she could be discharged, provided she came back every other day to have the socket cleaned and the dressings changed. Whistlehalt was much closer than Waterloo Street, so Freddie insisted on taking her back there.

Her nurses and the other patients crowded in on the last morning to say goodbye. Nancy had never realised that it was so easy to be ordinary.

Freddie and Guillaume and Mrs G had made up her Whistlehalt bedroom for her.

'Jake told me to buy you a present from him, something decadent and gorgeous. I chose this because I'd really rather like it for myself.'

Freddie draped a cream cashmere robe with satin revers against his lean body and spread the skirts. 'Mmm?'

'It is utterly gorgeous. If it's really mine, hand over, please.'

The robe had probably cost more than she had spent on clothes for herself in her whole life, in total. She would have liked to have her mother's old red robe. Perhaps Sylvia would send it.

Whistlehalt ran with its accustomed casual opulence and she spent her days lazing and watching the unfurling of leaves on the branches outside her window. It was still remarkably easy to be ordinary, and to be looked after by her friends.

She spoke to Gil on the telephone, sometimes twice a day. He had been dealing with the difficulties in Manchester and these were now resolved.

'I'll come to Whistlehalt tomorrow,' he promised.

Before he arrived Guillaume advised her, 'Do your hair. Put on something pretty.'

Cornelius and Jinny had brought her a small suitcase, packed by Jinny. Nancy dressed and stared at her reflection, having hardly used a mirror since the bandages had come off in the hospital. Uncertainly she rearranged her appearance and even tried out some make-up. Lipstick and one painted eye looked so wrong that she scrubbed it all off again. She heard a car turn in at the gates and watched the Bentley roll into view. Gil was wearing a soft hat with the brim turned down and he didn't look up to her window. She walked down the stairs to meet him at the front door.

When he visited her in the hospital she had been dazed by painkillers and intent on her own recovery, but now she saw him clearly without any surrounding halo of light. Her first thought was that he was as familiar to her as her skin. The second, hard behind it, was that in their long intimacy and then the drama of her eye injury she had stopped noticing his gloss. Celia and he had worn it the first time

433

she met them in her Palmyra dressing room, and now she noticed all over again how wealth burnished him. Every stitch and seam of his clothing was the best, his skin and his nails were polished, each movement he made expressed confidence.

She thought with slight bewilderment, *But we don't match. Not in one single respect.*

In the drawing room he took her by the elbow and led her to the French windows to study her face in the daylight. She had deliberately left off the dressings. She flinched only a little as he examined the ruined eye socket. Nancy had never been over-concerned about her appearance except when it exposed her status, and she held her chin high now.

'Does it hurt very much?'

'Not any more.'

They sat down in front of the fire. They knew Whistlehalt well enough but it was hard not to feel a touch of discomfort in surroundings that were not their own, where the theatrical decor featured oversized vases and Freddie's favoured drapes, as well as the new life-size portrait of Jake costumed as Hamlet. Nancy caught herself thinking that there was more fun and warmth under this roof than in all the grand rooms at Bruton Street.

'There must be something I can do,' Gil repeated.

She studied his face. She loved every piece of him. She didn't want anything done, only to be.

'Well, you could kiss me,' she smiled.

He leaned forward very slowly and pressed his lips to her forehead.

'When will you come home?'

*Home* being Bloomsbury, of course. She longed to be there, opening the windows to let in fresh air and arranging flowers in the vases.

'Oh, quite soon. In a week, perhaps. It's been lovely here with Freddie and the others but I want to set my life going again.'

She wasn't sure how that would be, sensing what she now did about the Uncanny, but she didn't mention that.

'That's good to hear,' he murmured.

Freddie looked in, wearing a loose silk shirt with his bare feet in Moroccan slippers. The two men shook hands and Gil thanked him warmly for taking care of Nancy.

'We adore her,' Freddie said, fitting a cigarette into its holder.

They began a conversation about a Cubist exhibition. Trailing in a robe, an actor called Frank brought in the tray. The last to appear was Guillaume.

He stopped as soon as he saw Gil's face, and there was a tiny break in the chatter. Gil accepted a cup and a plate from Frank before the talk resumed.

'Divine cake,' Freddie murmured. 'Feathery as angels' wings.'

After the boys had wandered away Freddie said that he must go and change.

'Do come any time to call on our darling girl,' he told Gil.

Nancy sat in her corner of one of the big sofas, still laughing at the nonsense the boys had talked.

'They're good fun, aren't they? Have you met Guillaume before?'

'No,' Gil said.

It was time for him to leave. He was dining in Kensington, he told her.

'How is Celia?'

He took her hand and turned it over in his, examining her fingers. Nancy sat more upright, wondering what was to come.

'Celia has taken a bad turn. I didn't tell you earlier, when you were in the hospital. Perhaps I shouldn't mention it even now.'

Her breath stilled.

'Yes, you should. What sort of a bad turn?'

'At the moment she is in a secure hospital. Her mother and the doctors are afraid she may do serious harm to herself, and I agree there's a risk of that.'

'Oh, Gil. Poor Celia.'

He was pale, frowning down at their linked hands.

'I have been thinking about a divorce.'

She stared, with wild hope leaping inside her. The first thought was, *At last*. Gil and she had both done wrong to Celia, but for the nine years they had been in love he had given every consideration to a neurasthenic girl-woman. If poor Celia was losing her reason altogether, that was not Gil's doing – nor was it hers.

A clamour started up inside her although she tried to silence it.

Divorce her. Marry me. I'll love you and care for you. You deserve to be happy. We deserve it.

He said, 'Don't look like that. Celia isn't getting worse because of what we did. She would have found someone, somewhere, to tell her what she wanted to hear. The damage is within her, and in the damned morphine, and most of all in me.'

He dropped his head into his hands.

'If I could take this into myself, I would.'

All the gloss of all the money in the world couldn't eradicate unhappiness, Nancy thought. She kissed him and told him she loved him.

'You are strong. You'll do the right thing, I know that.'

'Thank you,' Gil said.

A few minutes later the Bentley headed into the darkness.

That evening, after Freddie had gone out to dine, Guillaume slid into her bedroom. He took up his place next to her and tugged for a share of the eiderdown. She edged closer so she could lean against his shoulder. A strange tentative happiness hatched from hope was fluttering inside her.

Guillaume said, 'That wise old owl Freddie told me I should not say one word to you, but I'm going to anyway.'

'A word about what?'

There was a meaningful silence until she murmured, 'About Gil?'

Guillaume tapped her arm.

'I see the whole picture, dear. So handsome, *and* rich. And more than a tiny bit *triste*, which is always alluring in a boyfriend because you think you can be the one to make him happy. You know, I saw him only the other night. A week ago this evening, it was. And he knows I did, the wretch.'

There had been that little pause. A pause of mutual recognition, she understood.

Nancy said, 'Where was this?'

'I was meeting a Russian choreographer, very wicked, who invited me to a delicious supper at a secret place. I think you could take anyone there, the greatest criminal in Europe, and no one would murmur about it.' He rubbed his thumb and forefinger together.

'Fifteen.'

He flicked an eyebrow.

'Another couple was dining there *à deux, très intime*, and Sergei knew the lady, so he spoke briefly to her and I was also introduced.'

'To Lady Celia Maitland?'

But Celia was in a mental hospital.

Nancy traced the embroidered arabesques on the satin eiderdown.

Guillaume pursed his mouth. '*This* lady is an American and quite a patron of the ballet, Sergei says. A Mrs Thelma Auger. *Chic à l'extrème.*'

Freddie was right, he shouldn't have told her. Guillaume was fascinated by rich and titled people and couldn't resist the opportunity to gossip.

Nancy fought down the urge to bombard him with questions. Perhaps the patent holder of the Maitland Process was making a donation to fund an important avant-garde dance production. There was no reason in the world why Gil should not have dinner with a friend. An intimate dinner, even.

She inwardly shook herself.

'How fascinating.' She stretched, and produced a little yawn. 'Do you know what? I'd love a drink, wouldn't you?'

He squeezed her hand. 'Let's do that. I'm going to run and get us a glass of champagne.'

She drew the folds of the cream cashmere to cover her shoulders.

It was time, Nancy decided the next day, to think about going back to London. She had been away too long, and she was conscious that every day set her further apart. Her eye was healing well and Dr Pennington had been talking about modelling a glass replacement to hold the shape of the socket.

She would need to make decisions about the Palmyra, although Norah Vaughan was bringing in good audiences.

She wanted to be back with Devil and Cornelius, and Jinny Main.

And with Gil. Most of all with Gil.

Freddie tried to persuade her to stay longer.

'I'll miss you. Can't you wait until Jake gets home? It's only another week or so.'

She shook her head. Freddie looked shrewdly at her.

'You didn't pay too much attention to what Guillaume said, I hope? He talks a little too much, that one. Did you know that his real name is Kenneth?'

She smiled. Everyone needed a piece of unreality, his own illusion.

# CHAPTER TWENTY

A month after she left Whistlehalt Nancy made her carefully planned return to the Palmyra. She didn't want to spend her time fretting about Gil and Celia and wishing for their divorce, or even in reflecting on her own infirmity. Be strong, she told herself. To concentrate on work was the best distraction and anyway she needed the money.

Before curtain-up she stood at the peephole to study the house. The inverted palm tree suspended beneath the cupola was switched on and the clusters of electric bulbs lit every corner of the auditorium. She surveyed the scrolls of gilt plasterwork, and the coloured lozenges fronting the double tier of boxes. By candlelight or gas the effect was smoky and exotic, as Devil intended – his jewel box, he called the theatre – but under the electric glare it was gaudy. The down-at-heel impression was made worse by the scuffed walls and the chips gouged out of green-painted palm fronds to expose dimples of raw plaster.

Nancy turned her mind to this evening. She was apprehensive in a new and alarming way.

Since her injury the Uncanny had been fading. When she

440

tried to draw it about her it broke up like a morning mist, and when it crept up on her unawares it was tentative where it had once been overwhelming. Sometimes it closed her out altogether, and although the audible *click* like Cornelius turning off his wireless was only in her imagination, the effect was just as abrupt and absolute.

Her sparse audience was filing in. It was a wet evening and steamy raincoats dripped over the green plush seats. There were some drawn faces, people anxious for a message or a hint from the other side, but most of them seemed listless. She memorised as many sets of features as her confused head could hold, searching for the hook that would help her to begin a story. Here was a woman alone, wearing a pink scarf patterned with red roses. Perhaps her husband had passed, leaving her with a tiny pension and a legacy of loneliness. Two young girls came in, giggling together. They were making a joke of their night out, yet were still hoping for a word that might change their lives. A pair of elderly sisters, shop workers, were tired at the end of a day on their feet and eager for a sit-down. Perhaps they had misread the programme and were expecting an evening of Miss Vaughan's songs and cockney patter.

There were many more women than men. Male or female, none of the faces seemed to stand out except by their ordinariness. What could she tell these people?

The spot operators took up their positions and Desmond waited at the left of the stage. Five minutes to the up had already been called when Sylvia came to her side.

'I'm ready,' Nancy told her, although she felt far from it.

'You forgot.'

The dresser opened her hand. The new glass eye was cupped in her palm. Nancy already hated the thing with its fishy painted glare.

'I am going on in my patch.'

The triangle of black silk was threaded on thin elastic. She hoped by its plainness it could be excluded from Devil's prohibited categories of turbans and feathers and fringed shawls.

Sylvia reminded her of the doctor's advice to wear the glass eye and preserve the shape of the socket. Nancy stopped her. On the other side of the curtain the necessary stillness was gathering and spreading through the theatre. The rustling and coughing subsided as the swell of anticipation rose. She waited, as she had long ago learned to do, until the last possible second. Then she nodded to the curtain boy.

The green drapes parted and she walked into a column of light.

The words of her introduction came to her and there was the pressure of captured attention as her audience shifted forward in their seats.

'Who is here?' she asked. 'Who will speak to us?'

She could see her mirrors on only one side. She thought she knew where her targets were sitting. Sylvia and Desmond with the lighting boys and the stagehands were primed for her signals. At the right moment she would give the cue for the lights to filter towards blue and for colder air to seep through the ventilation grilles. Up in the gallery someone sneezed.

She attended to the Uncanny, urging it to swell around her.

Nothing happened. No one was there. She could hear a mutter from one of the boxes, even feel the scrape of stage dust through the thin soles of her shoes. Nothing more than that.

Anxiety crystallised into dismay, and dismay ballooned into a shocking wave of stage fright. She tried to remember where the woman in the rose-patterned scarf had been sitting, or the two young girls. Panic closed her throat.

'Lindley,' she managed to croak. 'Is there anyone called Lindley in the room?'

Two tickets for the performance had been paid for by cheque in the name of Mr Lindley Watts. She always memorised such cues and at least this discipline hadn't deserted her.

Mr Watts didn't want to put up his hand so his companion raised hers. The man was middle-aged and his mother might or might not be still alive. He might have fought in the war, or lost a brother or a friend. But it would soon be fifteen years since the armistice. Memories were fading.

'Lindley. May I call you that? I can hear the name Margaret. Do you know her?'

A popular name, even more so since it had been chosen by the Duke and Duchess of York.

The wretched man wouldn't speak. His face resembled a slab of rock.

'His cousin, in Canada,' his companion volunteered. 'Still on this side.'

Damn him then, and his bloody cousin and his entire family, dead or alive.

'Is it a family name? Margaret speaks up very clearly.'

The man folded his arms and stared back. In the wings Sylvia put her hands together and mimed a prayer. A shock of wayward amusement ran through Nancy. The evening's premise was ridiculous and she was the most ridiculous part of it.

*Do it,* she ordered herself.

Earn your money, keep them happy. Tell them something, anything that comes into your head.

Then get off this stage and never set foot on it again.

She took one sip of water and replaced the glass before raising it for a second sip. This was the cue for the change in lights and temperature. She walked forwards, almost to the footlights, and gazed deep into the auditorium.

'There are so many voices,' she softly confided.

She listened to the empty air before apparently suppressing a shudder. She pressed her fingers to her ears. This was another cue, one she rarely used, but Desmond didn't let her down. Immediately a fusillade of knocking ran through the theatre, amplified by speakers hidden in the walls. Several women gave little shrieks of alarm. Nancy took her chance. She shouted, 'Who is here? Who has come to speak with us?'

Walking the stage in sweeping circles she began a wild monologue, pointing at random and improvising from any clue offered by face or gesture. Sweat gathered under her eyepatch and a bead of it trickled down her cheek.

It wasn't the best seance she had ever offered – it might have been the worst – but somehow she carried it off as far as the interval.

The curtain fell and she tottered into the wings. There was some applause and even a little buzz of talk. Sylvia stood ready but Nancy had never been further from the Uncanny. She felt a wave of exhausted relief.

The act booked to carry the middle of the show was a magician. He made people disappear and materialise in different places and the stagehands were hurrying to put his apparatus into place.

Desmond looked harassed.

'What happened?'

'I dried.'

He patted her hand.

'The second half will be better.'

'I can't go back on.'

The manager and Sylvia stared. Even when almost too ill or exhausted to walk, Nancy would never miss a ticketed performance.

Desmond cleared his throat. 'Is it the eye that's troubling you?'

The lack of an eye, she inwardly corrected.

She was learning how not to be blindsided, not to swing her whole body when she turned to the dark side and how to cope with stumbling against obstacles. It wasn't the narrowing of physical sight that affected her tonight, but the certainty that Lenny's stone had cost her more than the eye. Somehow a window within her head had been smashed, and the sensory tumult that had blazed beyond the window was deserting her.

Her head was full of questions about how and why and there was only one person who could answer them.

She said hastily to Desmond, 'Yes. The eye.'

Sylvia fumbled in her pocket.

'Not the glass one. I don't want it. I'm going home now.'

Sylvia followed her to the dressing room. A message reading '*Welcome Back to the Old Palmyra and Good Luck*', signed by the whole of the company, was taped to the mirror and a half-bottle of champagne was set out for after the final curtain. Nancy looked at the dressing table, her outdoor clothes on the hook, the old tin kettle and the gas ring.

'Forgive me, Sylvia. Something has happened inside my head. After the injury, I think . . . I'm not sure I can do this any longer.'

'You're still recovering, dear. You're always so harsh on yourself. Take things slowly and gently, can't you?'

'I haven't always relied on the . . . ability, you know that. I couldn't have done. But it was always there, like the kernel in a nut, and by using it when I could I didn't feel a fraud every minute of my working life. Do you understand? If it isn't there, I can't go on.'

Sylvia wanted to understand her, but she half-shook her head.

'What will your dad say?'

This was the dresser's first consideration and Nancy had to smile. Sylvia hurried on. 'Well, I don't suppose he'll have much to say, will he?'

'I'm not sure.'

It was hard to predict how Devil would be on any day.

Sylvia's eyes glimmered with tears. 'It's been a good few years since I started work with your father and mother, dear. Marvellous years they've been.'

Nancy hugged her. The old woman was as light as a bird.

'There will always be a job for you, Sylvia, for as long as the Palmyra stays open.'

'No, dear. I worked with your mother and I've been your dresser all these years. Nothing less will do, thank you.'

'Then you can let Cornelius and Arthur and me look after you. The two of us can be retired together.'

Sylvia stepped away and began to tidy the dressing table.

'I don't know what to say, Nancy. Losing your eye was a shocking thing for you, but this company has been through as bad and survived for another day. Carlo died, remember, out on that very stage.'

'I know he did. I don't want to let the company down.'

Sylvia slid a glance at her.

'Go on. Get on home with you and have a good night's sleep and maybe you'll feel differently tomorrow.'

'All right.'

Nancy was already hurrying along the Strand by the time Desmond took the stage to announce that Miss Zenobia Wix was unfortunately indisposed.

Home?

Tonight she didn't even think of going to Bloomsbury and waiting for the telephone to ring. She wanted only to be safe at Waterloo Street with Cornelius and Devil.

In the morning she did put in her glass eye. It glittered disconcertingly when she peered in the mirror so she turned her back on her reflection. She walked down to Bloomsbury and let herself into the flat, where she could use the telephone in absolute seclusion. She could count almost on one hand the number of times she had spoken on it to anyone other than Gil, but today she gave the operator the number of Henley police station. A moment later she was speaking to the sympathetic officer who had interviewed her in the aftermath of the event.

In the presence of Mrs Templeton and Cornelius, Nancy had described what happened at the camp in the fields. She insisted that it was an unfortunate accident. The man Lenny Simmons had never intended to hit her with a stone propelled from a catapult. Everyone present had been upset by an argument about the sprits, even disturbed, but there was no malign intent.

The policeman had been deferential as well as sympathetic, because of her connection to Mrs Templeton, and also surprised that she did not want to pursue any charge. It seemed an unlikely accident, he said.

'Nevertheless, that was what it was.'

The policeman had kept her informed of the later developments. A few days after Nancy's injury, Lawrence Feather walked into Henley police station to give himself up.

447

In an interview he swore to the police that he had no knowledge of either Lenny Simmons' or his wife's present whereabouts. All the camp's occupants had panicked, he claimed. The husband and wife had run off at once while he and the others had done what they could for Nancy. One of them had rushed for help, and the rest of them had stayed with her until rescuers were almost at her side.

'Then we took ourselves off,' he said. 'That was a wrong thing to do, and so I have come to offer myself up. I am not a criminal. I am Lawrence Feather, the medium.'

He seemed surprised, at the end of an interview, to be told that there were no charges against him.

Feather gave as his address a street on the outskirts of Reading and Nancy now obtained that address from the policeman. Using a silver pencil she wrote it down on the leather-backed pad that was kept beside the telephone and had almost never been used.

Nancy took the train from Paddington, asked directions at the station and walked a long way down increasingly seedy streets lined with small factories and repair shops. She found the house in a brick terrace next to the railway marshalling yards. On the other side of a wire fence an engine shunted a line of wagons past clumps of ragwort and willowherb. It was the beginning of June, a day of blue skies and sailing clouds.

The house had no number but she checked those on either side to make sure it was the right one. When there was no response to her knock she tried to peer in through the downstairs window but the grey curtains were drawn tight.

She sat down on a low brick wall to wait.

A thin black cat purred and rubbed itself against her ankles before slinking away to chase cabbage white butterflies in the buddleia sprouting from the wall. An hour passed before she saw Feather coming down the road. A string bag of shopping bumped against his leg.

He started in alarm. 'Nancy?'

He had cut his hair and trimmed his beard. Although his face was increasingly haggard he appeared less unkempt than at their last meeting. He looked shabby but ordinary, like one of the workless men she had passed on the way here.

There was no shade in front of the house and the sun had reddened her face. She had discarded the grotesque glass eye and her black patch drew the heat to her throbbing eye socket. He stared at it.

She said, 'May I come in and talk to you?'

His mouth twisted. 'Really? Are you alone? Aren't you afraid I might hurt you in some way?'

'No, I'm not afraid of you.'

This was true. The bright sun and the bald, unremarkable street convinced her. The world had shrunk to what was limited and measurable. For her whole life the Uncanny had set her apart, and now it seemed she had joined the throng. She felt nothing but relief that her long isolation was over.

Feather led the way to a room at the back of the tiny house. A fly buzzed against the closed window and the clank of shunting drifted from the yards.

He put his bag down and looked directly at her.

'I am sorry for what happened to you at my camp.'

'Did you intend it?'

'That you should be half-blinded? No, I did not. Please, won't you sit?'

Two chairs were drawn up to a table covered with a

greasy oilcloth. It was a long way from the opulent Victorian rooms overlooking Gower Street. She sat down and placed her hands flat on the cloth.

He asked in a low voice, 'Why have you come here?'

'I want you to tell me what happened that night and before it. You sent that little child to me, didn't you, all those times? And you manipulated her mother and father. Why was that?'

He shifted, giving the smallest shrug. 'Why do any of these things happen? In the spirit world, as you well know . . .'

She cut him short. 'I laid no charges for assault against you or your accomplices. You will repay my generosity with the truth. Providing you know what that is. *Do* you know, Mr Feather?'

There was a metallic bite of satisfaction in provoking the clash at long last. His insinuating smile had faded altogether. There was a long pause.

'I find myself humiliated.' His voice was so low that she had to lean forward to catch the words, although his gesture at the dismal room spoke loudly enough. 'I was once the most celebrated. I had the best audiences. I commanded . . .'

She cut off the bluster. 'I know.'

'You took my success away from me. You double-crossed me.'

'I did not. The *truth*, I said.'

He bridled. 'Perhaps I made some claims I should not have done. I over-reached, you might say. My loss of favour was quite rapid and mostly unjustified.'

He told her a few details about his fading career, some of which Nancy already knew. Then he cocked his head at her, rediscovering his assurance.

'But I was never one to bow down to an ignorant public. I collected around me a small group of committed Spiritualists. Men and women who truly appreciated my gift. Lenny and Peg were amongst them, of course. They came to me first to contact their daughter, poor little Emmy.'

A drowned child, with her posy basket. The soaking girl, gone forever.

Feather said, almost wheedling now, 'You and I understand a little of the paranormal, Nancy. We know the margins, at least. We appreciate all that lies beyond the range for normal people, and we can estimate how much stretches beyond our own range. I had a channel to Emmy Simmons. Not a strong one, but she was an easy spirit. I was able to transport her, to will her into your presence. You are the adept, but I had my powers, didn't I? You kept my Helena from me so I sent Emmy to remind you of the *Queen Mab* and what I had lost.'

'You did.'

He chuckled. He might be humiliated by his current quarters yet his competitive vanity seemed undiminished.

'Lenny and Peg knew I could reach their girl. I assured them that I was her channel, and that you formed part of the connection because you were on the *Queen Mab* too. I brought them once to the Palmyra, remember?'

'I do.'

'They stuck with me for years. Them, and the others you saw. They looked to my guidance and leadership. I appreciated our life in the camp, you know. Raw, stripped to the bones, close to the bare earth. It was honest.'

Hardly, Nancy thought.

'Lacking my stamina, the others were tiring of it. Threatening to leave me. I needed my little crew, Nancy. I can't . . . I thought I couldn't be alone with the voices.

451

Then I woke up in the camp one night and Peg was sitting on my chest. The nails of her two hands were here, like this.' He dug his hooked fingers under his jawbone. Nancy could imagine all too well and she shivered.

'I promised to bring you to the camp. With both of us there, the connection would be so strong. I told them they would see her for themselves, Nancy.'

The poor creatures.

'I didn't expect Lenny to do what he did to you.'

Nancy raised her hand to the patch. The room was square, dull, grubby, with no shimmer or echo.

'Where are they now?'

'Lenny knows the country ways and how to slip into the empty places. Peg's people are Irish. Perhaps they have gone there. They won't come back. Not after what he did to you.' There was a final, heavy pause.

'I didn't know Lenny would attack you. The poor brute was usually docile enough. All I wanted from you was fellow-feeling and the respect I deserve. Is that too much, after the way you behaved?'

Everything about Lawrence Feather was disgusting, yet a worm of sympathy for him burrowed within her. Wearily she said, 'You always over-estimated my command of Helena. But even if I had had the closest contact I would have tried to keep it from you, because of what you did and were to her.'

His lips drew back. 'Do you truly believe I harmed her? The most precious and beloved creature who ever breathed?'

Nancy sighed.

'It doesn't matter what I believe, or what the truth is. I don't think truth is a concept you properly understand.'

Perhaps the misdefining of truth was – or had been – a failing of hers too. Yes, certainly it had been. No more.

She reminded him, 'I thought you said Helena was with you.'

His face seemed to collapse inwards. 'I try. I try so hard to believe she is.' He hesitated. 'Nancy, do you still hear her?'

'No.'

The man's skin was papery and creased with tiny lines. He looked old and frail.

Nancy said, 'I want you to answer one more question and then I am going to walk out of here. After the accident, after I lost my eye and all the damage happened inside here,' she gestured at her cheekbone, 'the other place began to slip away. Has it really gone? I have to know if it really is over and done with.'

The man seemed to reflect.

Rather than attempt words, he scooped his hands in the shape of a skull. His fingers tapped the imaginary bumps of bone and traced a net of blood vessels. He seemed to indicate that, in Dr Pennington's language, there could be a physiological explanation for the Uncanny. It was to do with small brain seizures, or the blocking and unblocking of neural pathways. Nancy already knew that the thick olfactory nerve controlled the most powerful of the senses, which was why the Uncanny was so entwined with her sense of smell. Then Feather's fingers fluttered and flew apart. Just as eloquently he sketched a different picture with his hands, this one of time's intersecting loops and swirls. Finally he smoothed the unruly strands to show her how they coalesced and flowed onwards in an unbroken stream.

Nancy exhaled a long, ragged breath. Her body yielded its stiff knots and kinks of confusion. Wordlessly, Feather confirmed what she had suspected: the Uncanny was gone. She was as light as air.

He asked, 'Do you regret the loss, if that is what has happened?'

A smile briefly transfigured her.

'No.'

Feather bowed.

'The child?' Nancy asked.

'At peace.'

There was a moment's stillness before she whispered, 'Helena too, I believe.'

Nancy stood up and pushed back her chair. She would never see Feather after today.

'How do you live? What are you going to do?'

'I live in a way. It is a temporary state in an endless continuum and I don't consider it important.' His shrug was preening. The same old fraud. 'I do a few tarot readings. One or two private sittings. It's enough.'

She nodded. Lawrence Feather could take care of himself. She was ready to leave but he restrained her with a touch of his hand. For the last time she managed not to flinch.

'And you?'

'I'm not sure. I can't pretend to be a medium any longer.'

'What will you do instead? What would you like to happen?'

*I want to be Gil's wife.*

She blurted instead, 'I would like a family.'

Lizzie Shaw was ripening like one of her own fruits. Nancy felt desiccated beside her.

Feather reached out and placed his hand on her head. He let it rest before stroking her hair. The gesture was so reminiscent of the morning long ago on the Kentish beach that she almost overturned the table in pulling away.

They said goodbye formally and without animosity. She left him sitting in the kitchen where the fly still batted against the glass. On the slow train back to London she fell deeply asleep with her cheek pressed to the dusty seat cover.

Gil came to Bloomsbury as he often did, in the hour after dinner. She had been reading beside the door into the enclosed garden. He kissed her before bringing up another chair and they sat side by side to look out into the midsummer twilight.

'What an old couple we are,' he remarked.

It was true. The rooms were layered with the years, their stolen hours written in the books collected on the shelves, the exchanged gifts, small pieces of furniture and china discovered in the cluttered shops of the neighbourhood. Even so there were only a few items of clothing hanging in the wardrobe. They wore only one version of themselves in this place.

'How is your father this week?'

Nancy sighed. 'He was on his way up the road this morning, still in his pyjamas. I had to run after him and beg him to come home. He said he was late for the theatre.'

'Poor Nancy.'

'Poor Pa, rather. Imagine losing your memory. All the precious moments of your life, melting away into a fog. Sometimes, when he realises what's happening to him, he weeps.'

Gil traced the line of her jaw before his mouth found the notch at the base of her throat. They rarely kissed on the lips now because Nancy was conscious of her eyepatch and anxious to keep it in place. After the one time at Whistlehalt she had never let him see the empty socket.

They felt a matching urge to deny ageing in the most primitive way.

He undid her buttons and cupped his hands beneath her breasts. He lifted the hem of her skirt and ran his hand from the knee up to her thigh, all the way to the tiny bulge of flesh above her stocking top. The whole of her immediately became concentrated in that square inch of skin.

The first time they made love had been in this room, and there had been dozens of times – no, hundreds – since that first discovery.

She wanted him as much tonight as she had ever done.

Nancy closed her eyes. The world contracted to the here, *here*, and now, this moment, *this*. She had been released from all the eavesdropping and the eavesdroppers, from the queasy shimmers and the insistent voices, and the consequent impression that she was never quite anchored in one place. She was free now. Desire, sex, the longing for physical gratification; urgency rushed into all the vacated spaces in her head and concentrated there.

He took off her blouse and slid the straps of her slip from her shoulders. Cool air touched her hot skin. Her fingers trembled as she made the equivalent moves with his collar and studs.

She broke away from him and took off the remainder of her clothes, deliberately slow with the hooks and eyes. The garments dropped in a heap at her feet and she stood naked. She indicated with a lift of her chin that he should do the same. Gil hesitated, the thumbnail dimple beneath his eye appearing and deepening, but she waited until he complied.

Then she took him by the wrist and led him to the bed.

For the first time, as she straddled him, she understood something that Lizzie Shaw must have known all along. Sex was for taking as well as giving. You could abandon yourself. She sat upright, looking down into his eyes through the fall of her hair. On an impulse she pulled off her eyepatch. Gil blinked, but that was all. He grasped her shoulders and pulled her down to him.

'Kiss me,' he said.

She was tired of the woman she had been. Goodbye, Zenobia Wix, she exulted, and gave herself up to the moment.

It was a good moment, perhaps the best.

When it was over they lay for a long time listening to their breathing as it slowed and separated and grew apart.

'Are you awake?' he whispered, with his fingers still wound in her hair.

'Of course I am.'

Her limbs were heavy and her body seemed all one valedictory smile, but she had never been more conscious. All was well, all would be well. Gil loved her, and she him. They would find a way to be together.

Gil sat up, tucking the covers over her so she wouldn't feel any draught. He swung his legs to the side of the bed and she studied the chain of his spine as he leaned forward to pick something out of the tangle of clothing on the floor.

It was the eyepatch. He fitted it in place for her and kissed her forehead.

'I have to go, Nancy.'

Even in her exultation she couldn't help but think that for all the time they had known each other he had been going, leaving her behind. It was on the tip of her tongue to ask him, *What about your divorce? Why do you always have to leave me?* But she had trained herself so assiduously not to put demands on him, and the words went unspoken.

'Are you staying?' he asked.

Sometimes she slept alone at the flat after he had gone.

'Perhaps.'

With a curled finger he stroked her cheek.

'Goodnight, darling.'

She did lie there for a while after he had left, but then she thought of Waterloo Street and very much wanted to be there. She flung on her clothes, tidied the bed and locked the door on the time being.

Cornelius and Jinny were playing chess at the kitchen table. The teapot in the old knitted cosy stood on the hob and the back door was propped open to let in the evening air. They were surprised to see her; Cornelius's beefy face was flushed and he pressed his glasses into place as if they might have become dislodged.

'Sorry,' she murmured. 'I wasn't going to, but I decided to come home. Carry on with the game.'

'She's beating me,' Cornelius complained, hunching his shoulders over the board.

'I am not,' Jinny said. She touched Nancy's arm. 'All well?'

'All well,' she answered.

Cornelius and Jinny were so tactful. They knew about her life with Gil and they accepted as little or as much as she wanted to tell them about it. She pressed her cheek briefly to the top of her friend's head, wanting to convey to her how much she loved her.

'Is Pa awake?'

Cornelius frowned at the board, made a decisive move and captured Jinny's rook.

'I took him a cup of tea half an hour ago. He asked if you were in.'

Nancy went to her room and took off her outer clothes in case any scent of Gil's cigar smoke was caught in the folds. She tied the sash of her mother's red robe before stepping across the narrow landing to tap on Devil's door.

'There you are at last. How was the house tonight?'

'Pa, I don't do my act any longer. Don't you remember? Desmond's looking after the Palmyra for us for the time being.'

For now. The theatre's rows of worn green plush seats were increasingly empty. The music halls were over and the craze for Spiritualism was fading. Everything seemed in flux.

'Come here,' he said. She went to him and he hooked his arm around her waist, letting his head fall against her red silken hip.

'Eliza, don't leave me alone all the time like this. Why are you wearing that thing over your eye?'

She stroked his hair. Devil had aged in the last year but he was still physically strong.

'It's Nancy, Pa.'

He stared up at her. There were cloudy rings around his dark irises and the black eyebrows stood up in wild tufts.

'Of course. What am I thinking?'

His gaze slid to Charlie Egan's drawing of his wife.

'I'm nearly seventy-seven,' he remarked, in a voice as plaintive as a child's. 'Nearly seventy-eight.' There was some confusion as to Devil's real age because he had chosen to amend it so many times. But he was quite certain of the day and the month.

'I know,' Nancy smiled.


Arthur and Bella came with their three boys to spend the birthday afternoon. They brought the good news that Harry Bolton's young wife was expecting her first child.

'That *is* marvellous,' Nancy smiled. They had begun to worry about the time it was taking, but now it seemed all was well.

The Wix boys loved visiting Waterloo Street because they

could race their toy cars up and down the length of bare linoleum in the hallway. They dutifully wished their grandfather many happy returns before dashing off to play. The cars flew against the skirtings and no one told them off. Jinny even sat on the bottom stair to look on and cheer.

'A trio of proper little officers in the making,' Devil remarked.

He was surprised by the two older boys' regulation grey flannel shorts and combed hair, and had to be reminded that these miniature gentlemen were his grandsons. He was careless with his own clothes these days, and he harked back constantly to his ragged childhood.

'What did he expect from Arthur and Bella?' Cornelius mumbled to Nancy. 'Urchins?'

Arthur stood with his back to the fireplace, out of uniform today but always with the impression of red-tabbed khaki about him. He was now a major, working in a capacity that could never be discussed and which involved prolonged absences overseas.

'It's quite a tribute to you, Pa, that Arthur's with us today and not riding his camel in the Empty Quarter.' Bella was a little plumper, which suited her. She was an excellent army wife.

'Don't listen to her,' Arthur said fondly. 'I've been at home for weeks, getting under her feet. She'll be glad to wave me off to Cairo again.'

The children thundered along the hall and clattered down the kitchen steps. The old house shook and a few flakes of loose distemper drifted from the ceiling like summer snow.

Cornelius was collarless and in his shirtsleeves with traces of the garden clinging to him. He carried a tray of cups and plates into the parlour and Nancy followed behind. She was bringing the birthday cake she had baked earlier and as she climbed the steps she felt suddenly dizzy. She had to steady herself with a hand against the wall, almost dropping the plate. Faith was sitting quietly in the corner. She had come for the family gathering, driven across town by her daughter although Lizzie complained that she could hardly squeeze herself behind the steering wheel. Matthew was too infirm to leave Bavaria.

'Are you all right, dear?' Faith whispered when Nancy came near.

'I am fine, Aunt Faith, thank you.'

Nancy knew how she must appear, even to her aunt. She had turned into the dutiful unmarried daughter, whose main function was to stay at home and care for her widowed father and war-damaged brother. She couldn't help comparing herself with Lizzie, newly married and blooming in her voluminous dress. Tommy Shaw Hooper was apprenticed in an engineering company. The boy showed real promise, Matthew liked to say.

Nancy lifted her chin.

'Wait and see,' she heard herself laughing, although she didn't know what she meant by it. Faith looked puzzled.

'It's my birthday. Am I going to get any of that cake?' Devil called.

Nancy had agreed with Arthur and Cornelius that they must finally raise with him the question of selling the theatre. As they were so rarely together it had to be done today.

'If only I were a banker or something lucrative I could keep the old place going,' Arthur said.

Bella's money meant that his family was secure and the boys' education would be paid for, but he had only his service pay to call his own. His fair, good face was troubled and Nancy hated to see it.

'You help us out quite enough.'

It was true. Arthur did as much as he could.

'And anyway it's not for you to worry about. I chose to give up the stage work.'

She had offered only the briefest explanation and her brothers had accepted it. They had never gone in for asking her a lot of questions. Nancy's real role was to be their sister, and the daughter of the house.

She said, 'We've got to find the money to pay the rent here and take care of Pa. I'll find another job, but the best answer is still to sell the Palmyra. We can't keep it going. I don't even want to do it. Do you?'

Arthur shook his head. The old theatre had already eaten up too much of their lives.

Cornelius stared at his big hands.

'I wish I could do more,' he mumbled.

Nancy told him, 'You do everything. You *are* everything, to me.'

Jinny leaned over his shoulder.

'Nancy's right. Let's not hear any more talk like that.'

'It won't be easy to convince Pa,' Cornelius warned them. 'But I know it's got to be done.'

David, Christopher and little Hugh Wix were clamouring for cake and sweets.

Jinny told them, 'Pipe down, you loathsome creatures, or there won't be another mouthful for any of you.'

They loved her mock strictness and acted up even more. With an iced bun in his fist the eldest ran at his grandfather and pounded his knee, scattering crumbs and sugar.

'Magic. Do magic for us.'

'Magic, eh? Let's see.'

Devil patted his pocket and brought out the three cups.

Nancy loved seeing him with the children. It was a joy for all of them to have the house full of family and noise and too much food. The middle boy was persuaded to give up a glass marble from his pocket and the shuffle of the cups began. However certain of its whereabouts any of them might be, the marble was never under the cup they chose. Devil hooted with laughter at their confusion, his eyes screwing up with alert cunning.

'No, it's there,' David yelled. Hugh stared from his mother's side, a little afraid.

Devil's finger oscillated over the cups.

'Here? There?'

Empty. All three children gaped. The marble could only be under the last cup.

Faith and Lizzie and Jinny insisted together, '*That* one.'

Devil slid it towards Hugh.

'Go on.'

The little boy flushed but he sidled forward and picked it up. There was no marble. In its place Nancy's glass eye stared at the ceiling. The cup clattered to the floor.

'Oh, oh, horrible.'

The children fell into paroxysms of delighted disgust. Devil sat back and beamed.

'Auntie Pirate,' David said. 'I like you in your patch much better than with that eye in.'

'That's enough,' Bella said. 'Put your coats on. We'll go for a little walk before it's time to drive home.'

Lizzie said that she would take a nap on Nancy's bed. She put her hands to the small of her back and crossed the room on splayed feet. Jinny and Faith went out to the kitchen to wash up and Devil was left in the parlour with his three children.

He spread his fingers and examined his hands, front and back.

'Wonder. Creating wonder in a drab world, that's what I do. You and me, Miss Zenobia Wix, eh?'

'I don't perform onstage any longer, Pa.'

'What? Why not? I should get back to the theatre myself. No reason why not. Work up a couple of new illusions. That'll bring them in. I'll talk to . . . talk to . . . what is his name? We'll need to get some flyers printed.'

He looked at his children, the light fading out of his face.

'Eh? What do you say?' He peered around the room and his hands trembled. 'Where's Eliza gone?'

Arthur sat down beside him and drew an inward breath.

'We've been thinking, Cornelius and Nancy and me, that the time might have come to sell the theatre. Let some new blood take charge of bringing wonder to the world. What do you say?'

Devil rotated his stiff torso and cupped a hand to his ear. Vertical clefts appeared in his cheeks, his lips drew back from his teeth. Nancy had a flash of the old illusionist, mugging at centre stage for a matinee audience.

'Sell? My *thee-aaaa-tre*?'

Arthur added, 'Times have changed. No one has much money to spare. People go to the pictures.'

None of them was prepared for Devil's outburst of genuine fury. When he realised they were serious the old man threw back his head and bellowed like an animal.

'Never. I will never sell the Palmyra. I would rather go barefoot and beg in the streets.'

'Pa, there's no need for anything of the sort . . .' Nancy tried to take his hand but he shook her off.

'You will have to kill me first,' he shouted.

'Come, let's talk about it, at the very least. There are some debts to pay. This house . . .'

Devil lurched to his feet. The loose flesh of his neck quivered and spittle flew from his lips.

'Is that what you want? To have me dead and gone?'

Arthur flinched. 'Of course we don't. Please don't say such a thing. We want the opposite, which is to secure your future and Nancy's.'

Devil shook a fist at him.

'I go before my theatre does. I've got a family, you know. My children will never let you sell my theatre. *They* know it would kill me.'

He groped for the back of the chair and used it to launch himself at the door.

They sat in silence as his carpet slippers slapped and shuffled up the stairs. Faith and Jinny's alarmed faces appeared in the doorway.

Cornelius raised his head.

'That didn't go very well, did it?'

Not long afterwards Lizzie came downstairs with combed hair and freshly reddened lips. Arthur and Bella took their children home and the rest of them gathered in the parlour for a conference. Nancy insisted to Jinny that she was family too and of course she should stay.

Faith pursed her lips. 'Devil always was a selfish, difficult man. He led your mother a dance.'

Lizzie frowned at her.

Cornelius was saying that they had sown the seed in Devil's mind and the best thing would be to let the notion take root. In a week or a month he would probably claim the idea as his own and insist on following it through.

Nancy's attention was taken by the sound of a car drawing up. She had to twist in her chair to see through the lace curtain at the lower half of the window. Not many cars came this way, and none like this one.

A moment later there was a knock at the front door.

'Excuse me,' she mumbled.

She rushed to open it but it wasn't Gil on the step.

'Miss Wix.'

'Lady Celia?'

The Bentley was drawn up behind her, the chauffeur standing bolt upright beside it. Of course Celia Maitland would not drive herself around London. Nancy knew that every eye in Waterloo Street would be on this apparition of opulence. The juxtaposition was brutal.

And then with a shock as sudden as the reveal in one of Devil's illusions Nancy saw the truth. For all her dreams she had never really, properly been admitted to Gil's world, any more than he had owned a genuine stake in hers. She felt stripped bare.

In a shock of anguish she dragged her gaze back to Gil's wife.

Celia's face was thickly powdered, her hair and brows hidden under a cloche hat swathed in net veiling. Her mouth was a crooked slash of lipstick. She held out a suede-gloved hand but it was not offered for Nancy to shake. It was more of a warning.

'I am so sorry. May I speak to you urgently? I didn't find you at the Bloomsbury address so I took the liberty of coming on here.'

Celia could never before have paid a visit in a street like this. Nancy glimpsed it through her eyes: the row of low houses, the corner shop with the rusty tin Fry's Chocolate sign, the public house with a bench placed against the wall where the men with no money for beer could sit down. How did Celia know about Bloomsbury?

A rush of emotions made her feel dizzy again.

'Is Gil hurt? I mean, Mr Maitland?'

Where was he? How was he allowing this scene to come about?

'No, my husband is not hurt or ill.'

There was no point in pretending any longer. Celia knew she was Gil's mistress. In a way, the knowledge came as a relief.

Peering over Nancy's shoulder Celia said, 'May I come in?'

'I'm afraid it's not very convenient.'

She tried to block the doorway, to head off the unthinkable collision between Celia Maitland and her family, but it was already too late. Devil came down the stairs, ordering Cornelius not to stand in his way like a sack of spuds. He put Nancy aside too.

'A Bentley,' he crooned. 'I've seen an earlier model very similar to this one. The same colours, cream and red.'

The chauffeur touched a smut off the gleaming bonnet as Devil approached.

Devil said to him as if he was talking to old Gibb, 'My word, look at this. A Walter Owen Bentley, four and a half litre. 1931, is it?'

He stroked the coachwork.

'Yes, sir. The year the company was bought up, of course. Mr Maitland is expecting delivery of the new model later this year. I'm not convinced it'll be an improvement, myself.'

'I had cars once, you know. There was a . . . a . . . I've forgotten its name.'

'Yes, sir.'

The man cleared his throat, shooting a look at his employer.

'Come back inside, Pa.'

Cornelius seized Devil's arm and drew his father back towards the house.

'Then won't you join me for a drive?' Celia begged Nancy in a low voice. 'I'd be particularly grateful.'

She answered wildly, 'All right. Yes, of course.'

A moment later they were sitting in the back of the Bentley. Celia leaned forward to the chauffeur.

'If you would drive us around for half an hour, Tate, I will let you know when to bring us back here.'

'Yes, my lady.'

She slid the glass panel shut and the Bentley purred down Waterloo Street. The men gathered outside the pub craned for a closer look.

How ridiculous I was, Nancy thought, ever to imagine I could shift out of that world into this. How lovingly naive.

Celia's gloved fingers tapped on the leather armrest.

'You will be wondering why I have chosen to speak, after all these years?'

It was even more absurd, Nancy understood, to have imagined that her liaison with Gil was a secret. It was as if she had been purblind before, instead of now.

'Yes. As you say, after all this time.'

'I have come to beg for your help. I need you.'

They looked full at each other. Celia was so heavily made up that it was difficult to read her expression. Through the net veil Nancy caught the glint of desperation.

'What can I do?'

'There is a woman called Thelma Auger. I believe she intends to marry my husband.'

They passed the turning to the old house overlooking the canal and the low buildings where the barge horses had once been stabled. The car plunged over the canal bridge and Nancy began to feel slightly sick.

'I don't think she can do that without his agreement, can she?'

Without warning Celia began to sob.

'He will agree. He intends to divorce me. I have been a terrible wife. I couldn't even give him an heir for the

Maitland Process. How I hate his damned Process, all those lurid colours and miles of cheap printed cloth.'

A hiccough of wild laughter cut through the sobs. 'I thought perhaps you and I might confront him together. Join forces as his wife and his mistress. We can go and confront him right away, don't you think? He's in his office in the City. We'll persuade him to leave matters as they are.'

She abandoned herself to weeping, the tears flowing from under the veil and dripping off her chin. Nancy tried to pass her a handkerchief and Celia suddenly flung herself into her arms. Nancy awkwardly held her as she gulped and sobbed.

She murmured, 'Celia, I'm sorry. It was a wretched thing to have done to you and I am ashamed of it. I was his mistress, but it's over now.'

Only at this moment did she know it. Deep in her belly, inside the nausea, she felt the first twist of desolation.

Celia's sobbing abruptly stopped. She threw her head back, staring in horror through the ruined veil.

'Oh, God.'

'What? What is it?'

'Don't you *understand*?'

Humbly Nancy said, 'I'm afraid not.'

'It was all right when he was with *you*. I didn't particularly worry about that. But if it's ended for you it must be because he plans to marry her. Don't you see?'

She did.

She felt cold, and gripped by the rising nausea.

She was a fool, because she hadn't learned her lesson from Lion Stone.

*I never thought of marrying you.*

Of course a man like Gil Maitland didn't marry a stage medium from a family like the Wixes.

Gil Maitland married into the de Laury family. A man

like Gil kept a woman like Nancy in a flat in Bloomsbury and once their liaison was properly established they went out and about a little, to the opera and innocuous public entertainments, to discreet suppers or even to stay abroad with similarly marginal people.

Everyone understood these things, including the man's wife. Except the foolish blind-eyed mistress herself.

And then, if he were driven through desperation to seek a divorce and if circumstances permitted, such a man might take a chic American lady, an heiress in her own right, as his second choice.

Celia read the signs correctly, Nancy knew it.

She was shivering and it was a moment before she could bring herself to speak.

She mumbled, 'I don't know anything about that. I do know that he was loyal to you, in his way. He always wanted to protect you. He's not a bad man. I think he's only a man.'

'Did you love him?'

'Yes, I did.' The car was swaying horribly now. Nancy swallowed down the sickness and the first great wave of loss.

Celia's face crumpled before the tears flowed again.

'I still do love him. If I didn't love him so much I'd have gone to join Richard long ago. He's waiting for me, you know.'

The poor demented creature.

'Don't say such a thing. I'm so sorry I can't help you, Celia. Nothing I could say to Gil would make any difference. Just try to be as brave as you can. Maybe the affair with Mrs Auger will blow over.'

Affairs did that.

Celia turned to stare out of the car window, her narrow shoulders hunched with misery.

She demanded abruptly, 'Do you think it is possible to have too much money, Miss Wix?'

'I don't know. It's not a question I have ever had to ask or therefore answer.'

'I think perhaps you can.'

The dingy streets slid past.

'How wretched it is,' Celia added. Nancy didn't know whether she meant her own life or those she glimpsed through the car windows.

Celia leaned forward and rapped on the glass. She slid the partition open and ordered the chauffeur, 'Take us back to that address, Tate.'

'Yes, my lady.'

The Bentley drew up once more in Waterloo Street. Nancy wound down the window and gulped some fresh air.

'I'm sorry,' she repeated.

Celia shook her head. 'I'm grateful to you, really. You kept Gil married to me for ten years. And you brought me Richard. I can never thank you enough for doing that.'

'I didn't. Really, I . . .'

The other woman's hand shot out. Her fingers gripped so fiercely it made Nancy wince.

'Yes, you did. Don't tell me otherwise.'

After so many years of doing it, Nancy wearily speculated, was letting Celia Maitland believe what she wanted any worse than doing the same thing for dozens of other people? It would never happen again. All that, and the Uncanny, was over.

She heard a murmur of voices and her senses instantly sharpened. The view through the window of the Bentley briefly shimmered, and then every last vestige of the Uncanny was gone.

Stepping down on to solid ground made her feel much better. Celia's ravaged face was framed by the open window.

'What's wrong with your eye?' she asked, as if she had just noticed that Nancy wore a patch.

'It was an accident.'

'Oh.'

The hand rapped on the glass partition once more and the car slid away. Celia didn't look back.

'Aunt Faith and Lizzie said goodnight,' Cornelius told her as soon as she came in. 'We weren't sure how long you were likely to be.'

Jinny sat at the table, stringing runner beans. Cornelius chopped them and tossed them into a saucepan.

'Where's Devil?'

Cornelius said, 'He was agitated. He went back to shouting about never selling and over his dead body, so I gave him a tot of brandy and some of my old sleeping draught. When I looked in a moment ago he was snoring.'

Nancy went into the scullery for the hoarded brandy bottle she and Cornelius kept hidden in a box of oatmeal. Alcohol was best out of Devil's way these days. She poured herself a scant finger of the spirit and placed the bottle on the table. Jinny helped herself and went on deftly stripping green spirals from the beans.

They wouldn't ask, but she could tell them.

'The woman in the Bentley was Lady Celia Maitland, Gil's wife. He brought her to one of my early Palmyra performances because she wanted to reach her dead brother. Gil and I became lovers not long after that.'

She had never told them how it happened. Nobody spoke for a moment.

472

'And did she reach her brother?' Cornelius asked in his flat tone.

'In a way, yes.'

Jinny's head was bent over the old enamel colander. She never judged, even when they had confided their early secrets amidst the oily clatter at Lennox & Ringland after big ambulance nights.

Nancy said, 'Anyway, I have just realised that Gil and I are finished. I have discovered how much I hate secrets.'

Cornelius carried the pan across to the range. He searched for the box of matches that usually stood on a shelf next to the gas ring.

Jinny said, 'I would like to see you happy.'

Nancy considered. Out of the mass of new shocking perspectives that confronted her it was difficult to pick a consistent angle.

'I am not unhappy,' she confessed, surprising herself. There would be pain to come, without the man she had counted as her dearest friend as well as her love, yet an unacknowledged green shoot gave her hope.

The air was spiky with a strange tension. Jinny raised her head.

'I hate secrets too. I want to tell her,' she said to Cornelius.

Nancy turned to her brother. His cheeks turned a mottled dark red but he went on mechanically searching shelves for the matches. Jinny put down the paring knife.

'Cornelius has asked me to marry him. I said yes.'

'Neelie?' Nancy breathed.

He pushed his glasses back up to the bridge of his nose. 'That's right.'

She was shocked almost to silence, where she had no right to be. She might have guessed, she realised, except that she would have dismissed the idea as impossible.

'I . . . That's wonderful news.'

'Do you mean it?' Jinny seemed hardly able to believe her.

'Of course I bloody mean it. Come here, both of you.'

She spread her arms wide. She kissed Jinny's cheek and rubbed Cornelius's heavy head as he laid it against her shoulder.

'I am so pleased for you.'

Jinny babbled, 'I love you both. And Devil, of course. I'll take the greatest care of him, Nancy, and of Cornelius, and nothing else will change, will it? Omadood barm, darling.'

'Besarves amather,' Nancy dazedly completed.

It *was* wonderful. Cornelius would have a wife and there could be no better woman for him. There might even be a child, she realised. Jinny was not yet forty.

A new family in Waterloo Street.

She pressed her hand against her belly. The tectonic plates of her world shifted. Where would her future place be? No longer in this house, surely? The immensity of change, the splintered perspectives of the new order swung at her and made her giddy all over again.

'Nancy?' Jinny was still holding her.

'Phew. It's a lot to take in. Pass me that glass, will you? I hope you will be very happy.'

They toasted each other in cheap brandy.

'My future wife,' Cornelius said, trying out the words. He put his hands on Jinny's shoulders and withdrew them again, awkward and affectionate as always. Nancy couldn't quite suppress a shameful quiver of jealousy. Jinny didn't see it and she was glad of that.

Cornelius muttered about this all being very fine but it

was getting late and if there were no matches there would be no dinner. He went off in search of a box and Nancy and Jinny were alone.

Nancy said, 'I didn't know, girl. I really am blind. I thought you and Ann were for ever.'

'Had she lived, we would have been. But there's more than one kind of love in this world, Nancy.'

'Yes,' she agreed. 'There is.'

# CHAPTER TWENTY-ONE

She didn't know what woke her, but in the tick of a second she was fully conscious and staring into the darkness. She lay listening to the tiny noises of the old house before she pushed back the covers and swung her feet to the floor. Devil's bedroom door stood slightly ajar and she padded in her pyjamas to his bedside. The bed was empty and the sheets held only a trace of his warmth.

Downstairs the house was in darkness. The clock on the dresser showed her that it was twenty to three. Devil wasn't there, and the garden door was locked on the inside with the big key still standing in the lock.

She turned the key anyway and opened the door, shivering a little in the draught of cold air. Beside the path she could see the steely glint of Cornelius's glass cold frames, and at the far end the massy bulk of the tree in the opposite garden.

'Pa?'

He couldn't be out here. She turned to face the back of the house, tendrils of association snagging her as she did so. The thought of Emmy Simmons came briefly before the Uncanny exploded around her. Without warning she was enveloped. It was denser and more potent than she had ever known because she had believed it gone.

In place of the house there was a burning building, exactly as she had glimpsed once before, with flames licking out of the windows to devour the oxygen from the heated air. With its greedy roar crackling inside her skull Nancy ducked, covering her face with her hands. Her terror of the fire was overpowering but she forced herself to take one step forwards and then another, as she had done onstage to meet the mirrors before escaping past them to Sylvia and the sanctuary of the wings. She peered through her fingers and to her horror she saw a human figure, tiny as a bird, embedded in the heart of the fire.

A voice thrummed, *Help me.*

Nancy staggered, but somehow she still moved forward. A second later she stumbled through the back door and the Uncanny lay behind her, shrivelling into tatters as it evaporated.

Gasping for breath she ran to the row of pegs and found that Devil's old coat was missing from its usual place. She was already on her way to rouse Cornelius when she remembered that Jinny might be lying in his bed. It was an absurd reluctance, when she didn't even know if Jinny had stayed or gone home, yet she couldn't make herself overcome it.

The urgent need to find her father took over. He was in danger: that was what the fire meant, and the figure at its heart. He might be hesitating at someone else's door, confused and lost. Or far worse. Without stopping to reason she slipped her feet into her boots and pulled on her coat and hat.

The thought of his frailty, the bewilderment he would be suffering, sent her flying out of the house.

Waterloo Street was deserted and there were no lights in any of the windows. She peered into the shadows, praying for a darker outline, but there was no one to be seen. At the corner she hesitated. A car raced past on the distant main road, its headlamps drawing a brief yellow cone. She drew her coat more tightly and hurried two hundred yards to the point where low-built houses like theirs gave way to bigger ones with steps protected by iron railings. She peered down into cellar areas, her eye accommodating enough to distinguish sacks of coal, piled logs, tin buckets and spindly shrubs, but no sign of Devil. The scrape of her breathing was harsh in her ears.

At the main road she paused near a lamp and gazed back into the recessed darkness. The stillness behind her was eerie. Another car swept by. She was standing so close to the kerb that the draught flapped her coat hem against her pyjama legs. The next car slowed and pulled up. Her imagination was racing ahead and it took her a moment to notice that it was a taxi. The driver peered out. He must have seen her nightclothes and now the collapsed socket of her eye. She hadn't thought to put on her patch.

'You all right, miss?'

'I need to get to the Strand.'

'I'll take yer.'

She patted the empty pockets of her coat. She must have looked desperate enough because the man said he was going up west anyway, to catch the gents on their way home. Good tippers, they were, at this time of night, if they hadn't spent it all. He didn't mind taking her along.

They whirled through Farringdon, past Lennox & Ringland, and swept up Fleet Street. Print workers were busy here. Vans were being loaded with the morning papers and all-night pigeons bobbed amongst the crumbs of late suppers and early breakfasts.

As soon as they reached St Clement Danes they saw it.

'Gawd, look up there,' the cabbie grunted.

A pall of smoke filled the sky, darker than the night, its underside burnished flickering umber. The cab nosed along until they could smell and almost taste the fire.

'I won't go no closer.'

Nancy gabbled her thanks and flung herself into the road.

'You watch it,' the driver shouted but she was already running. The fire was real. She heard its dull roar backed by the sharp snap of flames. Heat scorched her face and she fell into the partial shelter of a shop doorway.

The front of the Palmyra had been shrouded in smoke and even as she watched a wall of fire burst through the roof, roaring up like a living thing to snap at joists and beams. The ribs enclosing the cupola resisted for a moment longer before bursting into flames too, releasing columns of sparks and billows of acrid smoke. Chunks of smouldering debris rained down from the sky, setting miniature bonfires on the theatre steps and melting the tar in the street. A blackened poster shrivelled in the exploded glass case next to the foyer doors.

**Miss Zenobia Wix**, the posters had once announced.

Or *The Wix Family proudly presents*
**Illusions, Enchantments, Mysteries.**

She pulled herself together, covering her mouth and nose and stumbling ahead. Her blind socket stung and tears poured from both sides.

A helmeted policeman barred her way. Two fire engines blocked the Strand and firemen raced to unreel hoses. Their faces were pale sickles in the smoke. Nancy tried to dodge past the policeman but he stretched out his cape, arms wide to restrain her, like some giant bat.

She screamed at him. 'My father is in there.'

'You can't go any closer. It's too dangerous.'

High above them the cupola exploded like a piece of overripe fruit. The firemen fell back to take shelter behind their engines. Nancy stared up at the place where the dome had been, now a glowing furnace sending immense clouds into the darkness. Hot cinders and flakes of soot fell on her and on the policeman, dotting their clothes with smouldering points like the red eyes of insects. There was a stink of scorched wool.

The firemen ran out again and in a moment arcs of water were pumping into the heart of the fire. Plumes of steam hissed into the sky and the flames sank within the molten walls. Her throat was clogged with soot and she was hardly able to see, but she had no thought except finding Devil.

She peered sideways along the Strand to the gleaming windows of the Corner House. The polished sweep of glass was smirched with smoke, with the flames reflected in places so it seemed there was a second, smaller fire. She caught sight of a man standing under the arched entrance, his face upturned to the Palmyra.

It was him.

She yelled at the policeman, 'He's there. Just let me go to my father.'

'Go on then.'

She scuttled like a crab against the shopfronts and doorways. A window burst high in the theatre and diamonds of glass sprayed through the smoke. She shielded her face and plunged onwards to the shelter of the entrance.

'*Pa.*'

Her father looked round. At first his expression was

blank. He didn't mistake her for Eliza – he didn't recognise her at all. Grabbing him by the arm she swung him so that his back was turned to the blazing theatre. She shook him hard enough to rattle his teeth. If it wasn't Devil she had seen inside the blaze, who was it?

Sylvia. Oh God, it was *Sylvia*.

She screamed, 'She's in there. I saw her. We've got to get in.'

He only grinned, flames reflected in his eyes.

'You *saw*?'

'You know I see things. Help me. Help her.'

He shook his head, still dementedly smiling.

'No, no. I hunted through every corner. Jakey's old hidey-holes, your dressing room, under the stage where Carlo and your mother and I used to spring the boxes. There wasn't a soul there but me.'

His hand hovered over his pocket where the missing box of kitchen matches lay.

'The gas piping, you know. It was very old. Not safe at all.'

'*You* did this? You set the fire to burn down our theatre?'

She imagined her father fleeing down the old passageways for the last time, past Sylvia's little sleeping alcove, his shoes clattering on the bare boards as a tiny flame licked up in his wake.

A fresh corona of sparks shot into the sky. Devil sighed in awe, as if he were watching a fireworks display.

'There's no Gabe, you see. All's well. No one else shall have the Palmyra.'

There was no time for this. Nancy thrust him aside and raced into the road where the firemen wrestled with the black hoses.

'Help me. There's someone inside.'

'What's that miss? Stand back, now.'

Lent strength by desperation she hauled at the nearest man.

'This way. The stage door, at the back.'

Thank God, her anguish was eloquent enough. The firemen followed in her wake, clattering like an army, down into the cobbled alley. The stage door was locked and Nancy pounded on it with her two fists.

'Sylvia,' she screamed.

'Step aside, miss.'

An implement was hustled forward, a thick and heavy pillar that looked like a giant rolling pin. The men swung it, repeatedly smashing it into the wooden panels and within seconds the stage door broke into splinters and the rescuers burst in.

Fresh air collided with the wall of smoke and torchlight probed the swirling blackness. To her horror she glimpsed Sylvia lying in a ball, her head cradled in her arms, only a few feet beyond the stage doorkeeper's box. Nancy staggered along the wall, coughing and retching as the fumes flooded into her lungs. Within seconds she was sightless and suffocating. Falling on to her knees she reached out and her hands grasped the dresser's coat.

Men's voices bawled, 'Get out. Mind yourself.'

She was pushed aside as Sylvia's inert body was hoisted over a fireman's shoulder. Another man grabbed Nancy and manhandled her towards the faint rectangle of foggy light where the sweet air flowed. Thudding boots pounded in her head.

'Anyone else in here?' a voice in her ear demanded.

'No,' she choked. Sylvia, poor faithful Sylvia.

She was set down like a puppet against the far wall of the alley. She coughed and wept, her stinging eye and blurred vision just allowing her a glimpse of Sylvia's body as it was carried into an ambulance. Through spasms of coughing she gasped at the fireman who stooped over her, 'Is she dead?'

'She is unconscious, still breathing. She's inhaled a lot of smoke. They'll look after her. You worry about yourself for now, miss. You did a brave thing there.'

She clutched at the man's arm in desperation. 'I have to go back to my father. He's not fit to be left on his own.'

When they saw that she could barely walk they half carried her back up to the Strand. Devil was still standing under the Corner House arch and as soon as she fell against him he reached into his pocket and took out a handkerchief. As if she were a little girl again he dabbed the soot and tearstains from her cheeks and cleaned the puckered margins of her eye socket.

'There. That's better. My pretty one.'

Once he was satisfied with his handiwork he turned again to watch the fire. Pumped water subdued the flames although there were dark red seams glowing everywhere. The Palmyra had been devoured and the palm chandelier, gilt-faced boxes, plush *fauteuils* and hard gallery seats must all be in ruins.

Nancy gaped at the place she had known her entire life, unable to absorb the spectacle of its destruction.

Devil muttered, 'It's full circle, you see.'

'What do you mean?'

'There's nobody inside the barn. I made sure of it this time.'

Fury and frustration boiled up inside her as she recovered herself. She shook him again until his head wobbled.

'*Stop it*. Don't you understand what you've done? Sylvia

was in there. You might have killed her. Didn't you think of her for one second? Or about Neelie, or Arthur, or *me*?'

His milky eyes were glazed with confusion. Slowly she uncurled her fingers and pushed him away. Perhaps he really didn't know what he was doing. Yet with Devil there seemed always to be a shard of rational cunning embedded in the depths of his rambling, disconnected being.

They stood in silence, watching the fire's victory.

At last the hoses smothered the flames and the red chasms shrank. The pall of smoke shifted in the rising wind, turning from impenetrable black to grey. Nancy saw her father's white hair and whiskers in a less lurid light and realised that the dawn was breaking.

A uniformed policeman and another, obviously in plain clothes, were picking their way towards them.

She grimly ordered Devil, 'Say nothing. Not one bloody word, do you understand? I'll speak to them.'

'Good morning, miss. I understand these are your premises?'

The plain-clothes man had hard eyes. She explained that she and her father were the theatre proprietors. One of their employees had been inside the premises, but she had been rescued and taken to hospital.

'Where were you at the time the fire broke out?'

'We were both at home in bed.'

'How did you learn that the property had caught fire? By telephone, I assume?'

Nancy met his gaze. The man's focus shifted a little, away from her eye socket.

'We don't have a telephone. I woke up at half past two and I saw what was happening.'

'You *saw* it?' He consulted his notes. 'From Clerkenwell?'

'That's right. I am clairvoyant.'

The man almost sniggered.

Nancy never faltered. She had woken her father first, she said. Then she had raced by taxi to discover that the theatre was indeed on fire. Her father had joined her as soon as he could, she said. They had watched the blaze together from this doorway, apart from when she left his side to direct the firemen to the stage door.

'My stage name is Zenobia Wix.'

The plain-clothes man exchanged a glance with the uniformed officer.

'I see. Sir?'

Devil's old face was cloudy. His mouth trembled and there were tears at the corners of his eyes.

'Yes. That's right. My daughter and me. Who are you?'

'The police, sir.'

The man put away his notebook. He told Nancy curtly that he would need to speak to her again, but she should go home now and see her father back to his bed.

It was full daylight. The Palmyra was a black shell masked by lazy smoke. Nancy took Devil's arm and walked him slowly down the Strand. A taxi appeared in the distance and she waved her hand to it. At Waterloo Street Cornelius, and Jinny if she was with him, appeared not to have stirred. Devil was unsteady on his feet so she took him up to his room, removed his outer clothes and put him to bed. He lay down meekly and let her draw the blankets over him.

Nancy took her purse and hurried back up the street to the telephone box. It took a full half-hour to establish that Sylvia was very ill, but holding her own. She leaned against the heavy door of the box until her anxiety stilled and she recovered herself enough to walk home again. She looked in on Devil and found that he was asleep. In a few moments she would have to tell Cornelius the news, and once he had absorbed it they would need to think together about the statement she had made to the police, and whether or not the Palmyra had been insured. But before any of that happened she must have a few moments alone.

In the sanctuary of her room Nancy realised she was shivering uncontrollably. She peeled off her smoke-reeking clothes and wrapped herself in Eliza's red robe. Then she sat down and forced herself to think over the last hours.

The Uncanny had without doubt saved Sylvia Aynscoe's life. Its final, overpowering spasm was to be welcomed, therefore. She searched within herself for further intimations, studying the arc of light through her window and inhaling the room's smells of cold cream and bed linen mingled with the taint of smoke from her discarded clothes. That waft was freighted with the disaster, but there was nothing that was not physical. She couldn't find the Uncanny, not even a glint of it. The cool daylight was flat and reassuring.

After a little while she stood up and went to inspect the dressing table. It was bare except for her hairbrush and a hand mirror reflecting her ravaged face.

Her gift was gone, and this time she knew without any doubt that it would never come back.

Before the end of that same drawn-out morning of bad news and shocked faces, a messenger delivered a letter. Gil wrote that he was horrified to hear about the Palmyra and begged her for a word. She was glad to reassure him but it was a full week before she could agree to see him face to face.

They met at the Bloomsbury flat. He tried at once to take her in his arms and she might easily have given way because she had, and did, and for ever would miss him with all her heart. Yet she didn't yield, and his empty hands fell slowly to his sides. A tremor in his face was clearly visible before he regained control.

'Celia tells me she came to see you.'

'Yes.'

'You saw how she is. She is like that, and often very much worse. I am taking lawyers' advice about a divorce, Nancy. The de Laurys will do everything to oppose it, and it will take time, but at least it won't have to follow the usual course.'

She supposed he meant that the divorce would be on the grounds of insanity and so she would not be cited. She gathered herself, feeling her backbone firm and her intention strong.

'I'm sorry for Celia. Will Mrs Auger wait for you, do you think?'

He recoiled. This time the pain in his eyes was stark.

'You don't have to do this. Please don't. I love you.'

He did love her in his way – the way of a mistress, never a wife – and she loved him as she would never in her life love another man. Sadly in the end love hadn't been enough. Or not enough for a rich man who cared about the ways of the world. Poor Gil, she realised. He was trapped by his money and status, whereas she was at liberty to turn any way that life might lead her.

She did step forward now, taking his hands between hers and kissing his mouth.

'I'm sorry.'

'Nancy. Oh, Nancy, my dearest dear girl.'

She forced herself to break away although it felt like a limb being wrenched off. To contain the agony she paced the room, picking up and replacing their accumulated possessions and the years of happiness they stood for.

'We *were* happy, weren't we?'

Gil was in tears. She had never seen him weeping.

'Yes. We were happy.'

'Do you remember Rome? And the view from the villa?'

'I won't ever forget.'

'What shall we do with all these things?' she wondered.

'Things? What do the bloody *things* matter?'

There speaks money, she thought. She had carefully wrapped all the pieces of jewellery he had given her, including the cold sapphire pendant, and now she tried to hand them back.

With his cheeks wet and shining he demanded, 'Do you want me to take back the fish bag and the straw hat as well?'

The precious gifts lay in the wardrobe, wrapped in tissue. Nancy shook her head and bit her lip to hold back her own tears.

There were no more words to offer. Placing her key on the table she held her head high and her back straight. She kissed her lover on the cheek for the last time and walked away.

She took her newest and most precious secret with her, but that was hers to keep.


The smells of heated dust and wax and sawdust were the same, but there the only similarity between the Palmyra and the Ben Jonson ended. Backstage in this theatre the passageways were swept and free of lumber, and the light bulbs might be naked but they were all in working order. A passing stagehand led the way to Jake's dressing room.

'He's in rehearsal, miss.'

'I'll wait.'

Jake's dresser was a trim middle-aged man who made her

a cup of tea and seated her next to the mirrors. He went
back to ironing shirts and fussing with starched collars while
Nancy studied the make-up jars and brushes that were
arranged without even a dusting of surplus powder or a
misplaced lid. The messages and telegrams and scripts and
papers were neatly stacked. It was a tidy, workmanlike place
without unnecessary ornament, and therefore reminiscent
of Jake himself. It was Freddie who provided all the decor-
ative flourishes in their life.

'It's very sad about the Palmyra, miss,' the dresser said.
'How is Miss Aynscoe getting along?'

'Thank you. Sylvia's recovering well.'

The little dresser had been discharged from hospital. The
Wix family had sent her to recuperate at a convalescent
establishment near Brighton.

Thinking back over all that had happened in the past
month, Nancy regarded the fire at the Palmyra as a line
drawn under the last sentence of a long narrative.

In the immediate aftermath the police had interviewed
her, and Cornelius, and all the people who worked at the
Palmyra. They established that Arthur had been and
remained overseas, and finally they called on Devil. He
played the role of a sadly forgetful old man to perfection
– if a role was what it was. Enfeebled and rheumy-eyed,
he deferred to Nancy in everything and concurred with her
account of the night in every detail. Except for one thing.
Suddenly reviving, he leaned forward in his chair and
announced, 'I followed my daughter down to the Strand
by bicycle.'

Nancy studied her hands. Devil had never owned a bicycle
in his life. He would have considered it a very low-grade
means of transportation.

'I see, sir. Where is the machine now?'

'I have no idea. Perhaps you can help me with that, officer. I think I left it beside the doorway of Shepherd & Sanderson. The hatters in the Strand, you know? Some villain must have *stolen* it.'

He glared around in outrage, blinked, and subsided.

'What?' he whispered. 'Nancy, who are these men? Don't leave me here with them.'

The police gave up on him in the end, and on the question of arson.

Nancy and Cornelius were astonished to discover that the payments on the Palmyra's insurance policy had been kept up by Desmond. A series of papers arrived from the insurers. There would be a forensic conclusion in due course, but it seemed likely that the fire had started with an electrical spark from the theatre's old wiring in a spot tragically close to a slow-leaking gas pipe.

The dusty old structure had blazed up so quickly.

An insurance payout was unlikely to happen soon, but Cornelius took the view that they would get money in the end. Nancy had quietly confided the full story of that night and he considered it, resting his hands on his knees as he did when he was thinking.

'An electrical spark and a gas leak in an old building full of flammable materials? Yes, that would send the place up like a bonfire.'

Devil said, 'I had the wiring installed. Saw to it myself. We were one of the first to go over to the electricity, you know. After the Haymarket.'

'Yes, Pa.'

Devil's bewildered wanderings stopped as soon as they had better news about Sylvia. He presided over Waterloo Street from his kitchen chair, looking out at the garden during the day and with his sock-clad feet up against the warmth of the range by night. The clouds of his confusion sometimes parted to deliver needle-sharp memories of long ago although more recent events eluded him. He usually claimed no recollection of the night the theatre burned down.

'Gone?' he said. 'Is that so? The old place?'

Nancy took his hand. 'We are all still here, Pa. That's what matters.'

When Cornelius and Jinny told him their news he said, 'Good. It has taken you long enough.' He pointed a finger at Nancy. 'You next. Where is that young man of yours?'

'Lion? I don't think so.' She kissed him and he slid his arm around her waist.

'Zenobia, my Queen of the Palmyra. Born on the day of the old Queen's Diamond Jubilee.'

Whatever else Devil forgot, he tended to remember that.

Nancy's biggest concern now was the Palmyra staff and artists who had been thrown out of work. It was partly to seek Jake's help that she had come to see him in his dressing room. While she waited, Nancy reread the solicitor's letter which was the second reason for her visit.

Under the name of an important firm of City solicitors the senior partner wrote that he had some business to discuss with her, and he would be glad to see her at his offices at a date and time convenient to her. She had put it aside for a few days while she dealt with more urgent matters, and then made an appointment.

Across the expanse of his wide desk the solicitor informed her that Mr Gilbert Maitland wished to make over to her the ninety-year lease on a ground-floor property in Blooms-bury. Once the necessary paperwork had been signed, he would be able to hand over the keys. The man uncapped his gold pen and held it out to her, smiling like Father Christmas. Nancy thanked him, and asked if it would be possible to consider the matter before doing anything more. He looked startled, but he nodded and took back his pen.

'Of course, of course,' he soothed. 'Take all the time you like.'

Jake arrived quietly, dressed in an old jersey and flannels. He had come straight from rehearsal and she could see that he was jigging with the after-effects of performance. His face was that of a different man, the character he had been playing. Knowing a little of what the transition felt like she kissed him and he absently patted her shoulder.

'Just give me a minute.'

He sat down and drank tea and rubbed his face with a towel. The dressing room was scented with starch and ironed linen. Wholesome, everyday smells. After a moment Jake's features slid back into focus. He smiled at her.

'Shall we go straight to the nursing home? What time are we expected?'

'Visiting hours are three to five.'

'So we've got time to walk there?'

'Yes, I think so.'

He brightened further and took his coat from his dresser.

'Thanks, Bill. Billy knows everyone on Shaftesbury Avenue. He tells me there's a job in the costumes department here for Sylvia, if she wants it, just as soon as she's well again. They're looking for a lighting rigger as well, and maybe a props hand.'

Nancy begged the man to listen out for any other possibilities. Bill pursed his lips.

'There will be a few changes at the Lyric, I'm told. And there's that new show coming into the Haymarket. I saw your dad do *Charlotte and the Chaperone*, Miss Wix. It must have been the thousandth performance for him, but he made seem it as fresh as the first night. I thought my ma would pee herself laughing, excuse me.'

'Thank you, Bill. I'll tell him that.'

She shook the dresser's hand and they talked theatre until Jake seized her arm and led her out into Shaftesbury Avenue.

A trio of girls waited at the stage door and Jake signed their autograph books as they covertly peeked at his strange companion with the eyepatch. He was wearing a scarf to protect his throat even though it was barely autumn, but as he and Nancy set off he threw his head back to admire the china-blue sky above the rooflines.

'Thank God to be outdoors. So many darkened rooms. Another actress to kiss.'

'There are worse jobs than being a stage and film star.'

'Yes, *ma'am*, I dare say I deserved that. Come to Whistlehalt this Friday to Monday? No? Why not? What will Freddie do to me if you don't?'

They traversed Cambridge Circus and made their way south.

Nancy murmured, 'There are some things. Things I have to deal with.'

She didn't see his shrewd glance at her averted profile.

When they came to the florist's stall on the corner of Long Acre Jake halted in front of the banks of blooms.

'Roses, do you think?'

He nodded to the florist and the woman began to select crimson flowers.

'Not all red. We must have white ones, and pink, the buds and the overblown as well, those, and those, and those . . . yes, all of them.'

'Jakey,' Nancy laughed. It took two of them to carry

the enormous double bouquet over Waterloo Bridge to the nursing home.

Lizzie had given birth to her daughter in what had been a grim Victorian lying-in hospital and was now transformed into a fashionable obstetric clinic. They found her in a private room, arranged in a lace peignoir against a bank of pillows and looking as if she had just left her Mayfair hairdresser's. Her baby lay in her arms.

'Thank God you're here,' she cried. 'I don't want to drink champagne all on my own. Nurse, we need some glasses. And about a dozen vases. Gorgeous flowers, I must say.'

The nurse scurried off, hardly daring to glance at Jake Jones.

'Here she is.' Lizzie turned down a fold of shawl. 'Jennifer Faith Eliza.'

Nancy looked down at a tiny face, beautiful and crumpled in sleep. With a spasm of love and longing she reached out a hand and ventured the tip of one finger to a rose-red cheek. It felt infinitely smoother and softer than the rose petals.

Lizzie grinned.

'I know. A girl, a daughter. Aren't I lucky? Ray is already besottedly in love with her.'

Head on one side Jake peered down.

'She's you in miniature. I can't see the least sign of her father.'

Lizzie protested, 'Don't for heaven's sake say that to him. He thinks she's got his mother's eyes and mouth. The poor little lamb. Have you *seen* Myrtle Kane? Thank you, nurse. Pour us all a glass, Jake darling?'

Nancy found a voice although it came out reedy and muffled.

'May I?'

'Go ahead.' Lizzie readily exchanged the baby for a coupe of champagne. 'Cheers.'

Nancy cradled the little creature, standing beside the window to wonder at her in the full daylight. Jennifer responded to the sun on her eyelids by kissing the air, turning her head with a tiny nuzzling movement and making a sound that Nancy might once have thought of as a kitten's mew. Now it sounded explicitly human. This was a person, here and now, a miniature but complete new individual who was entirely herself, with a whole life ahead of her and a history yet to be written. Nancy stroked the baby's head with its nap like the inner surface of an unworn kid glove. She wanted to whisper in the dark pink whorl of the ear, promises of love and protection for as long as she was alive to give them. As she dipped closer she caught a primitive scent that tugged at her belly and made her heart drum even harder against her ribs.

'I hope you'll say yes to being her godmother, Nancy?'

The pigeonholing was no fault of Lizzie's. Of course she would regard her cousin as the reliable spinster aunt, suitable for the role because of her availability even though not godly in person. In the same moment Nancy stood apart from herself, looking at the person she had been and might easily have remained.

She felt a surge of simple joy.

The filaments of life were branching and translucent buds of flesh were forming within her body just as they had done in Lizzie's.

'Of course I will. I promise I will take care of her.'

She kissed her goddaughter's forehead and laid her in her mother's arms. As she straightened she noticed Jake's appraisal of her. She snatched up her champagne glass and the rim clattered faintly against her teeth.

Lizzie turned to him. 'And you, Jake? Her godfather? Do say yes.'

'It is the least appropriate choice you could make, but I'm flattered. Here's a toast to Jennifer Faith Eliza. Health, love and happiness.'

They echoed the words and drank.

Lizzie was ready for talk but Nancy could barely put words together. The prospect of approaching motherhood had been an abstract notion until this moment. And then in a matter of seconds there were curled baby fingers and a crescent of eyelashes, and the scent of recent birth that was as strong as anything had been in the lost Uncanny. Yet this was a real smell, of blood and flesh, and it was as visceral as love itself.

Even Lizzie was looking oddly at her now.

'Nance?'

She managed to laugh.

'Yes, look at me, smitten by my new goddaughter. When will you two be able to go home to Raymond?'

Lizzie waved a hand.

'In a few days I expect, as soon as the maternity nurse is ready to join us. I don't in the least mind being here. I'm thoroughly comfortable, as you can see. Tommy hasn't the slightest need of me nowadays and Jinny runs everything at Exotics with such frightful efficiency that I expect to be out of a job before Christmas. What news of the wedding?'

'Cornelius mentioned the beginning of December. A very quiet affair, just family.'

'I'll have my figure back by then, thank God. Any other news?'

Jake had stood up and moved to look out of the window.

He wasn't very interested in conversations like this. Nancy glanced his way and then said, 'It's not exactly news, but there is something you could both help me with. Some advice.'

Jake turned at once and Lizzie sat up. She was wealthy in her friendships, Nancy thought, and that would count even more in the future. She took out the solicitor's letter and smoothed the creases against the bedcover.

'What do you think of this?'

She told them about Bloomsbury, her visit to the offices in the City and Gil's offer of the leasehold. Jake picked up the letter and read it, then studied her again over the top.

Lizzie had learned about Gil only latterly and now she shrugged, 'Well, I must say. He redeems himself a little.'

She had been scandalised to hear about Thelma Auger, which given Lizzie's own history struck Nancy as comical.

Nancy said, '*I* am thinking that perhaps I should thank him and politely decline.'

Lizzie goggled.

'You think *what?*'

'It feels mercenary to me. You know, "Thanks for ten years. My fee is a ninety-year lease." I'm not sure I want to be paid, mostly because that isn't what happened. Our love affair came to an end and we are both sad, but Gil doesn't owe me a thing.'

A wing of Lizzie's hair fell prettily forward as she buried her face in her hands.

'No,' she murmured. Jake kept a straight face as she emerged again.

'No, no and no. Listen to me, my girl. It's not being paid off. It's a generous gesture you thoroughly deserve. Gil Maitland can afford it, from what I hear. You will accept his offer, in fact you will snatch off his arm, or I shall never speak to you again. Jinny and your brother are getting married, they'll be looking after Devil at Waterloo Street, which is as it should be, but you can't live there with them. It's hardly fair to Jinny, is it? What are you going to *do*? You haven't even got a job.'

It wasn't that Nancy hadn't considered the matter. These days Cornelius wore the little house the way a snail wore its shell. She thought of how it would be if he had to leave his garden and the quiet run-down street, beyond which he rarely moved, even if it were only to live safely with Jinny somewhere close at hand.

With *Jinny*, who would be his *wife*. She blinked, still getting used to the idea.

Her friend had left the flat near Shaftesbury Avenue because it was too painful to live amongst the memories it contained. Lately she had been occupying one room deep in the warren of Soho.

For herself, Nancy had thought she might return to somewhere like her old whitewashed place near the actors' church. Reflectively she smoothed the front of her skirt.

'Jake?' she asked.

He considered.

'I wouldn't go as far as Lizzie, because I'd miss you too much to be able to cut you off for life. Setting aside your natural pride, it is a generous offer and it might be churlish to refuse. Although I quite understand what you are feeling, and why.'

'You think I should let Gil give me a home?'

Jake looked her up and down, and this time she saw the question in his eyes. She glanced hastily away.

'I do, in the circumstances.'

'Hallelujah. Sense from somebody,' Lizzie cried.

Jennifer woke up and began to cry. Her lungs were powerful.

Nancy and Jake walked arm in arm towards the river and Waterloo Bridge. The streets were crowded with people making their way home from work. A scurrying boy with his nose in a comic slammed into Nancy and she almost fell.

'Watch where you're going,' Jake angrily yelled after him.

'I'm all right.'

'Shall we get a taxi?'

'No, thanks. Honestly, I'd like to walk.'

'Are you sure?'

'Jake . . .'

He stopped to place his hands on her shoulders. This time Nancy looked straight back at him. The crowd parted and flooded on towards the station, turning them into an island in a human stream. A news vendor was shouting the headlines from his pitch and sun slanted over the buildings to gild the crawling buses.

'Who is the father? Is it Gil? You don't have to tell to me if you don't want to,' he added.

It was a relief.

'Yes, Gil is the father. Of course I want to talk to you. No one else knows yet and I'm not sure how you guessed.'

'I just looked at you.'

She nodded. He listened and watched, and then used the observations to clothe the characters he played. That was what Jake did, and there was no better judge of people. She let her forehead rest against his shoulder and he held her in his arms, cheek against her hair. They must look like two lovers, she thought, about to tear themselves apart on Waterloo Steps.

'I am not going to tell Gil I am expecting his child,' she said.

'I see. There are things you can do, of course, to remedy your situation. Is it a matter of money?'

She pulled back and the sun flooded into her face. Even the dead eye seemed to see its brilliance.

'For people like us it's always a matter of money in some way, isn't it? Only people like Gil and Lady Celia think money doesn't matter. I'm going to have the baby, Jake, because I want it more than anything, and I am happy for it to be mine alone.'

Lawrence Feather briefly slid into her mind but she dismissed him, and all the memories. The dark past and the Uncanny all lay behind her now.

Jake sighed as he tried to angle her away from the un-ending stream of people. Whichever way they stepped they were jostled.

'This is a ridiculous place to try to talk.'

'Let's walk then.'

They linked arms and reached the bridge. Out here the sky was open and dust particles shimmered in the air. Sparrows perched on the ladder bars and globes of the street lamps, rising in twittering groups to circle over the water before descending again. At the midpoint of the bridge Nancy and Jake stopped walking, as if the equidistance from either bank lent them the privacy they were looking for. Tiers of windows glittered on either side, but out here the two of them seemed suspended in emptiness. They leaned on the coping to gaze into the foam-flecked water before Jake took her left hand and turned it palm down against the warm stone.

'I know this is 1933, and you are a modern woman. However, what you envisage won't be as easy as you imagine, for you or the child. Won't you be needing a husband?'

Nancy began a laugh, but it caught in her throat.

Long ago at Whistlehalt Jake had told her that if she needed him he would be there.

'Is that a proposal?'

Now it was Jake who laughed.

'How would you receive it, if it was?'

'What would Freddie say?'

'I don't suppose you will want to take on two husbands. But I am serious. The offer is there, Nancy. A nod to convention, a name for the child, a shell of security for you both. And a selfish advantage for me, of course. I am too old for it to be a matter of great concern, but the studio would be happy to see me equipped with a wife and baby.'

Their fingers interlaced.

Looking at him, Nancy saw as if for the first time his shrewd eyes and the twin vertical clefts between them, the light hair and the deprecating set of his mouth. She knew what it was to love a man, and that made her happy. She didn't love Jake Jones in that way, and she wasn't going to marry any man for his name alone.

There were so many different kinds of love.

'That is the most generous offer anyone has ever made. Thank you, Jake.'

'No, then?'

'No,' she whispered.

He kept hold of her hand.

'Look at what's happening in Germany, and in Russia. Another war is coming, Nancy, and the world will change all over again. You'll need me and you will need your friends, and we shall all need each other.'

She couldn't disagree with the prediction.

'I will be here,' she promised.

Jake kissed her knuckles and released her hand.

'And I will be here. This is our pact.'

The light softened as the sun slid down behind them.

'Shall we walk on?' he asked. He would have to be at the theatre soon. His resemblance to Devil in this made her smile.

'I think I'll stay and watch the river.'

Jake kissed her cheek and no one would have mistaken them for lovers this time. She watched him go, walking quickly with his hat brim pulled low over his forehead, attracting no one's attention.

When she could no longer pick him out she turned in a full circle.

Upriver to her right the burned-out shell of the Palmyra was hidden from her view by the great buildings on the Embankment. Beyond that she could see the white face of the clock of Big Ben and the spires and crenellations of Westminster, the sweep of olive-green water, and on the other side the blinding white slabs of the new building of a petroleum company. As she turned eastwards again she could feel the tug of the tide beneath her, drawing her with it as if she were floating on the water. To anchor herself she looked towards the dome of St Paul's, set like a pearl in the ring of the City.

She had no idea of the future and for the moment felt no anxiety about it.

She belonged here, on the bridge over the river in the heart of London.

'You and me,' she said aloud to the baby, and a passer-by glanced at the woman with an eyepatch who was exclaiming to herself.

It was her good fortune, Nancy understood, that she

belonged to a disreputable theatrical family like the Wixes. She could do what she liked with a reputation she didn't possess.

She was free.

It came to her, like a gust of wind off the river, that Eliza would have thought the very same thing.